"And there was the Brotherhood of the
Gatekeepers, masters of counsel and arms for
a hundred generations. Yet their gravest charge
was not the person of the Imperial family, but
rather the Portal Gate from whence came the
Shades, the Enemies of light. Should the power
of the Gatekeepers over the Portal Gate ever
fail, woe to the world of mankind, for nothing
would stem the black tide."

~an excerpt from Book 12 of the Kedassaic Texts.

80 CB

M.D.T. Johnson
THE LAST SON OF
ATLANTIS

The Last Son of Atlantis

Copyright ©2018 by M.D.T. Johnson

Book design by Mark W. Lambertson
with illustrations by Hetty Mitchell.

Cover art by Hetty Mitchell and Mark W. Lambertson.

ISBN-13:   978-1-7325955-9-0
ISBN-10:   1732595593

Library of Congress Control Number: 2018952556

Author's Website: MDTJohnson.com
Email: Matt@MDTJohnson.com

Publisher: Prodigious Motion LLC
                   ProdigiousMotion.com
                   mail@ProdigiousMotion.com

Minneapolis, Minnesota, U.S.A.
Printed in the United States of America.
First Printing: 2018

For my wife, who never questioned the effort and time spent.

For my mother, who always encouraged.

For my sister, who never complained about reading it. Again.

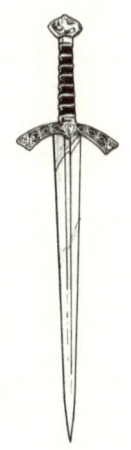

CHAPTER 1

"Let's be clear about this. Are you…are you asking me to kill your wife?"

"Only if I cannot."

~From a future conversation between two friends

ᚁᚂ ᚌᚏ

T he house was in a quiet little neighborhood. On that casual fall night an hour after dusk, they came to find it. The end of a long search was within reach.

Inside his home, Frank Blackman casually inched the curtain aside but failed to keep the tension from his voice.

"Do you trust me?" he asked his wife.

Adrienne Blackman had been restless since the sun had set, though she could not have said why.

"What's the matter?" she asked. "Of course I do."

In the furthest corner of their yard, a hissing intake of icy breath cut into the crisp air. A brooding silence crawled toward the lit house, driven by a sinister will.

"I need to tell you something." Frank adjusted the curtain and turned back from the window to look at his wife. "I should have told you before now."

Outside, a hooded cloak billowed in the night breeze. Among the folds of the cloak, an armored hand rested upon the hilt of a sword.

"Do you remember," continued Frank, "when we first met, and I told you I was an accountant?"

Adrienne Blackman crossed her arms, weight on one foot. One hand fiddled with the large green gem dangling from her neck in its ornate silver casing. "Yes…"

In the yard, the cloaked figure moved noiselessly forward. A stare more accustomed to darkness than light bore into the curtained window of the Blackman home. The eyes narrowed as it perceived the presence of the couple within.

"Frank, what are you trying to tell me?"

The hand opposite the sword hilt reached across the body and gripped the weapon's handle. Smooth steel scraped an ancient scabbard as a long and straight, double-edged blade was slowly drawn out with a familiar motion. The crickets ceased.

"Adrienne, I lied."

❧ ☙

Suddenly the hooded cloak halted mid-step at the sound of a motor, stiffened as headlights appeared and a vehicle came down the street, chasing the night out of the way.

A sedan with tinted windows came to a stop in front of the Blackman home. The engine idled for a moment and then shut off, but oddly enough the driver abruptly changed his mind after a few seconds and restarted the car. The shadow with the sword in hand stared evenly at the new arrival. For a minute the only noise in the yard was the rasp of the frosty breath, smelling out this new threat. The driver's scent ignited an arrogant resentment, but also caution based on previous experience.

The vehicle door opened and the driver got out. He was a tall, broad-shouldered man dressed in a long, flowing trench-coat. His square jaw was dark with stubble and his long hair was pulled behind him in a short tail. With a walk that feared no shadow, the newcomer closed the door of the car and came with confidence up the path toward the house. Across the yard the raised sword returned to its sheath. The cloaked trespasser moved a floating retreat back into the thicker cover.

❧ ☙

Inside the home, Adrienne watched with growing concern as Frank darted from window to window. Ironically, he narrowly missed the sedan as it parked. She hesitatingly followed him. *What is he looking for?* Five years of marriage and this was all an unnerving first. Her husband had not ever been prone to panic – until tonight.

"I'm not an accountant," he said as he left the kitchen, brushed past her and entered the den. "Well, not really. It is technically what I do now, but…" He came back into the hall and took her gently by the shoulders. "…but it's not the real me."

"You're making no sense-"

"I know, I know, and I'm sorry. But right now, I'm going to need you to trust me and do exactly what I say." His gaze locked onto her green eyes and his hand carefully moved some long dark hair behind her ear. "Please, we have to move fast, I...I think they're here."

"Frank...I don't understand. Who's here? You're scaring me-"

"I promise I'll tell you everything you want to know, but right now we need to get out of here. Now."

She nodded. "What should we do?"

He paused and looked toward the front yard, absentmindedly kneading the bridge of his nose. "I'm not sure, but we don't have much time. They're not just going to sit out there and wait...I'll get the keys-"

"Who's not going to wait?"

Their conversation was interrupted by the last thing they expected: the doorbell. They both jumped at the intrusion and for a moment stood gaping at each other. At length Frank gave Adrienne's shoulders a squeeze and moved toward the door.

"Frank, no!" she hissed in an ecstatic whisper.

"They're not going to ring the doorbell," he said dismissively over his shoulder.

Frank still checked the peephole, but then opened the door to reveal the driver of the vehicle. Adrienne gave him one look and moved back a few tactful steps, but Frank's mood dramatically improved. The stranger's face was expressionless as Frank moved aside, and he entered as if expected. He offered a respectful nod to Adrienne and then looked at Frank. He spoke with a calm authority and confidence.

"Greetings, old friend," he said as Frank shook his hand. "It is good to see you again, but I am afraid that now may not be the time for pleasantries. It is known that there are several Shades – legionnaires – about in your neighborhood – and I have found one in your yard."

Frank nodded. "How many? Are the others on their way here yet?"

The newcomer looked at Adrienne, then to the open door behind him. "Uncertain. This one is hanging back at the moment..." he said as if to himself, but then turned toward Frank. "I do not know, but it is my experience that waiting around for their arrival would be...unwise."

"Frank, who is this man?" asked Adrienne. She was past being polite. "How do you know him?"

Frank was not looking at either of them, but out the front window again. Still, he was much calmer now. His hand pointed to each respective party in turn. "Adrienne, meet my old and very good friend Orion Keldir. Orion, my wife Adrienne."

Adrienne failed to even acknowledge Orion Keldir standing there in her living room. After her husband was scaring her half to death a minute ago, casually introducing her now to a 'good friend' was insulting. *How good a friend could he be if I haven't even heard of him?*

If Orion was offended at the lack of acknowledgment on her part, he did not show it. Neither of the Blackmans had seen Orion at their own wedding, but he had indeed been there. Now five years later, Orion thought that at age thirty-two, Adrienne looked much the same as she had on her wedding day: still a beautiful young woman about five-eight with green eyes and dark hair several inches past her shoulders. For Frank, Orion did not see much change either. A few inches taller than his wife with short brown hair, Frank looked thirty-five and still had his characteristically lean but tough-and-wiry look, and that roguish, trademark grin of his – not that he was smiling now.

Frank caught the look Orion was giving him. "What exactly was I supposed to tell her?" he snapped, looking up from the window and letting the curtain fall back in place.

The question went unanswered. Both men had experience in keeping difficult secrets.

"Why are they here?" asked Frank.

"Who?" asked Adrienne.

"Only one of them is here," said Orion quietly. "That will not be for much longer, especially if the one in the yard recognized me; it would call the others here immediately. We must depart before the others join it." He looked out the open door and stepped out onto the stoop, staring into the far corner of the yard. He spoke back over his shoulder. "We must go. Now."

Frank nodded, and in crossing the room he had his wife firmly by the arm. "Adrienne, let's go."

Orion did not wait for the couple, but after surveying the yard from the stoop for a moment, he stepped down onto the walk toward his car. His eyes never left the black corner of the yard where the shadowy menace had withdrawn.

In passing by Orion, the wind gusted his coat and Frank saw a sword handle pointing toward the ground in a most unique upside down sheath strapped to his back. *Still gainfully employed*, Frank mused. His reminiscence was cut short as every light and electronic in his house and indeed the whole block, winked out. The moon alone shown down on the trio as the Blackmans left the stoop.

"W-what's happening?" asked Adrienne in a shaky voice.

"Make haste," said Orion quietly from behind them.

Even as Frank and Adrienne hurried to the car, Orion slowly reached around and caressed his weapon handle as he gazed toward the corner of the yard. His eyes could see better than a cat's in the dark, but no one he knew of could differentiate a black sheet as it lay on a black background.

Orion had an overwhelming feeling that he was locked in a cruel stare. He gazed back unblinking, tight-lipped. He could not see the Shade in the corner of the yard, but he sensed the unspoken wrath; a pure hatred. In his mind's eye he could picture the creature crouched like a panther ready to spring on him.

Ancient memories stirred within him and he had the urge to taunt it, goad it out into the open. Yet he recognized in the end this would be counter-productive.

These shadowy, other-worldly soldiers were venomous enough of themselves; irking one was a dangerous business. And now, the lights had gone out; unsurprising. He sensed the stare and its bellicose regard waver for a moment before leaving him, presumably to fix the Blackmans in its hold. Orion followed after them quickly, his hand still poised near the weapon, his eyes never leaving the blackness.

Frank positioned himself on the left, between his wife and the shadow as he rushed with Adrienne to the car. He almost threw her into the back of the sedan and clambered in after her. Orion wasted no time in pulling away from the property without so much as a word.

"Frank..." said Adrienne worriedly, "what about our house? My mother's cabinet is in there, and our photo albums – and Giovanni!"

"They don't care about our stuff, sweetheart – or the cat."

"You can regain all the possessions you wish when daylight returns," cut in Orion, throwing the car into a higher gear. "We are not going far – ah, here comes the devil."

Adrienne turned to look behind them and gave a soft involuntary gasp as a black shadow passed through their chain-link fence like a mist. It headed for their sedan as they peeled away. *What in heaven's name is that?* she wondered. In the midst of the terror of it, she could well have believed that Death itself was coming for them. As it reached the street and directly approached the car, its arms raised and its speed increased to the point that it stayed within reach of the fleeing vehicle. It lunged and a dull metallic screech could be heard above the gunned engine. But the reach cost it speed and the Shade fell back before regaining balance and continuing the chase.

"Two more!" called Adrienne as twenty meters behind the closest pursuer, additional black cloaks emerged from the darkness of a neighbor's yard and made directly for the car.

Frank could not keep from sounding worried. "How many are they bringing?"

Orion switched gears a final time, flooring it. "Enough," he answered shortly. "But there's a pair of shotguns under your seat if we need them."

Frank turned around to face the front and checked the speedometer. "Faster, man, faster!"

The car was going close to fifty and rapidly closing on the end of the block. The Shades chasing them began to fall behind, but as Frank looked forward he saw two more new shadows ahead of them, each floating out from the sides of the road to block the way, like a pair of Grim Reapers. They moved swiftly to the middle of the little suburban street, only Orion noticing the unmistakable action of drawing swords.

"Run them down," said Frank in a quiet voice, sitting rigid on the seat. It had been a long time since he'd dealt with this sort of thing.

Orion accelerated toward them despite the shortening block. Adrienne held her breath as her husband only encouraged him to go faster. Orion's fingers tightened around the wheel; he could see the two Shades outlined perfectly in the moonlight that bathed the street. Beyond the pair of legionnaires, an additional three individuals emerged almost simultaneously from the yards ahead.

As they closed so very speedily on the shadows, Orion flipped the switch for the high-beams. The tall black-clad night cloaks caught in the headlights, and the sword blades flashed red like firebrands. The one on the left uplifted its hand, despising the bright light rather than fearing the oncoming car.

The Shade on the right may have had the car pass through it, and as the lights struck the cloak and flashing weapon, it disappeared from their sight like a swirling vapor. The one on the left partly sprang aside as the sedan bore down upon it, a black sheet whisking over the windshield on the driver's side. At the same time, with a metallic shriek, Adrienne saw about ten inches of burning red steel knife through the side of the car at an angle where the door met the roof. Both she and Frank gave an involuntary cry at the sudden sight and sound: the blade was at the perfect angle to take off all or part of Orion's head as he drove.

At the last instant Orion tilted his head to the right, and the sword blade that the Shade had stabbed into the car narrowly missed him. It seared past Orion's ear as Adrienne grabbed Frank by the front of his shirt and yanked him toward her side of the car. He reactively pushed over too, and landed on top of her. The fiery red steel grated by them and wrenched out of the vehicle as it cornered hard to flee the block, tires squealing and drifting with their velocity.

Frank righted himself and searched behind them to see at least nine phantoms melting into the night away from the road. Orion was no longer being chased, but he slowed the car barely enough to round another corner, and then was back up to highway speeds. His passengers made no effort to get him to slow down.

Frank leaned back in the seat and sighed heavily, eyes closed. Beside him, Adrienne's hand closed around the familiar jewel about her neck. But she straightened and dropped it in surprise – the stone itself was strangely warm.

Orion drove, saying nothing. Eventually he reached up to touch the side of his head. His fingers grazed the top of his ear where a burning pain still lingered. He glanced at his fingers: blood. He could feel it trickling now, on its way to his shoulder. He sighed resignedly. *And I just bought this coat.*

℘ ℭ

Frank jerked as Adrienne gripped his arm. She was close enough to kiss his ear – but all she did was hiss into it: "What's going on, Frank?"

Suddenly ashamed he had not turned to her the moment the danger was past, Frank opened his eyes to meet hers. "Adrienne, I'm sorry. I never thought they would just show up one day – that's part of why I didn't tell you…I just didn't – they, uh – I'm not-"

"What's the other part?"

His eyes held hers. "There's no way you would have believed me if I told you how it was. How it really was. It was…I meant to…it's complicated."

He noted she had her arms crossed and was for once not playing with her necklace. Fingering her jewelry meant thoughtfulness and concern. To not be touching it but just sitting there… *She's furious,* he observed. *Why didn't I tell her before all this?*

"It's not a knock on you. No one would have believed me, even you. You may not believe me even now."

The shadows that had stalked the car flitted across her memory. "Try me."

Orion coughed and adjusted the rearview mirror, content to be no help at all. He said nothing, continuing to drive at a now law-abiding speed.

Frank leaned back, grateful to again have his eyes closed; that spared him the pain of meeting her glare. He mulled over how to begin – for only the thousandth time. But now the time had come to actually say something. Ten opening statements came to mind, none of them good enough. He paused and looked at her, fearing skepticism. Finally finding his train of thought, he spoke while kneading the bridge of his nose; his natural fidget.

"Adrienne, what would you say if I told you I had been part of a secret society?"

If the past twenty minutes or so had not happened, and if she had been sitting at home in her own living room, Adrienne would indeed have been skeptical – or even laughed. Now, she was speechless.

"It was a long time before we met…years before. Once I met you, once I wanted to marry you, I got out of it; retired." He paused and continued slowly. "I thought that if I told you, you would leave; I couldn't bear the thought of that. I also thought that as long as I got out of it for good, there was really no need for you to know about it. Ever. After five years I really thought it was over but – well, the Shades came out of nowhere tonight."

She said nothing. He went on.

"I joined when I was nineteen and stayed with the Society until we met. The organization is called the Dominos de Lumine; Lords of Light; it's dedicated to countering the Shades."

"Latin," she said.

"Part – and I admit, only part – of why I didn't tell you before was so you'd have what's called plausible deniability."

"Really, Frank? What, you're a lawyer now too? That's what you come up with-"

"Hey! I said it was only a part." He grabbed her hand as she tried to pull it away. "But it's true. I swear it is. Don't look at me like that…please don't look at me like that."

"Plausible deniability…" she said slowly.

His left hand went up above the window of his side of the car where the air whistled through the torn rent from the assault. He rapped his knuckles against it. His voice took on more force. "Remember what did this a few minutes ago? Red hot steel slicing through the car like we were a roast? What kind of creatures do you think we're dealing with? We had to stop them, and most of the time that meant very unpleasant dealings. Adrienne, I know you're mad and you have a right to be, but don't look at me like that when I'm finally telling the truth."

There was an awkward pause as neither spoke. At length she sniffed.

"So you were *fighting*?"

"No! Well – yes, sometimes, but that's not important now... Look, you've heard of counter terrorism?"

"Of course. So?"

"So the Lords of Light are into...counter *paranormal* terrorism."

CHAPTER 2

"Darkness cannot defeat the light. Its only victory is where there is no light."

~Frederick of Bavaria

ಠ ಣ

The origin and establishment of the Lords of Light was not a discussion for just anywhere or anyone. It was an old history, a long story that wove its way down through the centuries. Frank was very well acquainted with the Lords of Light's tale of years due to his own involvement, but Orion grasped it as intimately as a part of himself. Orion had been with them since before the council that created them, back when they were known as something else.

Europe at the time of the Middle Ages was a mix of civilizations ripe with corruption and decay that was tainted only too often with blood. War, plague, famine and death were known in every household, every land. Superstition ruled many hearts, violence moved many hands. In such culture the infiltration and influence of Shades was almost a natural progression.

The first step in countering a powerful enemy was to understand that enemy. Dukes and earls, even kings of Europe could fight wars well enough, but if they did not know their enemy, all their forced marches, sieges and cavalry charges did little good. There was, however, an albeit small group of men and even a few women that understood Shades, were aware of their purposes, and who had vowed to fight them. And they had.

It was hard, unmerited and unappreciated toil. More than once, plague crept through overpopulated and filthy cities, killing tens of thousands. History never recounted how such epidemics started, nor did she ever so much as reference Shades. Famines too had natural and unnatural causes. Crops withered and died, or even failed to rise in the first place. At one time the Lords of Light feared that the Shades had even managed to find a way to control the very weather to a point. They could also incite men to war; crusade after crusade savaged the land, depleted manpower, ignited hatred. The list of unnatural medieval woes that could be attributed to Shades was long and laborious to cite. Some, called Elders, could even take humanlike form...

Fighting them was more difficult, but measures could be taken. Many but not all advances in technology and knowledge – hygiene, medicine, herbal remedy, certain machines – were in actuality applicable counter measures. Agriculture could be tended to fight certain Shade-spread infections. Fire, the great equalizer, was always an ally. Inventions like the Byzantine Greek fire may have had historical fame for being sprayed at enemy ships to ignite them, but it worked just as well on Shades. And while what passed as human form could be used by the enemy, it was found early on that a woman's intuition or a dog's nose could unmask the foul creatures.

Frank paused in his narrative and asked if Adrienne were following him. She nodded, exhibiting a calm exterior while her stunned mind refused to get around the fact that her husband was a former member of a centuries-old organization that dealt with creatures like Shades – who were even worse than she had imagined after seeing one for herself.

"And this has just continued all the way to the twenty-first century?" she asked. "How does a small group deal against such astronomical odds?"

Frank went on.

While the Lords of Light had begun as really not much more than trained men and women in a special-needs war, the order expanded and grew with vastly increasing abilities and specialties among members. Secrecy remained paramount. The old ways still had their uses, of course, and always would. But when an order's ranks swell with talents of all kinds, martial skill becomes merely one of many things available. Soldiers, philosophers, politicians, scientists, inventors and artisans – all the kinds of beneficial people whose studies and pursuits were anti-Shade: military training, beneficial attitudes and understandings of thought, leaders with a grasp of the situation, advancing technology, useful inventions. The foundational members who had fought the Shades by any means at their disposal, however, would always remain in the bedrock of the organization.

As Frank went on, Orion remembered the progressions, advances, and other contributions to history that the larger part of mankind would never know to credit to a secret globe-spanning organization like Dominos de Lumine. He got the same silent amusement from articles and books he occasionally found which attempted to discuss secret societies like the Illuminati, the Masons or Skulls. No such writings ever named his own order – it was too clandestine, too well-protected.

The greater part of this amusement, at least for Orion, was when the readings made special note to declare what famous historical figure had been a member of the said organization: anywhere from Julius Caesar to Isaac Newton, Leonardo da Vinci to George Washington. Now he really did smile. If the masses only knew who had truly belonged to what.

Orion paused in his silent reminiscence, realizing that Frank had stopped speaking. His long secret history done, he now looked to the woman he'd hidden it from for so long. He'd been afraid to tell her for years; and now he had. What would she do with it? The following pause was so long that Orion wondered if he should be ready to stop the car and let her out if she demanded it. He would do so if she insisted, he decided, but could not let her go too far. At the moment, the November air outside would seem refreshingly warm compared to the car's female-fed atmosphere.

Adrienne sat without a word, arms folded across her chest and lips pressed. Had Shades not raided her neighborhood almost thirty minutes before, she would have sworn he was making it up – and she would have been angry. The fact that Shades *had* shown up assured her he was telling the truth – and she was livid.

Frank was not in the mood to sit, but he was trapped. He leaned forward, elbows on his knees, looking at his wife even as she had determined not to look at him.

"I'm really sorry, babe."

"Frank, stop saying that."

"But, Adrienne-"

"I forgive you, Frank. I do, but there's still a lot I deserve to know."

"Anything."

Her prolonged silence was killing him. Frank rocked a little, fidgeted, tapped his fingers. The car flew down the highway and he stared out the window, suddenly afraid to look at her. He'd waited five years to tell her; would she wait another five to ask her questions? An abrupt fear paralyzed him. *Oh man, what if she leaves me over this?* The weight of the revelation and Adrienne's ire made it remotely plausible, in the playing out of a worse-case scenario. If she thought she was in genuine danger...

"What are Shades?"

"I don't think anyone knows quite exactly what they are, or where they came from." He looked to Orion for help, but his oldest friend merely kept driving. Frank went on, "They've been troubling mankind since well before the Middle Ages – well before Dominos de Lumine was even thought of. They're...they're not human, Adrienne... I thought I'd never have to even see one again, but after tonight-" He stopped short. "Look, I swear, if I had known you would ever be endangered by what I did for the Society-"

She raised the hand that now held her necklace's gem. "Tell me about the shadows, Frank, just the shadows. No more apologies."

"If you really want to know about Shades you should ask Orion. He knows much more than I do. All I really can say about them is that they're very dangerous and that they're deadly enemies bent on destruction. As to why, Orion will be able to tell you better. And no, I don't know why they came to our house. Obviously they were looking for me, not you. But I don't know why. I don't even know how they would have known I lived there, or even who I was."

She suddenly cocked her head and looked at him. "Have...have you ever killed anyone?"

He did not have to speculate. "Yes."

She softly bit her lower lip, absently ran a hand down the seatbelt's shoulder strap. In the right scenario, the act itself did not really bother her; both of her grandfathers had fought in the Second World War. One had been at Omaha, the other at Okinawa; doubtless they had acted according to their role as soldiers. *But my Frank?* The hands that had held her close and stroked her hair had also ended a life? Maybe more than one. She could see his hands now, restless. That mouth that had smiled that same old impish grin of his was also the one that lied. *To me, good reason or not, he lied to me.*

But as mad as she was, she still loved those hands, that grin. The whole man. No one was perfect, but up until tonight Adrienne's complaints had been minimal. In spite of her anger, she had a clear idea as to the good past they'd shared. *He is still a good man. He has to be. I love him so much...*

"And Orion?" she asked.

"What about him?"

"How do you know him?"

"We're members of the same order. I know him."

"How, Frank?"

"We've worked together, on the order's business. We were partners once, though that seems a long time ago. I suppose it's actually only been...closing on six years."

She leaned back and looked at him. "Well, I can't say I'm not learning a lot about the man I married five years ago..." she finally said, a bit sardonically.

Frank tried to smile but avoided looking at her. Her expression was troubling, though all things considered she was taking it rather well. His throat tightened, a knot suffocating him. He was grateful for the lull in her questions, and that his wife's beautiful green eyes were softening an iota.

They lapsed into silence as Orion drove on through the night. The conversation in the back seat had taken long enough that neither of the Blackmans could have said exactly where they were at the moment; they had left the Cities and were hurtling down a remote country road. Only the distant light of a farmhouse could be seen out the windows.

Adrienne was simmering on the inside, but she kept her face blank and her arms again folded. Absently, she fingered her gem once again, feeling that it had cooled. Her mind was filled with conflicting emotions, half of her still seething at not having been told all this before, the other part of her trying to explain to the upset half that it was perfectly logical for her husband to not have shared any of it with her. *Betrayed and protected all at once,* she mused to herself. It was hard not to stare at him, trying to put a finger on what she made of the new man he had become. Well, old and new. Her peripheral vision could see he was not looking at her, but his arms were also crossed and he stared at the darkness beyond the glass. She wanted to be left alone and held all at once. She put her hand on his leg, sighed loudly, and said nothing.

Frank was preoccupied as Adrienne's reassuring touch warmed his rough hand on hers. *Retirement was supposed to be the end of it, but now it's all begun again...* The Shades had a talent for that; arriving unanticipated. It was bad enough that they had learned where he lived and had shown up. It was just as bad that he could not think of a viable reason why they should take the trouble. He had always thought that once he was out of the 'game' the Shades would simply have better things to do.

She turned abruptly to him. "Where are we going?"

"You'll see," said Orion quietly.

CHAPTER 3

"The man who crafted that gemstone would weep if he knew that all it was used for now is to adorn a neck."

~Orion Keldir

&⁊ ⳩

The new gravel road ground and popped beneath the tires, quickly losing itself among both thick and scattered trees. The hint of a distant bonfire touched the air. Looking out the window, the only illumination came from small lights lining the sides of the road. Adrienne thought the lamps made their journey eerie, a ghostly bluish twilight on the other side of the glass. Although they could not be that far from her own home, it was like they were on the other side of the world, lost in some forlorn countryside. *This is safer than our home?*

Adrienne and Frank both looked ahead with interest as they saw that the road was now blocked by barred gates. The gates were set into a massive brick wall twenty feet high, which spanned into the night to the left and right. Adrienne's suspicion that they were headed for some leaky farmhouse or barn vanished. The gates remained closed as the car slowed and Orion put down his window.

As he stopped at the console, a small screen snapped on at their approach. Adrienne could hear the voice that greeted their arrival, and it spoke in flawless Latin. Orion recited what was plainly a code. His clearance approved, a full conversation followed and went on for some time. The gates opened and the car passed through.

While the road onto the property was gravel and dimly lit, beyond the wall an entire compound awaited them. Lights shone from atop poles and numerous buildings. Grass and autumn shrubs lined the drive. They came a short distance past low bunkers and a cottage, and out into a wide area. The road broadened and wrapped in a perfect circle around a shimmering fountain. Adrienne's jaw dropped; on the other side of the fountain was a three story, old-style brick mansion.

The mansion had been built there in the middle of the huge two hundred acre property early in the twentieth century after the first war, in a time of remarkable prosperity. It and all other structures were surrounded by the perimeter wall, topped with barbed wire and lined every which way with floodlights and security cameras. The wall, of course, only encompassed the buildings and compound; not the property as a whole.

Once out of the car, Adrienne found herself clasping Frank's hand as she looked back at the wall. *I'd never get out of here if they didn't let me leave.*

Orion had also gotten out of the sedan, and was taking a careful minute to observe the deep slash down the left of his car. He paused at the back where the original first Shade had raked seven long, deep scratches across the entire width of the trunk. He sighed and patted the car resignedly, shaking his head.

As they followed Orion up to the mansion, Adrienne was too busy admiring the grand home's exterior to notice Orion scratching his left ear. Now, hardly an hour after a sword had sliced it, amidst the dried blood, the wound had not only sealed – it had completely disappeared as if never having existed.

ⅎ ℛ

The inside of the mansion looked to Adrienne as if a wealthy eccentric of good taste lived there. Upon entry they stood in a wide hall with rich carpet and dark wood paneling. The furnishings were immaculate, the art expensive and genuine originals, and what had to be an army of maids had done their job well in keeping all in perfectly neat and working order. She sat with her husband on a loveseat not far from a massive fireplace with a moose head mounted above the mantle.

Orion excused himself from the room and made his way up the carpeted stairs at the end of the hall. They sat and waited for him, listening to the crackling of the fire and the ticking of a grandfather clock of immense size. Adrienne distracted herself by looking at the various pieces of art on the paneled walls. From many of the frames, armored soldiers with swords gazed sternly back at her. The largest picture caught her eye in particular. It hosted a group of sullen men seated at a round table bearing the sigil of black bird – a crow or raven – upon its surface, while a handful of others across from them had left their places. Some turned and departed, others stood there content to lecture the sulking. Frank stared at the fire, kneading the bridge of his nose.

At length she whispered: "Where are we?"

"I don't know."

"What is this place?"

"I don't know, but I suspect it's a type of regional headquarters or retreat for the upper-level leaders of Dominos de Lumine."

"Why did he bring us here?"

He tried smiling. "Don't you feel safer here?"

She remained sober and her hand found his. "It frightens me that those shadows were after you."

"Me too."

"What are we going to do, Frank?"

He squeezed her hand. "There's no better place for us to be than here at the moment. Orion doesn't make foolish decisions. The Order is host to some of the most brilliant minds known to history, let alone our present era. We'll see what they have to say and then we'll figure it out, babe. We'll be okay."

She nodded as Orion came back down the stairs, flanked by two men.

The first moved slowly on the steps, grasping the railing as if the stair were likely to move. He was a distinguished-looking old man wearing a black turtleneck and blazer. His only colors were the white beard on his chin and the heavy, jeweled medieval cross on a gold chain about his neck. His free hand gripped a black cane by its inlaid gold and ivory handle. A natural dignity with which he carried himself made the awkwardness of climbing stairs fade instantly from memory.

Orion stood nearby and spoke. "Allow me to present my Lord Bohemond." The old man gave a nod of recognition. "My lord, the Blackmans; Frank you know, and his wife the Lady Adrienne Blackman."

Frank returned Bohemond's nod, but Adrienne only smiled shyly. She felt remarkably out of place, as if she were at an old-fashioned ball and no one had taught her how to curtsy. While the evening's events had put her in an ill-mood, she somehow perceived that to offend this older gentleman would be a terrible crime; she put her best foot forward. When Bohemond and Frank extended hands, Adrienne noticed that neither man's hand met, but rather had the other by his forearm. It struck her as an ancient method of greeting, along the same vein as her 'the Lady' title.

Bohemond spoke, his voice rasped with age, and there was the slightest hint of a German accent to his tone. "I am most sorry to have to see you once again under these circumstances, Frank." He turned to Adrienne and took her hand in an introductory fashion, quite unlike the formal clasp with Frank. "And you, my dear, I am grieved for your involvement as well. A most unfortunate business..."

Adrienne could only smile politely and he turned to the second man standing behind him, waiting patiently in silence. "This is my right hand, as we say around here, Doc Helms. He oversees our entire operation from here, or at least most aspects that don't need closer utilization. He is privy to all goings-on in so many of our associations that his presence here tonight will most assuredly be invaluable."

Long introduction for the lead tech-guy, thought Frank.

Doc Helms was as tall as Orion: a touch over six feet tall, but unlike Orion's long and dark hair, Helms' thin frame was topped with very blonde, close-cut hair. He had wire-rimmed glasses and was dressed in an immaculate suit and tie, a Rolex on his left wrist, a wedding ring on his finger. He was completely clean-shaven, and had an eternally serious expression. Helms was never without electronic access to the vast intricacies of the organization he helped to run. Both Blackmans nodded to Doc, who made the same gesture but then returned up the stairs.

Behind him, Frank turned immediately back to Bohemond, occasionally glancing at Orion. "We have much to discuss, gentlemen. I'm hoping some Shadow War intelligence can shed light on the fun we've had tonight?"

Orion nodded a bit grimly but said nothing, a depth of knowledge hidden in his face.

"You haven't been gone that long, old friend," said Bohemond. "You left us, the war did not. But you will not leave here disappointed, I promise you. Come! Doc is at this very moment probably preparing what we need to discuss. He will be underway, no doubt, by the time we join him. He's organized, that one."

With that, the old man turned and started back up the stairs, climbing as only an older man could. Doc could have told them that Bohemond had refused the organization's offer to put in a lift instead of steps. Orion stood there at the foot of the stairs, waiting to be the last one to go up. Frank had put a foot on the lowest step but stopped and glanced back at Adrienne.

"You want to come?" he asked.

Her arms were crossed, expression near sullen. "No...you go and just leave me here."

"Sorry, I was-"

Too far up the stairs to hear the talk at the bottom, Bohemond began speaking to Adrienne over his shoulder. "You are welcome to join us, my Lady Blackman, though I daresay you'll find most of our discussion tedious and obscure. Perhaps you'd like to retire for the evening in one of our guesthouses..."

Orion closed his eyes as he stood there, knowing this was not the thing to say just now.

Frank's left hand was in Adrienne's right, and she reeled him in so she could whisper in his ear: "I don't want to just toddle off to some guesthouse – not until I know what's going on. It is *not* fair to just take off with your friends and leave me somewhere. Not after tonight. I'm not going *anywhere* until someone explains this all to me."

Frank spoke in a low voice, thick with guilt. "Okay, okay, you're right. I'm sorry. Okay? Sorry. It's been a...a long night. Of course you should come with us-"

"If I may..." came Orion's voice.

The Blackmans stopped and looked at him, and he went on.

"The conversation to follow may very well contain highly-privileged information." He paused at the look Adrienne was giving him. "It is not that our discussion will be beyond your scope of understanding, my lady. It's just that your gaining the knowledge discussed may at some point become detrimental to your safety. Classified information can be very dangerous; people live and die for it – the latter not always by choice."

Frank stopped short. "I hadn't thought of that..."

Adrienne could not stand being patronized, but the tone and expression with which Orion said all this did not offend her. Whether or not he meant his tact to save face was irrelevant; his conclusion was rational.

She let go of Frank's hand and looked resolved. "So do I find my way to this guesthouse by myself?"

"You're sure?" asked Frank.

She nodded, now past the previous unintended offense. "What he says makes sense, I guess."

"Allow me," said Orion. He glanced at Frank. "Your destination is the fourth door to the left at the top of the stair." He then made a polite motion for Adrienne to come with him.

&0 C8

"What did Frank mean by 'Shadow War'?" she asked as they walked.

"It is a generic reference to anything concerning Shades," he answered, "particularly the intelligence network directly related to monitoring them."

"Isn't 'Bohemond' a bit of an unusual name?"

Orion had known multiple Bohemonds. "At this time in history," he finally said, "I suppose it is."

"Is that his real name?"

"Certainly not, my lady." And he said nothing more.

Quite the conversationalist. She encouraged him: "Soooo..."

"Here it is more a title than a name. There is not one leader of Dominos de Lumine, but four. The organization is too vast and powerful for one man. The four men who lead the Society take the title of 'Lord' and assume one of the four names reserved for their position. These four names are taken from the first founders: Robert, Godfrey, Frederick, and Bohemond."

She remembered the pictures she had viewed previously. "Ah."

&0 C8

The guest cottage was about a hundred feet from the mansion. Once again, Adrienne found that all was luxuriously decorated with fine taste: leather sofas, shelves with books, a kitchenette, rich carpet. Up the stairs were fully-accommodated bedrooms and a bathroom with a whirlpool tub large enough for eight. A full-scale grand piano sat in the corner; it made the last Steinway she had seen look like a child's toy.

The piano alone is probably worth more than our house...let alone everything else in here.

Adrienne was standing agog at the entry, marveling at the variety of antique vases sitting upon shelves and the corner table. Upon one wall were swords of various kinds, and she was reminded of the soldiering history of this mysterious society. She came back to the moment to find that Orion was still there with her, not watching her but rather looking straight ahead at nothing. He was impossible to read.

"A little wealth in Dominos de Lumine..." Adrienne said quietly, taking in the opulence.

"The Society has been around long enough to accumulate a few things," he answered.

She was wondering what Frank had earned in his time there, but what she said was: "How long?"

"The early eleventh century is when the four founders separated from their previous loyalties and began the Lords of Light."

"Previous loyalties?" she asked, recalling the paintings. "The men at the table with the bird on it?"

His voice had a sudden edge to it. "They are called the Order of the Raven. If we are not countering the Shades, we are dealing with their ilk..." He seemed to remember himself and his tone lost its passion. "Forgive me, but I must return. I trust this will suit your need?"

"Yes, thank you. Have you any idea how long it will take? The meeting, I mean."

"I'm afraid not. A most complicated matter. It is well that the Lord Bohemond is here amidst his travels. He is a far more wise man than myself. He will know what to do about tonight's...fiasco."

"See you later, then."

"Good night, my lady."

Orion closed the door and she watched through the window by moonlight as he walked back toward the mansion. She waited until he was a little further away before locking the door and drawing the shades. It was night, after all, and the lights were on in the cottage.

I should have asked him if any of these books are about these societies and orders...or the shadows hunting my husband...

෮ ෬

Frank had very few actual regrets about leaving the Dominos de Lumine for the purpose of marrying Adrienne and living a normal life. The regrets he did have were not related to her; Adrienne was the best thing that ever happened to him.

I've missed it, I admit it, he mused as he accepted the glass of brandy. He swirled and smelled it, hearing the crackle of the fire off to his right as he sank into the cushy armchair. Somewhere behind him, Doc was typing on a laptop.

Bohemond clinked a glass as he poured his own. The life of the Society had had its moments. His current job in accounting was a far cry from what he used to do. He had longed for the same sense of accomplishment, knowing that he was among the best at what he did – knowing that what he did mattered.

Orion entered the room and closed the heavy door behind him, and upon his arrival Bohemond struck up as if he had been waiting:

"Now gentlemen, let us begin. Frank, there is some troublesome news I must share with you now that we are all here-"

"James Talon is dead," interrupted Orion over crossed arms as he stood behind Doc.

Frank sat up, mouth open. "Dead! How? When?"

"Two days ago," said Bohemond resignedly, exchanging a glance with Doc. The unpleasant facts regarding their friend and long-time colleague was not news to either.

Frank leaned back again, eyes closed. His voice was quiet and tentative. "And...how?"

"He was working in Beijing and was found in an alley-"

"Suffice it to say he did not go quietly, as any of us would expect of him," Orion cut in once more. "The precise details are regrettable but irrelevant to our discussion here tonight. His living quarters were found quite disturbed; someone took the time to toss them very thoroughly."

"What were they looking for?"

"The place was such a mess it was impossible to tell what was missing," said Bohemond.

"We have our suspicions," added Orion.

"I hadn't spoken to him for six years," reflected Frank, searching for words. "This is...most regrettable." *Sorry, James. More than regrettable.*

"It gets worse," said Doc matter-of-factly as he looked at his computer screen, seemingly detached from the dark conversation.

Frank said nothing but looked around expectantly.

Orion's answer was grim. "James was two days ago. Marco was six months ago. And two months before Marco was Angelia."

Stunned silence met the declaration that three specialists had been murdered within less than a year. Frank was speechless – no one was entirely invincible, but these three were not the type of people to wind up on the casualty list, let alone within close time proximity. Angelia in particular he had been close to – but that ended years before Adrienne.

"It was obvious in each case that our perpetrator was clearly looking for something after the fact. As in James' case, the state of their living quarters made it difficult if not impossible to tell the point of the searches."

Frank wasn't sure he wanted to know, but he had to ask. "What's the analysis?"

There was a pause as they looked back at him.

"What?"

"Frank, I did not come to your home this evening because of Shades. I was already on my way when I was alerted there was a near battalion of shadow-legionnaires in your neighborhood. That is how the trip came out – but that was not my initial concern."

"I...don't understand."

"Every active time agent has been killed, Blackman," said Doc shortly, never looking away from his laptop. He sounded distracted and annoyed that Frank had not jumped to this conclusion of his own accord.

"James Talon," continued Bohemond with a chiding glance at Doc, "was the last active time agent still operating. In order, after him, you are the next closest thing to a time agent; you're the most recent to retire."

Frank stared straight ahead, stunned. The brandy sat shaking in his hand.

"We could not just call you," explained Orion. "We did not know if you were being watched, hunted, stalked. Various surveillance technologies we immediately employed showed us nothing; we had to come get you. As soon as we were in your region, I thought it best to bring you and Adrienne here before these murderers – or single murderer – located you. The progression seemed logical that they would find you next. My timing was unintentionally fortuitous."

"The Shades?"

"Yes. Though that in itself does not make sense. I do not think the Shades are involved in these recent deaths."

"How so?" asked Bohemond.

"Shades kill easily, especially legionnaires. But there is a...look, a feel to their heinous acts. Our brothers and sister in arms were murdered, surely, but the scenes were – forgive me – rather 'every day' as far as murders go."

"That's a little cold, Keldir-" began Helms, but was cut off.

Orion leaned forward, as he stood immediately behind Doc. "I know what a Shade can do to a human being, Mr. Helms," said the stern voice directly into the tech's flinching ear. "There are grievous types of wounds that cannot be inflicted without a shadow-legionnaire's blade." Doc remained still as Orion paused and moved from his left ear to the right. "We will not here dishonor the dead by discussing the varying degrees of trauma which resulted in untimely death. The Shades are not responsible."

Orion then straightened and stepped back. After a moment he crossed the room to be in more of a conversation-circle with Bohemond and Frank. Doc glowered shortly at his back and returned to his screen, now enveloped in his online work.

"So you're saying," said Frank, "that the murders and the Shades are unrelated, but both of you wind up at our house tonight?"

Orion sighed. "I did not say I could explain it."

"It was my concern that someone might be enacting an agenda specifically against time agents," said Bohemond, looking at his brandy swirl. "Perhaps that is the end of it now, given there are no more active time agents – present company excluded." He looked at Orion.

"I am not a time agent by definition. I take no serum," said Orion nonchalantly.

"But your longevity is greatest of any of them-"

"I take," Orion deliberately repeated, "no serum."

Frank abruptly sat up. "Elapsation serum! Could that be what the murderer wanted?"

"That was a primary suspicion. Unsubstantiated – but highly probable."

"As I said," Bohemond started in again, "a vendetta against time agents may be underway. But that theory was confounded when the Network confirmed the Shades being in this region for a week. They were widespread; not just in your neighborhood. That you were there in the area too did not stick out at first. It seems a good thing Orion came to get you anyway."

Orion looked out the window as he responded to this last statement. "If we had known they were actively pursuing you instead of biding their time as they usually do, someone on location would have arrived a day or two sooner and you both would have been spared the…excitement of the evening. As it is, it appears I got there just in time. I was not expecting to see them there."

"I doubt they were expecting you either," added Frank. "The one in the yard had its shot at you, but didn't take it."

"No," Orion said slowly, "no, it did not. It would appear I surprised them. That doesn't happen often."

There was a pause in the conversation as the fire crackled and the supply of brandy decreased by a few sips. Frank broke the silence.

"How would someone know the identities and locations of three time agents so quickly?"

"That," growled Bohemond, "would be our latest *inside* problem."

"Spy?"

"Worse," the old man said, but lapsed into silence.

Orion finished for him. "A covert mole. Someone with an impressive level of security and remarkable know-how."

Doc spoke up from the table, gaze not leaving his laptop. "I've been trying to catch the mole constantly since we discovered what had to be their handiwork. Heaven knows how long he or she has been active. Whoever it is has been very… thorough. I've not been successful. Yet."

Bohemond huffed. "You should have had them by now…"

Doc gave Bohemond as black a look as one could give a distinguished superior, but then lowered his gaze and began typing once more.

These two have had this discussion before, Frank silently concluded, but aloud he said, "So no one knows long has this mole's been in the garden?"

"Impossible to tell," said Orion. "With someone like this, who they'd have to be or what they'd have to know, it's likely they started legit. Someone probably bought them off. It's not unheard of, even in the Society."

"Could this murderer be one of our own?"

"If the purpose is to get serum, it would not seem to make much sense for someone with that kind of security clearance to have to kill for it. They would just steal it. Though it is possible that the one with the access gave names and locations to the murderer on the outside. And then the cur on the outside made his own move."

Frank stood up and angled closer to the fire, mulling the two situations – a murderer on the loose, possibly looking for him; and Shades at his own house looking for him. He spoke over his shoulder.

"Subject change; you explained what brought you to our place. So what were the Shades doing at our house?"

"I have ruled out vengeance and reprisals for your past service in the Society," said Orion. "It's petty for creatures like them. Regardless, that has to be the foremost theory until a better idea is proposed."

"Aye," agreed the elderly Bohemond. "Those foul creatures are far too practical to be concerned with mere retribution. It's not how they think, but that makes tonight's events all the more concerning: it means there has to be some special purpose for their raid on the Blackman home."

"And in a well-populated area," added Frank. "They never would have done that in the old days. Isolation always used to be their strong suit. Either the world has changed or they've grown much bolder."

"The world has changed," said Orion grimly. "The Shadow War has picked up in intensity remarkably overall in the last century, let alone the past decade. I fear this is reminiscent of some dark plan coming to fruition after long years…" He spoke this last part as if to himself.

Doc spoke up. "Could they want security information of some sort? Even after the debriefing for all retirees?"

Frank shrugged. "I can't think what they would want to know from me. Can't think of a thing I still know that they wouldn't already be aware of either. The debriefing did a very good job of relieving me of secrets I once had to know. I don't know what they'd expect to get out of me…"

80 Q3

Outside the tall stone wall that surrounded the mansion and its luxurious grounds, scattered woods and fields dominated the landscape. Moonlight on the branches and the wind that moved them made the autumn forest floor wildly alive. Yet the lone man walked along without so much as a thought to stumbling or tripping on anything in his way. His trek was filled with all the creaking and snapping that may have unnerved the average person when treading such places all alone in the dead of the night.

Cyprus was not an average person. He was, actually, very much like Orion: tall and dark haired, a bit grim of countenance – as though they were both from the same place. And unlike other men, but again just like Orion, he could see in the dark without enhancement. He wore a deep blue cloak about him, but beneath his raiment was close-fitting black apparel that a thief in the night might enjoy.

The anticipation in him was like a drug, and he licked his lips while two slow and heavy, twitching blinks stuttered his eyes. His plans that evening had taken an entrancing turn. Home invasion in the suburbs was not common for Cyprus, and he did not consider it overly stimulating – though that could depend on who happened to be home. So much for its being abruptly cancelled. But a visit to the regional headquarters of Dominos de Lumine? That would do just fine.

This night will be one for my memoirs.

The barrier of blackness before him was the perimeter wall which wound its way around the grounds of the Dominos de Lumine complex. He kept walking, his right hand going to his left wrist and tapping a couple buttons without looking, signaling his contact that he had arrived. He reached the wall and stood there in the dark, looking up the twenty feet to where the top of the wall ran with barbed wire, electrified. The slightest hum of generators somewhere on the grounds beyond mixed with the cool breeze. Before him in the wall itself was a heavy metal security door. It had no handle on the outside and was surely solid; there was no access that way except by help from within.

The gadget on his left wrist, the one he had tapped a moment before, vibrated to attract his attention. He had turned off the light and sound it would usually make, and silently promised himself that this device and the help it offered would be conspicuously absent from his pending written account of the evening's events. He looked down and read the short message that blinked across it: ***Priority One objective in eastern-most cottage.*** He tapped back his response with little exertion and waited. ***Port 3A access, point-five minute security negation window, engage.***

Within seconds, the door with no handle cracked open an inch, and Cyprus was there to help pull it out further, allowing him enough room to slip by. He smiled to himself, loving that at the moment, it was all just too easy. He entered the Dominos de Lumine compound, access Port 3A having its security latch and camera system negated for exactly thirty seconds, twenty-one of which were unnecessary.

CHAPTER 4

"Every man has his price, whether he is a cur or noble. Some men have a higher price than others, sure; but they still have one. You just have to be willing to find it."

~Cyprus Blackshaft

                                                  ℘ ℭ

A drienne used the accents and fortes to vent her anger, arpeggios to free her thoughts, and the rapid tempo of presto to focus and use up her tension. Beethoven let her mind wander and reflect, Mozart soothed, and Chopin…Chopin… *Chopin hated pianists, but I love him anyway.* That was what her mother always said. A joke about what the man had required one hand to do, from physical span to just intricacies. *Who writes a song in six sharps? Sadist.*

Some time elapsed and amid the fingering of *Valse Triste,* the timing and articulation of a later chord finally tripped her up, and the keys she pressed down insulted her ears. Good habit of practice demanded getting the chord correct before progressing. She pressed it again but it was tenths in both hands; her hands were just too small. She took it back a few measures to lead into it, but her hands would not cooperate. Her eyes watered. *He lied to me.* Her hands came down forcefully hard on the keys again and again, this time striking no chord but just pounding. The instrument filled the room with a dreadfully ugly, toneless blob of voluminous sound. One tear escaped her eye and she welcomed it with several more poundings of the keys.

The tension passed, alleviated by the frustrated tantrum. She let up on the keys and let the room fill with silence, but as she did so she cocked her head at the sound by the door: the inescapable sound of a cat, mewing incessantly. She sat there and listened to it for a moment, marveling that a cat would be kept on the property. *It is too serious of a place for pets...*

The feline continued its chorus to the point that she got up and went to the door, looking out the window to see it. There it sat on the cobblestones, bathed in the light from the bulb above the door, looking at the door and then Adrienne with large eyes. It was a white cat with blue eyes, tail flicking back and forth, voice plaintive. Adrienne's attention only made it cry louder.

Adrienne had admittedly always liked animals, and cats were among her favorites. Her family's Nebraska farm had well over a dozen in the time she grew up. She watched it for awhile and saw that the grimalkin had no intention of going away, so at last she opened the door just a bit to see what the cat would do. She was surprised when, instead of coming forward to get in, the feisty creature only stood its ground and meowed at her.

80 CR

Doc went on typing, although there was little to no further conversation. The fire crackled as Frank added wood. Computer keys clacked. Bohemond's glass was put down hard enough to crack the crystal; the old man was clearly accustomed to going to bed earlier. Frank was so deep in contemplation that he did not notice when Doc's eyes left the monitor for only a moment to look at him, and then returned.

Orion spoke up after his own moment of cogitation. "Frank, what if they were not looking for you?"

Frank looked up, attention grimly fixed. "You can't mean..."

"I was referring to your wife," he said plainly.

Frank stood up looking at each man in turn, rigid. "Have I been blind?"

Orion continued with his typical logic: "We have established the Shades would have no interest in you, the only answer left would be the Lady Blackman."

"Orion, don't upset Frank: that is ridiculous," said Bohemond.

"No," persisted Orion, however politely, "it is ridiculous to ignore the next logical step in the progression, if we have eliminated the steps before."

Frank's hands went to his head, pushing his short hair up between his fingers. "No, no, no...this is all wrong..."

"You're too rational sometimes, I think..." said Doc from the table.

Orion merely glanced over at him, deciding not to question aloud if it was possible to be too reasonable or logical. Doc had taken his eyes from the room and was focused on his screen, and so he missed the looks Frank and Bohemond were giving Orion.

"They plainly wanted Frank," Bohemond went on. "Simply because we do not know why does not mean he is not the reason."

"If neither option makes sense, neither is more or less likely," Orion said matter-of-factly.

Frank spun about and stalked to the door. "I'm going to check on Adrienne. She's been by herself long enough after what I've put her through."

"I'll show you where she is," said Orion.

⁜ ⁝

Adrienne crouched on the walkway with her back to the cottage, her favorite necklace dangling its green stone. She extended fingers up to the cat's nose while caressing the silken fur from the top of its head all the way down its back. It had stopped mewing and contented itself with sniffing her hand and occasionally purring, arching its back appreciatively into her stroke.

The light abruptly dimmed. She had only just noticed this change when the shadow immediately loomed larger around her; whoever blocked the light had come swiftly closer. An arm threw itself like a snake's coil around her middle, securely pinning her lowered right arm to her side. Her cry at this sudden intrusion was instantly stifled by another hand that roughly clamped a damp cloth over her mouth and nose, sealing tightly. The cat had vanished.

Her one free hand clawed at the chloroform over her features, nails raking at the gloved hand, but it was like tugging at a vice. The encircling arm lifted her bodily off the ground, eliminating the leverage of her legs. It was a comfortable, practiced motion on his part. Adrienne's pulse quickened as air became more important. Her free hand stopped clawing and took to rocketing her elbow again and again into the brick-hard torso behind. She thrashed for an excruciating, terrifying minute of struggle before the world faded into darkness.

Cyprus held Adrienne securely from behind, knowing he was perfectly positioned, and strength twice her own would not have helped her in that intense moment. He held on, head close to her own, hearing the panicked intake of breath, or at least the attempted intake. Her elbow hammered his ribs. It was an intimate moment, and he did not stop himself from admitting he enjoyed it. This one was not the first time he had done something of the like, but nonetheless each time it presented a certain thrill.

Once she succumbed, he held on a few precious seconds longer to make sure she wasn't faking, and then laid her on the ground. Cyprus stood over Adrienne, disappointed that his powerful self-created apparition of the cat had disappeared instantly once his focus was elsewhere; he should have been able to keep it there while subduing a woman. A temporary fatigue ached deep within his core; repercussions from projecting the image which Adrienne had taken for real, as most people would.

A normal man would not have been able to exude the power to make the apparition and still have the strength left to physically overcome a woman of Adrienne's strength in her resistance; the elbows she threw *had* hurt. She had admirable tenacity and a decent amount of strength for her size and build – but Cyprus was not an ordinary man, and he had no ordinary strength. He knelt beside the prone form of the woman on the polished stone of the walkway. After taking hardly a moment to check her pulse, he produced a handful of zip-ties. He cinched Adrienne's hands behind her, and then fastened her legs together at the knee and ankle.

A precious quarter of a minute was given to surveying his handiwork. *It's so much more pleasant work when they're pretty*, he silently speculated. Her green gem necklace had slipped out of her neckline amid the struggle, and he started reaching for it but then stopped himself. *No, not here. Later.* He picked Adrienne's prone body up, put her over his shoulder, and moved off the path into the shadows.

⁂ ⁏

Bohemond leaned back with his eyes closed, enjoying at one moment the comfortable chair, but at the same time troubled with Orion's suggestion. The very idea that Shades would be interested in Lady Blackman was ludicrous, as he and Frank had established. Yet somehow it unsettled him that it was Orion who proposed it. Bohemond had known Orion for a long time; indeed, he was among the oldest members of Dominos de Lumine. Orion over the years had been many things, and one of them was consistent. The man was, quite simply, rarely mistaken or wrong.

"Ridiculous," he said aloud, shaking his head.

Doc looked up from his laptop. "My lord?"

"Orion's suggestion that the Shades were looking for the Lady Blackman instead of Frank. Ridiculous."

"Aye, my Lord. Ridiculous." But Doc Helms had not spoken his own mind.

⁂ ⁏

"Adrienne?" Frank stepped inside the cottage with Orion close behind. They searched both floors and Orion noticed the piano keyboard cover was up, but otherwise it was like she'd never been there.

Frank called her name once more, more confused than concerned; she could not have gone far. "Where is she?"

Orion said nothing, but after glancing toward the wide open bathroom door, he looked back at Frank and gave the slightest impression of a shrug. He then turned and walked out the door, pausing in the moonlight, very close to the same place Adrienne had found the feline. He looked back at the house and then about the sidewalk, brow slightly furrowed.

"Something does not feel quite right," he said quietly.

"Adrienne!" Frank shouted into the night, fingers drumming on the banister of the porch. *Where is she?*

"I left her here," said Orion. "She would not wander off, would she? I do not know her well…"

"I doubt it," conceded Frank. "But where would she go?"

"She could not leave the property without us knowing. Back to the mansion. Security will have caught her movements."

✌ ☙

Cyprus paused just a moment to check his vibrating device: **She is missed.**

He frowned. *A little sooner than hoped for*, he silently groused. He did not consider Dominos de Lumine fools in the least. He would *never* attempt this sort of venture without inside help. But he had hoped for a little more of a head-start than this. He tapped back his response with some difficulty, as the unconscious Adrienne was over his shoulder.

I need an exit now.

The response was immediate and he followed its instructions, heading for the north end of the compound, staying in the shadows. He wondered in the back of his mind what he could do if his captive woke too early and became a nuisance before they were away. He had taken her by surprise the first time. He doubted it would be half as easy the second.

✌ ☙

"So bring up the camera showing the cottage then, Helms!" growled Frank.

Doc typed a few commands and sifted through multiple windows up on the screen. At length he isolated the right feed and began to rewind a square of video that showed the entry to the cottage.

"There! Stop!" instructed Frank, at a brief glimpse of Adrienne. Doc, without a word, rewound past her so as to watch the scenario from the beginning. "There, that's her, but…"

"What is she doing?" asked Doc.

They watched the video of Adrienne crouching on the cobblestone, one hand extended a bit and held still, the other combing the air in front of her in a specific motion.

"I don't understand," said Doc again.

"It looks like she's petting something," noted Frank.

Orion looked at it critically, frowning. "I don't like it…" He trailed off and then his expression changed as he came to an astute conclusion. "A phantasm… that's a phantasm."

A black figure emerged from the darkness behind Adrienne, grabbed her as she began to turn and pressed something over her face.

"Adrienne…" was all Frank could get out, his fists rolled so tightly his knuckles turned white. He turned away and looked back, two fingers pushing at the bridge of his nose. When the fearful scene ended, he turned to Orion. "What is a phantasm?" he hissed.

Orion stared at the screen. "It is an ancient and now lost art. Phantasms are mental projections that manifest for a short time. To the unsuspecting they are real enough, but they do not actually exist. That is why it did not appear on the recording. Come on."

"I'll sound the Lockdown," said Doc, and began typing commands. His eyes locked on the screen, flitting back and forth. He leaned forward, switched windows, and went down a line. "Uh-oh..."

Bohemond looked back from the chair in which he was about to sit. "What?"

"Someone else is in the system. They have security access."

"Can you trace them? Are they here?"

"One thing at a time..."

৪০ ৪৪

Cyprus leaned against the barracks wall, knowing that around the corner only a few feet away, the secured door would pop open. The floodlights came on all around him and an electronic alarm blared, but these were only prerequisites to what he wanted. He hoped it would be quick: with the illumination of nearly every last corner of the compound, he could not afford to just stand there with his captive. He was relatively sure that there was *some* camera that could technically see him. Fortunately, they had so many that someone would have to be lucky enough to look at the right monitor.

He glanced at the device and read: *Two will come out. Wait for both, but don't let the door close before you're in.*

Within moments, the secured door did indeed open and out came one armed guard, and a moment later the second. Cyprus smiled; it was most amusing that both were so intent on heading for the mansion that neither looked behind in time to see the dark figure slip from the corner and get inside the door before it slammed shut.

The closing of the door muffled the sounds and the lights that lit up the night all over the compound, and he was grateful for the break. Adrienne's captor carried his burden down a short run of stairs before finding himself in the barracks itself. To his left sat computer equipment and a command station. Every monitor showed a different part of the property, lit up in the night and dotted with running personnel.

He paid little heed to all this. Though the trespasser was momentarily out of sight, making haste was paramount. Recalling the instructions that had been written to him, he passed through the barracks, heading toward the end of the slightly submerged structure. Well below ground level, the building ended in a narrow tunnel that continued straight on. He had to take care in the low-ceilinged tunnel passage, lit only by little red lights that ran in a dotted line on the edges of the floor. It was not built for carrying someone while traversing its length.

Cyprus paused at the steel security door. A yellow light was blinking next to it and when he kicked at it, he found it was already cracked open. *I love computers.* In the midst of a security breach, any codes required to enter the door would be locked out; his contact had complete control of the mainframe and was one step ahead. He shouldered his way through the doorway.

Before him was the dark of night, made even more enveloping by the woods that crept in so close. He was looking down a hill, knowing that the river must be about one hundred meters distant. The perimeter wall around the Dominos de Lumine complex was behind him as the escaping intruder stood at the end of the emergency exit tunnel. Cyprus made off into the welcoming chaos of a windy, nocturnal woodland swept with searchlights.

ꚕ ꙅ

Orion stood on the terrace, surveying the scene of the entire property lit up as if for Christmas, with the added sweeping spotlights and glaring floodlights of a Lockdown. The sound of all the alarms was a poorly blended symphony of bedlam. Frank stood beside Orion, impressed that the man appeared unable to hear it all. In his mind, Orion had set aside the alarms as immaterial and unimportant, and locked them out.

"The question is," he said to Frank beside him, hardly loud enough to be heard over the bells, "of the dozen ways he could leave, which one would he pick?"

A quarter minute passed and the bells fell silent, though the lights all still remained on. There was shouting on the grounds below him, and he could see all types of personnel running about. The general situation had circulated by now, and each scanned the grounds in vain for a black-clad invader and his kidnapped victim.

Orion observed for a moment and then walked back inside without a word. Frank followed him. A moment later they stood in front of a whole wall of monitors, each screen divided into four; they could simultaneously observe the view of forty-eight cameras. Yet none showed what they sought.

Frank's stress could be heard in his voice as he stood staring at the monitors. "Adrienne...where are you?" He rubbed his eyes harder than necessary and returned them to the wall, looking disheveled.

"Courage," said Orion, also gazing at the screens. "The nature of the incident suggests they want her alive and well. Don't lose heart."

ꚕ ꙅ

Doc clicked on a window that blinked at him, and then glanced at Bohemond.

The old man sat in the large cushy chair with his eyes closed, listening to the commotion outside, muted by the closed door.

"Did you track where our saboteur is transmitting from yet?" asked the old man.

"He's in the city," said Doc. "It's closing on him. He's set up some deterrents. It's going to take another minute – no, wait, I have him."

Bohemond's eyes opened and he leaned forward. "Where is the rat?"

"He's at the Morgan Street building."

"So call and alert them!"

"If I make a call to the location," protested Doc, "our friend may be monitoring the calls."

"Don't have much choice, do we?"

Doc paused in the conversation as he grabbed the headset he always kept close at hand. He could use the laptop to make the call itself. "Dialing...yes, this is Doc Helms at Lumine One." Bohemond stared the tech down as he gave a number of clearance codes verifying his legitimacy. He concluded with "Initiate online access lockdown at your location immediately, Priority One. Do it now, Olson. And isolate console TF-952. Arrest the individual at that station immediately. I don't care who it is."

For a moment the only sound in the room were the shouts from outside the complex and Doc's fingers furiously clattering away as usual. Bohemond remained in his chair, eyes still closed, waiting for a good minute or two.

"Well?" he finally asked.

"My Lord...Port 3C has been opened."

Bohemond's eyes opened. "What?"

"Someone has either entered or left the property by Port 3C."

"The Tunnel?"

"Aye."

"Get a detachment down there, Doc."

At that moment Orion came in, followed closely by Frank.

"3C's been used," Doc announced.

"When?" asked Orion.

"Not even a minute ago..."

"Whoever it was must be in the woods and nearly away," said Orion, turning toward the door and speaking further over his shoulder. "We need to move. Now."

"So go," said Bohemond.

"Get a detachment to meet us down there. Standard night ops," said Frank, following Orion.

"Already on its way," said Doc, and the door slammed behind them.

Doc glanced after them and then at Bohemond. He typed a few things. When he spoke again, it was not to Bohemond, but on the line to the Morgan Street location now under lockdown.

"Is TF-952's user in custody? I see…what? But how?"

Bohemond looked up in surprise as Doc swore loudly and spiked his headset on the floor in exasperation. He took his glasses off and rubbed his eyes, swearing again.

"Yes?" asked Bohemond.

"Empty console. Remote access. And he'll be gone from his real location by the time we find it. This guy is good. And I thought I had him, after all this time waiting for him to be on at the same time I was."

"You're slipping, Helms," chided Bohemond.

Doc was hardly amused. "He's one of us, my Lord. He didn't have to hack into the network; it's already open to him, and so he has plenty of time to set up this kind of thing. If he puts up enough remote access and dead ends, there'll be virtually no way to find him. And even if we did isolate his feed, he'd have time to see it coming and be long gone." He sighed and looked hard at Bohemond. "Sir, this could be *anyone* in the Society."

⊰ ⊱

Adrienne Blackman made the slightest of groans and Cyprus made a concentrated effort to increase his pace. He had not reached the river yet, and he wanted to be underway. Amid the swirl of the wind in the trees, sounds of pursuit echoed after him. Distant pursuit, but they were coming nonetheless.

The moon broke upon the landscape before him as he came out from under the trees. Only a short way ahead the ground fell downward and soon met the shimmering river. Its surface was black glass, reflecting the stars and the pale moon.

Coming off the bank was a rickety old dock, and tethered loosely to it was a rowboat with oars lying alongside. While this land was technically on the property of Dominos de Lumine, Cyprus doubted they ever used this particular part. The little dock was not well kept, and probably dated back to the time when the surrounding countryside was part of a farm. The trembling wood creaked in protest as he walked out toward his small boat. He reached it and gently lowered Adrienne into it, noticing that once again she was gradually returning to consciousness. *Just in time.*

He stepped easily into the boat and looked shoreward, seeing flashes of light approaching through the trees. He cocked his head slightly. There were calls too, and he found himself wondering if the famous Orion Keldir was among those sent after him. Knowing that this was a distinct possibility, he pushed away from the dock and began rowing quietly out into the river itself. Here was where the oars in particular served: a motor would take them away faster, but oars were not to be heard.

Not tonight, Orion. You can read about this dazzling escape in my memoirs…

Part of Cyprus wanted very much to see Orion once again, though even without the present circumstances, he doubted the legendary figure would have anything to say to him. Not much had changed since they had last seen each other, but Cyprus could not help but want to discuss things with him. *We could accomplish so many things together – who could stop us? ...And there are so many opportunities to be had.* He looked at Adrienne. *There's even one lying at my feet.* Yet dwelling on it made him pull harder at the oars, knowing Orion would never betray his precious society. He had always been so...loyal, even from the beginning. He had to love Dominos de Lumine more than anything. But every man had his price, or so the old saying went. Some simply had a higher rate than others.

Not three feet away in the small boat, Adrienne groaned and lifted her head, eyes shut from the incredible headache that grated in her skull. She shook her head and then, much to Cyprus's amusement as he rowed on, noticed her restraints. He saw her arms twitch and heard the soft noise of her surprise as she did indeed discover she was hopelessly stuck.

"What...what is this?" she managed, shaking her head again. As coherence returned to Adrienne she saw she was not alone, and straightened with startled fear. "W-who are you? W-w-what's going on?"

Cyprus was impressed. She didn't sound too scared. He had expected she would. Well, good for her. Perhaps she had the foresight to cherish it while she could.

"This is a rowboat," he intoned. "And you, Adrienne Blackman, may call me Cyprus."

His methodical rowing continued as they entered the moving channel of the river itself and began coasting easily downstream. The surrounding night gave the illusion of the water moving faster beneath them. Flashlights had reached the bank.

"I meant – how did you know my name?"

"I really am impressed. No tears, no pleading, no begging. I appreciate that, believe me. Why, I brought duct tape just in case."

"I'm not the begging type," said she, but immediately wondered if she should be speaking her thoughts so easily. *It might encourage him. Think before you speak.*

"We'll see," he chuckled easily. "But in the meanwhile, consider this a simple invitation," said Cyprus. "I merely desired the pleasure of your company."

She sighed, already having reached her emotional peak for the evening, psychologically drained. *Haven't I been through enough tonight already?*

Her arms shifted as she uselessly tested the cuttingly-tight pair of zip-ties. They were so snug she had no slack at all, and her crossed wrists felt glued to one another. Her fingertips tingled, as did her feet. She had never had such a trapped sensation before, and a frightened chill went up her spine. She shivered uncomfortably, and her fists clenched in an effort to stay calm. She was helpless and she knew it, though she successfully kept her voice perfectly even. *I wonder if he would fall overboard if I could kick him just right...*

"If this is an invitation why am I tied up?" she asked.

"I did not want you going for a swim."

"Why would I do that? Looks cold."

Cyprus smiled the smile of a gentleman, and even he would have called it a practiced façade. At any rate, the rowboat was now far enough from shore. "Do you see those lights behind us?"

She looked, and it was impossible not to see them.

"Those are men of Dominos de Lumine. They did not care for my manner of inviting you out. Your husband is undoubtedly among them."

Her voice exploded into the night. "Frank!"

Cyprus continued rowing as if she were merely continuing a quiet conversation. "Well, you did ask," he said, nonchalantly.

From behind them across the water a distant call was heard.

"Adrienne!"

"Help me!"

Frank shouted something else but it was lost on the cold wind.

Cyprus rowed on, and in another minute or two Adrienne could not hear her husband's voice or see the lights that supposedly marked his position as he looked for her. She was glad that in the dark her captor could not see the water pool in her eyes as she lapsed into silence.

౭౦ ౪౩

"Adrienne! Adrienne!"

Frank stood with his hands on his knees, panting on the edge of the dock after the blind run through the woods, shouting toward Adrienne's fading voice. After a moment he could not hear her at all. He swore aloud.

Behind him, Orion made hand signals to the contingent of Dominos de Lumine who were going up and down the bank and shining their powerful flashlights every which-way. They noted his signs and without any further ado, turned their backs on the river and began heading back through the woods toward the compound.

"Are you coming?" asked Orion. Frank had a light but navigating to the correct entry point could be a challenge in the dark. *Best to wait for him.*

"I feel like I'm leaving her. I can't just…"

"Come, we're wasting time." He put a hand on Frank's shoulder. "We can't very well swim after them. This abductor was organized; we need to make a plan for our pursuit." *The list of those who can make a phantasm is short. I'd wager a night of peaceful sleep that Cyprus Blackshaft is nearby.* He kept this thought to himself: suggesting to Frank that Adrienne was now alone with that twisted scoundrel would not be productive.

"Will this night never end?" growled Frank. Forcing himself to entrust

Adrienne to her own capabilities at least for the moment, he followed after Orion back into the woods.

CHAPTER 5

"The legend of the Deathless Blade goes back centuries in these lands – even back to when they were called Belgica, and subject to Rome. It is said the guilty fear being hunted by an unknown man who is as old as the legend itself, or older. He carries a sword called Nemesis and is impervious to any weapon his prey may wield.

"Silly stories and nonsense, of course, but Raines Hobson has been missing for a week and people are once again recalling the ancient legend. That old Raines kept bad company and was said to speak in an unknown tongue when in his cups, only fuels rumor."

~an excerpt from the diary of Anna Kendall, AD 1620

৪০ ঙ্গ

BERLIN. OCTOBER 16, AD 1942.

The trials of the war were never too far away. The parlor was relatively quiet, and a rather nice sanctuary from the pressures of administration. It was well-furnished, a fire crackled in its place under the mantle, and there was a phonograph playing Wagner. On the loveseat lay a Nazi officer's cap and jacket, having been set aside by the room's sole occupant as soon as he had entered, as if he did not enjoy wearing them.

This was true; Orion did not enjoy wearing disguises, but he had not had much choice. He sat in the comfortable arm-chair facing the fire, able to hear the opening door behind him and to the left. He took his time with the evening, knowing he had nothing to do but sit and wait. He had helped himself to some of his host's wine, and was enjoying the vintage of it when he heard what had to be the approach of the host himself.

A man that had gone by the name of Hans Dietrich Buehler laid his hand on the doorknob to the room, smiled in serene anticipation of who was inside, and tried to imagine what she would be wearing. Something enticing, of course. He was most grateful that the German race was essentially rather close to his own actual ethnic background, so that he could successfully assume the names and guises he had for some years now. He had left behind the name of Falcius Kiriath a long time ago, and had recently found that Hans Dietrich Buehler was nicely inconspicuous. He did what he needed to do without any moral quibbles. As long as his drawn out lifespan continued, he was mostly uninterested in what he did to keep guises going. The Fuhrer would have marveled, completely baffled and utterly amazed, had he known that one of his own lieutenants here in Berlin was not forty-one years old as he pretended to be, but rather much older. Impossibly older.

But Buehler was not concerned with the Fuhrer or orders tonight. No, he had come to this quiet little parlor to have some private time with the niece of one of his captains, and he had deliberately given her ample time to do whatever she needed to do to prepare.

"Well, my dear," he said upon entering the room and locking the door, "we have the entire evening before us. What do you think we should do with it, eh?"

He was facing the fire, but before it was the large arm-chair with its occupant whom he could not see. The room was quite dim, lit only by the flames and a lamp in the far corner. He walked in a toying fashion toward the chair when out of it rose a shadowed figure who was both plainly too tall and too broad to be Fraulein Scherer. Buehler took a few steps back in surprise at first, but recovered himself, thinking the beautiful twenty-something had gotten one of her friends to play a joke on him. *Very well, I'll play along,* he thought, but his smile did not keep the surprise out of his voice.

"You are not Astrid," he continued in German, as the fellow got fully out of the chair and stood beside it to face him, only seven feet away.

"No," answered Orion quietly also in German, "but I am your date for this evening."

"Where is Astrid?"

"I convinced her to give us a few minutes; this will not take long."

"So she will be here…eventually?" Buehler asked hopefully.

"Probably," said Orion, dryly. "But in the meanwhile we have important business to discuss."

Buehler sat down in a rocker not at all far away and looked at the man, whose face he could still not see in the poor light against the flames. "So, sir, let us discuss this business of yours, if it is so important that my evening with the most beautiful girl in Germany must wait."

"As you wish…" said Orion, and took a few steps closer.

As he came near to within a few feet, he turned and his features were lit by the fire and the lamp in the corner. Buehler began to grow more and more alarmed, a fear spreading in his mind as he realized he recognized this man. Words from the past echoed in his memory: *You cannot hide from them forever, Falcius. They'll never forget about you, or stop looking for you…these men exist to hunt down people like us. People like you.* The stranger spoke again and Buehler had no doubts that his fears were confirmed.

"Falcius Kiriath, son of Meghanus Kiriath, the Order of the Gatekeepers has found you guilty of high treason against the Imperial Throne…and sentences you to execution immediately."

Buehler leaped up from the chair, but the tall man from his distant past placed a boot in his sternum as he did so, and he was sent back with such force that the chair buckled and tipped him to the floor.

"You!" was all he could say. "How can you b-"

"It is a traditional right that you may choose the manner of your demise, Falcius," said Orion in the same quiet but stern voice. His hand had reached around behind him and drawn out his weapon of choice, the short sword that he had to un-sheath upside-down. Nemesis. The traitor now called Buehler remembered that same eerily familiar motion. "Do you have a preference?" asked Orion.

"This is my preference!" snarled Buehler, and ignoring the pistol at his side, he yanked one from inside his clothing. From his place on the floor a few feet away, Buehler fired three shots without hesitation at Orion Keldir.

The roar of the weapon filled the small room to the echoing ceiling, and with each impact Orion lurched back slightly and gave up a little ground. He made no sound of pain. By the third shot he had fallen to the floor, flat on his back.

"You've waited a long time to fail, Gatekeeper," sneered the condemned man. He was going to say more, but he stopped short.

Orion had fallen to the ground, but he had never let go of his sword. Now, flat on his back and without moving his legs or arms, he simply sat up at the waist. His expression was only slightly changed: if the fugitive had not thought he was serious before, it was realized now.

"No…no…" said Buehler in unbelief, lowering the useless smoking pistol still in his gloved hand. He edged himself away from Orion, still on the floor. He was incredulous; his special secondary pistol carried no ordinary ammunition. "You… you can't just take…but those bullets were capped with gold!" The precious metal had saved him the last time a Gatekeeper found him.

Orion gained his feet and came swiftly forward once more. The expression on the face of Falcius was priceless, but Orion's amusement was limited – three burning holes in his torso soured his mood. "Falcius Kiriath, your traditional right of choice has been revoked. In the stead of your choice, I choose steel."

Useless or not, Hans Dietrich Buehler – the man who had never expected to again be called Falcius Kiriath son of Meghanus Kiriath – raised the pistol a second *time. He still lay on the floor where his chair had cast him. The agile blade of Orion swept sideways at an angle in a single, flawless strike. The gun and the hand that clutched it sailed up through the air and landed on the nearby loveseat. Buehler was able to make half the agonized cry of pain that he intended before the edged weapon put its tip into his chest and went through to the floor.*

Orion was on one knee beside him even as the traitor's last breath left him. Wasting no time to savor a long hunt now completed, Orion nearly tossed his sword aside. He thrust open the man's coat and began rifling carefully through the pockets. Surely Kiriath would not have stowed it anywhere but in his own keeping. But the dead man's pockets were empty. He paused a quarter second before almost chuckling to himself, and then put his big hand down on the corpse's chest. Why would he not wear it? That is what it was made for. *He felt the small hard block under the shirt and reached in past the neckline to pull it free, callously breaking the chain upon which it hung.*

Immense satisfaction, even more than in finally finding Kiriath, swept over Orion as he opened his fist and looked at the sparkling beauty of the oblong, green stone almost the size of his thumb. The gem itself was set carefully in an intricate, delicate-looking frame of shiny metal like silver.

"You use gold-capped bullets when you carry this around your neck?" he smiled at the corpse.

He stood there for a moment and then wiped his messy blade on the Gestapo jacket worn to gain access to the building. He detected some distant cries outside in the hall, and walked to the window. The cool breeze blew in as he opened the window, along with singing from the tavern down the street. Footsteps approached outside the door and there came a frantic banging, and cries in German.

By the time the guards in the building had broken down the door and entered the room to find the lieutenant lying dead on the floor, there was no one else in the room with him. The only exit was out the window, four stories above the pavement.

છ ભ

Cyprus and Adrienne continued their nocturnal journey down the river, Cyprus needing only an occasional pull on the oars to coax their direction. His mind wandered out over the black glistening water, stalking through the darkness and off to lands, places, and events that few besides Orion would have understood in the least.

The two of them sat in the boat facing each other as they went, several minutes passing. Adrienne had him locked in her gaze, unaware that Cyprus could see tears sliding down her cheeks. In the dark she could not tell that he was looking at her, observing.

"This is going to be an awfully long ordeal if you remain this miserable the entire time," he said.

At that, the tears stopped abruptly, as if she'd had complete control over them all along. When she spoke, her voice was not shaky, and it was hard to believe salty drops were still on her cheeks.

"Are you going to hurt me?" she asked.

"Pain is unnecessary in the presence of cooperation," he answered, pulling at the oars. "Just behave yourself, and the time will pass more quickly."

That's not an answer, she thought. She was afraid of him, but not in a way that he would be able to tell. Her wrists strained uselessly, by this time more from habit than intending to get free. *He could do anything he wants to me while I'm stuck like this…* That recognition brought repulsive and even terrifying pictures to her mind. She steeled herself but hesitated.

"Are you going to rape me?"

She immediately regretted asking. He cocked his head to the side to get a quiet crack in his neck, blinked obsessively a few times and licked his lips. When his eyes refocused, the look he gave her was predatory. The moon barely allowed her to notice.

Cyprus smiled just a bit in the darkness, and she missed the action of his eyes wandering. "You have very nice eyes…and a few other fine assets," he said. He certainly had not planned on hurting her in this or any other specific way. "But you have a more important purpose. That and I'm not one to make plans…"

This was true enough. After she had outlived her usefulness was a completely different matter. And to her credit, she did not appear to put much faith in his admittedly empty promise. She was innocent of this type of game, but apparently not overly naïve either. But Cyprus would be damned for a fool to think she belonged in the world he operated in with men like Orion Keldir and Frank Blackman.

"Why am I here?"

She could not see in the moonlight that his eyes went from her face to her chest and the necklace that hung there.

"That is a most beautiful green stone, my lady. Where did you get it?"

"My husband gave it to me on our wedding day," she answered, remembering the exact moment of the exchange. The very thought of that made her long all the more for Frank, recalling all that was said and done on that special day. When Cyprus said nothing, she added, "He didn't tell me where he got it."

He smiled darkly, humorlessly, with the slightest of nods as if to say he understood, but all he said was: "Didn't he?" It was hardly a question.

She shook her head, flexing her tingling fingers behind her back. *If he's talking, maybe he'll think less about what to do to me.* "Do you know him?"

Cyprus leaned back as he pulled a long steady drag at the oars. "Your husband and I go back a little way," he said, and then added with some hesitancy, "In his own way, he is…a remarkable man. We were…competitors."

"Competitors." Her skepticism dripped from the word.

"Aye, competitors."

In his mind's eye, Cyprus pictured himself with a scar. Given his current state of life, just like Orion, he actually could not get a scar without first a most grievous wound. A less than remarkable injury would disappear. Only the grave ones left any sign afterward. Nor could he get even a tattoo for that matter; his body would reject the foreign ink and exude it from pores in a cleansing. But if he had the literal capability, it would have been impossible to miss signs of his various meetings with Frank Blackman. The principal one would be right between the upper left pectoral and his left shoulder, where the arm met the body, and where the bursts of hot lead had passed through the body. His memory of the event, instead of a literal scar, would have to serve as his own reminder of Blackman's capabilities – and the manner in which they had last parted.

Reflecting on his own scars made Cyprus wonder how Frank pawned off the marks of his own past life. Blackman had been granted a longer existence with the 'modern' methods, but the ability to immediately heal was unique to only a few individuals, like Cyprus and Orion. At any rate, plainly Frank's female had been told nothing of what he used to be doing; else she would not spend the night asking foolish questions. *He probably told this woman that the scar at his front was his appendix having been removed-*

"Where are we going?"

The oars splashed a little. "Tired of our journey already?"

You can still feel your fingers and toes, creep. She didn't want him to see her fear, so she tried to keep it light. "You would leave me in suspense? It's not like I can refuse to go, what's the harm?"

"I'm taking you somewhere to show you off and gauge a reaction. And then we're going on another trip. Happy?"

"Overjoyed…"

He smiled. "I know, I know…jeans and a t-shirt was not a good choice for a trip on the river at this time of year. You should have planned better. Well, don't worry. I'll have you out of those clothes soon enough…"

She straightened, fears confirmed. *I should roll out of this boat and sink to the bottom before they find me naked and dead on the highway shoulder somewhere… or should I wait for a chance to get away?* She took a long slow breath on purpose, her mind running off on its own. *What if there's no chance to wait for? What would I tell Frank if he rapes me? What if I never see him again?*

He pulled on the oars. "Beautiful night, don't you think?"

෨ ෬

"So he came from across the river?" asked Bohemond.

"Obviously," Orion said quietly, looking over Doc's shoulder as he sat at the table rifling through surveillance files on the laptop. Frank had wanted to jump in the car but Orion was looking for a little more planning than that. They'd only been back a minute or two, anyway.

Behind them, Frank was pacing the hall, walking from one end to the other, his hands clasping, at his sides with balled fists, rubbing his eyes as if he hadn't slept in two days, in constant motion as if they did not know what else to do. Aside from trying to get in the car, he had not spoken since they had rushed back from the dock, up through the forest and around to the gate.

"Was it a Shade?"

Orion was certain, staring at the screen. "It was no Shade. They have a precise aura to their presence; you can *feel* them. I sensed no such thing with this intruder. Now then, the map, Doc, put the map back up…"

"I'm so sorry, Frank," said Bohemond, quite pained, "that this should happen, when she is here in the compound, and so under my charge. The resources of the entire Society will be at your disposal to get the Lady Blackman returned safely."

Frank nodded curtly but had been silently prepared to take whatever liberties were necessary to get Adrienne back. In his mind, there was no cost too great. *Some husband I am…how could I let this happen? I was fifty yards away.* He broke his own brooding silence. "What's across the river?"

"Farmland, for miles," said Bohemond.

Frank came forward and pointed on the monitor at the map that Doc had pulled up of the area. "He won't go upstream, not in a boat with no motor – from what I could hear. He wouldn't take her across the river to walk through empty farmland, not with potential pursuit so close."

"And the chopper is unavailable," added the old man.

"What is the nearest road downstream?" asked Doc.

"County 6," said Frank from memory. They had crossed it on the way to the property. He glanced at Orion. "Let's go for a drive."

Moments later they were in the car, Orion pulling away from the mansion so fast they fishtailed.

A sudden thought occurred to Frank as they left the gates. "We should bring some hardware…some gear…I want to be prepared for this guy when we catch him."

"You forget to whom you speak," said Orion sternly.

"So you've got weapons? In the trunk?"

They cornered at the end of the long driveway, spraying gravel out behind them.

"You've been gone too long if you think your old partner would go far without bringing a few tools of the trade. A sword is handy but occasionally something else must serve."

The tension was so great and was Orion so…Orion – that Frank laughed aloud. *Look who you're talking to.* Orion had always philosophized over his weaponry choices; he always said most weapons, no matter how different, were just varying ways of putting holes in someone else. The sudden but sincere laughter released the tension tremendously, though he never forgot himself – or Adrienne.

"The bridge isn't far," Orion added. "A rowboat can't be his only means of travel; look for something else when we get there."

૪૦ ૦૪

After a bend or two, Cyprus steered the boat toward the shore as the river began to creep toward a bridge spanning the water. Adrienne had been seriously pondering a perilous night swim, but neither courage nor good sense moved her in time to a commitment and plunge. They were quickly approaching the shore. In the dark and with her unfamiliarity of the area, Adrienne did not recognize that she had driven over the very same bridge earlier that evening.

Her kidnapper allowed the boat to scrape up on a pebbly shoreline, grounding it. He stepped out and pulled it further up on shore before turning to the device on his wrist and punching a few numbers on the panel, ignoring how she watched with interest. When he was finished doing this, he clipped the zip-ties about her legs and pulled her to her feet. He was not gentle, but could have been more rough.

Cyprus had her arm as she stepped from the boat, for being tied she was off balance. Her feet prickled with lack of circulation. Once ashore, she looked around for an escape route as he stood behind. He used the same snipping tool he had on her legs, and her hands were freed. She said nothing but reflexively rubbed her wrists, feeling her fingers tingle as well.

"Follow me," he said, and turned away, walking up a slope toward the road. "Our ride will be here soon."

Adrienne did not follow at once but looked around, back to the boat, to the sparsely wooded countryside that crept close to the banks of the river, all bathed in the star and moonlight. Her eyes strayed to Cyprus's back as he moved away; apparently not at all concerned that she might try and part company. His confidence that she would not was almost enough to tempt her to try running, but she thought better of it. She had reasonable faith in herself to know she was physically fit enough to take off running and not have to stop for quite some time, but she had absolutely no doubt that whatever her physical capabilities, Cyprus would have little to no trouble catching her. She was reminded of the unnatural strength with which he had first seized her.

And if pressed he would not be under any obligation to be half the gentleman he was now. *Well, not much of a gentleman – but I am untied...Is this my chance? No...too easy; he's probably waiting for it. But if there's a ride coming, he'll have help...now or never...* He would have few scruples about restraining her once again and forcing her to go wherever he wished. That had no appeal for Adrienne Blackman – especially when she now had the choice of obeying his command and merely walking under her own power. *And where would I run to in the countryside at night dressed like this? I'm freezing...* After second-guessing herself a few times, she followed.

The climb through the brush up the steep hill to the highway was a taxing one, especially in the dark. She was concentrating so hard on the labor of the climb that she did not notice how easily Cyprus stepped between shrubberies to various advantageous footholds, even though they were masked in complete darkness. She reached the top wet and dirty, having to use her hands every second step. Cyprus looked down the highway as if he expected to see something. They were on a remote country road in the blackness of an evening that was not yet very old, despite all its momentous events. It could not be more than a half hour since she had been first grabbed.

Then she heard it, and saw the lights. Not a car, but what was most certainly a helicopter. In no time at all it had approached and came to be directly overhead, slowly descending so as to land in the middle of the road. Contrary to what she had at first suspected, she soon saw that it was not a small air vehicle of the sort the local evening news team used to survey traffic. *Did Frank call the President? Look at the size of that thing...*

"You've gotta be kidding me," she said aloud.

Cyprus looked at her sidelong before gazing back at the helicopter as it landed. At the barely audible sound of an approaching car behind him, he glanced around to see headlights in the distance. He turned back to Adrienne. "Ladies first."

₭ ₮

Both Orion and Frank saw the helicopter in the road up ahead as they came over the top of the hill and sped on down the highway.

"That has to be them," said Frank.

Orion only nodded and turned on his high-beams to try and see some kind of insignia on the side of the chopper as it slowly lifted off. At that distance, Orion could not see the emblem on the helicopter itself, though plainly it was lavishly expensive. That and he could still make out the general design. If only they had gotten a closer look at the cur who took her. From what he had seen of the compound's security footage, only a black marauding figure could be seen. Perhaps a closer review would be advantageous later. Unable to follow his quarry directly, he continued down the highway.

Beside him, Frank released his frustration in a wordless growl. *I could put a bullet right there, and our pursuit would end.* He had the capability of shooting in just the right place to bring it crashing from the sky, or at least damaging it enough to force it to land. He had the know-how and the knowledge, and even the tools to do it – but knowing his wife was aboard nullified his desire to bring the bird down violently. That and he knew more than one enemy that in a dire situation would kill a captive rather than give them up. He watched with a grim expression as the lights in the sky disappeared into the distance.

Orion did not slow down. "That was a sky-hawk chopper or I have never seen one," said he. "The Raven have a skyscraper in the city. It's got to be where they're going."

"The Raven..." Frank was silent for a moment, brooding. "Those Black Chickens have a skyscraper here in the city not twenty miles from my own house? I suppose it shouldn't surprise me," he said quietly.

"Aye," said Orion, ignoring the irreverent nickname. "First Shades and now the Order of the Raven. Surely you did not think they would disappear when you retired?"

"At least that exhausts the list of whatever else could show up tonight."

"I hope you're right, but I wouldn't bet on it."

Frank leaned back in the seat as Orion drove on, exceeding the speed limit by twenty-five. "I'm not sure which I'd rather have to deal with, Shades or the Raven."

"There is great variety between them," said Orion. "It is well for us that they are not united in loyalty and cause, though at times their purposes would be better served were they together. There are those in the Society that theorize they *are* under one flag. It is an interesting notion – and terribly ironic if it's true."

"What side of the argument do you hold to?" Frank only asked to help keep his mind off Adrienne.

Orion continued. "That the Shades would be working with a human organization is possible, but I cannot see them doing so in a subservient role – and the Raven would never yield to being controlled from outside their own organization. No, I think the causes of bringing both Shade and Raven together in one night point to similar goals, not teamwork. But what those actual goals are, I do not yet know."

Frank nodded but closed his eyes and did not open them for awhile. He was suddenly very aware of how tired he was. It was not ridiculously late: perhaps nine, but he was much more suited to an earlier bedtime. He wondered if Adrienne would get any sleep. Poor Adrienne. She had to be frightened, worried, and confused all at once. *And it's all my fault.* Still, Adrienne was hardly the type to lose it in tense or even dangerous situations. She was quite independent, really, but Frank also had to admit that while fully capable in her own right, Adrienne could hardly be expected to be prepared for things like Shades or Raven operatives.

It was fortuitous, what with the Raven coming back into Frank's life that evening that he should be driving in a car with Orion looking for them. Of all the members of Dominos de Lumine, for all their knowledge and applicable experiences over the long years, Orion was undisputedly the foremost authority on the Order of the Raven. No one could relate exactly why he knew what he did, and few thought that questioning him would be fruitful.

Orion Keldir, for the years Frank had known him, was a very private man. He did not speak often, and when he did it was rarely not applicable to the moment at hand. He had no family. He had few friends. Frank recalled he had been married at one time, but where she was now he had no idea. Perhaps Orion hadn't an idea either. Frank suspected she was dead, though he had no idea how, and he could never get up the courage to inquire. Perhaps she had grown tired of the sort of life that Orion still lived daily, while Frank had left it behind for Adrienne. Or at least he had tried to leave it behind.

"I can't stop thinking about the day we met," Frank admitted.

"It was fortuitous I picked your tavern. But if you're still sore about the bullet holes through the oak panels, I would remind you I did have the Society pay to repair that-"

"Not you and me! Adrienne."

"Ah. That. Love at first sight, no doubt," Orion answered with no inflection.

Frank put his head back on the seat and closed his eyes as they shot along the highway. "It was actually related to some business with the Society. She had helped to organize a dinner function in Paris. That was back when she worked in fashion. I forget exactly why I was there, but it sure wasn't for whatever cause was going on." He smiled in the dark of the car. "She was twenty-five, flat-out gorgeous. Her dress didn't even have to be flattering, but it was. We talked a bit, didn't quite hit it off right away, but managed to get her to agree to coffee later. I still don't know why she settled for me."

"I believe the word at the wedding was she had lost a bet..."

Frank opened his eyes and looked at him. "You were there?"

"Of course I was. Did you really expect me to sit out your wedding?"

"Yeah," said Frank, flatly. "But you should have – that manila envelope: that was from you!"

"It seemed the right thing to do."

"We were *agonizing* over who that fifteen grand in cash was from!" He laughed. "Now I can send you that stupid thank you card..."

"Five years late. I have heard of worse delays. Neither of you has aged a day."

Frank smiled. "It's the cucumbers on the eyes at the salon that does it for me..."

"And what would your wife do if she ascertained how old you are?"

"I look like my mid-thirties."

"That," said Orion with a dry wit, "was not the question."

There was a pause as the driver glanced at his passenger.

"I don't know," admitted Frank, "what did yours say when she found out?"

"Those were different times; not like today."

Frank missed his friend's sober expression in the darkness of the car. "Sure, you don't remember."

"Our ages were never a concern."

"So you do remember."

Orion shifted only slightly, feeling the sword strapped upside down against his back under his coat. *Only when I close my eyes.*

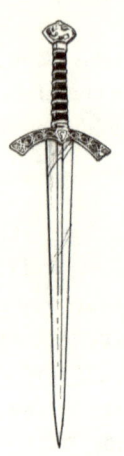

CHAPTER 6

"She is not mad, not yet, but she may be drunk with power. She asked me today: 'What good is power if not absolute? What good is freedom if we must answer to anyone?' I grow concerned about her boundless ambition. I would treat her as a rival and remove her - if not for her stunningly resplendent pulchritude. I have always had a thing for blondes."

~an excerpt from the memoirs of Cyprus Blackshaft.

☾ ☽

CONSTANTINOPLE. AD 1098.

Orion rested his hands lovingly on the hips of the woman that stood directly in front of him, her arms reaching up to rest on his shoulders as her hands caressed the back of his head. Her blue eyes were locked onto his, and in that moment he was convinced he'd never seen a more beautiful woman. But her eyes were sad.

"Must you really go?" she asked.

They stood on the side of one of the countless streets that wove among the towering buildings of the mighty city of Constantinople: churches, residences, palaces, shops, cathedrals, and all sorts of structures dominated their surroundings. The city of Constantine was a wonder of the world. In the distance beyond the hippodrome, identical towers jabbed into the sky above the cityscape, marking where the gates opened out of the strong walls of the city. Lines of crusader soldiers made their way toward the distant gates.

He let go of her and took her hands. "Yes, I must. But I shall return to you. I promise."

Her gaze was pressing. "This is not your war...and yet you march with the Pope."

"Great deeds are afoot, and about to come to pass. I have witnessed many things, and would yet see more. Would you have me lose this opportunity to witness history in the making?"

"These opportunities of yours will be the death of you," she said, though her tone was more of a playful scold. She was plainly not concerned with his safety. "And they will not return without you and tell me you were in the thick of the fighting?"

He smiled good-naturedly. "Alexander did not see me raise my sword against Persia, and Toulouse will not see me raise my sword against Muhammad."

Satisfied for the moment, her eyes fell to the one-handed sword at his side, saw the curve of the shield he had slung at his back, saw the battleaxe tucked into his belt opposite the sword.

She looked over his garb with a critical eye, her hands sought something to secure. She settled for straightening a fold in the cloak that had fallen over his shoulder awkwardly. As her hand caught it and fixed it, he noted as he looked down at her that she stopped and briefly touched the embroidered strap that crossed his chest. She brushed over it with curiosity, and then her hands snaked around behind him to what the strap held in place. He felt the slightest of adjustments as her fingers took hold of his oldest sword, strapped in its oddity upside down on his back, beneath the cloak and the shield that was slung over the cloak. She looked up.

"Expecting trouble, are we?"

He had hoped she wouldn't see it, but was not surprised when she did.

"You know she comes with me wherever I go. Some things are meant to be treasured – like you."

"Like me," she smiled, and pulled him in.

More than one crusader looked off the street to where the couple stood that day, envious of the soldier kissing his sweetheart goodbye before heading off to the Holy Land with the mostly French entourage, purposing to liberate Jerusalem from the infidel.

Orion was not nearly ready to let her go, but he somehow managed to tear himself away from her.

"I love you, Orion."

"And I love you, Attica."

ᙡ ᙏ

Adrienne, while still having her apprehensions, was beginning to find it hard to keep in the state of mind that continually reminded her she was being kidnapped. She was still tense, but in her darkest dreams, she had pictured a kidnapping as being in the back of a van with a sack over her head, tied up and drugged. Or maybe lying trapped in the trunk of a car waiting for some masked figure to open the lid, brandishing a knife.

She had certainly not pictured sitting in a multi-million dollar helicopter as it traversed the city ablaze with lights below. Under other circumstances, a ride like this could have been an anniversary present from Frank. The city below was admittedly beautiful. The buildings were lit up with the aggressive night-life and advertisements that a bustling metropolis of that size could offer. She could vaguely tell their direction from the black strip that was the river weaving its way on the far side of where the towering lights had just begun to fade into the night.

She yawned, watching the city lights pass beneath her feet. Five feet to her left, Cyprus sat reading a newspaper. At least, he was holding the newspaper up as if reading, but it was far too dark in the chopper for him to actually see the words. She wondered at that, especially when he maintained this façade for several minutes and periodically turned a page.

Who does he think he's fooling?

They had been flying on through the night for nearly half an hour. *I wish I knew downtown better; might have a chance to know where we are.* Adrienne had never liked the big city; she had grown up on a farm in Nebraska and was still a country girl at heart. The mayhem of downtown repelled her. Living in Paris for a time had driven any city-related curiosity from her.

"We should be landing soon," came Cyprus's voice, though he still held the paper up as if he could read it.

"Where are we going?"

"You'll find out soon enough."

And so she did. Not ten minutes later, the helicopter had landed on the top of a towering skyscraper. While it was not the tallest in the city, it was certainly in the running. Adrienne refused Cyprus's hand in disembarking from the chopper and looked out across the landscape from the rooftop on which they had landed. Had it been daylight out, she would have been able to see for miles. As it was, she could only see the general glow from the city and the occasional rooftops of skyscrapers that were as tall as their own.

They took the elevator down only one floor. The interior of the lift itself was a mixture of mirrors and gold-plating; immaculate. *I can't give him the satisfaction of looking impressed at all this...* It seemed unlikely that Cyprus would notice; she hadn't seen him look her in the eye since they had first boarded the chopper.

The elevator ride, short as it was, allowed Adrienne to see her abductor in actual light for the first time. He was just short of six feet tall and to her eye rather slim and wiry, though admittedly he looked strong. His hair was the same color as Orion's; darker brown, but unlike Orion's it was very short. His face was pleasing to the eye, though in its glance there was an undeniable air of superiority and smugness. He would have been handsome without that overall aura. His very dark eyes were never open very wide, giving him a slightly cynical look. Indeed, if she had had the luxury of looking very carefully at them – she avoided the appearance of staring at him openly – she would have seen they were actually not only dark but a very faded violet, as if he were wearing some kind of special contact lenses.

And he is not afraid that I can see his face. Now I can describe and identify him. He's not intending to let me go. The intuition steeled her desire to escape, eyes open for the opportunity.

Cyprus led her down a few corridors to a room he used a card to enter. He held the door for her, a hand extended into the room in the unmistakable motion of having her enter first. When she did so, Adrienne found a large suite that she could not have imagined how to make more desirable: it reminded her of the celebrity shows that Frank teased her for periodically watching.

Frank had always told her not to watch such things, as it would get her hopes up. She could see how, standing there at the entry with Cyprus closing the door behind. It was nicer than her home, and she had never been ashamed of her own house. The bed was king-sized, the bathroom having both a sauna and whirlpool hot tub, the living room had leather chairs and couches and a large flat-screen mounted on the wall. There was a full-fledged kitchen, two walk-in closets stocked full of clothing she could easily have worn, and a balcony beyond expensive glass doors that looked out over the city with a spectacular view.

"This is the penthouse suite," Cyprus confirmed her imagination. "I'm going to leave you here for a few minutes, and allow you to get yourself ready."

Adrienne, who had been standing with her back to him as she took in the suite, laid her eyes full on the bed as he said this. Their previous conversation from the rowboat flooded her mind, and she turned toward him with a clenched fist and the mental will to strike him if he touched her.

"Ready for what?"

He made an obvious gesture toward a table.

Adrienne looked, and her immediate fears of sexual assault temporarily paused. "You're kidding me…" she said slowly. Her tone was still defiant, but she was not sure he could be serious. Laid out very nicely on the table was the most elegant evening gown she had ever seen, almost as dark as the night into which she had been carried. A pair of heels lay nearby, potential ankle-breakers by the look of them.

"You'll look lovely, I'm sure," he intoned behind her, in such a way that she whirled around to face him again.

"You can't be serious," she said.

"I'm rarely not," came the humorless reply.

"I'm – you – I'm not just going to…"

"Yes?"

"I'm *not* wearing that for you."

"Very good, my Lady Blackman. No, you're not."

"I…don't think I understand…"

"You're wearing it for the party."

"The *what*?"

"Don't worry, we won't stay long. Just long enough for you to meet someone before we depart."

"This is crazy. I'm not putting that on-"

His voice was of such a tone she could not tell if he was joking. "You are a woman. You like nice clothes – you've worked in fashion. That gown is worth over ten thousand dollars. I am giving you the perfect excuse to wear it. I fail to see your dilemma." His eyes did a slow heavy blink twice and his tongue flicked like a snake's.

Adrienne was not the sort to be pushed into wearing anything she did not want to, let alone by a stranger who apparently knew even her work history, and the situation struck her as most suspicious. Her fearful ideas from the boat flooded back. He had mentioned getting her out of her clothes. *But not replacing them with something like this.* It was an exquisite piece of clothing. She did not know if Cyprus was telling the truth of its worth, but she could well believe he was. *I don't care if it's silken gold, that doesn't mean I'm wearing it.*

"And if I don't?"

He looked at her expressionless for a moment, but made no effort to hide how his eyes started at hers and then moved down her frame slowly. He got to her feet and started back up, and by the time his purple eyes had returned to her green ones, he was smiling.

He took slow steps toward her as he spoke. "So...you are refusing to don this gown...?" His hand went to his side and pulled a switchblade. "Oh...*please* tell me you're refusing." The blade and tongue flicked out together.

"Keep away from me," said Adrienne evenly. She took a step away and looked around for a weapon, but there was nowhere to go and no defense to be found. Frank's long-time counsel came to mind. *Groin if you can...if not, go for his eyes.*

"Stay still," said he, "I'll help you."

She was not thinking about technique when he took a step toward her and she lashed out. Indignant anger powered her blow to his face and her hand hurt as she backed further away, breathing hard and tipping over the lamp on the little table beside the bed behind her.

Cyprus ceased advancing on her, expression wiped clean. The switchblade fell from his hand and he blinked. The lamp tipping over seemed to tune him back to reality, and his brow furrowed infinitesimally. "What are you doing?" he asked. "Get changed."

He turned around and headed for the door.

What just happened? "I'm not wearing that dress," she said defiantly to his back.

Cyprus rested a hand on the door, and she noted that without the card in his hand it would not open – she was trapped without him. His voice was calm and quiet, as if he hadn't menaced her with a knife ten seconds ago. "I'm going next door. I need to change as well. I'm going to give you what I feel is more than enough time for you to get ready. Shower too, if you like. You'll find everything you could possibly need. This room has accommodated many ladies of high quality. When I return, I expect you to be wearing that gown. If you're not, Lady Blackman, I will be obliged to help you put it on myself. While not a completely unpleasant concept..." – and here she glared at him savagely – "...I am sure you do not wish any assistance from me. You can make it much easier on yourself by simply obliging to your host's request."

Does he not remember just a second ago?

Apparently he did not. Cyprus turned his back on Adrienne, ignoring her crossed arms and tilted hips. As he opened the door he gave her a predatory look.

"Make an effort in your appearance, or I *will* help you meet my standards," he said with a malicious wink, and then slipped out.

Adrienne held the dress up to herself and caught a sideways glance in one of several mirrors. Well, at the very least it *was* the most tantalizingly elegant and expensive evening apparel she had ever seen. In the mirror she saw his switchblade lying there, apparently forgotten. She cast the dress aside and picked up the knife. It would fit in a pocket of her jeans, but the confrontation and parting conversation had convinced her to wear the dress of her own accord; there was nowhere accessible to put the knife in or on the dress.

In the end she decided to put the switchblade between the pillows on the bed beneath the comforter. *I can't take it with me and I don't know what he'll do with my old clothes.* Her choice was based upon convenience; if he took advantage of her, there were worse places for a knife to be than under the pillows by her head.

౪ ౧

Against her instincts and with fear of Cyprus being good to his word, Adrienne made an effort. Their walk up the river bank had left her dirty enough that showering was necessary, and she had made use of the facilities after locking the bathroom door. A hair dryer, comb and brush, and curling iron had given her medium-long dark locks a more formalized look. She applied heartfelt skill to the process, as every time she blinked she saw herself sitting in front of the mirror with Cyprus behind her, doing it all for her. She had resolved not to leave him a single detail to attend.

It was a shock to find that the dress was precisely her size; down to the slightest measurement. She had only barely gotten the dress on – not even entirely – before Cyprus returned unannounced and clad in a tuxedo, slipping inside as if he owned the place.

"Midnight blue suits you, Lady Blackman. You clean up well."

Adrienne said nothing, being of a slightly different opinion. Yet she preferred straps over her shoulders to none at all, and though the front was low, it was not nearly as low as it could have been. Honestly, there were far worse dresses one could be forced to wear. The tastefulness, for what it was worth, made her wonder at the nature of the coming party.

He stood there for a moment, arms folded as he looked at her standing by the bed where she had been finalizing her appearance in front of the large mirror. She had whirled to face the door when he entered.

"Turn around, please," he said.

Her expression alone told him to get lost. But when he came slowly toward her, she turned.

Standing in front of the mirror as she was, their eyes met even though she faced away. There was, for her, an uncomfortable silence broken only by the sound of the dress's zipper as he pulled it upward; it was the last part of wearing the dress and she had not yet gotten to it. Then he stepped back and his eyes drank her in.

"I could have managed," she said curtly.

He pulled from his pocket what looked like a dog collar. It was a small belt of leather, with notches to be tightened snugly around something the size of a neck or thigh. She had the brief glance of some interior wires. Adrienne had never seen anything quite like it. She barely caught it when he tossed it at her.

"Let's see what else you can manage. Strap this to your upper leg well above your knee." He paused. "If you do not do it correctly, I will do it for you."

She held it there and looked even more suspicious than when he had made her wear the dress.

"Why am I wearing this?"

He spoke matter-of-factly. "The gathering we are going to, already in progress, is attended by many people. While there, you will be my date and I shall be at your side at all times. I can assure you none of them will be concerned in the least bit for your well-being. That does not mean we want our guests disturbed. Should you attempt to inform any other guests of your predicament, I will activate the device on your leg. It will induce unconsciousness immediately."

He stepped away and made the meaningless gesture of turning his back, since all he did was turn toward another mirror and straighten his tie. Adrienne comprehended that he did this to give her the opportunity to strap the device to her leg. Rather than give him the excuse to do it, she put her foot up on the bed and modestly raised the dress.

"How would you explain my unconsciousness?"

"That is the least of my concerns. A medical condition, an allergy to the foreign food, the stress of how that dress can't possibly be letting you breathe well, or my personal favorite," and here he turned with a patronizing smile, "the thrill of being with me all evening."

Task done, she put two feet on the floor again and glared at him. "*Thrill* isn't quite the word."

He smiled again, and it annoyed her. "We will at some point be better acquainted. Then we'll see." She shivered as he held up the remote and hit a button; it vibrated slightly against her upper leg when he turned it on. "Shall we go?"

ⅎ ⅛

"When did Lumine get this building?" asked Frank.

"By definition it only possesses the top few floors. It took years to acquire, even with the Society's connections."

Frank and Orion stood on an observation deck twenty stories above the buzzing of the city's vibrant nightlife. It was right around ten give or take a quarter hour; not yet terribly late and all below and before them was ablaze with lights. Frank might have found it relaxing under different circumstances.

"So what are we doing here?"

"You'll notice we have a nice view of the skyscraper two blocks down."

Frank used the binoculars that Orion had readily produced to scan it up and down. If the traffic was limited at its front he could see individuals entering and exiting. They were in the perfect location to survey the other building: they had a good view of the entire west side. There was a consistent stream of eloquently-dressed people going in and out on the first floor, as if they were going to a Hollywood awards ceremony or highbrow opera. He nodded in response to Orion's statement.

"The Raven own that building," Orion continued. "The whole block, actually, but the skyscraper in the middle there is what they primarily use. Other unrelated businesses rent out from them on the other lots. This building's upper floors were acquired by the Society as an in-city observation location."

"Some big to-do over there tonight, eh?"

"So it would seem. But more importantly, we already know they have a helicopter pad on the roof. That's where they have taken her at the moment. It's the only sizable facility they have in a fifty mile radius. Regardless, I'm not sure how to proceed. It's a major headquarters for the Crows in this region, let alone the state: they're not going to let us just waltz in there and take her back. At least, not until that social event is over, and that may go a long while yet."

Frank lowered the binoculars and leaned on the banister again, thoughtful. "I'd still give anything to find out why they took her in the first place." He placed the ocular tool in Orion's extended hand.

Now Orion was looking carefully over the skyscraper. "Patience. This will take some precise execution." He looked back over at Frank. "I'm not sure this is a just a two-man operation. There are too many variables. They may have a skeleton crew, or they may have a full regiment there. If they're looking for us, we won't get in period."

Frank looked up toward the stars, nearly invisible with the city lights. "This takes me back, planning stuff like this. There's no small number of ways we could go about it, of course, but there I'm preaching to the choir."

Orion said nothing to this, continuing to scan the building with the binoculars.

"We won't be able to land on it ourselves, and jumping won't do with the wind this evening. And I doubt they would let us in to the party if we asked nicely..." Frank trailed off.

"When have you ever asked nicely? But what are you thinking?"

"Don't know. But it's going to take time and planning, that's the problem. At the least I'd want the blueprints of the building. But if I know the Raven at all, they won't keep her there long. When they would kidnap people like this, it's not twenty-four hours before she'll be out of the country."

"They do have many offshore places from which to pick," admitted Orion.

"If only we understood their purpose in the first place. It would be undeniably useful, if only to be ready for them at another location. We're not going to be able to plan this before midnight, let alone with the party or whatever they're having over there. But maybe we could-"

"My word."

Frank looked back at Orion to see him looking through the viewer.

"What is it?"

"It's Adrienne."

"What? Let me see!"

"And you won't believe who's with her."

⁖ ‘’

Ever since Adrienne had been a little girl, she had always had the fantasy of attending a Cinderella-style ball. Per his earlier command, she had her arm in Cyprus's and walked with him through the largest and most extravagant party of which she had ever heard or dreamed. What she would not give, she lamented, to exchange Cyprus for her husband and the situation to be legitimate. Having lived in Paris for a year while in the fashion design industry, she had attended parties like this one, but none had quite reached the grandiose heights that were before them now.

They were in a large hall whose ceiling soared high over their heads, upheld by lofty Corinthian pillars. The carpet was red and the tiles were marble. The double doors that opened into the wide space were of rich mahogany and twelve feet tall. The room was almost large enough to extend from one side of the skyscraper to the other, and where it came to the walls there were utterly gigantic towering windows stretching the entire height of the room, practically making up the entire wall in and of themselves. Through this tremendous conglomeration of windows peeked half of the downtown area.

All around them, the other party guests mingled. Not a single man was without a tuxedo, and every last woman wore an elegant evening gown, some of which Adrienne could not help but notice. The former designer in her came alive as she looked around at numerous styles and patterns. She had once met the man who designed the silky flowing blue dress that cascaded down the young blonde off to the right; he had been a complete jerk; his secretary had been kind. The green embroidered purity that was worn not far from Jerk Designer cost more than her Honda. And who could miss the Charisse Bachmann waltzing across the floor away to the left?

And for all the power and class in this room, not one of them would lift a finger to help me.

There was no shortage of servers walking about with trays of gourmet hors d'oeuvres – caviar, fruits, shrimp, shellfish – and drinks of every last concoction. In the exact middle of the room was a tall sparkling fountain, and spaced among the pillars and in strategic locations were tables covered in white cloths, laden with a feast that would have made the Queen of England envious. Amidst the foods were full-scale ice statues of various themes, most of them reminiscent of classical Greece. Off to the side, a portion of floor had been set aside for ballroom-style dancing, and a small orchestra was playing a waltz by Strauss.

Adrienne really was impressed, but she was still in a foul mood and begrudged every last marvelous accommodation thrown at her – as if she were allowed to partake in any of it. The more there was, the more she was reminded of how she did not belong and was there against her will. She wanted to ask Cyprus why they were there, but decided this would somehow only give him more strength in the situation.

They crossed the width of the hall filled with people and came to a tall, narrow set of doors which opened inward with a push from her abductor. No sooner had she passed inside than he closed them behind her. They had entered a plush, quiet library whose tall walls kept out every last hint of a party outside. Now that they were in private once more, her open-toed heels echoed on the hard wood floors as she took quick steps away from Cyprus. Upon entering the room she felt a twinge in her core, like a sixth sense. A strong feeling of discord perturbed the young woman.

Curiosity and frustration overwhelming her, Adrienne opened her mouth to ask him what the point of it all was. But she stopped short; they were not as alone as she had at first thought. Across the room and looking at a large book on a podium, there stood an exceedingly tall man.

Cyprus was almost six feet tall, but this new man was a head over him, and terribly thin; so lean he would appear awkward if not for his overall aura of decorum. While all the men in the other room wore tuxedos, this fellow wore – what was he wearing? Even with a fashion background, she could not describe it. It was a twist between a collar-less dress shirt and a robe, quite fitting to his lanky form. In short, very high-quality attire that may have been a tuxedo of sorts from a non-western culture. To Adrienne it looked like a combination of Asian, African, and Middle-Eastern garb. Solemnity was evident in his poise. Cast behind him was a cavernous hood, neatly fitted about his narrow shoulders. He appeared to be of European descent. He was older, certainly, though with few lines and short gray hair.

In all, he had an intimidating appearance, and he struck Adrienne as rather grim before she even heard him speak a word. The most striking thing about him was his eyes. Adrienne had heard that to look into one's eyes was to see into the windows of the soul, but if so this man's soul was surely missing. Her spine tingled. His eyes were dark and unfeeling, empty, as if there was a nothingness to the intelligence behind them – not a nothingness of nonexistence, but an emptiness of darkness, void of heart or kindness. It struck Adrienne that the tall frame before her was not a man at all, but a shell set to hide what was truly there – but what that thing was she could not guess.

It's cold in here – or maybe it's just those eyes, she thought, thoroughly chilled.

With morbid interest, Cyprus noted the change in Adrienne. She stood rigid, looking at the formerly sole occupant of the library. In their brief time together, she had always been controlled – even in her fear of him there had never been a sense of panic. She was good at covering this newfound agitation of hers, but she was plainly more afraid of this new man than she had ever been of Cyprus. Well, that was fair; he could recall no one living who was completely at ease in the presence of the one they were now approaching, let alone someone meeting him for the first time. Her eyes told him everything.

The tall man had noted their approach, and with long strides glided over the wood floor toward them. She would have felt more comfortable in a shark cage approached by a titanic great white. Where her heels had resonated throughout that quiet space, this fellow's steps could not be heard. The empty wells in this tall man's eyes were locked onto her as he randomly halted his approach at a distance of several meters. Adrienne could not put her finger on it, but something about him was obscure and out of place. *He is like someone wearing someone else.* A smile molded itself across his mouth and her hearing came back to catch Cyprus: he was speaking to her.

"My Lady Blackman, allow me to present Memphis." They remained a good twenty feet distant from the tall man, who held her in his regard. The crawling apprehension would not leave her, and indeed was only growing. Now Cyprus spoke to Memphis. "Sir, the Lady Adrienne Blackman."

Memphis' voice was terribly deep; almost too deep to be human in Adrienne's mind. "Lady Blackman, the pleasure is surely mine."

Adrienne returned nothing as she held her breath and tried very hard to master herself. The hairs on her arms were straight up, but she was silently grateful he seemed content to remain there in his place. *Why won't he come any closer?*

Memphis was still completely enveloped in his regard of Adrienne. The empty eyes took her in from her feet to the top of her head, his manner impossible for her to ascertain what intention was behind the gaze. On their way back down, the dark eyes halted a few inches below her throat, where her green gem rested. Even at this distance, it was obvious that was where he focused.

He spoke to Cyprus, his eyes still scrutinizing the stone.

"Found it at last, have we?" he asked.

"Was there ever a doubt?" smiled Cyprus, but his mirth faded when the cold eyes of Memphis left Adrienne's gemstone and went to his own. He sobered. "I said I would find it, did I not?"

"Indeed you did – just as many other servants of mine claimed."

At this point, Adrienne randomly noticed that the jewel around her neck was growing warm. *Not again! This is too weird…*

Cyprus blinked slow and hard twice and his demeanor seemed to change a hint, as if he suddenly resented Memphis's reactions hitherto. His captive jerked involuntarily as he stepped in close, snaked an arm around her waist to hold her right up next to himself, and then took hold of the green bauble. It took all her control not to put her elbow in his ribs again – for all the good it had done before.

"Pretty, is it not?" asked Cyprus, cheek to cheek with her as she grimaced. "Now, what do you think we should do with it?" His grip around her tightened as he suddenly took a few steps forward toward Memphis, virtually carrying her against his hip with ease. "Would you like a closer look? Make sure it's real?"

Memphis, for all his decorum, tensed as the woman and her jewelry came three feet closer. His big hands made fists and then relaxed again, and one eye twitched just an iota before returning to its cold glare. But he did not draw away, standing his ground like a massive oak against a thunderhead.

But his tone was sharp and perturbed. "Enough of your foolishness!" he snapped.

Unable to just stand by any longer, Adrienne sensed Cyprus's grip loosening and roughly shouldered herself free. She moved a few feet away to lean against the back of a nearby leather couch. Her own hand touched her small adornment, now strongly warm.

Memphis's overt anger abated as suddenly as it had manifested, now that Adrienne had moved a few feet further away. But the gaze he now held Cyprus in was a murderous one.

"Perhaps you recall," Cyprus coolly began once more, "the…finder's fee that was placed upon our happy little trinket."

"My recollection is flawless, Blackshaft."

One slow hard blink squeezed Cyprus's eyes shut and popped them open like window shades. His tongue licked his lips and slunk back in. "In the name of ancient tradition and solidarity, I would have *you* formally declare it."

"As you wish…" said Memphis, sounding amused but still deadly serious. "Cyprus Blackshaft, I hereby aver that We now owe you a Favor."

Adrienne saw Cyprus's whole frame relax considerably, as if this declaration was all he had wanted to hear in the entire world. Indeed, she herself felt certain of the veracity of the proclamation. Cyprus smiled again – but this time it was a genuine, honest upturning of his mouth's corners – as if every like-action she'd seen before that had been contrived and wily; his first honest, real smile.

Sighing deeply, he looked content. "Our business is completed, then." He looked at Adrienne. "Woman, remove your necklace." He dug in his pocket and pulled free, to Adrienne's surprise, an identical green jewel.

Adrienne would have parted with many things before willingly giving up a wedding day gift from her husband. She didn't move, and stared back at Cyprus coldly as he came toward her. Her fist was prepped for another confrontation with his jaw, but Memphis interrupted them.

"Leave it with her," he said.

Cyprus had reached her but turned to look back. "With her? But we're leaving. My lord, she *is* coming with me; she must."

"Is your master aware you are on your way with this…prize of yours?" asked Memphis.

After what Cyprus had just said, Adrienne could not help but wonder if he were referring to her or the necklace bijou. It was difficult to decipher, given Cyprus insisted she leave with him. At the same time, she had another overwhelming feeling in the depth of her being that this adamant statement by Cyprus was indeed the truth – just as Memphis's earlier affirmation had been.

"…Undoubtedly…" came the reluctant and sullen reply, as if the title granted to this 'master' individual irked Cyprus. "The resources available make that a foregone conclusion."

"Then you must not disappoint, as you have a habit of doing lately; this female," Memphis said, indicating Adrienne, "will be delivered wearing the legitimate piece. Your master is more than capable of determining a forgery. It would not do."

"That capability is debatable-"

"It is not. A detected forgery will result in the ruin of my carefully laid plans, as your master will not act accordingly without the real gemstone."

So it is the stone that matters, and not me, pondered Adrienne. *Why am I coming along, then?*

"Deliver both the legitimate stone and its bearer to your master. We will speak later on this, but for now, go."

"Then why," growled Cyprus, "did we come here in the first place? We could be well on our way without this unnecessary pit-stop-"

"Mind your place," came the curt reply, and there was a pause as the two men stared at each other in a brief test of will. "I do not command useless, unnecessary things. I had to know for certain it was the proper element myself. No one who actually knew you would be fool enough to take you at your word, Blackshaft. And now that I do indeed know it is genuine, I am sending it on for the purpose I intended all along."

Cyprus gave a nod of understanding. "So what we had discussed previously along those veins remains? Once the position is vacant, I will have your support to…fill it?"

A sinister smile oozed itself across the blank face of Memphis. "Of course. *I am always true to my word.*"

That is a lie, Adrienne immediately intuited. She did not understand how she knew, but she was certain that she did indeed know. As she marveled at her own surety, she at once recognized when Cyprus answered with mendacity.

"I never doubted it, my lord."

With a half bow, he immediately turned about and grabbed Adrienne by the arm. She had no choice but to stagger along with his quick pace toward the door, barely able to look over her shoulder at Memphis. Behind them, the tall grim tower of spite had turned away, giving them no more thought. In exchange, Cyprus seemed to have forgotten him as well.

"Our lucky night," he told her as she opened the library doors and followed her through, assuming her arm in his again. "I get a Favor and you keep your necklace. How auspicious."

"Not the word I would choose," she said quietly, to herself.

Adrienne was dazed and numb, but the twinge in her insides that was so present when in Memphis's presence was now fading. Still, she felt as if caught between getting violently sick and having just had a terrible fright – like driving after a nearly fatal car accident. Her ankle trembled as she took a step trying to keep up with Cyprus's stride. The heels were going to kill her before Cyprus could. Passing through the hall to the elevator, guests and party festivities sifted around her like a dream. She walked almost not seeing, mind filled with images of Memphis and Cyprus arguing over what to do with her.

Her ankle nearly buckled and she spoke without thinking.

"Please slow down, I'm going to hurt myself."

To her surprise, he obliged. She breathed a hair easier, not having to watch her step every time she planted her foot.

"You need a stiff drink," he chuckled.

"That…" she answered slowly, "is not the problem."

They had reached the elevators and entered the car when the doors opened.

"Maybe you should get off your feet."

"Perhaps-"

It was as far as she got. In mid sentence her voice caught in her throat as a very sudden and sharp pain – like electric needles – inserted itself in her upper thigh. She swooned, a cry of pain caught halfway out of her mouth as the unlooked for surge interrupted her thought. She buckled like a house of cards, and would have reached the hard floor if Cyprus had not caught her easily.

"I insist," he said to the unconscious woman in his arms. "It seemed a pity to make you strap on the device and not show you how it works."

"Well, at least he can't hurt her in such a crowded setting…" Frank offered after a long silence.

"The Order of the Raven will do what they like in their own building," said Orion grimly. "If Cyprus wanted Adrienne dead, she would be so by now. They are intending to use her for something, I'll warrant."

"Use her for what?"

"At the moment," said Orion dryly but without humor, "for a date."

"Don't remind me -- Adrienne, where is he taking you?" Frank asked aloud as he watched through the glasses while Cyprus accompanied his wife across the floor through the party.

"She appeared unharmed," recalled Orion, leaning on the banister with his back to the street, arms crossed. "But it troubles me more that Cyprus is with her."

Frank paused in his watch as Adrienne walked out of his view on her way from meeting Memphis. The giant window in the skyscraper provided a wonderful view for Frank and Orion, but it did not allow them to see every last thing. Because of this neither caught Adrienne losing consciousness by the elevators.

The two stood there, Frank with the binoculars and Orion watching with his arms crossed, both waiting to see if Adrienne would reappear.

"It will be hard to get over there with the party going on."

"Much traffic in the sewer, do you think?" asked Frank.

"There will be too much security that way. But we have discussed this. She's going to be gone by the time we would have a team down here. When we first saw her, they were crossing the room from the left, and now they've come back from the right. I think they are leaving already. Whatever purpose he has in mind is already accomplished."

Frank had left the railing and was headed off the balcony back inside, talking over his shoulder. "We've waited long enough. If anything happens to her, I'll never forgive myself."

Orion came after him, slower and reflective. *You never do*, he thought.

CHAPTER 7

"You have forgotten our purpose. Are you a Raven, or just some greedy crow?"

~Robert of Manderly, AD 1201

&❧ ❧

CONSTANTINOPLE. APRIL 11, AD 1204.

There were worse cities for a council than Adrianople. Orion found the solar of their hostess to be comfortable enough, furnished and amiable. Open windows and cool air made for pleasant accommodations. Callia's beautiful young daughter had placed bread and fruit on the table, enough for all eleven men present. Her long blonde hair and kind countenance reminded him of Attica, who at the moment was a little over one hundred miles away in Constantinople.

Safe where he'd left her. There were few safer places to be in these dangerous times; the latest crusading army had gathered in Venice two summers prior. The crusaders were now at Constantinople, but this was typical of a crusading venture: they would rally there, squabble with the emperor over common goals, pending territorial captures and supplies, and then they would depart across the waters of Marmara and the Bosphorous toward Anatolia.

There were few worse topics for a council. His own beloved Order of the Raven was at war within itself. Discontentment only began to describe the angst that men like Arman and Philip had with stubborn conservatives like Robert and Frederick. And Orion, they considered him a relic.

We oppose the Shades for centuries, *thought Orion.* And the ancient Order of the Raven dissolves because of pitiful infighting?

"Your greed shames us all," snarled Bohemond from the corner where he poured more wine. A fiery Norman named for but not related to the crusader of years past, he was a broad-shouldered man who fancied wine to fuel a notorious ill-temper. He wiped his bearded mouth with the back of a rough hand and lumbered back to his place, glaring at Arman and his five compatriots. "What's become of your honor?"

"You presume to lecture me, you Norman sot?" answered Arman, a scowling Frenchman both tall and thin. His sparse mustache bristled indignantly. "Take your filthy-"

"Yes, Arman," came Robert's calm but stern voice. Everyone looked at the English duke sitting there, arms crossed beneath grim expression, surveying Arman and Philip across from him. "We do presume to lecture you. When you turn your back on this Order's history, on her men, on her very purpose and propose to set out on a brand new venture of pure self-interest...we do presume to lecture you."

Arman was more calm when addressed with respect. "Robert, you don't understand-"

"What's become of you, my old friend? We have done many a noble thing together against the shadows down through the years. And you would throw it all away? Things of this life are fleeting-"

"All the more reason to seize as much as possible," said Philip, fat fingers slick with juice as he hovered over the fruit bowl.

"We have given our lives for the cause," Arman answered Robert. "The Order of the Raven controls wealth and resources beyond that of a hundred kingdoms, yet we live like paupers driven from town to town. I did not join this order to die young and penniless. We chase the sunset in the hope of stopping some atrocity, but when dawn arrives we only gallop madly for the opposite horizon once again to face the next oncoming night. It is tiring, thankless work. And I am weary of it."

"As am I," said Philip.

This last sentiment was echoed by multiple supporters about Arman and Philip, six men strong.

The stout and lordly German, Frederick, toyed with his beard thoughtfully. It was far more gray than it had been but a year before. He glanced at Orion.

"And what does our Gatekeeper friend have to say of all this?" he asked. "If the ancient and sacred Order of the Raven belongs to anyone, it is you."

What good was it to encourage weary, bitter men to maintain their thankless workload? Orion looked from face to face about the room, knowing it was indeed his part to say something. Orion knew as he sat there that continuing to debate was more useless than a wooden sword; this was not the first council on the subject. Men like Arman and Philip were growing more bold and more common: good soldiers of the cause but weary and mostly empty-handed after years of service. They had a fair point.

"I cannot tell you that people will eventually be grateful for our work; it is indeed thankless. But it is needed. If you cannot see that in the years of your own experience...

nothing I say will sway you. I and the other Gatekeepers did not help enact the Order of the Raven so we could become rich. We did it because the greatest kingdom of men had fallen and the Shades were unopposed in a world of fledgling civilizations just gaining its feet. If we did not devote our time to opposing the shadows, the world we know today would not be-"

The door of the solar banged open violently and their serving girl nearly fell into the room. She looked as if she'd seen a ghost, and was breathless from a run. Callia's brow furrowed as she came to her feet from her place between Robert and Orion. "We are in the midst of council, child. What's come over you?"

The girl held a piece of rolled parchment in a clenched fist. "Mother...my lords... the crusade has turned on The City. Constantinople is besieged..."

Attica. *Orion lurched to his feet and almost flung Bohemond out of his way as he made for the door. "Godfrey, Robert," he said over his shoulder, "your horses are coming with me."*

℘ ☙

Frank had always known that for the remarkable life Orion had lived, he was not much of a conversationalist, nor had he ever been. He listened halfheartedly as Orion spoke to the Bluetooth hooked over his ear, communicating back with Doc and Bohemond at the Dominos de Lumine headquarters miles away. There was a pause for the hundredth time as Orion sped down the highway, passing cars left and right, weaving.

Frank tried to pay attention, knowing the potential passing of information would be beneficial in finding Adrienne, but he was distracted. To see his wife with a man such as Cyprus was downright disturbing. Frank had known many logical enemies in his own time, but Cyprus had always been a trifle unhinged. *Hang in there, babe, we're coming...*

"No, no..." Orion was saying with slight exasperation. "Just listen to me: isolate the flight clearances out of the nearest airports...no, I don't know where to. Just do it-" He paused and his brow furrowed infinitesimally. Frank of course didn't catch what it said, but plainly Orion did. "I do not understand this difficulty of yours at this task, Helms," he said, a smidgen of annoyance in his tone. "They arrived at the headquarters via helicopter, and it is a high likelihood that they will leave after it has refueled and they've accomplished their purposes."

"I saw the chopper lifting off again when we were back in the car," Frank reminded him.

"And Frank says he saw it take off again, so wherever they're going, they're already en route...no I'm assuming they're taking her out of the country, or at least out of the city. Now utilize those codes of yours and access the information...yes, get back to us when you're in. I'm headed for the Harris Airport."

He hung up with the touch of a button, and replaced his grip on the wheel.

"Impossible man," he said with a shake of his head. As an afterthought he removed the device entirely and tossed it in the cup-holder.

"Is Doc always difficult to work with?"

"No, he's the best tech-man the Society has, and it has a lot. He seems distracted the last few weeks. I think his wife is pregnant."

"So where are we at?" asked Frank.

"I suspect the Raven are moving Adrienne at the very least out of the city. The chopper is going to be the fastest way to the airport, and the nearest airport is Harris. A large organization can get clearance for immediate departures if it likes, but it still needs clearance. Those records, if we find them, will tell us where they are going."

"Isn't that a long list to sort from?"

"At times, but we can isolate a period of time for the departure, as well as types of aircraft. The Crows favor a number of small private jets. They're very exclusive, but in the end inconspicuous if used under the right cover."

"Couldn't they just give a false destination and change in mid-flight?"

"True, but the false destination would still be informed they're on their way; when they fail to arrive, problems arise and it's often not worth the trouble. It's a relatively safe way of gaining destination."

"How long will it take Doc?"

The cell rang.

80 03

A loud rushing of air greeted Adrienne's return to consciousness, and she realized she was on a plane. Her eyes fluttered: she was on a small, well-accommodated private jet, seated in a large cushy chair. There were fewer seats and more specialties: a wet-bar was close to the front of the cabin and a forty-two inch plasma television was mounted nearby.

A glance out the window placed her above the clouds somewhere in a nighttime world. The lights of the jet traced shadows over the billowy clouds below; stars shone overhead. *Where are we?* Weariness curbed her curiosity. The seats in the plane were not in rows as a normal passenger jet, but were large, padded, comfortable, and few in quantity. She could stretch her legs out easily, for there was nothing before her but space. She was still dressed in the formal gown, the garment wrinkled and bunched against her after having slept in it – as if the choice had been her own. When stretching forced her to move, she saw that next to her seat lay a folded pair of jeans and a T-shirt, as well as underwear.

A presence at her left side made her glance over and she saw that Cyprus was standing beside her, holding a large bottle of water out to her as he looked down at her. She could not read the look in his eyes, but for some reason it troubled her. It was mildly disconcerting that his contacts made his irises appear a shimmering dark purple. Decorative contacts – what else could they be? Still, at the same time she wrote him off a little more; decorative contacts were something she had always considered juvenile.

"Being debilitated can cause extreme thirst," he said.

She was tempted to refuse, if only to express outrage at the continuing indignity of her kidnapped state. But hearing him say that made her pay attention to the possibility of being thirsty, and she found she was parched. She took the bottle with an air of resentment that was mostly a principled facade, and emptied a significant amount.

"Where are we?" she asked.

Cyprus had turned away and seated himself across the aisle not far away, pulling a leather-bound book from the side-pocket of his chair. Ignoring her, he opened it and pulled a pen from its place and began to write.

"Over the Atlantic Ocean," he said at length.

"And where are we going?"

"East."

He still hadn't looked at her. *Aggravating jerk.* The nerve of the man not to oblige a simple question when he plainly could without difficulty! Knowing that she could not coax any answer out of him – and hardly being in the mood to even pretend to try – she crossed her arms and lapsed into silence. A moment later she remembered that the device was still strapped to her leg. Considering the removal of the device reminded her of the spare clothes and the gown she still wore.

Without a word, she took the clothes and went to the back of the plane. She changed in the roomy bathroom, removing the device from where it throbbed around her leg. There was a plastic bag with toiletries by the sink. Taking the liberty of not asking, she used all: floss, toothbrush, deodorant, hairbrush. *How did these people know my size?* As with the evening gown, everything fit perfectly. By the time she left the bathroom some twenty minutes later, she almost felt herself.

"Feel better?" Cyprus asked as she sat back down. He didn't look up.

"Considering I've been kidnapped, almost literally scared to death by some creepy stranger, and am now being illegally transported right out of the country," she said coolly, "I feel well enough. Though I think you could afford to cut me some slack and at least have the decency to tell me where I'm being taken."

Cyprus said nothing, turning a page to continue writing. He made a sideways glance at her for an instant, amused at her silence. "I liked you better in the dress."

Adrienne wanted to punch him again. "So you're not going to tell me?" It was hardly a question.

"You will find out soon enough," said he. "You are a more curious sort than I thought you would be."

She crossed her arms again. "And I'm sure you'll explain that comment, as you've been so forthcoming with every other nature of this journey."

Cyprus smiled in a sinister way. "You're feisty. I can see why he likes you."

"Who? That creepy Memphis?"

"No! Your husband."

He enjoys being vague purely to enrage others. Probably considers himself witty...

She knew better than to say it, though she nearly did. Adrienne's anger at the whole affair barely kept her from caring whether she remained tactful.

"You don't know anything about us."

His eyes blinked their heavy double-blink, his tongue worked slowly over his lips before he spoke again. "That you believe that is truly amusing, but don't overplay your hand. It would not do for me to grow tired of you. We've some hours before us yet. Don't force me to look for methods of entertainment." His free hand went to his side from where he had pulled the switchblade, back in the suite. Cyprus's fingers closed on nothing, and he looked down. "Where is Annabelle?" he asked, looking for his knife.

Why do men always insist on giving a woman's name to their toys? It's insulting...

But given he was looking for his knife, Adrienne decided she'd pushed enough. Cyprus did not give up, but searched a number of places on his person while she looked on. He turned away to dig through a bag next to him.

Does he not remember dropping it? She recalled how Cyprus's whole mannerism had changed after she decked him. He had walked away without it after giving her a look as if she were the one behaving oddly.

"My husband will find me, you know."

"Oh, I'm counting on it," he said, turning back to look at her. "It will be just like old times, only now you can replace what's-her-name."

Adrienne discerned almost immediately that he was lying to her about the other woman, playing games in her head. At the same time she was angry with herself, because as soon as he said it there was the one percent of her brain that suspected it was true. She had recently been learning a lot about her husband, after all.

But what she said was, "There's that classy wit from earlier. And here I was afraid it had gone away."

"There'll be little enough wit when he sees me once more." There was no humor in his statement.

The lying jest about another woman – of course it had been a lie – had stirred spousal possession within Adrienne. Her voice took on a tone so low and dark he would have thought it was someone else. "If you hurt him...so help me..."

"You are worried about hurting him after what you and I did?" he asked, a mischievous glance in his eye.

"What...are you talking about?"

He smiled. "Coy...I like that."

"I don't know what you're talking about." But she could not decide if he was lying or not. *I don't like where he's going with this...did he do something to me while I was unconscious? Oh...no, please...*

"You threw yourself at me," said he.

Her fears vanished like smoke, and she gritted her teeth. *This one is twisted.* "That's what you've come up with? You seduced me? Really?"

"I seduced you? No...no...*you* were most insistent," he chuckled, and picked up the notebook he'd been writing in. "I was just recording it for my memoirs." He found the page and began to read aloud: "'*Her beautiful green eyes sparkled as she searched my own for approval. "Do you like what you see?" she asked, refusing to don the dress I had gotten for her-*'"

"You're delusional-"

"'*She had her arms around my neck, whispering in my ear to-*'"

"Oh my word," exploded Adrienne, "you are an absolute *nut-job!*"

He was looking at her in that horrid way, where she could not tell if he were serious or not. "I could make you happy, you know..."

He can't possibly believe what he's written... After a deep breath, her voice regained composure. "Going home is all that would make me happy."

"What were we talking about...oh yes...you protecting your husband from me..."

She glared at him derisively, but said nothing. Obviously she was in no such position, though with that look of hers he did not doubt she would have the will to do it at the time. He went on.

"I wonder where you got the idea that Frank Blackman needs your help? What do you think he's been *doing* for the Society, teaching kindergarten?"

Adrienne had resorted to fingering her necklace gem once more, inhaling slowly. Losing her temper like that had not happened in a long time, and she was taking purposeful steps to calm down. Her anger had left her flushed.

"I can't imagine what he was doing if it meant having to deal with a man like you," she finally said.

He was both surprised and amused. "You really don't know, do you?"

She knew it was taking the bait, but she had to. "Know what?"

"What did your husband tell you he did when you met him?"

Adrienne had sat back, seeing no reason why she should not say, but returning his gaze with suspicion. "He was an accountant at the time."

Then Cyprus really did laugh. "An accountant! How amusing..." He leaned toward her indignant glare. "The partner of the immortal Deathless Blade and his wife doesn't even know! Too hilarious for words, really." He paused and she was slowly shaking her head, but he continued. "In a way I can't blame him for not telling you. He couldn't be expected to tell you, even now, I suppose. How could he?"

"What wouldn't he be able to tell me?" asked Adrienne, now defensive. She was interested, admittedly, but she had also begun to see that her knowledge of her own husband was being called into question. Although it was not her fault, the prospect of it was rather insulting. In her own turn, she had never thought that her husband's enemies might have something specific in mind when it came to him.

"What wouldn't he be able to tell you? Why, what he's been doing for the past two centuries, my Lady!" He had looked away and was facing forward, finding great entertainment in this revelation of which Adrienne was unaware.

The reference to time was the last straw. She had been angry enough when he'd inferred she was an adulteress, but to be made fun of further… She could not fathom how she had almost believed the cur. "Now I know you're lying." But in her heart she was convinced he was not – but how could he possibly be speaking truth? *He has to be lying.*

He shook his head, still finding the situation humorous. "Oh, you can't make this stuff up."

"Two centuries?" scoffed Adrienne. "Frank isn't even forty yet!"

He suddenly recovered from his delight at her lack of knowledge pertaining to her husband. "I'll grant you he looks very good for a man approaching his twenty-sixth decade. How intriguing. I would love to hear you ask him about these things, since you were plainly unaware. Too bad, really…" he trailed off and picked up the book again.

Adrienne was not in the mood to be placated, but she did want to know. "What's too bad?"

Cyprus looked back at her once more as if it were a foolish question. "Why, that you'll never see him alive again to ask him about these things." He squeezed his eyes shut for an instant, as if trying to clear them.

Adrienne sat there both frightened and infuriated at the very same moment, looking at Cyprus. He spoke of terrible things with an ease that sent a shiver up her spine. She somehow managed to console herself by staring out the window at the passing clouds, fingering the green gemstone and trying to process too many thoughts at once.

ಹೋ ೞ

Frank watched out the window of the small private jet, seeing the technicians finish their last minute work. Orion sat nearby, phone in hand, fingers busy tapping away.

"I prefer laptops," he said randomly. "My eyes are not what they used to be; phone screens are too small. At least for mapping they are."

"What maps are you looking at?"

"Portugal. A century ago I could not expect to be in Sintra for weeks. But now we shall be there within a number of hours."

"Sintra?"

"It would appear Adrienne is bound for southwestern Europe, though where exactly we are not yet certain. We have a place in Sintra – as usual, I suppose – and by the time we get there, we'll have negotiated the next step."

"How do we know that's where she's headed?"

"Doc hacked into the arrivals and destinations and has verified the departure of a Raven jet. Its destination is also Portugal."

"Seems a little too easy."

Orion spoke as one with experience. "If one knows how…many types of things are 'too' easy."

"I meant they don't seem interested in covering their tracks."

"Who told you they didn't want us to follow them?"

"No one, I just-"

"This is bigger than Adrienne. While she may be valuable to them for a number of reasons, rest assured she alone cannot be the only thing of interest. They have to be using her for…something."

"So?"

"So someone is probably preparing to have you and I as guests as well."

There was a pause. "I still don't understand why Adrienne was taken at all."

"That reminds me, now that we will have some time to ourselves, I need to catch you up on something. It may explain much, though not all."

"Catch me up on what?"

"The necklace I gave to you when you retired, the one your wife now wears."

CHAPTER 8

"...madmen raging against the sacred..."

~Niketas Choniates

☙ ❧

CONSTANTINOPLE. APRIL 13, AD 1204.

he mighty city of Constantinople was in utter chaos. For centuries, foreign armies had attempted to break inside at one time or another, but the massive Theodosian and Constantinian walls were a formidable barrier. Yet the city was not invincible. In the end, it was more complicated than most of the history books would come to tell, but at length the armies of Europe entered the ancient city, sacking it.

Orion was exhausted, having ridden virtually nonstop from Adrianople. Godfrey's horse had died beneath him, poor beast, but the need for speed spurred him on with Robert's. Attica had never begrudged him attending to the business of the Order. She accepted it was for good, though he could be gone for long periods of time, as was the latest occurrence from which he returned. Yet they always took up again upon his coming, as if he had never left. At any rate, it would have been far too dangerous for her to accompany him. Regardless of destination, most roads had perilous stretches.

He and Attica had stayed in Constantinople for years – decades. They had moved away once or twice, but they always found their way back. The location made sense for a traveler that might head off at the last minute to a plethora of places; the city was between two continents and not far from a third. The home to which Orion was returning this particular time had been their abode for thirty years by the time the Fourth Crusade came along.

After riding the hundred or so miles from Adrianople, Orion's approach to Constantinople was toward the end of that fateful day. The few people he did pass told him there was great trouble in the city. Still miles away, he could see the smoke of countless fires. He rode his second and last horse to the point that it fell dead beneath him about a mile out.

His thought was so intent that upon reaching the gates, he hardly noticed how blown he was from the run. Without pause he passed through the arches, staggering over the gates themselves, cast down with violence and partly burned. Crusader soldiers were everywhere, but he saw few Byzantine soldiers. Those that he did see were not armed. The streets near the outskirts and walls were littered with corpses. Not just soldiers. Women. And children. The very sight of them made him race harder down the familiar city streets, weaving through their maze.

Nothing had been safe within the city. Orion passed even the doors of churches that had been broken in the onslaught. Some lay on the streets where they had been pulled, some were half on their hinges, some lying in the doorways of the places of worship. Drunken singing came from the dark entries of more than one chapel, screams from others. It was well known that the churches of Constantinople contained treasures worth countless fortunes, not only gold but also innumerable relics of Christendom. Everywhere was the smell of fire, the sight of rubble, evidence of death, ample destruction. Cries of a woman in the agony of loss came from his left. The city was dead, but it had not gone quietly.

Orion could hear the cries of children off to his right as he rounded the corner of the street and ran straight toward the familiar door on the edge of the market square, the same door where eight weeks before he had kissed his wife goodbye. The business with the Order had called him away just in time to miss all that had gone on, and had ended only for him to come back too late.

He had reached the square and was running across it, eyes locked on the small house on the edge and – the door was open, half torn from its hinges. For the first time in a long time, his stomach turned with a sudden onslaught of sick fear from deep within his being. He staggered to the ground in his weariness and panicked hurry as he tried to rush on toward the door of the home. Ignoring his scraped palms from the fall, he got up and ran to the house. His house.

৪০ ৫৪

Adrienne had never slept well on planes, and with Cyprus so close by, slumber was difficult to achieve. At the same time, she was so exhausted that eventually she did drop off. How long she had been asleep, she did not know, but she did find that when she awoke the plane was much closer to the ground than it had been. They were still over water, but a mainland was approaching.

Where are we? Is that Europe? Africa?

She glanced toward the front of the cabin to see Cyprus talking with a member of the flight crew. Instantly she thought of informing this new fellow that she was being kidnapped and that he ought to do something to help her, but that fancy passed quickly. They were on a private craft. The fellow was an employee. She sighed, annoyed at herself for even contemplating saying anything.

Neither man, at any rate, paid her any attention. They spoke in voices too quiet for her to hear over the rush of the air overhead. The conversation soon finished anyway, and she found that Cyprus had once again sat down in a nearby seat across the aisle and picked up his fallacious journal.

"We'll be landing in Lisbon in twenty minutes or so. From there, we have an hour's drive, and after that we shall remain at our destination. There your role in future events will be revealed to you. You of course realize you are not here simply at random choice."

Obviously. Her mind was bursting with questions, but the real trick was to ask one that Cyprus might actually answer. He was not very adept at small-talk, but Adrienne had exchanged enough words with him to begin to conceive she understood him a little bit. He would not talk for pleasure or to be polite, but he had proved more than willing to give information when he considered it to his advantage – or when it proved his resourcefulness or cleverness. *Or when the information gives him some sort of malicious satisfaction or enjoyment. I wonder what he really knows about Frank.* She tried again.

"Is Frank really almost twenty-six decades old?" she asked. *He can't be, of course, but if it makes this one keep talking...*

His eyes did not leave the book. "He looks good, does he not?"

"Please. Tell me."

"He's around that age, yes."

She had to hand it to him; he looked very serious, and held the pose well as if he meant what he said with all sincerity. Once again, as earlier, in her heart of hearts, she was convinced he was telling the truth. It was eerie, as of course he couldn't be. "You're either a very good liar or the world is a very strange place."

Cyprus smirked and put down the book, glancing over at her at the same time. "Your questions betray you. You are not as skeptical as you would have me believe."

"Lots of weird things have happened to me over the course of the last day. It is only natural that I should have questions."

Cyprus's next statement was flat and sincere, and carried no explanation. "When I first met your husband it was in 1772, in Boston before the American Revolution. It was during a very temporary truce between our two societies...the fate of America warranted discussion."

Adrienne said nothing. She didn't believe him, of course, but what he said was in such a tone that he could have suggested anything and she'd have to think twice before dismissing it. She was not above suspecting that some of what he said was true while some was not. He continued without even looking to see if she was still listening.

"Dominos de Lumine was all for the coming revolution in America, for a new power in the West to be born, helping to break apart the large British Empire. The Order of the Raven was more of the mind to keep the British dominant, for at the time it served our purposes." He stopped and looked over at her again to find she was looking back at him, but he grimaced at the amusement in her eyes. His own eyes squeezed shut convulsively and popped open like window shades.

"You doubt me?" he asked, and his voice had taken on a different feel to it, as if a dangerous individual's good graces had been insulted.

"I-I didn't say anything."

He cooled to a sneer. "It matters very little if you believe what I say or not. Though you may have yet to play a very important, critical role in the course of history as we know it. Few people can say they have accomplished something like this in their lives."

"Will this historic role explain what Shades want with me?"

He looked at her with a mischievous glint to his eye, and Adrienne saw that she had finally said something that piqued his interest.

"It is plain I have not given you enough credit, my Lady," he admitted at length. "What do you know of Shades?"

"Not enough," said she. *And that's me being generous...*

"Nothing at all, then..."

"I won't dispute that."

Cyprus smiled. "An interesting history, that," he went on, almost as if to himself. "Once you hear of them, you never look at the Grim Reaper the same again, do you?"

"What?"

He looked back in mild surprise. "Death," he said expectantly as if she could have guessed. "The Grim Reaper. The tall robed and hooded being that comes to harvest souls, with the sickle." Now he stopped short. "Well, where do you reckon such stories originated from? Shades have, after all, been in the world since before civilization as you recognize it came into being. They had a hand in its evolution, you know. They had to leave a recognizable mark on it somewhere. The closest thing one can point to is the death cults: the aspects of death and the Grip Reaper. Even that Dickens fellow's Ghost of Christmas Yet to Come or however he called it. The tombstone and all. Western literature especially has too many references to count..."

Adrienne would have had to admit she was listening intently, and while she did not understand everything he said, she did find it interesting at the very least. He merely went on in his condescending tone.

"'Not enough' indeed," he laughed, but paused. "Of what were we speaking?"

She didn't want to discuss it anymore but he wouldn't look away.

"My…tremendous role to come."

"Ah, yes. The honor is yours, Lady Blackman, the honor is truly yours."

"I've got so much to be excited about, I should be writing it all down…"

"Of course you do not understand now, woman, but you will. Aye, you will."

"How would I come to understand if you won't explain it to me?"

His eyes narrowed a bit. "I'm going to let someone else do that…"

"And who might that be?"

"You'll meet her, rest assured."

Adrienne turned to look at him. "Her?"

"The Lady Triassa looks forward to meeting you. Take care not to disappoint her."

How am I supposed to avoid disappointing someone I know nothing about?

"Does Dominos de Lumine know about this Miss Triassa?"

Cyprus gave an amused half-laugh. "Dominos de Lumine? A bunch of old men who cannot see the power at their fingertips, and thus all fail to suitably use it. Robert and Godfrey and Bohemond and Frederick…what *would* they say? Fools, all of them, though perhaps they would have the wit to grant the Lady of the Raven proper due. You can never trust what one's enemies say about him – or her, you know. On one hand, they may praise him excessively – but only because he has outfoxed them and so they will look better by being topped by a genius rather than a fool. Or when they are victors, that they have bettered a great man, and so are great themselves. On the other hand, they may speak poorly of her as an enemy, as they simply don't like her.

"But consider this: Dominos de Lumine is mastered by four different men at the same time, but for an organization roughly the same size, the Raven have only one master, and need only one master. Our lady holds together for the Raven what it takes the Dominos de Lumine four men to control. Tell me, who is the better leader?"

Adrienne remembered her own ancient history courses. *The Roman Empire adopted the tetrarchy to assist administration, why not a Society?* She remembered so readily because the idea of having essentially four rulers had struck her as a clever solution to succession problems. *He'd probably tell me his fancy Raven Order cut the empire in halves to suit some whim…*

The plane had begun to descend and it was obvious they would be landing soon. With that expectation, Adrienne chose not to divulge that from *her* understanding, it might be very purposeful that more than one person control a vast organization, and probably advantageous in ways beyond those she could name at the moment.

"Choose your words carefully when you speak with her, Lady Blackman. Whatever her design, your part is important enough for you to be brought to the Lady Triassa personally. To disappoint her would be…unwise."

"If you're trying to frighten me…" began Adrienne, originally intending to sound defiant. She trailed off and realized she would only be fooling herself. "… just cut it out," she ended lamely.

Cyprus had a smug look on his face that annoyed her incredibly. "You master yourself well enough. We shall see."

With that he lapsed back into silence and once again picked up his book. Adrienne found herself in no mood for further conversation. Her thoughts dwelt on Shades and the Raven, who they were and what they were going to do with her – but mostly on her husband, where he was and what would happen if and when she was able to see him again.

CHAPTER 9

"I do not know what unspeakable crime fueled the rage of the Deathless Blade in the Tavern Street Massacre, but nothing quite like it has ever happened again; nor has he been the same since."

~Robert of Manderly to Frederick of Blois in a personal correspondence. December, AD 1243

༄ ༅

CONSTANTINOPLE. APRIL 13, AD 1204.

O rion stood in the doorway of his own small house there on the edge of the square of the ransacked city. His hands were on the door-frame itself, his breathing increased from his run through the city, his eyes critically searching, confirming his fears. The destruction and chaos that had torn through the city like an eruption had reached his own door and not slowed.

The door had been literally hacked from its hinges with something so heavy that it was irreparable. The table at which he and his wife had eaten so many times was tipped over, legs snapped. Everything that had been on the table, the shelves in the room, and in the larder was cast rudely about. It had happened long enough ago that flies had taken to the scattered foods, though decay was not yet rampant.

He called Attica's name aloud many times, even as he saw that the other three rooms were equally ransacked. Furniture and clothing had been destroyed, shelves of books overturned and partially burned. Some favored scrolls, he saw at a glance, were still smoldering. Everything he could see, touch, hear, and smell confirmed that chaos had reigned and been the victor in what must have been a brutal battle with his belongings.

His eyes were on the floor, among other places, when he turned the corner down the short passage to their bedroom. If not for other circumstances, Orion would have assumed it luck that he saw it – although he had never believed in luck. The small jewelry chain that was most familiar lay beneath a smashed vase, and he pulled it out by the broken clasp. He had given this very necklace to her very early on in their relationship, and she had never taken it off. Not once. To have it lying on the floor with a broken clasp could only mean it had been torn from her neck. Orion looked at the adornment with a special appreciation, but most of this enamored stare was tied in with the woman he had given it to years and years before. Monetarily it was not worth much; its value was sentimental. Yet he was troubled and continued down the hall, for if it was torn from her neck, what had been going on at the time?

Attica was in the last room. He had called her name numerous times, but upon entering the bedroom and seeing her, his chilled veins were warmed. But why had she not responded to his call? At the very first, seeing his wife lying on her side in the bed with her back to him, he had thought that she had come upon the disaster as he had, and exhausted and stricken with grief, had at last after much toil to salvage, lain down to sleep. Then he saw the blood and his heart that was beating so ridiculously hard in his ears, stopped.

Her favorite shawl lay on the bedroom floor, twisted and bloodstained, slashed. With all the ripped and torn clothing scattered all about, all their garments ruined, it was impossible to tell what she had had on. But it was plain she no longer wore it. Her most natural state was obscured only by the sheet that had been sloppily drawn across her middle as she lay there, and the whiteness of it was splotched everywhere with the red of blood.

He did not have to see the actual physical signs on her body to tell that she had been violated and abused with reckless abandon, and by more than one offender. How long it had gone on he could not tell, but he doubted it was short-lived. That they had taken the time to slit her throat when they were done was no consolation. It came as mere spite that the weapon, or one of them, lay there on the bed beside her. A fine dagger, ornate and upper-class with a signet in the pommel, the blade red with her blood.

The anger in his innermost being was so cold it burned him, feeling like a physical presence lurking between his sternum and lungs, making it hard to breathe. For the longest while he could do nothing but sit there with her head in his lap, smoothing the long beautiful hair out of her face.

Vengeance had always been a strong and valid emotion in the back of Orion's psyche. Over the years betrayal and treachery had never been far away; he had had his share. Perhaps more than an honest man's share, but of course his life went on longer than any honest man's. For the first time he was consciously aware that he did not desire that long lifespan to continue, not anymore.

He half-imagined that she would tell him it was okay, that she would open her eyes and smile and put her arms around him. That the whole moment would be over was his most intense desire. As a soldier of many years he had seen this sort of thing many times, give or take specifics, and it had always been bearably terrible. Women were often among the first to suffer when a city was taken. And now it was Attica who was given the place of such a condition, and while the previous travesties of war had not wrung so true for him in the past, now with his own wife dead in his arms, he understood the atrocity more clearly than ever before.

Time elapsed and Orion truly did not know how long he sat there cradling her body, one hand absentmindedly holding hers as she could not squeeze it back, the other unconsciously moving through the long hair that had always – always – delighted him in such times as he was taken to notice it. There were innumerable other things about her, of course, but her hair had always been a point of adoration.

Time passed, and as he held her hand, he realized her right fist was closed tightly, unyielding. With great trepidation as if it somehow disrespected her last moments, he forced himself to pry open her hand, which was no small task. A barely audible sigh that could have been described as sadly mournful escaped him as what she had clung to slipped from her dead fingers. It was her wedding ring.

৪০ ৫৪

The tavern was loud and jovial, as usual. Ironic, really, that so many with sorrow came to such a place for solitude, to drink and forget the hardships of life. Yet in his despair of loss Orion had admittedly come to drink oblivion on himself and the world he had so recently come to despise. He had seen much loss in his life, but little that was so personal and so recent. He could have burned the house and everything in it and missed very little, but she with whom he had shared the house had been irreplaceable. He would trade it all for another day in her company, if only to better prepare for her unexpected departure. Had he told her he loved her at their last parting? He could not remember.

The strength of the Geneva liquor was not strong enough to alter Orion's mindset or body chemistry at all, though a mere quart of the stuff would have killed most other men. The fact that he was who he was, a man and yet a different kind of man, severely limited the ability to intoxicate himself. He had never tried it before – had never felt the need to try it before, but now that he had, he found it was quite the task. No matter; it had only just begun to get dark outside, where the city was still in the throes of barely-restrained chaos. Looting parties still roamed near and far. Those who had slaked their lust upon the city and had no more will to continue for the evening had found a place to drink.

The establishment was filled with crusading soldiery, the many races of the men of Europe who had come all this way to the edge of western civilization, purposing to recapture the Holy Land, only to fall short of even arriving there. Exactly why Constantinople had been turned on had not been revealed to Orion at that time, and he frankly did not care why such events had transpired. He could think only of Attica, but he was suddenly aware of a conversation in which he quickly took interest.

At the end of the counter was a group of five crusader knights, their helms set aside at a table as they got more beer, all armed according to the day and their business: swords and knives. One had a crossbow over the back of his chair, slung with a strap. Another had a Danish battle-ax, as Orion had seen Richard the Lionheart carry at the siege of Acre, not fifteen years prior.

They were enjoying themselves, laughing and boasting of past deeds. Orion became aware they were discussing what they had done that day. One bearded knight drained his mug and slammed down the empty vessel. The others laughed as he belched and picked up again where he had left off.

"So what happened then?" encouraged one knight.

"It was truly amusing," said he, wiping his mouth with the back of his hand. "The little vixen actually tried to stop our entry inside. The house didn't have anything to interest us on the inside, but after going to the trouble of getting in, we didn't want to come away empty-handed. A mere glance at her made it easy what to pick."

There was laughter all around. Orion sat there ten feet away, eyes closed, breathing slowly. His empty mug sat in front of him, between his hands was the signet dagger he had found beside his wife's body. It still had her blood on it. His hands made fists that rolled tighter as the story went on, beginning to tremble with a barely suppressed wrath.

"We had a little sport. The little siren actually pleaded with us to stop in four different languages. Let's see…Greek, French, Italian, and some fell dialect I've never heard."

"I was most curious as to what it was," said another.

"Aye, for myself as well. Like nothing I've ever heard."

Orion got off his seat and slowly walked toward them. The fourth spoken tongue was from a place that no longer existed. There were few left in the world that would have been able to recognize it. That Attica had used it at all only pointed to the level of her stress at the time; she would have known no European would recognize it. She had surely not been addressing any of these men when she used this last language.

"Even after we'd all taken a few turns she was still crying. Thought she'd have run out of tears by then!" The bearded man pulled at his beer as his fellows laughed again. "Anyway, so fine a thing is not to be discarded easily, so when we'd all had done, I couldn't just leave her in such a state."

Not all of his friends followed his meaning perfectly. "So you…?"

"Like the little whore when we came through Zara. Would have been faster for her if she'd stopped moving. We should have brought rope…"

"Pity you forgot your knife," said his friend.

"Aye, a good signet dagger of my House it was," said the knight. "I'll have to go back and get it. Perhaps her sister is in the city…"

His fellows laughed uproariously at that, but they gradually quieted just a bit as the tall dark-haired stranger approached. Orion smiled as he leaned on the table.

"It sounds as if you have misplaced a fine weapon, friend," said he.

"Aye," said the nearest man to him, right before him, *"it was that."*

"What was it like, this dagger?"

"A steel four-inch blade, double-edged, sharpened to the point it could cut hair. An elegant ivory handle, inlaid with gold, laced with red leather, and a pommel with the standard of our family name, in Chartres."

"Finest dagger money could buy," added another knight, *"but a family heirloom, this. You really will have to go back and get it."*

"Why such interest, friend?" asked the first and nearest knight, the man who had so brazenly boasted.

"I wanted to make sure it was yours before I gave it back to you," said Orion, and with the swiftest and most controlled motion any of them had ever seen, he put the point of the four inch blade straight up through the knight's jaw at the top of his throat behind his chin, up into the bottom of his mouth, through the tongue, and into his palate.

⁐ ⁃

Orion sat in the comfortable chair on one of many planes belonging to Dominos de Lumine. It was a small but highly efficient craft, hurtling them eastward over the ocean at speeds that would bring them to their destination in mere hours where the rest of the world would have taken nearly half a day. Such technology was not unique, really, but it was expensive.

He and Frank were the only passengers. Orion reclined and looked at the necklace of gold that ran through the circle of the beautiful ring he turned in his fingers. Its precious stone was still as brilliant as it had been the first day he saw it, so many years before. It still made him reminisce about Attica. The series of events with the Blackmans made Orion ponder his own married days.

But one regret.

Eight centuries earlier he had stepped from the tavern doors, covered in blood up to his elbows. Three crossbow bolts stuck from his back – he had not bothered to turn around and face the shooter until his business around the bar was done – and multiple lacerations and wounds that would have crippled several normal men. He did not regret the action, having killed no fewer than thirteen foes.

But now he could not think on her without seeing the faces of those men as well – her very memory was scarred. He regretted that.

Most men had experiences in which they wished afterward – with the full advantage of hindsight – that they had spoken or acted differently at the time. They were always wondering what they could have said better, or more suitably advantageous. Orion rarely experienced such remorse.

Even years and years later; he lamented none of his acts in Constantinople, regretted none of his words there. The first knight, after being informed that his dagger was to be returned to him, had gone down with hardly more than a wet squelching wheeze. In hindsight, that had been too fleeting; but in the end good enough. *I should have gelded him first.* The others had leaped up, spilling drinks, staggering in both stupor and the awkwardness of the moment combined with violent surprise, all reaching for one weapon or the other. Not every last man slain that day was personally guilty of assaulting Attica; only four or five of them had actually been there. The other eight or nine had joined the melee because the strange man at the bar had suddenly gotten to his feet and started killing. *Guilt by association.* Attica was not the only woman raped or even murdered in Constantinople during the sack, nor was their home the only ransacked property.

I did not tell those men why they were about to die. How could I not? I always declare that to the guilty. Perhaps I regret that as well, not telling them...

He had not spoken a word after the first strike, from beginning to end. Stony silence the entire time; not even the slightest sound of physical exertion as he went about the slaughter. Like some dread angel of death just going about its business. The mannerism had been detached, but in reality it had been an idiosyncratic moment – the first of its kind: the single time that the punishment for a crime was personal. The one time the fear in the faces of the condemned had pleased him. All the times before and after had really been Justice catching up to do her duty, but at Tavern Street she had brought her estranged sister Vengeance.

True Justice takes no joy in her administrations. That day was beyond mere Justice. You should have permanently retired then; your credibility did...

"You really think it's her necklace," said Frank from his seat a short distance away. He sounded troubled. "Why they took her in the first place."

"I suspect so," answered Orion, slipping the ring inside his clothing. "I am more troubled over the murders of the time agents, and if those are not connected as well."

"Do they have to be?"

Orion gave a half shrug. "No. But in my experience, coincidences are not as common as people tend to think."

"Why keep Adrienne alive? Why not just take the gemstone?"

"Did you not hear me telling you the nature of it?"

Frank's eyebrow raised. "Of course I did. What are you getting at?" he asked.

"It is a magical jewel that explicitly protects the person in whose possession it is – to a point."

"So?"

Orion gave him a look. "You think they can just rip it off her neck and be done? Cyprus would know better than that – he wouldn't want to continue his long years of life with only one arm. Or hand."

Frank leaned forward. "You think if someone tried forcibly removing it from her neck it would *blast* their arm off instead? Geez, what if I was playing around and accidentally snagged it..."

"There is something to be said for intent – it was initially given to a little girl."

He grew satirical. "Back in the days when children ran around playing, rather than looking at phones…"

"Ha-ha, but listen, you – what? What is it?"

"Cyprus…"

"Man, your whole face changed just now. What about him?"

"The time agent murders…suddenly make much more sense if Cyprus is involved."

Frank sat back, looking grim. "We've known him to be a murderer before these latest killings."

"He was a murderer since the beginning. But you had mentioned back at the mansion that maybe it was elapsation serum that the murderer was after in the first place. That makes logical sense if the one interested in the serum is Cyprus Blackshaft."

"Why would he want elapsation serum? He's already immortal, or so close to it that it shouldn't matter…I mean, he's like you in that way, ain't he?"

"He is for all practical purposes immortal…but unlike myself, he is not a sustained immortal; he has to take continuous steps to assure his ageless passage through time."

There was a pause. "His old source dry up?"

"I don't know. Perhaps in his own twisted way, he is doing his 'due diligence' and pursuing a back-up or fail-safe plan. But again we must ask; why now?"

"Fair question," acknowledged Frank, "but my first priority is still Adrienne. I hope she's been paying attention. Maybe she heard something."

"And if she has, perhaps it is only what they wanted her to hear. They are cunning enough to set up something like that."

Frank spoke his suspicion aloud. "A setup, like our knowing to come to Portugal, possibly."

"I have given that consideration," said Orion. "Perhaps I flatter myself with delusions of importance, but I suspect a trap."

"I wouldn't put it past Cyprus." Frank shook his head. "I never thought I'd see him again, not even in a bad dream. That and I sure as heck didn't think Adrienne would ever meet him, let alone spend some time with him."

"I just hope she doesn't remove her necklace for him."

Frank paled. "How would she know not to…"

"Don't worry too much. She is worth much more to our enemies alive than dead. Even if they get hold of her jewel, I believe they will want her to remain."

"Let's hope so. In the meanwhile, what about our next stop?"

"Even if Portugal was not a modern country, the Raven would have some sort of quarters there." Orion was silent a moment. "With a population like that, one could expect numerous holdings, I'm sure. If my memory serves me, the Raven should have a fortress or base of sorts in the back-country of western Spain; driving distance from Sintra. And that's not a figure of speech: it's literally a fortress, a restored castle that once kept a watch on the southern frontiers with the Moors. I imagine it was once open to tourism, being one of the last standing castles. But since then, it has been bought by the Raven and 'modernized'. I doubt they give tours."

"And you propose to go to this place?"

"It is not the only location they have in the region, but it would be the one to take a hostage that could attract attention. They are not going to walk Adrienne down a main street in the downtown of the capital where she can be noticed or request assistance. I am not certain, of course, but the fortress to my mind is a very logical step. And I've not yet been there personally. There could be a better course of action, but if there is, I am unaware of what it would be." As an afterthought, he added, "We will rendezvous with our man in the area and get an update on their holdings. I have not had dealings with the Raven in southwestern Europe for quite some time. Things may have changed since I was there last."

Frank let his head tip back and stared at the cabin's ceiling. "Storming a castle for my damsel in distress. Terribly old-fashioned. And it's been a long time since I've done anything like it."

"Castles are more the domain of my own antiquity. They are almost always individually different – and with modern techniques and so forth, our strategy of invasion must be altered, especially if secrecy is to be maintained."

"They say pick your own battles. This one, my old friend, has been chosen for us."

Orion got up to get himself a drink. "If life were fair, Frank, we'd both be dead."

೮೦ ೞ

The ride in the back of the limousine had taken about an hour before reaching the property. Adrienne was too tired of traveling to force herself to pay much attention as the guard box was passed and the gates were opened. The vehicle passed on down a gravel road surrounded by trees. *It feels like going to visit Uncle Harvey and Aunt Jane in Duluth – but that's a world away.* She could see nothing but trees, and for all she could tell, they stretched on forever.

It did not help that the car ride was dragging on into eternity in its own right. Cyprus's company made the ride longer. He had not spoken a word since they'd gotten in, except to tell the driver to drive. The road they were on now wound back and forth, and Adrienne sat back to keep herself from getting sick. The constant grinding and popping of the gravel road became a consistent background noise.

A few miles passed and she at last saw their destination as the road curved its descent into a small valley, and then crossed a bridge over the river that ran along the bottom. Across the bridge and up a twisting passage stood a castle, its towers rising high above the wooded landscape. In a time when there were fewer trees about, it would have been visible for miles.

Adrienne had seen her share of castles, having lived in France not that long ago. Still, she did not appreciate them enough to recognize this particular design. *Good luck getting rescued from there, girl.* The massive structure of yellow-brown brick and stone from the Middle Ages had a perimeter wall and four towers, and beyond there was a keep as well as many other more modern additions: garages, glass windows, electricity.

Yet Adrienne had ceased to be dazzled with the wealth of the Raven since Memphis had scared her half to death. After that frightening meeting with the old man whom she really wasn't convinced was actually an old man, she had a dwindling appetite for the strange new world to which she had been so rudely introduced. Thus, Cyprus observed a very unimpressed woman looking out the window as the limousine came up the roadway and slowed just enough to make the turn to go right in through the castle gates and on into the courtyard.

The doors were opened for them and the two got out of the car, Adrienne reluctantly following Cyprus up the steps and into a large hall. She watched his back as they went. *He's totally unconcerned that I might try and slip off without him. It's almost enough to try it, but where would I go?* The mere size of the place was intimidating; navigating her way as a first-timer would be difficult, let alone as an escapee on the lam.

"Where are we going?" asked Adrienne as their footfalls echoed off cavernous walls.

"It is amusing how often you ask that," said Cyprus as they continued walking.

"Not nearly as amusing as it would be to get a straight answer for once."

"I am taking you to meet the Lady Triassa, and then I'm taking you to your quarters. Would you like me to make you a schedule?"

You don't want to know what I'd truly like...

Their walk went on and on, because the fortress was so large. They passed few staff, and everywhere they came the halls and corridors and rooms were nicely furnished, mostly in the old style as if they were centuries in the past. Eventually, the grand corridor they were walking down – slung with shields and banners on the walls, suits of armor standing like silent sentinels, rich thick carpet under their feet – brought them to two exceedingly tall and narrow twin doors. Cyprus opened them and entered.

Before them was a wide room with tall double doors in three of its four walls. Straight ahead was the largest indoor fireplace Adrienne had ever seen, in the wall where there was no door. It was nearly twenty feet wide and gave the room most of its light, as it was blazing with flame. There were also electric lights, but they were hardly needed. The ceiling was high overhead, and on the wall hung long, dangling tapestries to the sides of each set of doors. A coat of arms was over the fire with an elk head on either side.

Before this fire on a slightly raised section in that part of the room was a very large banqueting table, with places for fifty. Only one of the places was occupied, and that chair had its back to them as they approached.

She had been told little of all there was to know about the Order of the Raven's shadowy lead figure, the Lady Triassa. Adrienne did not know it at the time, but she was the first non-member to even see their leader in many years; decade upon decade. Not even Orion had seen Triassa up close – though surely he had heard of her. Regardless, Adrienne could hardly have been more apprehensive, even if she had heard what her friends in Dominos de Lumine would have told her about the one in the chair before her – a vicious, sadistic genius if ever there was one, and more dangerous than a den of starved tigers.

Probably a withered, bitter old crone, brooded Adrienne. *Intelligent, perhaps, but worn down with a combined weight of too many years and too much power.*

The chair pushed itself away from the table as its occupant stood, turning toward her.

Adrienne balked, and for an instant her jaw actually did drop, though she covered it up rather well. Her eyes, however, could not conceal their surprise. Standing beside the chair and then coming toward her was the most stunningly gorgeous young woman Adrienne had ever seen.

She was a little taller than Adrienne, and looked to be in her late twenties; certainly not a day over thirty. Her long blonde hair was pushed back, spilling like silken gold down behind her to within a few inches of her waist. The business attire of blouse and skirt could not have complimented her flawless figure any better. Her very step was confidence itself, her face lovely, her eyes predatory.

Having worked in the fashion industry, Adrienne had seen her share of beautiful women. But this one before her put them all to shame. Some models had a way of showing that they were aware others were inferior to themselves. This woman did not have to treat others as if she considered herself better. They already knew.

The thing that caught Adrienne's attention most was her eyes. The other woman had cool blue eyes, both fierce and dazzling. They were cold and calculating, daring whoever saw them to cross them at one's own peril. The intensity behind their chilling glance made Adrienne nervous. She caught herself wishing that Lady Triassa had turned out to be a man. A thuggish jerk would have sufficed.

The blonde came within five feet and stopped, looking at Cyprus rather than Adrienne. When she spoke, her voice was still feminine, but smooth and rather sweet.

"Greetings, Blackshaft," she said, and Cyprus inclined his head in polite acknowledgment. "I trust there were not unforeseen problems with your travel?"

"None, my Lady," said Cyprus. He put a hand between Adrienne's shoulder-blades, enough to incline her to step forward. "Allow me to introduce Adrienne Blackman. She was good enough to return with me."

What could qualify as the slightest hint of a wolfish smile touched Triassa's features. "Ah, the Lady Blackman. I thought as much. Greetings to you as well."

Adrienne did not know if she should offer her hand or not, but Triassa did not lift her own. The two remained standing there looking at each other as the latter continued.

"It is by my design that you are here, Adrienne."

The familiarity with which this woman used her name troubled the captive slightly. The blonde circled Adrienne at this point, slowly, looking her up and down as if appraising her worth.

Triassa continued: "If you manage to behave yourself and do as you're told, you may well find your time as my guest will not be too intolerable for you." She paused and Adrienne realized she was immediately behind her. The voice spoke almost directly into her ear. "I trust you have the wisdom not to try my patience, for unlike my power it is very finite."

Adrienne didn't know what to say, but she could tell that for the first time in the large room, she was expected to say something. She inwardly wished to tell Triassa exactly what she thought of her, but since that would plainly not do at this point in time, she swallowed and managed: "I'm sure we can reach an understanding." She didn't know what else to say.

"Excellent." Triassa completed her circle and once more stood in front of Adrienne. "Remove your necklace."

Adrienne's hand went to the green gem that hung around her neck, hidden underneath her clothing. She hadn't the slightest idea how the woman had known she was wearing it, nor why she wanted it removed, but her hand betrayed its existence. She had a multitude of things she would rather give away.

That, and a sudden, strong, unprovoked desire to *not* remove it rose in her heart. Did Cyprus look tense?

"What?" she heard herself say, hoping that somehow it would make Triassa change her mind.

"Finite, Lady Blackman. Very finite." There was a menace there, though her tone and body language had not changed in the least.

"I…I-" Everything within Adrienne told her not to.

The cool voice seemed to zero-in on her anew. "*Remove* it, or I will have this man remove it for you."

Finite indeed, Adrienne agreed, and in looking at Triassa she missed how Cyprus gave her a look of some apprehension. Her hands moved hesitantly to the clasp behind her neck, moving under her dark hair. In a moment she had released it and held the necklace carefully, lamenting. Triassa held out her hand. Her arrogant expression was of the sort that suggested it was utterly unthinkable that someone might withhold from the hand whatever was desired. With a great inner reluctance, Adrienne set the gem in the palm.

She did not know why, but as soon as the gem was out of her possession, she was oddly cold. A little afraid, even. As if all the trials thrust upon her in the last twenty-four hours had not gotten through until now. *Get a hold of yourself. These are Frank's enemies. Best not to give them any satisfaction.*

"Cyprus," said Triassa, "I am sure the Lady Blackman is in need of rest. Show her to a guest suite. One she will be comfortable in." Adrienne was tired and distracted, and she missed the eye-contact exchange between Cyprus and Triassa.

Cyprus bowed at the neck. "Something in the lower levels?"

"An excellent idea. You may go."

That last comment Adrienne did not miss, and she shivered. There was something about the tone she did not care for in the least. Cyprus gave her that look of his, tilted his head to the side to crack his neck. Adrienne started walking when he did, not wanting to know what would happen if she did not. She followed him without a second glance at Triassa, who was content with the necklace and was less than concerned with proper good-byes.

Behind them, Lady Triassa did not sit, but rather leaned her hip into the end of the table, looking at Adrienne's necklace. *Strange, and perhaps ironic*, she thought, *that something so small could be so detrimental*. Yet the gem dangling from the chain she grasped was not just important in its size. It was imperatively pivotal to Triassa – and she smiled as she recognized the completeness the stone brought. Not just the polished green gemstone caught her eye, but also the shining metal that wrought the small but robust frame encasing the bauble. *A magic jewel and Atlantean silver together.* She smiled. *Two birds with one stone.*

ᛒ ᚲ

The man that both Orion and Frank called Trego Macleod looked to be in his early sixties and still sported the full beard he had back in the years Frank had worked with him. It was still as orange in color as befitted a full-blooded Scot, especially one so proud to be truly of the Old Country. Frank had always laughingly thought that Trego had missed his purpose in life: he did not belong here in the modern world. He belonged on a pre-firearm battlefield somewhere, shouting threats at the enemy and posturing defiance in a manner as boisterous as possible; such was the old way of war in the highlands and many other places. He was over six feet in height and broad-shouldered with large grasping hands. He still wore his full head of long, almost mangy, fiery hair like it was the twelfth century, could drink almost anyone under the table, and had a laugh that carried down the block and onto the next street.

Trego was the Dominos de Lumine contact in southwestern Europe, and he welcomed both men hardly an hour after they had left their plane at the airport. His place of operation was out of a large private home made over into a military-like barracks, equipped with fortifications and generators, all surrounded by a perimeter wall. The barracks was on the outskirts of the city close to several main roads and almost qualifying as being in the countryside. Trego led an elite corps of Dominos de Lumine field agents, commandos. They were immediately based in Sintra but operated in regions all around. It had been quiet in Trego's general radius the past ten years – he had done a lot of traveling with his corps to stay busy.

His men joked about his pending retirement, a humorous inclination that Trego laughed off every time.

The table in Trego's kitchen was long enough to seat six to a side, and when Orion and Frank first arrived it was laid out with every accommodation they could offer. That said, it was not extremely lavish; the property, home, and barracks served a paramilitary purpose and were not places for creature comforts: the last man to try and bring such things with him had been laughed out of the building. The team that lived in the barracks had little actual company. Still, there was beer and meat, plenty of each – Trego would periodically pause in his discourse to lower the contents of his mug significantly.

A map was laid upon the table and kept from rolling up on itself by a combination of several tall beer mugs and a boot-knife. While the barracks had tech at need, its commander was partial to traditional means of a sort. An additional few agents stood nearby in the hall, chatting quietly among themselves, ready to serve if needed in the conversation.

To Trego's left, Frank's feet ached and his legs were stiff. He hoped the fatigue didn't show. He wanted little more than to sleep in preparation for what he and Orion purposed to do the next day. He leaned in on the table, chin on his left hand while the right held a mug. He listened to Trego discuss the layout of the Raven fortress and tried to concentrate, even chasing thoughts of Adrienne out of his mind. To Trego's right, Orion looked to the map, following Trego's direction and large finger as it went here and there. He appeared neither interested nor disinterested. He merely looked on. Frank envied his ability to do this in nearly all situations.

"It is an older castle," said Trego in his deep voice, his Scottish accent tainting his speech at all times. "Thirteenth century or so, quite restored, of course. No telling how many personnel are there at any time. It could house hundreds easily. But with technology these days the whole property could be manned by a minimal staff from one room. There is no telling. That's why the whole operation's going to be rather delicate."

"What of the property itself?" asked Orion. "The file I looked at was done recently but did not reflect any change for the past two decades. Has it really just sat there so long without alteration?"

"Twenty years ago was the last detailed surveillance of the area, and since then periodic satellite pictures and some observation is used." Trego bristled at the look he was then getting from Orion. "When something is not in operation, it falls off the radar to make way for things that are priority. We were familiar with it being the Black Chickens who owned the property, but they've never done anything with it.

"I can update a little bit for you that's not yet in the record, only because I sent some lads out there for some reconnaissance. When the Raven jet's arrival point was calculated and later confirmed, a convoy was tracked from the airport to this property. My boys reported in only two hours ago. And of course there's the satellite photos and heat-signature surveillance. This Adrienne lass is at this location; they aren't even trying to hide her being there."

Frank and Orion exchanged looks. If the Raven were not even trying to hide Adrienne, that she had been found in the first place was met not with so much joy but rather suspicion.

"Now, the castle, as noted, is roughly in the middle of lands in the countryside that are about five miles square. They used it much more in years passed, but in the last two decades, I have been unaware of anything of significance going on there. That said, there is still security. The twenty-plus miles that make up the perimeter is fenced off from the public by a chain-link about ten feet high with barbed wire running across the top – not that there's much public in the area." He paused to take a long draught, belched loudly, and went on. "Like I said, it's in the countryside. Most people would consider it a nature preserve, as there are only a few roads going in, and these are clearly marked private with guard boxes and gates and such. There is also the matter of a number of helicopters that have come and gone over the past few days; someone important is there now, I believe."

"What about the terrain itself?"

"At one time long ago, it was farmland. But that was a long, long time ago, by my guess. The few roads that enter the property make their way to the castle and really nowhere else." He traced one idly with a finger on the map. "What is not a road, a small building near the road, or the castle itself, is wild. A better description is simply woods. In some places, the patchy forest has been there for literally centuries. That's why nothing has changed; it's just undeveloped land, little more than overgrown farmlands with just a lot of brush. There are no paths that I know of that go through the woods themselves, though there very well may be. I was on the property once long ago for surveillance purposes, but that was too long ago to give you a good idea of what may be there now."

"This is the only Raven location in this area?" asked Frank.

"It is the only place they would take a prisoner. They have a warehouse in the city, a few businesses throughout Spain. All legit. That castle refuge on the private property is the only place they would be, and like I said, the car with your wife was tracked there."

"What about security on the perimeter?" asked Orion.

"Aside from the fence there are cameras, but twenty miles of perimeter is a hard distance to cover with surveillance. I doubt there are cameras covering much more than the gates themselves. It should not be hard to get in – they don't man it to keep people out especially, because no one is crazy enough to want to get in. The castle itself, however, will undoubtedly be fortified against gentlemen such as yourselves."

"The circumstances of our arrival at the castle itself may not be covert," mused Orion. He glanced at Frank. "It might be desirable for them to know we are there."

"But-" began Trego, but Orion cut him off.

"We do not know what they want yet. If we can bargain to retrieve the Lady Blackman, I think we should. The possibility may reveal itself, eventually."

"Until then we sneak in and don't get caught," said Frank.

"Aye."

"When are you planning to do so?" asked Trego.

"It is the morning now," said Orion. "We'll sleep here until dark and then go in tonight."

⁕ ⁖

Adrienne walked beside instead of behind Cyprus. Some of the passages and corridors of the castle were poorly lit and dim. Along their way, the lack of light cast all types of fell shadows across their path when passing through rooms with suits of armor and statues. It was eerily quiet most of the way except for echoing footsteps. She never would have admitted it, but she was grateful she was not walking through the fortress by herself. The place was absolutely cavernous. Even without being lost, she had the urge to look over her shoulder.

"I thought you had pointed out my necklace as a mere change of conversation," she said, referring back to their original meeting on a rowboat.

"It is a curious process when events make us realize how mistaken our past thoughts can be," said Cyprus philosophically, knowing the number of people willing to have a casual conversation with him was not large. "I do not know what your husband paid for that necklace when he gave it to you. Yet I assure you, whatever he paid for it or however he came by it: he did not pay enough. I find it amusing you wore such an artifact regularly without knowing its significance in the world."

Does he mean it, or is he just trying to get to me? Adrienne wondered. *Well... asking him straight will be a waste of time. Stirring my curiosity and then closing down is a game for him. I wish I still had my necklace, though.*

"Perhaps if you press Lady Triassa about the properties of your necklace, she will divulge further," he smiled.

Purposefully hazardous advice. She rolled her eyes beside him. "You don't think much of me, do you?"

He stopped as they came to a single wooden door in the corridor they were walking along. He opened it and Adrienne looked in to see a narrow passage of descending stairs lit only by eerie, faded blue electric lights sunk into the right wall. It went into darkness around a corner. A chill went up her spine and a musty wet smell met her nose.

"Down you go," he said, and made the unmistakable gesture that he wanted her to go first.

It was noticeably cooler in the dark tunnel as the two descended down the stairs. Adrienne, as she went, was less and less comfortable with each step. She was remembering Triassa's comment about a 'guest suite' and Cyprus's suggestion of 'lower levels', and her imagination began to run away with her as to exactly what the latter pertained. Her history of the Middle Ages was good enough to know she did not want to find out what lay at the bottom of the stairs.

The passage wound on for awhile, always down at the same steady pace. *We've got to be underground by now. It's colder too.* They descended on, as if seeking the Gates of Hell. She shivered harder than when Memphis had been so close, and made the mistake of putting her bare hand on the chilly, slick wall. She had a constricting tightness of the chest that annoyed more than worried her, and she made the effort to control her breathing. Her breaths partly fluttered and wanted to panic, but her mind's voice was stern. *Don't you dare. Not now.* Still, she could not shake the desire to go running back up toward the real light. Cyprus was behind her, potentially for that very reason. *And where would I go even if I did get back to the top?* She walked on, listening to the echo of footsteps and the rare drip of water upon cold gray stone.

A wide hall of dark stone awaited them at the bottom of the stair. The same blue lights shone from the ceiling here, and security cameras hung in all four corners. Down the side walls was door after barred door. There looked to be twenty cells down here, and the far end of the large room was barred off floor to ceiling to form a small compartment that sported chains and benches and what she took to be a wheel of wood and iron.

Adrienne crossed her arms and put her weight on one foot. A week ago, if she had seriously considered that mere days into the future a strange man would kidnap her, bring her overseas, and lock her in a castle's dungeon deep beneath the ground with nothing but shaky light and perhaps a rat for company, she would have pictured herself as terrified. Now, she was too angry to be scared. Frightened, certainly, but not too much or noticeably. *These people want me alive, they won't kill me yet.* At some point, maybe, but not yet. A comforting thought, despite the topic, calmed her: *He wouldn't march me all the way down these stairs if he was going to kill me – he'd just have to carry my body back up.*

"Nice dungeon. Where's the torture chamber?"

"The barred-off enclosure at the end of the hall, of course," he said nonchalantly, as if it had been a serious question. "This way, my dear," he added snidely as he took hold of her upper arm and began walking toward one of the cell doors.

The cell to which Cyprus pushed open the door was of cold gray stone, ten by fifteen with an eight foot ceiling. Above was a poorly-working light fixed in the ceiling protected by a metal grating. An old bench lay on its side near one wall, equipped with half-rotten legs and cobwebs. There was hay underfoot, but most disturbing were the chains dangling from the wall, equipped with rusty shackles. A squeaking helped both of them notice a rat in the corner a moment before it disappeared into the hay.

Adrienne stopped short and stared at the dangling chains. She knew voicing her current thought aloud just might encourage him. She stepped inside before he could push her.

"Classy organization, this group of yours," she said, turning to glare at him. "A dungeon, really? In this day and age?"

"The Middle Ages had its efficiencies." Cyprus closed the door and looked through the head-level barred window as a bar was slid into place. "My quarters are more desirable, if you like."

"Hmmm, exchanging one cold, dark, rat-infested depravity for...another cold, dark, rat-infested depravity."

"There would be a difference," he added darkly.

She didn't even have to create a response before it was spilling out: "Only the size of the rat," she said, glowering back at him.

He cocked his head to the side, neck cracking. "Mind your place, woman. I'm leaving you down here – but I don't have to leave your clothes."

That blink of his kicked in again, only this time his eyes were not in perfect sync. One closed and opened as the other closed. He stared at her long enough that she thought he might follow up on his threat, but then abruptly he turned and left, footfalls echoing off the damp walls.

Adrienne stood for a moment as he disappeared and his footsteps vanished. She sighed, shoulders heavily lifting with the frustration of the past few hours, and then looked around again. She propped the bench on its legs, testing it hesitantly with her weight. For a minute or two she busied herself cleaning the cobwebs away with a handful of hay – Adrienne could not abide cobwebs, especially in something she sat on. Then, looking about the cell for anything else to do, she sat. The single light illuminated poorly, but her eyes had adjusted and while she could not see well, she could still see.

As she sat on the bench with her knees up to her chest, hands folded around her shins, she sighted the rat resurfacing. *At least you're not a spider.* She could see no arachnids, and that was some comfort. Rather, the whole overall situation was the sole reason alone that a single tear somehow coaxed itself out of her clear eyes and slid down her cheek. Now that there was no one there to see them, hiding the accumulating droplets was a waste of time and effort.

The rat stood on its hind legs and cocked his head to the side, not having heard any sound like sniffling in a very long time, if ever.

"I don't suppose you have any Kleenex?"

CHAPTER 10

*"And there was the Brotherhood of the Gatekeepers, masters of counsel
and arms for a hundred generations. Yet their gravest charge was not
the person of the Imperial family, but rather the Portal Gate from
whence came the Shades, the Enemies of light. Should the power of the
Gatekeepers over the Portal Gate ever fail, woe to the world of mankind,
for nothing would stem the black tide."*

~an excerpt from Book 12 of the Kedassaic Texts.

৪০ ০৪

ROCKFORD ASYLUM, AMERICAN EASTERN SEABOARD. AD 1826.

"**O**f course, Master Dirks, you understand that what you see may be
disturbing."

Orion sat across from the doctor in the other man's office, legs
crossed and fingers forming a steeple under his chin. He was doing his best to look
thoughtful – but also to appear just a bit like he was trying to do so; a sincere but
concerned visitor out of his league but trying to do the right thing. Trying to show
that he was not as nerve-racked as he probably should be. Never convey your true
purpose, wherever possible, *the traveler's mind advised him.*

Rockford Asylum had been there for only a quarter century and had originally been a hospital, but was later converted to the madhouse that was its current
designation. Its history was long, dark, and disturbing. As well it should be; Orion
happened to know they had a special wing reserved just for the criminally insane.
Maximum security in such a place was nothing to be trifled with. Rockford had only

had one escape in her twenty-five years of history. A difficult feat, surely, undertaken by desperate men with nothing to lose. Aren't we all, he silently admitted.

That was Doctor Andrews's mistake, Orion decided. He prattled on and on, talking of what to expect, what not to expect. The man may have been a brilliant psychiatrist, but Orion's psychology in his entry interview was too devious. The fellow concluded that he comprehended nothing about this place, the nature of it and so on. In reality, Orion had an acute perception of and proficiency regarding insanity; he understood it better than most people and had been exposed to things that would have surely given this doctor a massive stroke.

The inmate James Whittaker was a special case, Andrews said, and began a discourse as to why. Orion nodded and gave every appearance of listening intently, but mentally he was correcting the doctor as the man went along. While the doctor worked under the impression that Whittaker was a misunderstood and eventual candidate for massive rehabilitation after his initial snap – an unfortunate affair for that particular general store – Orion did not particularly care about his latest crimes. The details were absolutely hideous, but in the end unimportant. Not that long ago, this American society was more likely to convict a woman of the same crimes by proclaiming her a witch. For a man, insanity was not an unlikely designation. He had probably narrowly escaped a proclamation of possession or some such determination. Orion had seen both many times before. Yet Whittaker's early nineteenth century sins were not what brought the Deathless Blade to America looking for him. His old crimes were what brought the Gatekeeper to him. It had taken many years to arrive, but Justice was indeed knocking at the door. As soon as this doctor grew tired of hearing himself talk. Well. What were a few more minutes after so many years?

Sometime later and after being depleted by guards of anything he might have been able to bring in with him, Orion looked through the tiny window in the small room's only door. There he saw James Whittaker for the first time since Avignon and the 1600s. The man was not born James Whittaker; he had not gone by his birth-name for years: Sarn Dorme, son of Dalien Dorme. The chains suited him. The man sat there in the corner of the empty room, staring at nothing. Well, the eyes did not see, but they would move. They would periodically double-blink slowly and heavily, and then flutter open and shut a few times before coming back to the dead stare. If anyone could fake it, Sarn Dorme could, but faking was hard. Orion stood there watching him for what he felt was a long time.

"What's wrong with his eyes?" Orion asked rhetorically.

"We don't know. He has always been like that, even before the incident. Or so we were told."

It looks like stutter-flutter to me. An ironic fate, but not undeserved.

"Would you like to speak with him, Master Dirks?" asked the assistant.

Orion had known upon entering Rockford that anything he carried with him – money, ticket for passage, pipe, whatever – would be taken from him when he passed the security areas and entered the asylum itself. He had come to kill Dorme, *of course. To give the whole enunciation of presiding justice over high treason against the Imperial Throne, and then to achieve the man's sentence – his death. That he could not so easily bring weapons in had not dissuaded him or changed his plans in the least. He had been doing this sort of thing for a long time, and a specialist that could not kill without a weapon was no specialist at all. No weapons, the presence of the assistant, the other staff; none of these struck Orion as reasons to desist.*

"Sir?"

Dorme was not faking. His centuries of life, falling gradually further and further into futility and ultimately insanity, had taken and were still taking their heavy toll. Just look at his face…he cannot remember yesterday, nor his actions so long ago. *Gazing at him, it was hard for even Orion to believe that this man was a war criminal from an old and forgotten civil war, and a former commander that laid siege to no fewer than three cities.* The man can no more remember his own name let alone what he has done.

"Sentence commuted," said Orion aloud, and turned his back on the surprised assistant.

"Mister Dirks? Sir!"

"I'll see Mr. Whittaker another day, perhaps," said Orion over his shoulder. *If he ever recovers, that is.* "I was going to give him something, but I think what he has now is just as good."

€ Ↄ

"How much further?" Frank asked as they went.

"Two miles by my count, and that is to the property itself. Once on the property I'm not sure how much further tonight. We will sleep once we have secured entry. It would be foolish to try and navigate the forest by night with whatever security network they've set up."

Six miles of farmland had passed by since Trego dropped them off on a random roadside, and Frank was beginning to appreciate that he was not in great physical shape. Five years had gone by since retirement, and accounting as a cover did not provide exercise. *I had a feeling a desk job would be the end of me.* Still, approaching by foot in the dark had presented a better option than driving up in a car with headlights on. Even now, the sun was setting.

Several hours later, both men were on the inside of the perimeter fence of the Raven property, their journey only postponed long enough for Orion to replace the section of chain-link that he had removed for their entry. All around them the darkness closed in as they stood on the edge of forest. The sounds of a wood at night, mixed with a distant car blended all together. Orion twisted a few branches about the chain-link, disguising the cut section, and then trudged past Frank into the dense trees.

Orion's ability to see in the dark had always been a beneficial advantage. Frank followed after him with a hand on his shoulder. *Just like old times,* he recollected with a smile. He had once tried to get Orion to explain his ability, but Frank had been unsatisfied. Orion had explained that his eyes did not stop adjusting at a certain shade of darkness. He could just…see in the dark.

"This will do well enough for the next few hours," said Orion at length, and they abruptly stopped. "We're at the base of a pine. There's shelter beneath the branches. You may sleep again if you wish."

"Unlikely," said Frank using his pack as a pillow and reclining nonetheless. "I always feel bad sleeping knowing Adrienne was having a hard time. With anything. Sick. Work. Anything. Didn't sleep so hot this last time either. I'm not going to get more than a wink knowing she's in the castle somewhere, probably scared out of her mind."

"Don't underestimate her. Women in general can be exceedingly resilient when they have to be." Orion was looking out into the forest, scanning, but now he looked down at Frank. A slight smile crossed his face. "You said she was a Nebraska farm-girl. She's tough."

Frank laughed. "Tougher than me, anyway. Well…minus spiders and she is."

"Worry serves little purpose. I want to see this fortress for myself before drawing conclusions or an actual strategy. Our intelligence and blue prints are too old to go by. We'll see what's what tomorrow."

"Maybe, but I think even Adrienne might be in over her head. The Black Chickens aren't exactly something you deal with every day." He sighed. "But I'll try to sleep. I never could sleep on planes, especially going overseas, and I'm still feeling it from our trip. If we can end this whole thing, I'm going to sleep for a week…"

Orion listened with silent amusement as Frank trailed off about hating trying to sleep on airplanes. Orion himself had trained specifically when and when not to fall asleep. There would be time enough to rest later, but for now…

"Where are you going?" asked Frank.

"To take a look around. I'll be back soon."

୫୦ ୦ଓ

The forest looked very different at first light. Frank had somehow managed to sleep on the bed of needles, however lightly, and at once began eating one of the rations that Trego had been kind enough to provide. He took a few swallows of water, crunching the cracker-like food and swallowing more to get free of the taste than anything else. *What I wouldn't do for some eggs and bacon right about now.* But so went life in the field.

"The good news," said Orion as he walked up, "is that there are a few paths that cut through the woods. It should not be hard to find one that meanders in the general direction we desire."

"And the bad news?" asked Frank, standing and shouldering his pack.

"The day is young. I am sure we can find some before it is old. But I think that some of the paths might not be as ill-used as others. It is possible there are patrols that walk the property."

For about an hour there was no path to be found, and they slipped among the trees, under low branches and leaning trunks, over logs and patches of thick shrubbery. Above the cover of the trees it was a drizzly, overcast day, as those lands tended to be in November. Beneath the overlapping branches provided for a drippy, cooler, dimmer atmosphere, not without a touch of mystery.

Behind Orion, Frank was pondering Adrienne and a dozen questions that kept resurfacing. *Does she know we're following? What's happened to her? What's Cyprus done to her?* Cyprus was an enigma at best. Frank had never been certain of Blackshaft's sanity, and given his mood Cyprus could leave Adrienne anywhere from terrified to beguiled. *If anyone's hurt you, I'll never forgive myself.* He gritted his teeth and kept walking.

In time the forest opened up a bit on their left, and they were walking along the top of a small ridge. A valley of grass and a few shrubs fell away from them before rising up a quarter mile away and ending in a line of trees. Orion paused and looked out, after a moment taking up the small binoculars he kept inside his outfit.

He handed them to Frank after a moment. "Base of the tree line about eleven o'clock."

Frank scanned and saw a pair of men walking a German shepherd, quite some distance away. They were walking away from him, and to Frank's eye did not appear worried about stealth.

"Reminds me of the bloodhounds on our trail in Louisiana," he said.

Orion's glance in his direction was droll. "An accursed place if ever there was one..." he said in his driest tone. "But as to the matter at hand-"

"On a circuit, do you think?" Frank asked, handing the binoculars back.

"Probably. I'll warrant there is more than one team out. We'll see. Last night I had found a motion sensor camera on one of the paths – which is why we're not using it." He turned back to their path. "Fortunately, this large an area is hard to keep a close eye on."

    ⅓ ℤ

An hour later, their dirt path was narrow, winding its way amidst the trees. They had gone on for only a little while before the path went down into a bit of a valley, the forest creeping close at the sides and going uphill steeply. They were in a near trench, filled with shade and the closeness of the foliage. Even if the sun had been straight above them, the thickness of the forest roof would still have left them in shadow.

Orion had slowed his pace. "I was here last night," he said. "This whole stretch of the path had numerous motion sensors scanning across it at various places." He spoke over his shoulder as he kept walking.

"And why did we go this way?"

"It is the quickest way by my reckoning. Besides, I was able to aim them all away from the path. A bit of a risky business, but one can do it if careful. Most are scanning a plot of ground immediately in front of them."

Frank could not resist asking. "What if you missed one in the dark?"

"An interesting possibility," admitted Orion, and kept walking.

"Would it kill you to-"

Orion raised a hand and Frank fell silent. His friend's head was cocked ever so slightly to the side, and he was listening hard. Frank listened too – and heard the voices. They were distant, but after a moment's hesitation of listening, each man could tell they were getting closer.

Neither had to inform the other he intended to hide. Both Frank and Orion stepped off the path and slipped beneath the underbrush. It took only a moment to become situated, and then they lay still, listening intently for the approach of what both assumed to be guards. By the sound of them there were at least three, speaking in French. That French was used instead of Spanish or Portuguese surprised neither of them; the Order of the Raven employed men of countless nations and used them in many places. Orion eavesdropped easily, being fluent in many languages; his lingual talent was a result of his long life and a phenomenal memory that almost never misplaced anything, words included. Frank had met his wife in France and had spent much time there in the not too-distant past. His French was passable though not fluent. He caught the gist of the conversation.

Frank lay flat on his back amidst the ferns, his heart not even beating fast, knowing he was completely hidden from anything but an actual underbrush-thrashing search. If they didn't look for him, they would never suspect. On the other side of the path and a few feet further up, Orion lay on his side, his bent arm underneath his head as if he were reclining. He lay quiet, concentrating on the discussion.

Both men doubted they were in active danger of being discovered. Guards present or not, they were not at the moment actually looking for anyone. It appeared to be a random patrol, though both wondered at how many such patrols walked on the property. Then the dog barked and Frank's heart sank.

He almost groaned aloud when he heard it, and he craned his neck. At the top of the hill, he could just make out four guards come into view, and about their legs came a German shepherd. *Great...just great. That bark is probably for us already.* The dog suddenly began in earnest, and Frank freed a weapon from its holster. *But Orion is closer – it will head for him first.*

The guards, however, were unimpressed.

"C'mon Jacques," came the French from the handler to the dog, "another rabbit? It's almost lunch. Don't spoil your appetite."

"Cut him loose," encouraged a second guard. "I get a kick out of watching him catch the things."

"Yeah, go get 'em, Jacques," laughed the fourth.

"Don't encourage him! Oh, fine..." conceded the handler.

"Go Jacques!" yelled the others.

Adieu, Jacques, thought Frank as he listened to the frenzied bark, knowing Orion would be left with limited choices. *He won't run, not from a dog. The guards would see us climbing trees, even if these trunks weren't too big around.* He checked his clip. *If we play it right we should at least have surprise...*

Orion was not ignorant of the situation. He could hear the canine approaching, crashing through the brush. The shepherd closed the short distance as any trained patrol animal might. In a moment it had taken its last leap through the air that, with its current trajectory, would bring it right down on top of him. It left the ground, and so did Orion. The guards had the surprising sight of a man in black rise from amidst the ferns and spin around as he came up. This twisting as he rose brought the sword about in perfect form and the point pierced the shepherd's side above the left front leg and continued on, effectively cutting the animal in two as it sailed toward him through the air, mouth open. It was surgical precision; the animal barely had time to emit a half-yip in response.

Completing his strike brought Orion into a half-crouched position there in the bushes, red sword held out at a lateral angle, ready for further action. Yet the guards were ten yards off and a sword might not have been the most-choice weapon for such a conflict. At any rate, the guards carried shotguns, and at the death of their shepherd, two of four men had the weapon off their shoulder and swinging into firing position.

Orion had not gone onto the property with just his sword as a lone weapon. His free hand went to his side and liberated his Glock. Frank cradled his own firearm, hearing the sudden shouts at the ceasing of the barking, listening as to when he might reveal himself advantageously.

Even by himself Orion was too fast for any of the guards, although they were actually quite rapid in relation to the surprise they received. But as he surveyed the scene he was strategizing speedily. The dog handler did not have his weapon off his shoulder yet. The other three, who were standing on the path, did. Orion zeroed in on the guard with the weapon in the foremost firing position, and the Glock erupted twice in rapid succession and dropped the fellow for his efficiency at being fastest. The unlucky man fell backwards howling – Orion had either missed in his precision or was feeling particularly merciful. Regardless, the man was out of the fight.

The others shouted and scattered in different directions off the path. Orion stood without saying a word, resuming his full height as his weapon took the dog handler into its full attention and discharged at him. A red spray of blood exploded out of the man's upper leg and crying aloud he went down, his shotgun falling from his shaken hand. With that, Orion fired multiple further rounds while he twisted about and put himself behind a tree as the other two guards came up, shotguns blasting. They fired impulsively, pulling the triggers before they had fully taken in the scene. This action in and of itself confirmed in Orion's mind that none of the four were serious professionals, or adept at the art of a close-quarters firefight. Good.

Orion stood with his back tight up against the shielding tree, listening to the disruption of gun fire and noting the vibrations as the repeated shots hit the tree. He blinked to avoid the splintering of bark as one blast skinned off the surface near him. His face was calm, his breathing slow as he quickly stuck his sword upright in the earth before him and in the same motion with the other hand, disengaged the empty clip of the Glock. From up his sleeve came a second clip, and he thrust it easily into position, locking and loading.

While this occurred, the guards were alarmed to see a second man on the other side of the path come up from amid the shrubbery, this one bearing no sword but having instead two firearms. This newcomer also fired without hesitation but he hit nothing as his remaining two targets each found their way to a tree. He noticed they made no effort to drag their two wounded compatriots to safety. Frank advanced, firearms raised and echoing with the vomiting of lead, until he also had found his way to the thickness of a tree. He was at the same time struck at how loud gunfire could be – it had been a long time.

The forest was then for a moment quiet. The trespassers heard the crackle of a radio. Now, as all combatants found a momentary solace behind tree trunks, there was a pause in the chaos. The only sound was the muted moans of the injured, even as Orion was wondering if he had been too kind. Even as he listened to them, he doubted the courtesy would be returned if the guards were given a chance.

After a minute of mental sparring with the silence, the first guard peeked his head cautiously around the side of his tree trunk, shotgun at the ready. He had taken the moment of peace to reload and say a prayer or two. Now as he brought the weapon up and his eyes moved from one tree to the other, going from Frank's known position to that of Orion, he suddenly saw a black coat come out dangerously far from Orion's tree trunk. He reflexively fired a couple times, striking the coat so hard that it fell halfway off the stick propping it up. In the instant that he realized his mistake, the real Orion came from the other side of the tree and fired at him, one shot bursting the bark of his tree into splinters and the second ringing against his weapon's barrel. The harsh vibration and shock caused him to drop the suddenly useless weapon, vigorously rubbing his pained hand.

The second guard took that moment to try and draw a bead on the momentarily revealed Orion, but Frank timed it perfectly and was there to greet him with a hail of lead. The bullets kept him back behind his tree, and by the time he leaned out, he could not see if his two enemies had remained in their places. He looked around one side of the tree and saw Frank move a moment, and then ducked back into place. He then turned around only to see an eighteen inch blade resting gently against his breastbone. Orion stood not four feet away, his left hand holding the sword ready at this nearest guard, his Glock pointing at the second man who had dropped his ruined shotgun as he stood twenty feet away.

His voice was neither superior nor cocky, nor pleased with the apparent victory. It merely spoke an order in fluent French, and in those circumstances neither enemy dared defy it. "Drop your weapon."

The remaining guard dropped his weapon sullenly, and the guard with the broken shotgun under Orion's watchful eye very slowly drew out his own secondary sidearm and let it fall. "Thank you, gentlemen." His voice increased in volume as it called his compatriot in German – just to mess with them.

"Frank, what about the other two?"

By aiming his weapon advantageously at the dog handler, Frank had already assured that his shotgun was not to be picked up. The man that had been shot first was no longer moving at all. "Taken care of," he answered in German over his shoulder, keeping an eye on the one.

Orion was still contemplating what to do with them when shouts came from two separate directions. From atop the hill and up the path, the same place from where the first set of guards had come, there came five more men trotting down the trail, also bearing shotguns. Clearly they had heard the commotion. From down the path and nearly at the same time, other shouts came on, and four guards came running up from the opposite direction.

"Apparently they have a few more patrols than I thought," said Frank, looking at both oncoming parties as they closed the gap, plainly catching up on the whole situation. He was exhilarated by the recent action, but these new enemies disappointed him. Two on four with surprise was one thing for a shootout in the woods, but eleven against two without surprise was another matter entirely. It was over.

Orion said nothing, his sword blade still held out in perfectly steady synchronization with the immediate guard's sternum, the Glock leveled at the man twenty feet away. His options with the shepherd had been limited. His choices in this new scenario were depleted from the start.

"Surrender," said the guard with the sword at his chest.

Orion was not looking at him, sword doing the watching for him in close quarters. But he did just barely glance at him. The point of the sword, already resting against the shirt, pressed infinitesimally deeper, pushing the man against the tree.

The poked guard smiled snidely but said nothing further.

Orion ignored him, looking at the rapidly arriving reinforcements. The new men up and down the path spread out and aimed their weapons, not firing outright, as they recognized two of their own. The third and fourth wounded men still lay on the ground, beneath the cover of shrubbery and unseen by the newcomers. It was now the guards' turn to give the orders.

"Drop your weapons!" came a call – still in French – from up the path.

Neither Frank nor Orion moved, for it was plain that their position of holding weapons on the two standing guards stopped their being shot at, at least at the moment. Frank was wondering how long the sanctuary status would last, and whether or not the new guards would simply blow away their compatriots along with the trespassers if they had to wait too long. Orion had a lifetime of experience with the Raven: best not to keep these men waiting.

"If you have any suggestions," said Orion to Frank, remaining in the same position without wavering, "I am listening."

Frank had retrained his Glocks on the second guard, who was between himself and Orion while Orion held the first in close proximity. The conscious injured man, at the urgings of Frank's weapon, had tossed his weapon far out of reach, and so was not gauged as a threat. He thought for only a few seconds. "Even if you could get away alone, they'd only be ready at the castle when you got there."

That was true. The new patrols were distant enough that a man like Orion might have a chance if he had just taken off into the forest. And yet Frank would surely be captured or killed straight away, and Orion would have a waiting host prepared for his coming when he came to the castle. Orion acknowledged Frank's statement with hardly a nod.

"Plan B, then."

"Just give up," said the first guard again, and this time Orion turned to stare him down.

"For one with nothing to say, you speak often," he said.

But even as the guard expected the point of the sword to shove inward, he was surprised to find the weapon suddenly withdrawn. He opened his eyes after having closed them in anticipation. He breathed a sigh of relief at seeing that Orion had thrust the blade into the earth at their feet, and cast his Glock to the ground. With a nod of understanding, Frank followed suit with his own weapons.

CHAPTER 11

"Consul Aurelian of Rome, successor of the late Consul Faeryn of Iratha,

"To the Eternal and Sacred Order of the Brotherhood of the Gatekeepers, in whatever places they may be found throughout the World:

"Greetings. As you know, our lord Consul Faeryn of Iratha wearied of his long years and took his serum no more some five years ago, and he died. Now, Gatekeeper Tylaean Monsir was found dead among multiple fallen assassins, all of whom were armed with knives carved of birch wood. Additionally, in the pocket of one assassin was found an exhaustive list of the various Gatekeeper banes.

"Our mortal secret is out, somehow discovered by our enemies after the death of Consul Faeryn. All of the brethren are to take warning; your enemies are aware how to bring about your demise. Take precautions and act accordingly."

~From a letter to all Gatekeepers from Consul Aurelian of Rome, AD 623

&0 C8

THE LUCKY DRAW TAVERN IN BOSTON, MASSACHUSETTS. AD 1772.

Orion entered the tavern and made for where Cyprus sat with his back to the room at a small table in the corner. He took in the rest of the room with a trained eye and promptly identified that at least three of the five patrons spread throughout the large room were Raven agents. There was a big burly man in the corner taking pulls at his mug between scowls. For the other two average-looking colonists, Orion had ascertained in the glance of the left one that the man was far too interested in the newcomer to be just another customer. Additionally, both carried pistols while the former had a blunderbuss propped against his table. That Cyprus had company with him in the room only made sense, since he confidently sat in the corner with his back to it.

Orion did not even look at Cyprus as he passed alongside him and sat across the table. Orion was now situated in the corner of the large room, facing out. It was a few hours after dark and Orion had little interest in making the day much longer. Still, Dominos de Lumine and the Order of the Raven did not speak face-to-face often; he was under the impression this was going to be important.

"Good evening," said Cyprus with that smile of his. He had been looking at the fireplace to the left, but now turned to see his nemesis. Orion was not in the mood for the almost playful tone that greeted him; he locked his steady and impassive gaze – the same gaze that men died under – at Cyprus.

"State your purpose," Orion answered, and then motioned to catch the barkeep's eye.

"Past your bedtime, is it? Well, don't worry. This shan't take long."

The barkeep placed a mug of ale on the table in front of him with a friendly nod. Orion hoped the dark-haired twenty-something proprietor would have the sense to stay down if the meeting had an unscheduled hiatus.

Orion took a long steady pull at the mug, draining it significantly. He set it down and finally looked again at Cyprus: "I'm going to leave when this mug is empty."

"We want a truce in Pennsylvania, and we are willing to make it worth the trouble for you light-lords."

Pennsylvania was home to many places, but foremost among American cities in the area was Philadelphia. There were numerous things in that city in which the Raven could have interest. However, Cyprus had said 'Pennsylvania' and not 'Philadelphia' so perhaps there was a broader scope to be considered.

He went over voluminous things in his mind, but aloud all he admitted was, "I'm listening."

"If hostilities are called off in the bounds of Pennsylvania," baited Cyprus, "we will yield our influence in the French and Spanish courts: no more stonewalling support for the colonies."

Now he had Orion's attention, and he leaned forward just a bit. "A tidy sum to be rendered," he acknowledged. "To what New World industry would you dedicate such a ransom?"

"All that matters," said Cyprus coolly, "is that we have purpose there and would simply like to continue it unmolested for a time."

"Yet another mining operation, nephew?"

That Cyprus straightened in his seat was proof enough that it was indeed such an undertaking.

"So many mines all over the world…" chided Orion, "…and half of them so recent.

South America, Africa, Asia. What metal is so precious that you have launched such an exhaustive search?"

The younger man scowled back at him, blinking. "You may find out some day. But in the meanwhile-"

Orion leaned forward infinitesimally. "Looking for Atlantean silver, are we?"

"That is not your concern-"

"I think we both know it is." Orion smiled, and Cyprus straightened. When men like Orion smiled, men like Cyprus could die – and they had. But Orion went on. "Not easy to find, is it? It's almost like someone planned on it being elusive to people who were looking for it..."

"You ask foolish questions when you should be giving me an answer-"

"What's truly unfortunate, nephew, is that the one reliable source for that special, shiny little metal is some distance beneath the Atlantic Ocean..." Orion said this easily, perfectly aware that this was something Cyprus already knew. "But one has to wonder how you are hoping to find it in American mining."

"What say you to the truce, Gatekeeper?"

Orion slowly shook his head. "Did you not think I, let alone Dominos de Lumine, would not realize what you are looking for?"

"What is your answer?" Cyprus half-shouted.

Orion sat back, his residual seriousness solidified once more. "If you don't yet know, you've lost your touch." Cyprus said nothing. "A truce would make no sense if it only exists to let you search for Atlantean silver. No. I cannot acquiesce to this proposal." How foolish, he cogitated, does my own nephew think I am?

The color of Cyprus's face was gradually turning crimson as a silent rage filled him. He appeared controlled, but Orion had inwardly braced himself; this Raven lieutenant had always been a highly volatile man. So much for a quiet evening.

"You'll regret this," growled Cyprus, teeth gritted.

"As long as your silver search is fruitless, I think not."

From across the room, the young bartender could see the two men at the small corner table. To his surprise and consternation, he could also see that both men had drawn a pistol under the table, and were likely to at the very least blow one another's kneecaps off. He purposefully did not step from behind the bar; behind the counter he had at three separate locations a musket, a pistol, and a Cherokee tomahawk. Placed for exactly this type of thing, it never hurt to have a little reassurance available for particularly raucous patrons. Stepping outside the bar would take him away from these handy tools; staying behind the bar allowed him to approach the hostile duo and at the same time have a weapon close-at-hand.

The barkeep called across the ten foot space between their table and the nearest section of the bar counter, "Gentlemen, I don't know what you're on about, but you need to take it outside this establishment."

Neither man looked his way, their eyes locked on one another. However, they *both heard him. Out in the larger room, the two actual customers of the establish-ment left their drinks un-emptied and vanished out the door.*

"Ironic, is it not?" said Orion to Cyprus. "We're each about to shoot the other when we both know it will do no good and cause no lasting harm."

Cyprus sat still, but suddenly smiled broadly as if he were having a good time. Uncannily, his anger had evaporated in an instant, perhaps squeezed out of him by that slow, heavy blinking of his.

"Seemed worth a try."

At that point the largest Raven member, the scowling man in the opposite corner, abruptly got up from the table as he hauled his blunderbuss into firing range. His surly expression, sudden movement, and audible growl left no question as to his intentions. Even as the barkeep's face changed when he began to see no troublemakers were interested in leaving at the moment, Orion made his own sudden movement from the corner where he sat.

His right hand clutched the pistol aimed under the table at Cyprus, but now he swung it up and around to aim over Cyprus's shoulder at the man with the blunder-buss. The other two Raven men leaped up from their places, brandishing their own weapons. Orion's pistol fired as Cyprus leaned a bit out of the way, and at the same time under the table Orion's opposite hand took a hold of the table leg and thrust the entire structure so that it spun a full half turn. An oaken leg pushed against Cyprus's own pistol and forced the barrel off target as it fired; it emptied into the wall behind Orion.

Orion's pistol shot really only made the fellow with the blunderbuss duck beneath his table. He lurched up again an instant later as Cyprus left his seat and dived out of the way, shouting, "Shoot him! Shoot him!" As Cyprus left the table, Orion flipped it outward onto its side as a shield. He crouched behind it as the blunderbuss pelted into it with buckshot from across the room. The table moved with the impact as Orion got up immediately after the resounding blast, and launched himself up and over the bar counter.

One of the two pistol-carriers fired at Orion as he vaulted for a new refuge, and a bottle behind him against the wall shattered. The second man leveled his weapon at the bar, but as he focused on the place Orion had disappeared beneath, a short distance down the barkeep came over the top with the musket leveled.

"Get out of my place!" he roared.

The man with the unfired pistol made to retarget upon this new threat, but having offered a warning already, the barkeep pulled the trigger as the Raven agent ignored his order. Even at that distance the notoriously inaccurate musket was aimed well. The lead ball hit the man square in the chest and took him off his feet, never to rise again. The remaining pistol carrier and blunderbuss man dived for cover.

Behind the bar, the barkeep had ducked back down to find himself almost face-to-face with Orion, the man the entire bar was after. He had already seen this athletic stranger spin a table around with one hand, and then leap wholly over the bar as if it were two feet tall and not four. Now that he looked the man in the eye in close quarters, he did not seem unusual. Just popular.

"Offering a warning after shots have been fired," said the stranger, "was bold but honorable." He was reloading his pistol and was almost through.

"Waste of time," said the bartender. He found Orion's mannerisms slightly calming in the midst of the chaos. As if he'd done this type of thing before.

"Any other weapons back here?"

"Pistol and tomahawk, neither in reach at the moment."

"On my mark, make for the pistol," said Orion, pocketing the ramrod.

"But what is go-"

"Now!"

This sudden cry was rushed, for at that instant the blunderbuss-wielding Raven agent had appeared at the end of the bar, seeking those sheltered behind. The barkeep had the sense to scramble for his stashed pistol as Orion fired his own weapon at the blunderbuss man. The first shot Orion had leveled at him earlier when the fight began had missed, but this second volley hit him in the head and he went down out of sight without a sound.

Orion rose up from behind the bar to take in the new situation: two of four Raven were dead and one remaining man had already used his pistol shot. That left Cyprus, but as Orion rose above the counter to survey, he found that the wily devil was nowhere to be seen. The final Raven agent, the one who had fired his pistol as Orion vaulted over the bar, now had a knife in his hand and was closing on the bar. The barkeep's pistol went off from twenty feet away, but the ball narrowly missed the lunging assailant.

As the attacking Raven agent jumped up to clear the bar, the savvy Gatekeeper reached under his long coat and from this unlikely place drew out his double-edged sword with its tempered blade. This drawing motion was so very swift that the Raven fellow had not even cleared the bar before the sword point extended toward him.

The foe stopped short, having only a four inch dirk to defend himself from an eighteen inch sword; he dropped his knife before Orion could order him to do so. The battle appeared to have abruptly ended.

"Where is your mining operation?" asked Orion, sword still pointed at the man from only a few feet away. "How long has it been in use?"

The fellow's mouth opened, but instead of audible words, a shot rang out. The man barely made a sound as a lead ball hit him square in the back and he slumped forward over the counter stone-dead. Orion looked to see Cyprus in the door of the establishment with a smoking pistol in hand. With a bit of a smug look, Cyprus disappeared out the door and into the night.

Orion checked the man face-down over the counter in front of him. "Well," he said after a moment, "I think that's enough fun for one evening."

The bartender was the only one there to hear him. Orion looked at him a little more critically now that there had been an exchange of weapons fire in close quarters.

The battle had lasted only about a minute or two from first to last shot. Even now, he was reloading his weapons with tension-sore fingers. Admirable dedication and poise, all things considered, Orion silently admitted.

"Friends of yours?" asked the barkeep.

"Yes, very old friends," answered Orion. He looked around the bar, noticing multiple places that were damaged. "I'll see to it this establishment is restored. Don't trouble about that."

He hesitated but admitted to himself that Dominos de Lumine was not without its needs for field operatives; the war with the Raven and Shades were not without casualties. This fellow had behaved in excellent fashion for someone without training who was thrown into an unexpected fray.

"I am Orion Keldir," he said after some silent debate, and extended a hand.

At that moment a newcomer came in the door. The tavern keeper reflexively raised the reloaded pistol at him, but Orion recognized the encroacher and pushed the barrel back down. Standing in the doorway was a tall, broad-shouldered man with flowing red hair and a bushy beard. He looked at the weapon being aimed at him for a moment, and then took in the bar with its three dead men lying about in their throes. Then he looked at Orion with a chiding eye and spoke with a thick Scottish accent, exasperated in tone.

"For crying out loud, man, can't you ever talk these things out?"

"If that is an apology for being late, I accept."

"Diplomatic negotiation my eye..."

"And that is an actual old friend, Thielen Macleod," Orion informed the barkeep. The fellow extended his hand and clasped Orion's firmly.

"My name is Franklyn Black."

∞ ↯

Adrienne had composed herself long before she heard the approach of footsteps outside her cell door. It was easy to hear the slightest thing in the consistent quiet of that dim place. Her own hushed breathing struck her as especially audible at times. But no more so than the creeping of a rat here or there, or the occasional drip of water on stone.

The guards that arrived took her from the cell and escorted her up the stairs, back to the daylight world. She blinked intensely for the first few minutes when they passed the door and walked on through the castle. Even the air was cleaner and less stale up here, and every window they passed blazed with light. *Have I only been down there one night?*

Neither escort spoke to her, and their five minute walk was punctuated only by echoing footfalls through cavernous spaces. In the end they climbed a short stair, at the top of which beyond a pair of double doors was a spacious chamber with tall windows in three of four walls. It looked like a study; shelves with books, desks piled high with papers, a few comfortable chairs, and tables all sat well-used.

Many old maps were hung upon the walls where space allowed. There was a dry, musty smell that blended almost harmoniously with the eggs and bacon that sat on the smallest table. Sunlight flooded in and reflected at so many conflicting angles that she did not at first see the two people standing by the desk in the corner.

Triassa and Cyprus did not look up as the guards left the room and closed the doors. Both her captors were looking down at a decrepit, leather bound book of immense size, neither daring to touch the fragile yellow-brown pages. Triassa was looking carefully at something on the page when Cyprus glanced up to see Adrienne standing awkwardly in front of the doors, staring at them.

He smiled at Adrienne. "You look awful, woman. You should have taken my offer."

Triassa spoke before Adrienne could return a clever retort as to why she had preferred a dungeon cell for the night instead of his own quarters.

"Break your fast, Lady Blackman." she said, not looking up.

In truth, the smell of the piping-hot food was part of the reason Adrienne had no response for Cyprus's barb. She did not know how long it had been since her last meal; she was famished, and obeyed the command quickly. Neither captor troubled to watch her devour some bacon, eggs, and a warm biscuit slathered with butter and jam. Rather, they continued their discussion in low tones that Adrienne strained to hear.

"It is a complex of immense size," Cyprus picked up again. "The imperial palace makes us here at Raven's Roost look like a summer home. I know some of it, but I confess for your purposes there I will be no substitute for Keldir's guidance. Without him I might have a chance of finding the Stair, but even if I did pick the right level after all that, we would surely run out of time and be sinking before ever glimpsing the chamber."

Triassa contemplated that, still yet to raise her head. "It is just as well," she said slowly after a pause. "I need him alive and in the chamber when all is said and done."

"He is not a fool. What makes you think he will guide us there?"

"The same advantage we have extorted from the weak a hundred times before," she said tersely, and looked up to meet his eye. "Compassion."

Cyprus was not so sure. "That is not a word I would have applied to the Deathless Blade."

Triassa reached up and patted his cheek patronizingly. "Not for you, Blackshaft. No fool would have it for you. Compassion for *her*."

Now they both looked over at Adrienne, who could only look back uncomfortably. Triassa looked back down at the massive book but Cyprus remained staring. Adrienne looked down at her lap when he gave a twitching, heavy blink – like a power behind his eyes was interrupting his brainwaves.

"I knew we were saving you for something special, Lady Blackman," he hinted darkly.

"You are too short-sighted, Cyprus," chided Triassa, again without looking up. "She is a former bearer of an Imperial Gemstone, which as you know does not find its way into the hands of just *anyone*. That quality alone is enough to keep her around. That and the fabled residual effects of such exposure." She looked up. "Now, make yourself useful. Go get them, but give us some time alone first."

"Your wish is my command," said Cyprus with a playful half-bow.

"If only that were true," Triassa snapped once he was completely gone. She finished looking at something on the same cracked page and then came and sat down across from Adrienne. "He does not think I see what he wants. Men rarely do."

"Rarely think or rarely see?" asked Adrienne.

Triassa gave her a fleeting glance and then a nod of acknowledgement as she placed some food on her own plate, and then poured some juice into a tall silver goblet. "You play your part well," was her answer. "I hope Orion Keldir will not force us to hurt you." The casualness of this remark made Adrienne swallow hard.

Me too, was her immediate thought. Briefly mulling over whether it was wise to do so, she spoke her previous worry. "Why do you…think Mr. Keldir is concerned about…my well being? I mean, we don't even know each other. And what's a Deathless Blade?"

"You ask many questions for a guest at my table," said her hostess between sips.

Adrienne dropped her eyes to her lap, recalling their last brief conversation and not wanting to antagonize – as if that were difficult. "I'm sorry."

"Orion Keldir is an enigma, one thing to some people and something else to others." She looked at Adrienne with what could be mistaken for pity. "For unimportant, 'innocent' people like you…there is something of a protective instinct present. In the end that is the essence of much of the work that Dominos de Lumine performs." Her face now hardened. "For those deemed enemies, he is practically death-incarnate. And the Deathless Blade title" - and here she viciously sliced a biscuit in two – "is because Orion Keldir carries a sword and does not die, despite various efforts to assist him on his way. There is a power within him that resists death." She said this last part as if to herself, but in hearing it Adrienne believed her.

Adrienne reached for her necklace to hold it, remembered that the gemstone was gone, and wound up circling the rim of her cup with one finger as she held it nearly in her lap. A hundred questions fought for her vocal cords but somehow none seemed worth the Lady Triassa's time. At any rate, Orion Keldir did not seem to be a favorite topic of discussion. *I wonder if she's ever actually met him.*

"May I ask one more thing?"

Triassa meticulously spread jam on her biscuit, taking more care than a woman of her temperament had a right to take. "A fifth question remains? You've had a lot of time to think, haven't you?" She spoke this, again, without looking up. "Go ahead, amuse me."

"You said I was a bearer of an Imperial Gemstone. And there were residual effects."

Adrienne said this also without raising her head, but when she finally did, she found Triassa gazing at her evenly. She had a fierce natural glance but her expression was neutral. *Well, perhaps with a hint of amusement. Be careful,* Adrienne advised herself.

"That is not a question," Triassa replied, dark humor tainting her tone. "But your statements do have some entertainment value. I shall oblige you."

She reached up to her own neckline and pulled out a golden chain upon which hung Adrienne's emerald jewel. The silver frame in which it had been originally encased was gone; the Lady Triassa had removed it and refitted it with one of her own.

"I can see in your eyes you still consider this trinket your own." The pendant dangled between her fingers, sparkling in the sunlight of many windows. "I cannot say I blame you in your desire for its return. It has served you well over the years, hasn't it?" The only answer to Adrienne's inquisitive look was a smile. "Ah, that's right…Frank Blackman doesn't tell you every last thing, does he?"

Adrienne made no reply as the reflected green light matched that of her eyes.

"Let me guess…your husband gave this to you on an important occasion early on?"

Adrienne swallowed, not liking the turn in the conversation. It had been their wedding day.

"A noble gift," admitted the hostess. "I suppose you never would have equated this pretty little green gemstone with your well-being this day, did you?" Her voice was now almost taunting, fully enjoying the conversation. "I'll bet…you aren't even aware how many times it's saved you since you got it, are you?"

Adrienne was not amused, though she controlled her rhetoric. Holding back was better than a hard slap in the face – most of the time. "You're wrong."

"Six months after your marriage you were in a car accident, were you not?"

Now Adrienne was stunned.

"What happened to the car?"

"How…did you know about…that?" asked Adrienne slowly.

"*What* happened to the car?"

Adrienne was slowly shaking her head. The car had been totaled, absolutely totaled. Triassa only looked superior as she read the lovely green eyes with her cold blue ones.

"You walked away, didn't you?" It was hardly a question.

"I did…" admitted Adrienne. She remembered the accident like it was yesterday. She'd walked away after the machines tore the two cars apart to get her out. The paramedics had been amazed, unable to explain. She hadn't even been sore – and she hadn't given the remarkable good fortune of it all another thought, aside from counting her blessings as anyone would.

"So…why did you sell your stock in Andromeda Enterprises?"

Now Adrienne truly was stunned into silence. This too she could remember, having the sudden interest not in all their investments, but in that one in particular. A burning interest, satiated by neither research nor countless experts acknowledging it was a wonderfully intelligent investment that had gone from five thousand to twenty-six thousand in three years. And yet at the start of the fourth year she hadn't even been able to sleep, unexplainably. It vexed her every waking moment for a week. Frank had at last acquiesced and sold off all but one thousand dollars. He had been uncertain but Adrienne had at last been able to sleep again.

Lady Triassa smiled as if she read the mental processes like a book. A week after the sale and their impressive profit, the company's CFO was indicted for fraud and the whole thing tanked to practically zero in a matter of days. Adrienne stared at the pendant with a fresh sense of awe, realizing with a new light that only recently after the wedding had she surprisingly and inexplicably no longer been severely allergic to nuts.

Adrienne had felt naked without the gemstone once it was taken. The trials she had experienced had weighed on her more heavily in its absence, but that realization hardened her resolve. *Just because I loved it doesn't mean I'm nothing without it. Keep it, you nasty blonde harpy.*

"What good…" began Adrienne at length, "would something like that do for someone like you? Someone who has everything?"

Her meaning was even more tearing to her, for she had loved the gemstone before she had known it was something special indeed. Now to have had it taken from her by force was even more maddening. A sense of violation grew up now, where before it was just another wrong on a growing list.

"Mere protection of every-day things is not what the ancient magic was meant for," the Raven woman said, "only what it results in when its chief purpose is not being fulfilled."

That statement, to Adrienne's ears, had the ring of truth.

"And what is this chief purpose?"

Triassa leaned forward clandestinely as if it were a secret. She nearly whispered: "It keeps Them away." Adrienne's brow furrowed, and her hostess sat back once more, adding still quietly, as if to herself, "*That* is what good the gemstone will do for me. It keeps Shades away." She held the pendant outward, letting the jewel dangle at Adrienne.

"This precious little bauble has had many owners before you. Not even I can name every one, and in the end it really doesn't matter. Still, a variety of ranks and walks of life, cities and countries." The Lady Triassa looked at the stone herself, thinking back. "Let's see…there was the daughter of a Russian czar, in the family for over a century. She survived three assassination attempts, all by poison.

"It was carried by a nurse in the 'first' world war. Her convoy was ambushed by Germans and despite eight bullets in her, she lived.

"It has been also in the Qing dynasty – the last dynasty of imperial China, for all their years in power. A daughter of that house who wore this gemstone was unconscious under the water of a river at flood stage when she fell from a bridge. She was not pulled from beneath the surface for nearly twenty minutes, but she was revived with no ill effects.

"From China it reached Central America from the west, and in time was given to the queen of Spain when the conquistadors returned from the New World, where it had been taken from among the Aztecs. The Aztecs had not the sense to know it should be *worn* and not stored. I have no particular knowledge of events in the queen's life once she began wearing it, but I've no doubt there are tales enough.

"I can never remember if the Egyptian princess who possessed this jewel was of the Middle or Old Kingdom dynasties…but I digress.

"There are many more…but in the end you are the least significant of all bearers," she concluded with another superior smile. "You…who had no inkling of how beneficial it has made your life. One can practically trace the history of the world through this sparkly rock, Adrienne Blackman. All the way back to *truly* ancient times, when it was borne by an heiress of the imperial royal line of the great Lost Isle. And that is where this particular green mineral initially comes from; the Lost Isle."

Adrienne was too staggered at that point to offer much of a reply. Before her kidnapping, the world had been a much less-complicated place; she would not have believed the Lady Triassa's statements. Yet she did not believe in coincidences, at least not ones that negated serious repercussions. Her mouth had been open with a sort of awe for much of the time her hostess spoke. The realization that she'd been unwittingly wearing a magical gemstone around her neck for five years was flooring. That, and while the woman was speaking, Adrienne had been confident in the veracity of her words; she was not lying.

Have I accomplished anything on my own since our wedding? Disturbingly, a few things that had occurred in her life were beginning to make perfect sense when viewed through the lens of a magical gemstone. She suddenly wondered as to whether the 'protective' character of this gem had anything to do with why she and Frank had no children – for which they had tried and hitherto failed. Her mind was so full with the weight of it that she did not reflect until much later as to how Frank would have gotten his hands on such a marvelous thing. *Say something.*

"May…I have some more juice, please?" she asked. She didn't even want more, but could conjure nothing else to say.

Triassa looked at her with a quizzical glance, as if surprised that Adrienne could be interested in thirst when she was revealing the marvels of a past age. Without a word, she filled Adrienne's cup.

For several minutes the two women ate and drank together in silence, one watching the other while the other tried very hard to look nowhere in particular. Conversation for the sake of itself was out of place and stank of wasted time. Adrienne randomly thought, *I should have asked more about these residual effects.* But queerly enough the idea of them terrified her. Something in the context suggested regrettable outcomes.

A door opening interrupted her thoughts. A guard came in carrying something Adrienne could not make out, and she refused to let herself stare. He put the item on the table and with a slight bow of his head, excused himself. It was a sword, sheathed in a leather scabbard. Adrienne did not recognize it as Orion's weapon when Triassa stood from the table, picked it up, and drew it out. To do so, she actually had to push the weapon an inch deep into the sheath, twist counter-clockwise, and then pull outward.

"Have you seen this weapon before?" asked the beautiful hostess.

"No."

"This blade is the oldest thing you have ever seen, aside from perhaps its owner. The art of its forging has been forgotten with the place of its birth on the Lost Isle, and its craft can never be duplicated, for the tempered steel of this particular element can no longer be found among the races of mankind. It has only recently come into my hands, though I know it well. Its owner follows closely."

She held the sword as if it were sacred, caressing the blade with her bare hand, fingers running down the relatively short, eighteen-inch length. Triassa held it so Adrienne could see a number of foreign, unrecognizable characters etched in the steel.

"'Siaktria' it is named in the runes of the Lost Isle," Triassa said, reading, "But I like the name in English better: *Nemesis.* A fitting name for such a tool." She twisted it in an arc with the skill of a master. "The carrier of this weapon has borne it through the ages with him, opposing the Order of the Raven, and eventually myself, in a *most* aggravating fashion.

"It was not always so, but all that lies in the distant past and is of no further consequence. What matters, my Lady Blackman, is the here and now. Soon he will be here, and he will do for me what I wish." Her face hardened. "And then he will die."

"What do you intend?" Adrienne asked, and a free hand went up to clasp her necklace out of habit – but her fingers closed on nothing. She clasped her hands in her lap to hide her nervousness; she didn't want Triassa to see her fidget. Magical gemstones and Lost Isles and men that apparently lived 'through the ages' and weapons that lasted to make the time journey with them were quite out of her reckoning. *Will she make me watch as she kills someone?*

"I am having some prisoners brought in here. You are going to witness their interrogation. You are going to give your undivided attention to their answers when I speak to them. And if I ask you what you think, you are to tell me openly, honestly, and immediately without thinking as to how to craft your reply. If you speak out of turn, these prisoners will experience varying degrees of pain. If you hesitate or reply deceitfully when I ask you questions, these prisoners will experience varying degrees of pain. Do you understand?"

"No," admitted Adrienne, but also added quickly in the same breath, "but I will obey."

"Wisely spoken. They will not be able to see you, at least at first. Remember your place is silent as a grave until I inquire of you. Wherever possible you will nod or shake your head, rather than actually speak."

"Yes, of course," replied Adrienne. *Who are these prisoners?*

"My guards found them wandering through the forest. Foolish of them not to ask for assistance sooner. Some aggravation may have been saved, not to mention one of my German shepherds." She said this last part as if to herself, musing over the situation. "I will bring you in on a little secret, my Lady Blackman. I did not have your person brought here for the pleasure of your company, however charming. While I desired your stone, your personal presence is also of some benefit. Those residual effects you are so keen to learn about may eventually become known to you. Remember this when you answer my questions."

☝ ☜

Even as the Lady Triassa finished speaking, the doors at the end of the hall opened and several individuals entered. The first was Cyprus, immediately followed by guards walking alongside Frank and Orion, these latter two being handcuffed with their hands behind them; both prisoners were also securely blind-folded. Further behind in the procession were several more guards, their shotguns aimed at the backs of the cuffed men in front of them, poking them if they walked too slowly.

"Fr-!" began Adrienne, and clapped her hand over her mouth with a look at Triassa. The other woman only gave her a sideways glance as if in warning.

The men came forward, reaching a proximity close to the table. Adrienne was surprised that Triassa said absolutely nothing; she only nodded to Cyprus. It was Cyprus who turned to the two men and addressed them. A handful of the other henchmen departed without a word, though there were three that stayed with their firearms in position.

"A pleasure to see you once again," said Cyprus. "I was hoping we would be talking before long. I've missed you both."

Both Frank and Orion obviously recognized Cyprus's voice. Apparently he had been walking with them to the hall but had said nothing to announce his presence. Orion said nothing but Frank sounded as if he were rolling his eyes.

"Oh, you gotta be kidding me…"

"Frank…Frank…is that any way to treat an old friend?" Cyprus smiled. He leaned against a desk a few feet away with arms crossed and a most amused grin. "Really, I expected better of you."

A glance at Triassa with her folded arms and tapping foot made Cyprus pick up the pace a bit.

"The esteemed Lady of the Raven has desired to meet you two men for a very long time," he said to them. "The honor is yours. But first, Orion, we are interested to know whether or not you remember your way through the palace."

Orion stood still as a statue. "Palace?"

"The imperial palace. You spent much time there. Surely you remember it..." prompted Cyprus.

"I fail to see how that could possibly matter now."

"It matters if you wish to stay useful to the Order of the Raven. If I were in your position, I would be most interested in staying useful. The obsolete tends to disappear here at Raven's Roost. Don't waste my time."

To Adrienne's surprise, Orion actually gave the hint of a smile and even the slightest of half-laughs.

"Outliving my usefulness..." he said aloud, "...that will be a glorious day." His amusement then vanished like a scent in the wind, the mirth dissipated. "I should be so lucky."

Cyprus sounded genuinely confused. "You wish to die?"

"Now who is wasting time?" answered Orion.

"I'd like a room near the pool, please," added Frank.

Cyprus nodded his head to the guard behind Frank, who promptly put the butt of the shotgun hard between his shoulder blades, driving him to his knees. Adrienne put her hands over her mouth, catching her breath in a kind of stifled gasp. Frank made a bit of a groan, shook his head and coughed, but then made no further indication of pain.

"Don't feel left out, Frank, I was getting to you," Cyprus said. "All the time I've spent with Adrienne has made me worry about you. Have you missed her?"

Words failed Frank. "If you've hurt a hair on her head...I'll kill you..."

Cyprus only chuckled. "Hurt her? Me? A little credit, please. What do you take me for? If I was going to hurt her, don't you think I would do you the favor of letting you watch?"

"You vile piece o-" spouted Frank, but Orion interrupted.

"Now you really are wasting our time...nephew. Kindly come to a point, if it is not beyond you."

"An excellent idea," Triassa now cut in, her clear and stern voice pushing Cyprus's smooth one out of its way. "Gatekeeper Keldir, you remember the imperial palace at Iratha and would be able to navigate your way through it?"

Blindfolded, Orion turned his head in her direction. Even masked, intrigue blossomed on his features at the very sound of her voice. An infallible memory stirred and there was only a slight pause before he asked:

"To whom do I speak, please?"

She came slowly forward, his confiscated sword over her shoulder as if she approached home plate. "And why would I trouble to mask your sight only to assist you in this way?"

"Your voice…it is – no, it is impossible. A mistake."

"No doubt of it, but as to introductions, the guest should speak first."

"As you wish," he answered. "I am Orion of the House Keldir, Justice in the Eternal and Sacred Order of the Brotherhood of the Gatekeepers, and for your purposes representative of Dominos de Lumine. Does that suffice?"

"No one uses titles anymore…" said Cyprus under his breath to Adrienne. "How I miss long introductions…"

"It will serve, Gatekeeper Keldir," answered Triassa. "I am the Lady Ravenslord, Master of the Order of the Raven." She came a bit closer, amusement on her features. "Minister of Injustice, Scourge of Nations, Imperator Extraordinaire…I could go on."

Orion would have been staring her in the face but for the blindfold. "Undoubtedly. But I am sure one so important has better things to do, like using her real name."

"Well spoken," she acknowledged. "That you shall know if I deem it necessary. But back to my initial question. You know and remember your way about the imperial palace at Iratha?"

"The city and all within it is lost. What of it?"

"Answer my question."

Orion paused, as if measuring how an affirmative could possibly be detrimental. At length, he admitted, "I know it well enough."

"Like the back of your hand, you mean," interrupted Cyprus.

"Peace," Triassa ordered him, and then looked to Adrienne. "You there, does this Gatekeeper speak the truth?"

Startled but not forgetful of her previous commands, Adrienne gave a nod. *How am I supposed to know?* But if she pondered on Orion's words, she was indeed outright confident. Unexplainably, inextricably sure of it.

"You are certain?"

Another nod. Triassa turned back to Orion.

"You will lead me through Iratha and take me where I wish to go," she informed him.

"Doubtful," said Orion, and once again Adrienne found herself believing him.

Triassa did not ask her this time, though. She glanced at Cyprus, caught his eye, and then gave the slightest of indicative nods in Frank's direction. Without hesitation, Cyprus moved to where Frank sat on his knees, took him by the back of the head and drove a knee succinctly into his face.

Adrienne gave an involuntary half-scream as her husband took the blow full-on to land flat on his back.

"More along the lines of…what I expected," he groaned from the floor, blood streaming from his nose. "Not bad for a girl. You could teach Cyprus something, lady."

Cyprus gave him a sharp kick in the gut at that, but Triassa raised a hand. Her eyes were on Orion, who was of course not deaf to any of it. Neither was Adrienne. She sat rigid, eyes closed, head turned slightly away. *If I make a sound, they will do something worse.*

"Uncivilized in this day and age, I admit," said Triassa, "but it is in your power to make it stop."

Adrienne gripped the edges of her chair. *You have to agree, Orion. Tell me you're about to agree.*

"Or," said Cyprus as he circled Frank, "your friend *and* his wife can suffer together. Perhaps that will tug your heartstrings."

"No!" said Frank, but Cyprus kicked him again.

Orion remained standing there silently, though it was plain to look at him he was not immune to actions around him. Triassa gave a scoff of derision.

"It is true then," she laughed, "the Deathless Blade has a heart of stone."

"If your ears will not serve," said Cyprus, "perhaps you can watch Frank watch me when I turn attentions to his lady fair."

Triassa fell silent at this, any hint of amusement gone. She glanced at Adrienne, who appeared more worried for Frank's welfare than the hint at her own abuse. Cyprus, in the meanwhile, was more intent upon getting to Orion than reading female facial tells.

"A wife's suffering won't bend your will? Unfamiliar with the idea, are you?"

Orion said nothing, but anyone looking at him could tell the comment bothered him.

"You were married, were you not? Do you miss her, uncle?"

"Be silent...nephew..." came the newly cold, menacing reply.

Frank was about to say something but the tone of Orion's voice shut him up abruptly.

"Don't worry, Blackman," said Cyprus to Frank. "I'll make sure you're at least there to watch when we kill your precious sweetheart."

And with a fierce look he put the toe of his boot hard into Frank's ribs. Adrienne sat not ten feet away, both hands over her mouth in an effort to make sure she remained quiet, her troubled eyes portraying everything she was not able to speak.

Cyprus went on. "I'm sure Orion wished it was the same for him."

Orion's voice was so dark it could have belonged to someone else. "Is your desire to live so depleted that you dare speak to me of this?" Orion's blindfolded gaze turned toward the one who was actually talking to him, instead of looking straight ahead. "You will never again even *refer* to my Attica, or I will have your head. My poor sister ought to have thanked me for never telling her what a treacherous, insolent little coward her son was before she died in the war."

Triassa's head snapped around to stare at Orion as he spoke these words.

Now it was Cyprus's cue to take on a hateful glare, interrupted by a pair of slow heavy blinks. His tongue pushed out of his mouth slowly – but it had to wedge itself past gritted teeth. While he had slowly backed away when Orion spoke, now he stalked toward his uncle with murder in his eyes. His mother was apparently a sore spot.

But Triassa now stood absolutely transfixed, staring at Orion with newfound shock, as if he had materialized out of thin air right then. Cyprus was in the midst of walking past her on his way to Orion, but the sword she was holding came off her shoulder and placed itself in his way, across his chest. He stopped short, turning to look at her. Her eyes never left Orion, head cocked to the side ever so slightly. Her voice was clear, deliberate, slow.

"What did you just say?"

"It is not your concern, Ravenslord," said Orion tersely. His blood still ran hot.

"Speak the name of this woman you mentioned once again," she ordered, coming forward step by step. The sword was at the ready like a Roman legionnaire's.

"Leave my wife in peace."

"If she is dead, what harm are you concerned about?"

"Enough," said Orion, teeth gritted.

"Tell me her right name and I'll pursue her no more." There was no taunt to her tone; she was merely adamant.

He hesitated, as if surrendering the name of his beloved would somehow mar her memory. But in the end Orion also saw he was in no position to bargain. That and Triassa's avidity was clear. The imperial palace at Iratha now seemed an afterthought, since he had mentioned the other woman's name. Her hand pointed at Adrienne to assure she was focused on the matter at hand.

At length he spoke. "Attica Triassa."

Triassa whirled toward Adrienne with the intensity of inspired rage. "Does he speak the truth?"

Adrienne would not have dared to lie, not to that face. And, once again, she was confident; she gave a nod.

Triassa turned about and walked right up to Orion, right in front of him face to face, put the sword blade to the side of his head and neck, and tore off the blindfold as if made of wrapping paper. Her free hand grabbed the front of his clothing and pulled him within inches of her face as she looked up into his.

"Then what bewitching trickery is this?" she roared in his face. "I *am* Attica Triassa!"

Orion's voice was incredulous, and no one present had ever heard him speak in such a tone. He spoke a limited question, almost as if he were afraid as to what the answer was.

"…Attica…?"

That face was permanently etched in his memory. He had looked into its eyes countless times, lost himself in their love, had stroked the long entrancing hair. Could it be her?

The beautiful woman who had been referred to as 'the Lady Triassa' within her own professional network for years and years looked deep into his eyes, cocked back the balled fist of her free hand and hit him so hard his head snapped around and he staggered a pace back before going to one knee. It was the only thing that he could have done without falling flat on his back.

Beside him, Frank had gotten to his knees without any assistance from the guards behind him, one of whom took off his blindfold too. At his particular angle, Adrienne was not immediately visible. The first thing Frank did see was a flawlessly attractive young woman with flowing blonde-hair, icy but beautiful blue-eyes, and a fierce expression. Frank gaped; she was absolutely gorgeous. The famous Lady Triassa Ravenslord – Dominos de Lumine's greatest foe – was always pictured as some severe old hag; none of her enemies knew what she looked like. That she was more comparable to a centerfold had not seemed plausible.

A number of things immediately jumped to mind, but Frank was not so much of a fool as to say any of them. Nearby Cyprus looked smug, but the blonde was plainly incensed. She gave Frank a look of barely suppressed ire, the sword *Nemesis* trembling in her hand.

"I just came for my wife," he heard himself say.

Cyprus scoffed, but Attica Triassa took a long, deep cleansing breath. She turned and gave a flick of her head in Frank's direction. Adrienne was on him in an instant, on her knees in front of him with arms around his neck.

"You're okay!" exclaimed Frank. "Oh, I've missed you."

The Blackman's joyous reuniting was a secondary sideshow for all other parties. Orion was not speechless for long, but when he spoke he was looking at Cyprus, and his voice was dark and wrathful. In a man of few emotions, it was a stark contrast. "This latest deception of yours is low indeed, even for you."

"A cruel twist, perhaps," admitted Cyprus, "but it is none of my design."

"How is it *you* are my husband?" asked Attica fiercely, sword still in hand. "That cannot be. He *must* be dead by now, whoever he was. What sorcery is this?"

Orion came to his feet, looking her in the eye. "The sorcery is yours," he said grimly. "That you clothe yourself as she is an insult to her memory." He spat the blood from her punch off to the side. "To what gain do you take this disguise? It is *not* possible!"

She was still perturbed but now in firm control of herself once more. "Well, we agree on *something*."

Orion muttered slowly and hesitantly, as if he wanted to convince himself simply by saying it: "It's not possible…it is *not* possible." He had his eyes half closed, but then he focused them on her and spoke decisively, "You are not her. You cannot be her. A remarkable, accurately portrayed deception, I grant you, but a deception nonetheless."

Not even looking to see if Cyprus was, she sheathed and tossed *Nemesis* to her subordinate. She then began to walk slowly and casually in a semicircle around Orion.

Despite his words, Orion was honestly beginning to be torn. *What vile sorcery is this, that she is not only returned but now my implacable enemy? It is some abhorrent deception, this…creature that mocks her memory. Identical to the eye and ear, but this one's spirit has rotted from the inside.* His wife Attica had been as sweet and gentle as they came. She had been a very kind woman, the sort that endeared herself without even trying; it was just who she was. This woman he was looking at now made no attempt to hide the spite in her voice.

"You are perhaps right," she said at length. "The woman I once was, whom you supposedly knew, is dead. And has been for some time. The question is, even now do you believe me, or are you still clinging to your suspicion of my veracity?"

He said nothing to that, but was looking at her in very deep thought; in a way that troubled her. His eyes were not portraying what she had expected, and in the years of dealing with him impersonally as an enemy from a distance, when he did not behave as expected there was trouble brewing. She frowned, looking at him and then Cyprus.

At length Orion spoke. "There is one manner in which I can make sure you are no deception."

Attica placed her hands on her hips and cocked her head ever so slightly, her weight on one leg. *That is her stance,* he silently acknowledged, *the one she always used. That in itself cannot be a lie…* A true mannerism of someone dead for hundreds of years could not be faked. In the meanwhile she spoke slowly, eyes narrowed a bit.

"Do tell."

Orion said nothing, but admittedly he looked confident. Cyprus was taking this all in carefully. He could not help but state his amusement at his uncle's proposal:

"What are you going to do, ask Them?"

"This is your plan?" asked Attica. "The Different Place?"

"There is no hiding there," answered Orion.

She pondered. If he, here in the twenty-first century knew of the Different Place and was really her husband from ages past, that was actually logically coherent. That, and a willingness to go to such a location was indicative of genuine intentions to search out the truth.

"Go then," she said at length, "but with condition."

"I'm listening."

"I do not know if we were married in a past life, but I am Attica Triassa. If you learn this to be true from Them, you will return here and when I desire it, you will guide me in the palace of Iratha and take me where I wish to go."

He considered it. "Agreed," he said at length. *That place is under a thousand feet of water; she must know something I do not – or thinks she knows what I do not.*

"Swear your swift and peaceful return to me, on your honor as a Gatekeeper; swear it on the Portal Gate." To her knowledge, for such a man there was no more precious an oath. And this man came from a time when oaths were truly sacred.

He gave a solemn nod. "I swear it as so."

"Release this man," she ordered the guards, her own confidence emanating. "You may go, Orion Keldir, but keep in mind that while you are gone, your friends are my guests. Don't tarry on the way; my patience can wear very thin. When you return, come alone or your friends will pay the price." She glanced at the lead guard. "You there, see to it this man finds his way off this property."

Attica was leaning on the table with her arms crossed as Orion was freed, and she did not watch as he nodded once to Frank and made for the door. But he stopped as he passed her, pausing very close to speak in her ear as she refused to look at him – portraying no worry that her freed captive might turn on her in such a position. Her clear blue eyes looked straight ahead.

"You two here can lie to me, but They will not," said Orion in her ear. "And if I find that you are lying and are using my wife as your façade, all the while poisoning her memory; if I were you I would not be here when I return."

With that he turned and left. He did not see, but Triassa only smiled serenely, a look of superior confidence on her face. *He could be lying, but I am not. Either way he returns here. Did I really marry the Deathless Blade all those years ago?*

Adrienne knelt beside her husband, concerned at the blow he had taken to the head. One guard seized Adrienne as she held Frank, the other two grabbing Frank and hauling him to his feet.

"Take them to the cell," said Cyprus.

"Lady Blackman, a word," said Attica.

Adrienne stood by a moment with a pair of guards. Frank stared back at them while they dragged him away. She looked at her captor with a different air after the intense exchange a moment before.

"Do you recognize your newfound talent?" Attica asked.

"I was monitoring the conversation a little too closely to pick up on this supposed talent of mine."

"Really? You did not find the residual effects beneficial in the least? I did."

"What do you mean?" queried Adrienne.

Attica only looked at her. "You did not even notice your ability to tell whether or not an immortal is lying?"

80 C8

Upon the departure of both Keldir and the Blackmans, Cyprus laid the Gatekeeper sword on the table as the other Raven personnel departed.

"The Different Place…" he said aloud as if to himself. "…Keldir is original, I'll give him that. He will be hard pressed to-"

He had looked up at Attica and his voice suddenly stopped. Her blue eyes gazed unblinking at Cyprus, accusation swimming in the deep pools. He thought of the sword on the table; with that look in her eyes, he wondered if he should have kept it close.

Her steps as she came toward him reminded Cyprus of a lioness stalking prey. The sword may not have served him anyway, given that glare. But she was still ten feet away when she asked.

"Well?"

His dark violet eyes met hers. "I did not know."

"I trust you are clever enough not to attempt lying to me, Blackshaft."

"It is so, I did not know. How could I?"

Now she closed the distance with a few echoing steps and slapped him hard across the face.

"How could you not?" she thundered at him. "How could it *possibly* have escaped you, in all the years we have known each other, that you not only knew my former husband but were *related* to him as well?" She grabbed his throat with a hand that trembled with anger. "And you thought not to tell me? For what insane reason? The man was right; even for you, this is beyond."

He tore away from her grip – no small task. "Did you think I was invited to your wedding? After years of enmity with the groom?"

She scowled at him, but was done shouting. She turned abruptly aside and went to the table.

"And besides," he continued, "when you and I met, he had been a widower for nearly two years. I had heard of his loss and did not think more on it. A tragedy, surely, but none of my concern." He gauged her movements carefully, the side of his face burning still. *But does she believe any of it?*

"It is those cursed, ragged shadows," she said as she looked at the sword on the table. "They are the ones who have robbed me of remembering my own past. When I was mortally restored, I was able to see that I had lost much; many original memories, desires, some temperament. I used to think it was just their failure when all that I lost was not restored to me. Now I see it is all by cruel design." She shook her head resignedly. "This truly is a game."

"You could say that now the game has truly begun."

"It ought to be in my favor," she acknowledged. "I've spent enough time setting the board."

"Are you not concerned that Keldir will not return?" he asked.

Attica had already considered this and answered confidently. "A Gatekeeper has honor that a man like you cannot fathom. He has pledged on the Portal Gate that he will return. He will."

"Fair enough," said he, blinking once. *My time will come.* "Pardon me; I think I might retire for a while." He turned around.

"Before you do, check on the blacksmiths in the armory and see if they have completed my blade. At this rate, I will need it sooner rather than later."

"Yes, Lady Triassa."

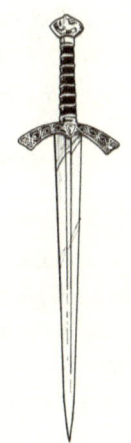

CHAPTER 12

*"Enough of your doubt, Blackshaft. Are you a man, or not? That the
Portal Gate exists at all is enough to drive me mad. Open or closed, it
leaks paranormal energy into this dimension like cracks of light about
a shut door. This seepage empowers the Shades on this side of existence,
gives monsters like Memphis his strength. The Seal keeps the rest of
them out of our dimension, perhaps, but the vile shadows here with
us are still fed enough to remain. Do you see why this must be done,
Cyprus? If the Portal Gate is no more, the Shades in this existence will
wither and fade – and once that war is at last over, we shall be free to
live this immortal stretch our own way."*

~Attica Triassa, AD 1994

୫ ଔ

VALLEY OF DANDRALIA. 6 DAYS BEFORE THE FEAST OF HIN, 3654 BC.

*T**he roar of battle echoed off distant hills, amplified within the confines of the
rich green valley. The lines were mixing and confused; the cavalry was lost
amid the curve of the flooding riverbed; the conglomeration of ballista and
scorpions, catapults and mangonels were hardly useful on the bulk of enemy forces;
not once the men were engaged, already red to the elbows with the blood of the slain.
Swords wove in and out, spears launched above the shining helms gleaming in the
sunlight, only to drop down to the battle-level to pass through throat or breastbone
with a burst of red. Axes cleaved helm and shield with mighty strokes. Random arrows fell everywhere. Thousands and thousands went back and forth in a massive
free-for-all, though the commanders were trying to keep it more organized than all*

that. Cries of rage, pain, and loss echoed all over the field. Death was omnipresent.

On a hillside above the action but still close enough to be shot at, Orion's mind was occupied by a hundred details as he gripped his sword more tightly than usual. He still had pain in his leg from the fall by the gates of Lynsaelyn, and that ache distracted him now. It was part of the reason why he was not down there wading shoulder-deep in the blood and guts, as he was formerly accustomed. The Dandralian Campaign had entered its second week and this was the third pitched battle he had fought. At least he had started the first two – but this morning they had finally surprised him. It had only cost them a few thousand men over the past ten days, but life itself had never mattered to the rebel Separatists. The Shades, of course, valued nothing more than victory in their feud with the royal line. He could see the vile cloaked creatures moving about the flanks of their rebellious horde, slashing at any that ran from the imperial Loyalists, their occasional shriek haunting the thoughts and dreams of Orion's soldiers.

He looked down the line and spoke just loud enough for his aide to hear him. "Torch it."

"Torch it!" shouted the aide loudly.

To their left a man with a torch lowered the flames and sank the fire into the small narrow trough at the men's feet. Other torch-holders further down the line saw the action and read the signals, and dipped their torches into the trough as well. The oil snaking its way through the trough ignited and a slim line of pure fire rushed unbroken all the way down the thousand man front, to the very end. The archer captains looked toward Orion at the south end of their lines, awaiting the order that was swift in coming.

"Light."

"Light!" went the cry, and it was answered by captains shouting the same thing. The entire front and second line dipped their specially-constructed arrowheads into the trough, setting each ablaze. Within thirty seconds of lighting the oil, two thousand arrows were alight and on string ready to fire.

"Make it rain, Carlian my lad," said Orion to his aide. "Target their flank-"

The order was not even complete when the aide turned just in time to have a rogue arrow hit him just underneath the chinstrap, and he went down with a gurgle and a spurt of gushing blood. The general blinked at the foreign blood in his eyes, wiped the running red just enough so that he could see, and spat some out angrily. But cleaning himself up could wait till after the battle, as could mourning the loss of another young friend. If the special fire-arrows were left burning on-string for too long, they themselves burned up and became useless.

"Archers ready!" Orion's roared like a dragon, louder than the din of the very battle before them. His captains answered and the longbows of horn and wood were raised.

A glance toward the enemy told Orion that at least seven Shades were on the north flank of the opponent. "North flank!" he directed the aim of his archers.

"North flank!" answered ten captains' voices. Two thousand arrows aimed toward the river directly behind the foaming lines before them down the hill.

"Loose!" roared the commander, and with a synchronous whoosh!, a hazy thicket of shafts vanished from the bows. One could follow their two hundred yard flight path and the general color of the rushing flame as the flanks of the army of the Shades – and three Shades themselves, fell beneath a snowing inferno of incinerating arrows.

Orion watched with an anticipation of which he was partly ashamed. The fire-arrows were the best repulsing weapon against the Shades aside from actual magic, and Orion had employed them multiple times. There was always – always – something a bit theatrical about being able to incinerate multiple Shades in the heat of battle from a distance of two chariot-racing tracks. He watched with grim but secretly elated satisfaction as he saw one shaft come along straight down through the top of the hood of one of the Shades, igniting it literally from hood to boot. Another burst asunder and went wild, flying about every which way until it eventually collapsed to burn to cinders. He fancied he could even hear the death-shrieks the vile creatures made at such times. Those that had not been incinerated scattered, leaving behind the black smoldering ashes of their former compatriots. Some of the nearest soldiers panicked; some dropped their weapons and covered their ears amid the tortured shrieks of their twisted, black-shrouded masters; some lay dead as the arrow shafts in their chests slowly burned out.

Good, but not good enough. He would drive them into the river to end the threat on the Dandralian Provinces at least until next spring. The emperor had already lost his favorite son in the great civil war of which they were all a part. Orion wanted to bring him some good news, for once. He looked down the line of his archers, raised his sword high overhead to gain attention, and shouted again like a thunderclap.

"Archers ready!"

℘ ℘

Adrienne sighed as she leaned against Frank and warmed to his arms around her. She was back in the dungeon cell once again, but she had to admit the company was infinitely better than before. They held each other for a moment before Frank's legs practically buckled and he collapsed onto the bench. She realized he was exhausted – and, as she could tell by the hug; a bit tenderized by Cyprus's assault.

She sat beside him, wondering if the bench would take both of them at once, and at length, being so glad to see him she smiled playfully. "Tell me this is all part of your plan to rescue me," she said.

Frank did not open his eyes or unfold his arms from across his chest. "Don't you like it here?"

"There are a few places I'd rather be."

"Well, I got news for you, babe. I'm afraid we're going to be here for awhile."

Her smile faded. "That's your plan? My hero."

He glanced sidelong at her but in the end returned to his relaxed state. "Ah, affirmation, a relationship's lifeblood," he said dismally, "I'm afraid that the plan at the moment is, if nothing significantly changes, to wait for Orion to return."

Adrienne experienced a pang of guilt. She took his arm. "I'm sorry. I've just… been down here awhile, you know?"

He put his arm around her again and they sat for a moment. "I'm the one who's sorry. It's really all my fault you're involved in the first place. I haven't been fair to you. You know if I had any control over the past couple days, you would have been spared all this." He stood up as she nodded. "But at the moment, Orion really is the best hope."

"And you think he'll come back?"

"Even if Attica wasn't here, I'm sure he would be back."

"So who is this Attica?"

"As far as I know, she's Orion's wife."

"They have a falling out?"

"I suppose you could say that."

"How would you say it?" Adrienne asked.

Frank hesitated. "She died."

"Come on, Frank, you don't really believe that?"

"I didn't say I could explain it, but I believe it. You can't work a lifetime with someone like Orion and not see some strange stuff. Besides, you saw his face; he believes it."

Adrienne stopped short. "A lifetime," said she. "That reminds me. I heard I missed some of your birthdays."

Frank's eyes were closed, and he wondered who had told her. "Adrienne, please don't start with that…"

"Frank, you are *not* making me the bad guy on this one – but I won't push you. We'll talk about it later, when we've nothing better to do."

"And for now?"

She pulled him back down to the bench and leaned in close, her head on his shoulder with his arm around her. "You can tell me how much you missed me."

80 CB

Cyprus squeezed his eyes shut and leaned heavily on the counter of his private quarters, listening to the faucet empty an endless stream of scalding water into the basin. The bathroom door was closed, locking in the warmth. Rushing was not Cyprus's style; his was a cool and calculating, well-developed strategy that in the end was inexorable in its advance. *Hurrying only creates mistakes.* And mistakes could hurt. In this world they could kill. And yet he had rushed to his own chambers to report this latest piece of news – this final step in the process.

He opened his eyes and looked at the mirror. His reflection was clouded by the fogged glass, the heat doing its job. He focused hard and closed his eyes again, remembering how challenging this skill had been to learn. It was an unnatural way to communicate, but then, Memphis and the other Shades were not natural creatures. Over the years, Cyprus had learned that only the Elders like Memphis had the skill and focus to answer back in kind. At any rate, what were they supposed to do over long distances, email? Call? Those would never do, not given their topics of conversation. In his mind, a clear thought produced itself. He opened his eyes.

Across the mirror, his thought literally appeared written in the condensation:

THE LAST GATEKEEPER HAS MET TRIASSA.

A moment passed, and Cyprus remained leaning on the counter, a bead of sweat trickling down his brow. Soon, more words appeared, but these were not his own. Somewhere, Memphis was concentrating.

Does he know her?

Cyprus focused again. His words wrote themselves.

YES, BUT HE DOUBTS. EVEN NOW HE HAS DEPARTED TO TEST HER VALIDITY.

Once he finds that it is she, he will return. At which time you will encourage Triassa to depart for Iratha with all due speed.

A mirror conversation was no time to waste space and energy arguing, or in this case defending. *I won't always be your messenger-boy*, he reminded himself off-handedly. Unless he gave his entire being to the concentration, thoughts would not appear written; it took serious effort. Little mental trivialities always flitted across his subconscious during these sessions, and were never remotely close to writing themselves out. Cyprus pushed ahead, feeling the beginning of a migraine. But that was typical of the strained back and forth.

AND IF SHE IS NOT ENCOURAGABLE TO THAT END?

We finally have what we need to realize the Great Intrigue. The city may grow permanently inaccessible if we wait too long. While I am not in the position to appear in person as initially intended, we must push forward with all haste.

There was a pause in Memphis's flowing thought.

Arcanus will go in my place. His very presence will make her realize she has little time to use, and she will act accordingly.

Cyprus took a few breaths, struggling for the strength and concentration that humans required for this kind of correspondence. The deathly face of Arcanus flashed in his mind and shattered his acuity. *I have not seen that monster in years.*

ARE WE SO CLOSE?

The Great Intrigue must come to fruition. The board is now set; it cannot fail. Attica Triassa must now play her part.

Cyprus thought too naturally and quietly for the flow to show up in the glass: *She may play her part, but will I get my coveted role when all is said and done? Or is this one using me as he uses her?* Sweat trickled down his aching back, the mental strain translating into tensed muscles. He mustered an effort for one last push.

AS YOU WISH.

Memphis's response was immediate.

You will see that it is.

He continued leaning on the counter, glad the conversation was at an end. These discussions drained him like a sieve. Panting, he reached up to wipe his brow, and his eyes fell on Memphis's continued correspondence, changing the subject abruptly.

And what of your favor? Have you decided?

While he was still very pleased at the prospect of having an immortal race like the Shades owe him a particular favor of his own choosing, Cyprus was disappointed at the timing of the question. The narrow glowing eyes of Arcanus still stared at him whenever he blinked; he could think of nothing else.

NOT YET, MY LORD.

There was amusement behind the response:

Pity.

Cyprus turned off the water, hurriedly wiping the mirror clean. The pending headache abated, his mind no longer agitated. That was how those mirror conversations went – they were so unnatural that making the specific required effort could literally hurt. *Human psyches are not meant to perform this way.*

80 C8

Trego did not know how fortunate he was that Orion bothered to stop the Raven SUV outside his gated property, taking the trouble to assure the guard that he posed no threat by entering. Of course, it was easy to believe that he had stolen the vehicle from the Raven, which he had; no one had stopped him. The front bumper hung precariously from the reckless driving it had seen, and the front of the car was dented and crimped as if with a sledgehammer. A branch or two was wedged under the right front wheel-well and there was mud spattered everywhere. Someone would have put fewer scratches on it by grating a rake over the hood. It had been an uncharacteristically frenzied drive that had not yielded to trivial things like the Raven front gate.

Orion did not knock as he walked in the front door of the residential section of the property. There was a barracks built onto and adapted into the original homely structure. The corps had a job to do in the region, but they also needed a place to call home; there was still much on the property that qualified for domestic needs.

"What happened?" asked Trego, looking up from his chair, unperturbed that Orion merely came in. He could tell something was not quite right. "Where's Frank?"

Instead of answering, Orion merely asked straight away: "A bathtub, do you have one?"

"Of course..."

"Get all the ice you can."

Without further conversation, Orion marched to the bathroom and began running only the cold water into the tub. When Trego walked in with a large bag of ice that had been recently acquired for his own needs, he found that Orion had cleared the bathtub and the area around it of any free items. Soap, a washcloth, and two towels had been tossed out into the hall. The tub itself was half full of water and not even plugged.

"I don't like the look of this," said Trego, but still emptied the ice into the enclosure.

Orion pressed the plug into the drain and only said, "More ice. And a chair, get a chair."

The orange-bearded host muttered to himself as he looked through his freezer for anything that would be just as cold as ice. There was not much, though he did find a couple cold packs – his back was not what it used to be. His mind was wandering about trying to find a practical reason why his oldest friend was trying to make his bathwater frigid. What could he want to make that cold?

Returning down the short hall, he dropped the cold packs upon entering the bathroom. Orion was already stripped to the waist, and making short work of what remained of his clothing. *Still built like a tank*, Trego marveled, *with never a sign of rust*. Even with the evidence of vague but numerous scars from close-calls, the immortal body proved resilient in every way. *Those scars there have to be bullets, that there a knife thrust, surely.* And that long one some sort of slashing weapon. Deep in his side, Trego noticed, there was a short succinct scar that was not reddish or pink, but powder blue as if it had been caused by an icy dagger. Sure, he could be shot or stabbed, but the man healed almost at once, and usually completely. He could still scar, but the marks that still remained were from grievous afflictions indeed.

The Macleods had been Dominos de Lumine men for centuries; Orion had worked not only with Trego, but his father, grandfather, great-grandfather, and so on. Back fifteen generations. Trego did not know the exact nature of Orion's long-lived existence. However, he did understand that Orion's longevity came from a different source than that of time agents like Frank Blackman or James Talon: Orion had been old beyond reckoning since before time agents were even conceived. He was also tough as a grumpy wolverine wrapped in barbed wire.

"What are you intending to do?" asked Trego, already realizing full-well what he most likely had in mind.

"Set some coffee brewing," answered Orion, "and come back straight away."

When Trego had done so, upon his return Orion had immersed himself up to his neck in the very full tub. Water spilled over the sides onto the tile floor. His head was leaned back against the end of the tub and his eyes were closed. His breathing was purposefully slow.

"For the last time, man, what are you doing?" yelled Trego, tired of being uninformed.

"Give me no more than twenty minutes, and keep my head above the surface."

Trego gritted his teeth and spoke slowly. "A man can't withstand that temperature for long."

"A normal one, no," agreed Orion.

"What do you intend-"

"Sssssslowing my heart…old friend, I'm slowing my heart."

"B-b-but why?" Trego stammered.

"Because…" said Orion slowly, "they have to believe it has stopped…"

"Who? Why? How long will you have to take?"

No answer.

"Keldir?"

Silence.

Trego left for only a moment to get a chair and sat down close by the tub. He was pleased to see that the size of the tub and the manner in which the man sat would make it surprisingly difficult for him to slip beneath the surface of the water. The Scot put two fingers to his neck for a pulse. He had to hold ten seconds to get a single beat. This went on for almost a minute, and then the beats came gradually slower. Fifteen seconds. Twenty. Forty – but no slower. Trego checked his watch; it had taken five minutes to reach his slowest.

&) (%

Attica stood and stared at the giant map on the wall. Behind her a few feet and seated comfortably at a table upon which sat many books and more maps, Cyprus looked on. Before them on the wall, the map showed what might have been best described as the Roman Empire at its height, though this was not its purpose:

Great Britain was in the high mid left region, and Egypt in the lower right. A generous portion of the Atlantic was also shown.

Attica's laser pointer made a miniscule circle in a small uncharted region about five hundred miles westward off the northern coast of Spain. She spoke quietly, almost more to herself than Cyprus.

"This point appears to be the foremost choice for the location. The research points here, as do the seismic measurements and sonar." She turned back toward Cyprus and smiled. "It is most plausible. Agree?"

"Thousands of years can change many things. I really couldn't say."

Attica looked defiant, but had to admit he was right. There would be no way to tell until they were there. Even now there were crews and Raven ships doing excavation work on the bottom of the ocean; they had been there for months. What he said next only annoyed her.

"Keldir will not know for certain either."

She walked toward him casually, but Cyprus was shrewd enough to be a bit on edge as she came close. Not that he showed it, of course. He had spent many years in Attica's service while she ruled the Order of the Raven with an ingenious hand under the name 'Triassa', a name which at one time in the archaic past had been fairly common. They had come to the Raven together at first. He was her greatest lieutenant, her right hand. One did not maintain such a position by showing weakness. But he was still watching his step now, after that slap earlier.

"I will raise that section of the city, and your uncle – my former husband – will take me to the chamber."

She reached out and Cyprus almost stiffened in his alerted state, but all she did was lay a finger upon the lines of the largest book. This was the same book that Adrienne had noticed when first brought in; it was large, thick, and exceedingly old.

"According to the Kedassaic Texts, an immortal's lifeblood will completely seal the Portal Gate. Permanently." She looked at him with a slight smile. "Relax. As you know, since you are not so much truly immortal but rather merely a cheater of death, your lifeblood will not do."

She turned back to the book, but Cyprus shivered. He remembered the first time they had had this discussion, when she had read the Texts' claim that an immortal's lifeblood would forever seal the dimensional Portal Gate. The look she had given him then was outright predatory. Immortals were, after all, hard to find – and here was one sitting across the table from her, in her employ as it were. It had to be lifeblood, not just blood from a wound. Lifeblood: the immortal doing the bleeding would be dying. Had to be dying. That was why Attica could not just use her own immortal blood; she was going to live to see the deed done, and therefore needed someone else. Another immortal.

Cyprus did not qualify, not because of lifespan, but rather due to *how* he achieved his long years. The Shades' venom avoided death, held it off, abused life in its own way. True immortality was not accomplished by a dosage, no matter how long ago he had swallowed the venom – or how often he had to swallow more.

That was why he had sought out a new life-enhancing method from the various time agents of Dominos de Lumine; as time agents they would have their own serum that he could use instead of depending on that of the Shades. Of course, virtually none of the time agents he encountered had offered or allowed him to share; each one had fought him tooth and nail. Each had been left dead and Cyprus had been left without a single dose of elapsation serum. That plan had failed miserably.

"Cyprus, it is just as well you could not serve in this fashion. Did you really think I could slit your throat after all we have been through together?" She said these words kindly, sweetly.

"And sleep like a baby afterward, my dear Lady."

There was an abrupt halt in the conversation as they both looked at each other. At length he gave a dark chuckle and she a musical laugh. Shortly, all merriment departed as quickly as it had arrived.

"Orion Keldir's lifeblood will serve marvelously. And then, my old friend, we can live our lives free of unneeded influence." *I will seal the Portal Gate, and then Memphis and his black drapes will answer to me, for once. Then the shadows will pay.*

Cyprus looked contemplative. "I have seen the end of many things in my ageless years. The end of the Eternal Order of the Brotherhood of the Gatekeepers will be a glorious day. They are responsible for much. Now, to think that they are at last down to one sole remaining member – and that it happens to be the last of my kin. There was a time when I would have considered that…unthinkable, maybe even impossible."

Attica smiled like a lioness. "As impossible as the entire land being buried deep beneath the Atlantic Ocean? And your race lost?"

Cyprus neither smiled nor gave much of a sign. He found neither of her historical notations amusing.

She went on, unperturbed: "Tell me, Cyprus, did you even see it coming?"

Cyprus only stared for a moment, but Attica would not cast her gaze away. At length he said with a bit of a shrug, "I suppose some may have claimed that such a thing would happen. The great war went on for so long, took such a devastating toll. How could magic not have been used to bring about victory? Yet the strain of powers…and the dark influence of the Shades themselves proved too much for even the very land itself. Only some were saved when the Cataclysm began and sent it all beneath the waves." He was reflective for a moment, and then eased back in his chair, crossing his legs. "I would give much to see the Gardens of Kel-Monsir again," said he. This was as close to sentimentality as he allowed himself.

"You may very well see what is left of them by the time I get the seafloor to the surface," said Attica, and her compatriot only gave a single nod. "Then perhaps the rest of that decrepit old book will at last have found a use."

Her irreverence irked him. "You should not berate it so. It is one of the greatest literary works ever written, and the last of its kind. I had to go through many things in order to bring it to you. We are fortunate the monks on Sicily had copied it at all over the years – they thought it was a lost prophet. And their whole monastery and every book in it were burned to the ground by the Muslims only a decade after I gained it."

"It shall be yours once again when I am out of uses for it. Then you may read all the useless charms and spells to your heart's content," she said callously. "The only purpose of that book is to help me craft my own destiny of my own accord, not learn as to what ancient pages dictate it should be."

CHAPTER 13

"Immortality is not for everyone. The years go on and on with no end in sight. Why, a man could go mad just thinking about it – and some have."

~Cyprus Blackshaft, ca AD 826

෨ ෫

O rion blinked and found a different place awaiting him as his eyelids lifted. As his consciousness faded in the waking world, the enveloping cold that he had pushed to the back of his mind slipped away to the point that it entirely disappeared. He was no longer slouched in the tub but standing erect, and in an arched stone doorway. He inhaled deeply and decided nothing was askew on his person; he was the image of health. Of course, he could hardly recall what being sick was like; it had been multiple lifetimes since he had been under the weather. But here there was rejuvenation in the very air, though it was a dark atmosphere.

The arched doorway he stood within opened immediately into a large circular chamber about forty feet across. The ceiling was high and domed as if with glass, and above the glass the universe itself was pressing down: stars stretched into eternity, a few smallish globes that had to be moons, or perhaps even very close planets could also be seen, and a pinkish stretch of anomaly was visible in the background. One had the sense of looking out into nothing and yet everything all at once. It was a galaxy, surely, but a different one – not in the sense of being far away from Earth, but in the sense that it was in a Different Place that could not be reached simply by astronomical travel. A separate dimension.

Orion stood in the doorway. Straight across from him stood the only other way in or out of the round chamber; another identical doorway. The opposite doorway passed into nothingness beyond, not into another room or tunnel, but into a blackness which leaned and pressed up against the archway itself, held back by an invisible force. Orion glanced behind him quickly and saw that stepping backward would apparently pitch him into a similar blackness, though perhaps not so sinister. He stepped forward to get away from it.

Built into the very walls of the room in stone, and running all the way around the perimeter was a shelf of rock. It was interrupted only by the entrance in which Orion stood, and the other doorway. Upon this shelf, spaced evenly at about one every foot or so, were smallish, polished and glassy black orbs. They were about the size of a croquet ball, and were so shiny and glistening with the flicker of light that one might have sworn they were wet. The room was dimly lit, though what actually provided the light could not be identified. Occasionally, deep within a sphere, a very dim but distinct flash of color would barely surface and then be swallowed back into the core. There were perhaps one hundred twenty spheres around the room.

In the middle of the room, standing there watching him as if it were the most natural thing in the world, was a Shade; a tall gangly figure in a sweeping, all-encompassing black robe and hood. Orion had noticed it, but as it had made no move he had almost forgotten about it while taking in the wonder of the room. He was especially entranced by what pressed in from above. The view was magnificent. But as he stepped into the room, he reached behind him for the old familiar handle of his oldest friend slung as always upside down against his back. His fingers closed on nothing. It was a dreadful shock, and he strove to cover his reaction. Showing weakness in front of a Shade could be perilous.

The Shade did not move, but its gaze enveloped him. Eventually it spoke, and the cruel, sinister voice croaked its way out from the cavernous hood in a hissing whisper grated with malice: "Enter in, Orion Keldir."

Orion took a few slow steps into the room, keeping half the room between them. Other than their voices the room was utterly quiet, and it was not hard to hear the slightest thing. *The silence itself means me great violence...the very stones hate my presence here.* A random glint of intuition came to him: *This must be where Consul Faeryn came upon his death – where they stole the Gatekeeper mortality secrets from him.* The darkness at the doorways was trying to push its way in. The dazzling display overhead encroached down upon them. He waited a moment before speaking, although his task was urgent.

"What is this place?"

"This?" asked the Shade, indicating with a partly raised arm not only the room, but the Expanse above. "It is a different place for many. For us, it is Vengeance, but for you...it is Clemency."

Orion had recognized the voice; Shades, as in any civilization, were similar in appearance but in the end they were all individuals, however with an ability to be part of a collective of sorts. Having dealt with Shades for as long as he had, both in the recent present and the ancient past, Orion had learned a few of their names.

"Edramyn?" he asked.

The Shade lowered its arm and began walking, almost casually, always looking at Orion. Orion in turn countered its every step as the two began to slowly circle. Shades could move like a sudden wind, and he had no weapon.

"You are perceptive, for a human."

"And you are not all as mysterious as you would wish to be. Now what is this place? Of what clemency do you speak?"

The Shade's voice was like someone doing a bad impression of a monster. "Yours, human, yours. We have waited so very long for you to come here, that we might have this conversation with you. But first tell me: how did it happen?"

"How did what happen?"

"Your death. What was the nature of it? I have waited especially long for it, being here with only the occasional visit to the Earth Realm. How did you come to…expire?"

"That is no concern of yours," said Orion haughtily, as if he had lost some pride in the said event. He was also too distracted to conjure a plausible answer. "But why am I here?"

"I can usually get a glimpse of what occurred," said Edramyn curiously, "but with you…I read nothing…"

Because I am not actually dead.

"You may keep the secret of your death," the Shade went on, undeterred. "The next journey I take to Earth Realm, they will tell me. I can wait another seven years until I journey back there again, it is of no consequence. But as for now, after years of defying our Purpose, in this place you are offered Clemency for the deeds of your lifetime."

"Clemency for what?" asked Orion, defiantly.

A dark amusement surfaced. "Your pathetic human civilization only resists the inevitable when it refuses to bow before our domination. You have spent your outrageously long lifespan actively working to sabotage our overthrow of your civilization, your very species." It kept walking, and Orion stayed opposite the tall Shade. "Admirable from your species' point of view, but ultimately futile. Now that your mortal coil has been severed, you are left with a choice."

There was a pause, and Orion looked around the room, in particular observing the orbs. Edramyn stood and awaited his reply, which came hesitantly.

"I'm listening."

"That archway," said Edramyn, extending a long, thin, black-wrapped arm in the direction of the doorway opposite the one Orion had used to enter, "is the Doorway into eternity. All of your species are bound by their very nature to die and pass on into the Void of everlasting emptiness. That is what lies on the other side of the darkness: eternity itself. All mankind must come to that in the end, though not all will reach it by coming through this place.

"This dimension you are now in, Orion Keldir, is a space within Time itself. It is so contrary to the rules and laws of both your and our own dimension, that one can virtually *feel* how the universe itself seeks to abolish it, pressing in upon us. At one end of this chamber, the door you entered only minutes ago is the mortal realm, the Earth Realm. Those that come through this gap in Time are privileged, for they are given a second chance."

"So…what kinds of men come this way?"

"Only humans that are aware of us, or the ones close to those that are aware of our War with your dimension."

That includes Attica. Yet it was hardly confirmation that she had come this way. Edramyn went on, the unseen gaze from beneath the hood always boring into Orion.

"Such humans can serve a purpose to us if they are returned to Earth Realm with the right motivation. They die, come here, learn of the futility of the resistance against us, and instead of opting to pass into the nameless Void of eternity and snuff themselves out forever, they choose a second chance at life: enhanced, rewarded, free – and for only a *small* price."

The amusement in its voice at this last comment was unmistakable.

Orion named the price: "To be a slave to your will is not much of a bargain."

"There is the occasional fool that chooses to pass up such an extravagant offer," said the Shade. The long, thin, gloved hand now indicated the orbs about them that encircled the room: "But most are wise enough to take us up on our Clemency."

"What are these spheres all around us?" asked Orion.

"Each has its identity in an individual that we have returned to the Earth Realm, formerly dead and now there with a second chance at life – with that small price occasionally woven in as a task to complete."

"So they are annals of what has transpired here," said Orion.

Edramyn hesitated. "In a way," it said, sounding as if something cryptic was being admitted.

Orion turned and walked close to the edge of the room, looking at each identical orb as he passed it. If one happened to be Attica's, he would have his answer as to whether the Raven woman he had met was really her or not. *Then I will end this pretender's shameful deception.* But it pained him that his beloved wife had been drawn to this Different Place after the trials of her death, only to face a Shade like Edramyn alone. *She must have been terrified,* he thought. The reminiscence made the anger related to her death slowly begin to rise to the surface from beneath his calm exterior.

He paused in his step, knowing Edramyn was watching him, and reached out at random toward one of the many orbs. The dark amusement surrounded him like cold water, even as Edramyn spoke from across the room, a good twenty feet away.

"You cannot touch," said the Shade from behind him. "Your spirit is here; nothing more. What you see here as your body is your own mental projection of yourself; you will find you cannot touch anything here."

Orion smiled inwardly. *Amusing, this ignorance to the deception of my appearance. They will protect this place more vigorously after today, once they divine that an enemy would actually will to come here and so gain access.*

Still facing away from Edramyn, he finished his reach. He took hold of one of the dark orbs, removing it from its place on the shelf. The orb was like ice in his hand even as his fingers encircled it, and without even trying he derived in his mind a name that belonged to it: *Larius Kiriath.*

The Kiriaths. Orion was familiar with the family, and had spent much time in their company both before and after fate had changed the world in which they all lived. Meghanus and his sons Falcius and Larius had been among many Separatists, rebels against the empire. The entire family had been condemned to die for treachery by order of the crown and the Gatekeepers as well – and not without reason. They were murderers, seditionists, enemies of the purest form – and Larius himself was even after this infamous list, a rapist as well. But in the end it was only one more crime at the bottom of a long list.

Meghanus had been tracked down very speedily after the Cataclysm; Gatekeepers had found, cornered, and finished him off within a few years somewhere in what was lately called India, though it was not called this at the time. As the numbers of the Gatekeepers gradually dwindled over the years, finding fugitives became a much more prolonged process. Larius had been located in Italy at the height of the Roman Empire. Orion himself had caught up with him in a dark alley not at all far from the Coliseum. Falcius had taken nearly another two millennia to find. Masquerading as a member of the Nazi secret police, Orion had also fulfilled the order of the court upon him in Berlin in the midst of the greatest war the world had ever seen. The line of Kiriath had thus ended, or so he had thought.

Orion was suddenly chilled by the fact that every man he had dispatched could merely come here and return to the waking world. He had accomplished so much, so many honorable fulfillments of duty, as he considered them. As an officer of the court, and for many of the past years the *last* officer of the court, he had had a long list of assignments to accomplish. And now, as he saw, had it all been wasted? The very idea of it made him incredibly irate, though in his own way: masked. *Aggression is nothing without surprise, not here.*

The orb was heavy in his hand, but not overwhelmingly so; a couple pounds. He hefted it easily enough, and turned to Edramyn with a blank expression. The Shade stood rigidly, staring. There was nothing but blackness under the hood, but Orion could easily perceive a general sense of utterly shocked surprise.

Edramyn immediately confirmed Orion's intuition. "What sorcery is this? How can you take up the orb?" The Shade stalked forward menacingly. "Carnality is not possible here! Put it down!"

"As you wish," said Orion, and let the orb fall from his grasp, destined for the stone floor.

"No!" rumbled Edramyn, but was far from fleet enough to stop its perilous fall.

The orb of Larius Kiriath burst asunder in a flash of blue fire as it met the stone floor and impacted with a sharp crack. The orb sounded like glass, but only partly burst without scattering pieces, like a heavy hardboiled egg. From its shards, wisps of purple smoke trailed up toward Orion, and he smelled something that he would have put between lavender and gunpowder.

With an expression that meant no such thing as he looked back up toward the Shade guardian, Orion spoke his answer to Edramyn's gaping amazement.

"Oops…sorry."

ᛒ ᛃ

At the very instant the orb of Larius Kiriath cracked and broke violently in the Different Place, in the Earth Realm there was quite a disturbance in a hotel ballroom in New York, where Lance Krause had been addressing stockholders of his multi-billion dollar shipping company. One of the top CEOs anywhere in the world, the man who in a previous life had answered to Larius Kiriath struck most people not only for his apparent luck and success in business, but also for his incredible youthfulness. No one knew exactly how old he was.

But whatever he was supposed to be, he was in perfect shape for a man ten years younger. It was eerie, in a way, how everything fell into place for him in automatic fashion; and he always made the right moves. But however old he was at that moment, it became very clear that he would become no older. The man gave an agonized cry and toppled from the podium in mid-sentence, coughing and gagging on the floor. Someone called for an ambulance. Others shouted for staff and aides. To the utter amazement of all, among the coughs and death rattle crept a sort of purplish mist that barely wisped from the dead man's nostrils.

ᛒ ᛃ

The wrath in the room was so strong that Edramyn would not have had to say anything to communicate it. But speak the diabolic voice did, and it was torn between incredulous shock and barely suppressed rage.

"Your Clemency is revoked, Orion Keldir. Now I see why I could not read you earlier. I do not know how your carnality has made it here, but I assure you, it will not remain with you for long."

Edramyn's ire was unmistakable as the Shade slowly and deliberately began to stalk toward Orion. It did not rush; it was in no hurry; the mortal's fate was inevitable. Just as Orion had learned that his sword had no place in the Different Place, so also Edramyn did not have the typical long cold steel to draw upon. It was of no consequence. The Shade was perfectly aware there was more than one way to kill a human, even a special one. Why, the creatures could sustain many an affliction in the body – but the mind, as the fitting proverbial phrase went, was a terrible thing to waste. It was a remarkably fragile part of the psyche if one grasped where to…poke. Death could be drawn out for a very long time, given proper technique and the gritty will needed to inflict such a fate.

"You are truly resourceful, Orion Keldir," Edramyn acknowledged, "but you will not leave here alive."

"If I found a way to arrive here alive, I will find a way to leave," said Orion. "But first, you will assist me."

Edramyn said nothing.

Without hesitation Orion reached out and took hold of another orb. It was not Attica's, if hers was here. He tossed it to the floor where it burst in pieces as the first had, and then he grabbed a third and held it menacingly.

Edramyn stopped advancing and eventually spoke. "What do you want, Orion Keldir?"

"Do you know which orb is which?"

Edramyn said nothing. Orion took that as an affirmative.

"Give me the orb of Attica Triassa."

Edramyn still did not move.

The third orb crashed to the floor like a little bomb, tossed close enough to the Shade that the purple smoke and eerie smell wafted about its black robes. A fourth orb was in Orion's hand before the third had struck the floor. This latest orb, he noticed off-handedly, was also a former acquaintance from the distant past.

"Very well," said Edramyn, and with apparent hesitation, moved a short distance toward a part of the room. Stretching out an empty hand, a particular orb lifted itself from its place and sailed gently and safely to the waiting spindly fingers. Edramyn took it up and turned to stare at Orion, who watched apprehensively.

"Put it down and step aside," said Orion.

Palming the orb, Edramyn outstretched an arm and turned the hand upside down, as if purposing to smash it upon the floor as Orion had done to several already.

"Proceed," said Orion calmly. "Send her to her rest. That is something you took from her, something she deserved." *If it does not smash her globe, I should. I want her back, but the one I met is no longer her.*

There was a pause, while Edramyn measured intentions – not a suitable task for a Shade. Truth would be required. It was not a sentiment that was a proactive element for that particular species, the truth; measurement took a little while. At length the hand turned back again and set the orb down, and then very gradually withdrew. The blackness of the stare gripped Orion with a nearly physical hold, but despite the hostility he came darting forward and took hold of Attica's orb.

The black sphere in Orion's hand was Attica's. As the other orbs had done when he picked them up, it manifested its person upon him, and he had every confidence that it was indeed hers. It was unmistakable. He had locked out the other orbs except their identity, but Attica's he let in. His strong arm trembled violently with the power of the experience, and despite his utmost effort, Orion was overwhelmed and he swayed as he stood there. In a moment he was on one knee, the power of the unconscious element of the orb acting like an electric jolt to his mind.

His conscious reality in the room took a hideously twisted turn. Attica was there before him in that very room, her mindset almost crippling him in her unspeakable terror. The darkness was powerful. He shook his head hard as if he could clear it, but at the same time he had to try hard to stay with it, for a grasp of Attica's situation would be priceless in unraveling the mystery of her death and apparent reappearance. It was like watching a scene but being part of it all at once; the character's thoughts and emotions vomited into Orion's own mind, and he was not prepared for the agony they brought.

Several very sharp but real, physical pains suddenly erupted in his back, and he threw back his head. Looking over his shoulder he saw Edramyn from across the room. His free hand clawed at the pain in his back and he cut his fingers on the embedded shards of former-orbs. Edramyn stood beside a pile of shattered orb and with a hand motion, the rigid projectiles rose from the floor. With a flick of the Shade's wrist, the second barrage hurled themselves across the room directly at Orion. Only a body roll and an uplifted arm kept most of the shards from chocking themselves into his neck. But then the essence of Attica's orb took him again and he sprawled.

&) (8

Trego dropped Orion's wrist in alarm as he noticed that the icy water in which the man sat was no longer as clear as it had once been. He traced the intrusion to multiple swirls of red that crept from behind Orion into the water. It took him a moment before he realized that Orion was bleeding profusely from a great many places on his back, to the point that the water was gradually growing more and more clouded, turning sanguine.

He stood up and then sat back down, unsure of what to do. What could he do? Orion was not sleeping. A slap to the face would do nothing. Trego cursed aloud as he suddenly remembered that while Orion had told him to give him 'twenty minutes' he had said nothing about how to bring him out of it. On top of it all, he was not sure if this was the plan or not. But how could bleeding profusely be part of the plan? Trego had confidence that Orion could handle himself. *I've only watched him do it for years untold.* He stood again and paced with his hands on his hips, watching the water darken.

৪ ৫৪

Everything that had happened to Attica in the chamber of the Different Place was inundated into Orion's mind like a technological download, her memories exploding in and out of his physical eyesight. It was an utter psychological and physical onslaught, Attica's experiences assailing him one instant, flashing back into bleary-edged visions of Edramyn as he threw the last of the broken shards at breakneck speed.

Edramyn had at last run out of broken shards to hurl at Orion, and now returned to a personal advance, like a lion stalking distracted prey. In the meanwhile, Orion was out of his element. He would gain his feet only just in time to have the orb throw him one way or pitch him the other.

The Shade had been across the room but was now most close. Edramyn would have bore down on him at once like lightning, but fear stopped him. *If Attica Triassa's orb breaks in the midst of the assault, the Great Intrigue will not come to fruition.* Threatening Orion with its destruction earlier had been a mere ruse – one that the Gatekeeper had called out.

But as for the Great Intrigue, the vast web, they were so very close to completion as it was. No, the guardian of the chamber could not simply bear down on and finish Orion Keldir. It had to stalk him and pick its moment.

To irk the Shade in the midst of its predations, the human occasionally managed to come to himself enough to grab a random orb from the shelf and hurl it at his attacker. Edramyn could stop the orb in mid-flight and put it harmlessly aside, but in order to do so concentration was necessary, and the stalking would stop at such intervals.

After a most agonizing minute, it became clear to Orion's beset mind that he had come to understand in its totality Attica's experience in the Different Place. There on his knees from the weight of the strain, he clutched the globe, staring at it. *I should smash it to pieces here and now. I must.* But all his minds-eye could see was her face, looking up into his. She smiled and pushed his hair out of his face. *Crack this orb like an egg, you stubborn fool. The Shade wouldn't do it, they need her still.* And that alone was reason enough to break the globe into fragments.

The hand with the orb raised overhead, poised to slam the sorcerous contraption into the unforgiving stone. But almost in the same motion he brought it safely back down and held it in two hands as if it were crystal. *Coward.* It clinked softly on the stone and rolled a short distance away.

৪ ৫৪

Trego had decided that flowing blood was enough reason for him to try and gradually bring this strange exercise to a close. He reached into the tub and pulled the drain ever so slightly, getting the water to drain very slowly. He then turned the faucet on, setting the temperature to warm. He checked his watch. Twenty minutes would have its completion in five.

℘ ℂ

Physically speaking, Orion recovered from the onslaught nearly at once. Very soon after dropping the orb harmlessly to the floor, he could stand. When he did, his eyes focused on the slowly advancing Shade. If Edramyn hoped to see prey in those eyes, the Shade was sorely disappointed. Rather, a raging fire bore into the blackness beneath the hood and the advance stopped to consider.

Orion Keldir had never been a man taken to emotion, but he was now in this Different Place. Every human had a breaking point, and the capable ones could even be considered actually dangerous when they reached it. Had this one reached his?

"Satisfied with what you have learned?" asked the Shade, tone exhibiting no pity whatsoever.

Orion said nothing for a moment, and then much to Edramyn's alarm he gave a cry of pure fury: raising his arm he ran for a short way along the wall, dragging his forearm across the orbs and sending them flying. More than twenty had crashed to the floor in smoking ruin by the time he stopped, shoulders heaving with the intake of furious breaths.

The Shade moved to stop him but the human invader, plainly mentally unbalanced at that particular point, stood his ground beside the shelf of spheres and threw one after another at Edramyn. Edramyn could stop them, but not in such rapid succession. A strong effort managed to stop three before a fourth flashed past the defenses and disappeared into the blackness beneath the hood. The Shade twisted as a ghastly shriek split the air of the Different Place, there was a bluish flash in the dark shadow that was Edramyn's face, and the Shade itself reared back as the orb popped back out from under the hood and fell to shatter smoking on the floor.

Orion was still beside himself with rage with what he had learned. Managing to keep from uttering aloud, with another sweep of his arm he knocked five more spheres to the ground. He was about to do more but a very strange warmth began to creep over him at that point, and a queasiness deep down that he had never quite known before. A particularly intense surge gripped his insides and he staggered to one knee, gasping. Over half of the last thing he had eaten came vomiting out onto the stones he knelt upon.

Across the room, Edramyn had recovered enough to rise once again. Wisps of bluish smoke trailed from beneath the hood, and the advance was now very slow, as if it had trouble seeing. But the menace and murderous ire was still there. The

Shade bent its head and returned to the prowl at once, noticing Orion's sudden trouble. There was no endangered orb to slow the storm now.

Orion realized what was going on, even if it wasn't technically happening in the Different Place. The strange sensations and overpowering sickness meant that in his own dimension, in Trego's tub, his body was trying to bring itself out of the voluntary coma-like state he had induced in himself. Trego, he realized, was probably doing what he could do encourage all this. *If my body comes to consciousness while I am still here in this Different Place, I will die* – the body could not live without the spirit or mind.

He rose to his feet and staggered like a drunk toward the archway through which he had come. Edramyn saw his action and followed his movement.

"You cannot help her, Orion Keldir," hissed the Shade. "She is beyond your influence now."

Orion stole a scornful glare at the Shade as he struggled toward the door, nearly overcome with nausea. The room was spinning. He retched hard but nothing further came. The Shade was closer – was able to move so much faster than he. It would surely beat him to the archway...but he could not simply stand there and let it. He had learned what he needed. How could he not return to the Earth Realm to deal with what the Shades had done? No, he would *not* allow this experience to be useless.

There was the archway, right before him. And there was Edramyn closing rapidly on his right. The darkness of the doorway loomed up in front of them. Both of them lunged at once.

৪০ ৫৪

Trego was just making the water that much warmer when Orion abruptly gasped loudly and gave a violent spasm. Water sloshed over the edges of the tub and spilled onto the floor. Orion's hurried and frenzied taking of breath was joined by Trego's own cry of surprise. Before either could say anything, Trego gave a secondary jolt of horror. Protruding from Orion's bare chest, coming essentially from beneath his breastbone, was a long, thin bony arm that moved of its own accord. Its twisted greenish-black flesh, like a dried corpse, extended a hand with six grasping fingers of more than five joints. It grabbed at the air for a frenzied split second before Trego shouted the first audible word of the moment.

"Shade!" he bellowed, so loud the neighbors might have heard.

Orion was fresh from his unconscious and in little position or mindset to do much of anything. He was still coming to himself; it was a very disorienting experience. Trego, on the other hand, was fresh and awake – and more than prepared for living remotely as an international specialist for Dominos de Lumine: he and his team had weapons set aside in virtually every room, the bathroom being no exception.

Quick as lightning he pulled a Beretta from its place taped in the cabinet under the sink and flicked off the safety. With astounding noise the handgun emptied its clip into the grasping arm. One flailing finger was even blown clean off, but as it left the limb it vanished into a mist that disappeared just as completely. Trego was cursing himself for not having an extra clip around when the arm grew rigid and drew itself back into Orion and vanished entirely, leaving no sign.

It had all taken such a short amount of time that Trego was not sure Orion even noticed the grasping arm protruding from his own body. The deafening eruptions of the Beretta had definitely woken him up, however. He sank back, gasping air as if he'd never breathed before. Trego's adrenaline drained fast and he fell to his knees by the sink, still grasping the empty gun.

"Is that what I thought it was?" asked Trego.

Orion nodded, eyes still closed. In a moment he had kicked the plug to the tub with his foot, and the cold water slowly drained. A moment later he was sitting naked in the empty tub.

Two armed men rounded the corner, weapons in hand. Finding no Shade, they stopped to stare at Orion sitting there with Trego kneeling nearby.

"False alarm, lads," said Trego.

They didn't move.

"What do you want, a photo op?"

"C-c-c-coffee p-p-p-lease..." stuttered Orion.

"You heard the man, make yourselves useful."

A few minutes passed before one returned with some coffee. Orion was still in the tub, but this time he was filling it very slowly with lukewarm water. He did not touch the coffee for a good ten minutes, knowing that coming out of the awful cold as he was, lukewarm in and of itself would burn like lava to the touch. At first the frigid skin could not tell him if what he touched was cold or hot. It was a good half hour before he left the tub and had his accustomed strength and constitution. In the meanwhile his body temperature had gradually been restored. A normal man would have had a much more difficult time, but Orion was after all rather special.

Trego helped himself to some coffee as Orion dried and dressed once again.

"Every detail, lad. I want every detail."

"Lamentably you shall have precious few," said Orion succinctly, "but some-day perhaps I shall tell you the whole tale. Right now, I need to be headed back to the Raven stronghold."

Without waiting for permission he left the room, followed by Trego at his heels.

"Can you tell me nothing?"

"I'm sorry, my old friend, there is precious little time. Suffice it to say that what I wanted to accomplish was completed. The Shades have a space setup within... Time itself; they intercept departed lives as they pass on into what awaits us all after death. I...I was there."

Trego stood spellbound. "You...*saw* it? It's been speculated about, but...you were there?"

"The theories that they *could* do it are true, as are the theories that they *are* doing it. I was there."

"That means that all those that have passed on have been..."

"Intercepted, yes. Well, those that had something to do with the Shadow War."

"So..."

Orion turned away and began gathering the last of his things. He could not bring himself to describe in detail exactly what Attica had experienced. Most of his colleagues were aware he had been a widower for many years now, but their knowledge ended there. No one had ever asked details, and Orion would not have given them anyway. The trip into the Different Place had brought up every emotion he ever had about the whole terrible event – and inundated him with the horrors that his wife had experienced about the same thing; she had had the worst of it.

The past could not be changed. Upon Attica's death, the Shades had intercepted her spirit on its way into eternity. Certain individuals were offered another chance at a lifetime, guaranteed to be prosperous – for a price of serving the purposes of the Shades. Attica had come to such a place because of her association with him. Still recovering and somewhat disoriented, Orion sat down on the nearest chair of the living room, eyes closed again, brow furrowed. He looked as if he was in pain, but he could not stop dwelling upon it.

"This is troubling," said Trego, also sitting.

Attica was still in physical and mental anguish from her death. Orion had never known anything like her experience in that accursed room; horror, confusion, fear. But she was always strong of will and spirit – while the Shades had succeeded, it had taken everything they had to do so.

The problem, thought Orion, *is that if they could bring her back on their own terms, what pieces of the original Attica could they leave out?* Shades would surely have no need for her kindness and love. Her mirth. Her giving heart. *Are these all gone?* Briefly he wondered whether her being a woman would further confuse their process; they had plenty of men to have honed their skills upon, but women had their own intricacies that were well beyond the scope of Shades.

"What is this going to mean to the Shadow War?" asked Trego.

"There is no time to explain now," said Orion, and he made for the door, the car keys in his hand. "At the moment, I must return to the Raven fortress, and see what remains to be done. It is, perhaps, fate that this has all been revealed to me. In the meanwhile, I cannot accept that I am not meant to see her again, knowing what I know now."

"But...what..." began Trego, but Orion had opened the door.

"Frank and Adrienne are also counting on me. I will not leave them to their fates either. But Attica has some underlying purpose in all this, and I must find out what it is."

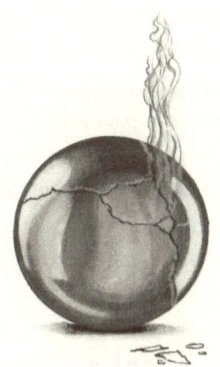

CHAPTER 14

"The Order of the Raven began ages ago, only a year or two after Atlantis had vanished beneath the waves. Its founders were veterans of the recent wars, many being Gatekeepers. My own uncle was among them. Even with their homeland sunk into the great ocean, the wars over, the Shades weakened and dispersed – even then they would not rest. The Order of the Raven from its birth was dedicated to the destruction of the Shades and the opposition of everything they stood for. That…and finishing off old war criminals and traitors like me.

"I only joined the Raven in the early thirteenth century after the Lords of Light broke off from the corruption they saw within their own order – after their original purpose was swept aside to enjoy the riches and luxuries they had built up over the years. They had been ripe for change and new leadership after the Lords of Light departed. That was when I and the Lady Attica Triassa joined them…made the Order of the Raven an organization to be feared once again."

~an excerpt from the memoirs of Cyprus Blackshaft.

℘ ℭ

MOUNT ALIAH, SOUTHEAST EDGE OF THE ATLANTEAN PROVINCE OF CYNAVIA. 3658 BC.

The mountain that was called "the Forbidden Rock" by so many was a towering heap of gray stone, but one in the long chain of craggy foothills that lay between the farmlands of Atlantis in the west and the great salt water in the east. Since ancient times the priests of Atlantis had used it for a temple, and within it were carved passages, halls and rooms. Generation after generation had abode and *delved there, still the furthest reaches of its extent were known in their entirety by no one. More than one man had disappeared around a corner and never returned.*

That was why the place made such an excellent base of operations for the rebel Separatists, the fathers of the great insurrection against the imperial line of the Atlantean Empire. Their numbers were rivaled only by the Loyalists far off in the capital; hundreds lived in the mountain itself and thousands more lay in the military encampments about the feet and spur of the cavernous fortress. The rebellion had made its headquarters there since the beginning of the civil war, some three years earlier.

On the furthest heights upon the top of the mountain, there was a paved area of large expanse, and built in the middle of this was an open circular stone dais with a partial roof upheld by granite pillars. If one looked up, there was a wide circular gap in the roof for stargazing, which was the structure's original purpose for the priests. One could sit or stand in that place and look around, watching the landscape for miles in every direction. Unseen approach by a great force was virtually impossible, unless done by night. And that would be remarkably unwise given the swamps and bogs, or countless pitfalls that opened up in the ground throughout the mountainous country.

But none of the twenty-five present rebel Atlanteans was hoping to view stars that evening, nor was anyone looking about for enemy campfires in the lands below them. No, all sat in their customary seats and listened to the Shade called Memphis as he laid out a grand scheme with which to penetrate history itself.

Cyprus sat with a leg crossed and arms folded. The wind blew across the open area on the heights of the mountain, and it was beginning to be later in the year. He was chilled and in no mood to continue listening to one of the top Shades carry on. That did not mean, of course, that Memphis was not right in his assumptions. So far he had identified each and every man or woman there as an enemy of the established state, most of them already condemned to death by the Imperial Throne and its at-hand agents, the accursed Brotherhood of the Gatekeepers. The Gatekeepers were not merely the administrative arm of the royal line, they were also enforcers and the strongest judicial hammers in the empire. If you were a criminal on the run, a Gatekeeper would find you. If you were condemned in the courts, a Gatekeeper would execute you. Every man and woman sitting there hated the Order of the Gatekeepers with a passion. Men of the Gatekeepers were often the commanding officers in the war against the Separatists; some rebels, like Cyprus, had Gatekeepers in their own families.

Cyprus looked around to see what the other Atlanteans may have gleaned from this presentation. Of the other twenty-some people there, only three looked back at him for hardly a moment. Sarn Dorme, Larius and Falcius Kiriath all met the eye of Cyprus before turning their gaze back to the Shade. Dalien, the father of Dorme was among the Loyalist forces, and had pledged to hunt his only son down and rid the human race of him. The father of the Kiriaths, Meghanus, had nearly been killed not two months before in the press against the walls at Ajtelon. His own cousin had been leading the emperor's army and had thrown a spear at him; it went through his thigh. He now had a notorious limp. By that day and year, family ties in powerful Atlantean families no longer ran nearly as strong as they had at the beginning of the war.

The Shade's plan was cunning and intriguing. Being immortal creatures in the Earth Realm, the Shades had a methodology by which they could bestow a lasting state of existence upon a human being; they could stop one from aging. They called it an enhancement but Cyprus saw what it truly was: an abuse of life. Still, he admitted, you cannot argue if something works. *In some ways and fashions, the manipulation of this continuous state of existence could be used to keep one from being hurt by weapons. Not only would he become immortal, but also fairly invincible. Not purely invincible, there was a limit to what one could withstand, but it was still intriguing. Invincibility, even partial, was incredibly alluring to men and women in an ongoing war facing death sentences regardless of the war's outcome.*

Memphis went on about this for quite some time before he stopped and indicated the pitcher on the table around which they all sat. There were twenty-five people seated, and twenty-five small glass vials around it. In each of the small vials could be seen the luminous green venom of which the Shade had spoken. That is proof, wagered Cyprus silently, that this proposal of the Shades is surely unnatural. A venom…that bestowed life? Or rather, that prolonged life. First one man and then another took the vial, looked at it closely, and then downed the toxic elixir of poison.

The Shade Memphis was not watching as they took it, but instead he had locked eyes on Cyprus as the Atlantean sat there watching the others. The two stared at each other for quite some time, expressionless. Cyprus looked long at the vial that was his to take by choice, telling himself he was weighing consequences even though in his heart that he had already made his decision. Even while the proposal was still being expounded, he had chosen. He did not hesitate to get up and reach for the vial, even when the first of the drinkers nearby coughed and convulsed onto the ground in writhing seizures. Memphis stared at Cyprus coldly, not without a look of amusement as the last Atlantean took in the suffering of the previous drinkers one by one, and then swallowed his own ration of venom with a gulp before smashing the glass vial on the stone at his feet.

୨୦ ଓଌ

Attica struggled as she lay on her back, the muscular forearm across her throat, keeping her pressed down. Tears streamed into her vision and she could hear laughter and things breaking. Her air intake was so limited she couldn't even scream. Her body was in hell. There was a sharp sting in her cheek as someone slapped her hard.

She choked with the pressure of it and came to herself sputtering, the weight gone. She sat bolt upright in the bed, the sheet half on the floor, the rest of it tangled amidst her legs. Sweat tickled her back while one shaking hand clenched a pillow with an iron grip. She looked down at the knife clasped in her other hand, a weapon she always hid nightly under her pillow. *Dreaming again. You're going to stab yourself one of these nights.*

A growing frustration seized her, and the knife went clattering across the floor. She brought her knees up and rested her elbows on them as her hands smoothed the long, damp hair out of her eyes. Her breathing was hard, as if she'd had a horrible fright. Now, the tell-tale signs of fear abruptly gave way to vicious anger. She had never truly mastered these foreign but genuine memories. Visions of knights hurting her erupted periodically, unlooked for, particularly when she'd been stressed – and stress came with her acting on her own designs. She knew what stress did, but sitting back and resigning to whatever might come was not in Attica's nature. The more she pursued her own ends, the more stress occurred. And the more stress, the more the fitfully horrific memories haunted her sleep. It was like she willingly chose to be reminded of something terrible, just so she could accomplish her own desires.

But nightmares were a side-effect of allowing the Shades to reproduce her life-cycle, along with their tweaks. Well, not all nightmares. These *memories* of her own death were revisited upon Attica randomly and unbidden throughout her new span of years. The details of it all still escaped her. She did not know *exactly* where, when, who or what had *precisely* gone on, but the clarity of what she did know left little to the imagination. Hundreds of years ago in her first life, she'd been assaulted, defiled, and murdered. And then she had met the Shade in that Different Place.

It is not important what I was, she told herself yet again, *it is only important what I am now. And what I will be.* She grimly calmed herself and at length lay back down. *And besides, those men are all dead now.*

Her subconscious flashed disturbing details at her when she closed her eyes. For a second night in a row, she forced her lids open and stared at the ceiling. Only last night she'd awoken nearly choking on feathers from the shredded pillow. Her original death was always there with Attica, shadowing her like a monstrous vulture. She put one arm behind her head, the other resting on her stomach while fingers drummed restlessly on the sheet. And they wondered why she could be so irritable in the morning.

It was not difficult to determine what had stressed her this time, resulting in another of these accursed nocturnal interruptions. She had met her former husband. He'd stood there right in front of her and surprised her; and she'd promptly punched him in the face. Attica had known she was married in her former life. In lost recollections at odd times, at best she could recall a form, but never a face or voice. No pleasant memory ever came easily; clarity was reserved solely for the agonizing. *And where was this husband of mine while all this went on?* Not home, obviously, wherever home had been.

Orion Keldir himself was not new to Attica. His own organization had sprung from the Order of the Raven almost immediately before her sudden and abrupt rise to power with Cyprus. Now rival powers, the Raven and Lumine had been at war since the latter's birth. Orion was a founder and chief operator within the bounds of Dominos de Lumine; of course Attica as Triassa had heard of and familiarized herself with him. As head of the Raven, not doing so would have been irresponsible and foolish. He was an infuriatingly sagacious and formidable enemy. An original Gatekeeper, no less.

And one of a handful of remaining true immortals in the world. Not merely a cheater of death, like Cyprus and other ilk. A true immortal. *And I need an immortal's lifeblood to permanently close the Seal of the Portal Gate.*

But her actual former husband? Attica knew that her original husband once existed long ago, but had also thought him dead for centuries. As a result, whenever her mind wandered on the mysterious topic, Attica had simply dismissed what they had meant to each other. She didn't love him, she didn't hate him. She didn't know him. He was dead and even she herself was now someone else. She had no idea whom he had been – or whom she herself had been either. What had it mattered?

The irony was that now of course, it did matter, since he was not dead but very much alive. *I've considered him dead all these years, and he has thought the same of me. And now he is off somewhere trying to prove to himself that it is now really me again. His face changed greatly when he saw me. What was the nature of our last meeting, before I died? And what was I like then? I was married to an original Gatekeeper. How did that come about?*

While these questions were real, in the end they changed nothing of Attica's plans. She lived in the here and now, and while she had fleeting curiosity regarding a past life with someone she could not remember, that said life was dead. Literally. *What I am now. What I will be. This is what matters.*

Attica was fully confident that Orion would return to Raven's Roost, and once he did she would enact the last stage of the plan she had concocted and plotted for multiple standard lifetimes. It had taken many years to acquire the Atlantean gem and its silver clasp. The green bauble hung around her neck even now, never leaving her person, not in sleep or even the shower. At all times Attica wore it. It was, after all, protection; better than any money could buy. The ability to keep Shades at a distance was not one to be taken lightly.

Her drumming fingers became a fist, and she turned on her side. Shades. That was *one* thing she was not going to dwell on, especially not alone in her room at night. The thought of caution made her suddenly wonder at her own mortality. In truth, Attica could not be confident as to how old she actually was. She had conscious memory back to the thirteenth century, when she had been 'reinstated' by Shades after her initial death. But she could not recall the specifics of her life together with Orion, or how long it had lasted. A decade? A century? A millennium?

One would assume, she mused as she lay there, *that all this time in the world would have helped me reach a reasonably composed state of being.* It was a long-standing desire to be master of herself by now, to have some sort of command of her own destiny. She was master of many things; why not her own fate? Most of her subordinates would not have doubted she already ruled her own path with an iron will.

How untrue that was, even after all this time. Attica was annoyed to admit to herself that even after her long life, her trials and her triumphs: she was still human. *Still vulnerable. Still weak.* Her representation to the world, to the Order of the Raven, was of a strong and independent woman, fierce and determined, confident in her power, woeful to any who might cross her. And this was indeed who she was. A strong and worthy leader of men, exceedingly capable, having wisdom surpassed by few.

And yet it was not. It was part of her, but it was also a plain and simple façade. When the Shades had returned Attica to her waking mortal life, she had been given everything she could use but little she would need. She had unspeakable riches; but she had little desire for material things. She was at the head of a powerful organization and thousands hearkened to her every wish; but she had no friends. Her most trusted associates were nothing better than fair-weather friends at best. Even Cyprus would betray her if he decided it would profit him. *He plots against me even now. How naïve does he think I am not to see it?*

She could buy whatever or whomever she wanted, afford to do virtually anything with anyone; but she found no pleasure in anything for its own sake. And after the passage of long years, she had lost her desire for this sort of thing; riches, friends. Power was a different matter. Attica was obsessively driven to free her life from the influence of Shades, and would pour her limitless resources toward that sole purpose – even when it was they who had given her domain over all these things. She feared in her heart that when she was at last free it would be only to find that her craftiness and cleverness had merely gained her enemies over the long years it had endured.

She laid there, long hair spilled across the pillow, hands folded behind her head, staring up at the ceiling. A single tear trickled down her cheek out of the anguish in her mind and the emotions of earlier in the day. Of all the thoughts that went through her mind that night, none of them marveled at why she could not sleep.

� ෪

Adrienne was sleepy enough to move her hands to pull the blanket up higher, but all they found was her husband's forearm wrapped around her. The effort and momentary confusion caused her to open her eyes, and she was disappointed to find they were still in the cell. She leaned against Frank laterally across the bench while he sat normally, so she couldn't actually see him. Given his movement and breathing pattern, he was asleep.

She sighed. Sleep was nearly impossible and non-refreshing in the cell. The bench was the only thing upon which to sit, and it was too small for even one person to lie comfortably. Her knees were bent and her feet still barely managed to stay on the end. Her husband was on the edge to make room for her position. And neither would sleep on the floor itself. Even now in the corner she could hear what had to be the rat, whom she had christened 'Cyprus'.

"If you can't sleep," came Frank's voice, apparently not asleep after all, "I have a rude suggestion."

"What?"

"Give me the room to try."

Adrienne did not want to stand, but her husband had had a difficult time the last two days. Well, she had too, but she had been *driven* to their present location. He had hiked there and been shot at before he could arrive.

"I suppose…switch."

Adrienne immediately had an appreciation for the position he had been putting up with for the last two hours. She sat on the extreme end of the bench, more off than on. His head was in her lap, arms folded, legs bent double to avoid uncomfortable dangling.

"You looked much more comfortable than this…" he said.

Even this was almost too playful for Adrienne's mood in that moment and place. "Frank, we're in a bad spot. Can't you just-"

"Wait…" he interrupted. His tone made her stop short.

"What is it?" she asked quieter.

"I thought I heard someone coming."

They listened for a bit and both could eventually hear the gradual echo of footsteps. Voices approached, neither taking care that anyone – at least anyone down here in the dungeon – might hear.

"But think of it, uncle," said the first, and Adrienne identified Cyprus's superior tone, "a new world for both of us. She has spurned you long enough; you and I are family. Am I not better than my word?"

The voice that cut him off was quiet but unwavering, the very air of confidence itself. *Orion's come back, at least*, Frank thought. *I hope he found something worthwhile.*

"It amuses me, my dear nephew," Orion said, the term of affection a formal nothing, "how readily betrayal presents itself as an option in your mind. You and I have been enemies for ages now. But as you say we are family, so as your last remaining kin perhaps you ought to listen to me: be true to something in your life. Gaining the ascendancy of the Raven will gain you everything at the same time as it brings you nothing."

"The measure of power is what you do with it," said Cyprus, undeterred. "I will make peace with Dominos de Lumine. You shall see! If you would but help me remove her-"

"The road to Peace is paved with the blood of those who got in her way," Orion quoted an old proverb, referring to a personified Peace and not Attica.

"You and your poets! If you will not assist me in this noble task, Orion, you have changed much."

"I wish I could say you have. Abandon this quest, nephew. You are the last of my kin; do not persist in giving me reason to remove you from the world."

It was now plain to Frank and Adrienne that the two men were at the very door of their closed cell, standing and talking and no longer walking.

Cyprus's voice took on a little more agitation. "You have sealed your fate coming here and yet you refuse the only way out that would have given you a benefit. Your foolery increases with your age."

"And yours knows no bounds. Now, is there a purpose why we are walking further down into this dark, or did you bring me here only to weary my ears?"

"She has the Kedassaic Texts, uncle. They tell her everything she needs to do to seal the Portal Gate – and you bring the required immortal lifeblood. She wants you back here at Raven's Roost for what runs in your veins, not your company. Can you really not see it? Finding her again will be your end."

"Have you truly lived so long that you do not gladly anticipate an End, my nephew?"

There was a short pause, as if Cyprus was pondering the concept. "My time has only begun."

"Your time," said Orion dryly, "might be better spent studying the Texts for any reference to the Kyrian Shore. You will be there before long, doubt it not – if you do not instead go somewhere…warmer. Why, you might be there in…in the blink of an eye."

While neither of the Blackmans understood the Atlantean afterlife reference to the Kyrian Shore, Cyprus plainly did, and he grew irate. Or perhaps it vexed him that his incessant blinking had been noticed.

"I will recite a psalm at your funeral," he snapped. "Think on my proposal. It is your only hope."

There was such a pause that Frank stood up in the cell and took a step or two toward the door. There was no sound outside for the longest time. At length Orion spoke.

"Everything you have said dictates you are a man who cannot possibly be acquainted with hope."

The cell door's lock snapped in the keyhole and the door was pushed open. Frank and Adrienne watched Orion walk in while Cyprus held the door. Orion looked no worse for wear, though his hair was disheveled and he was in need of a shave. Sleep would not have hurt him, surely. His expression was of mild annoyance, doubtless due to the conversation in which he'd been participating.

"My offer remains on the table at the moment," said Cyprus, and closed the door. "Better to betray something and live than stay loyal and die, uncle."

His departing footsteps echoed in the passage. Soon they were gone.

"What really irks me," said Orion to the Blackmans without looking at them "is that he seemed to know I would not require extra security in the escort, as I am resolved to remain throughout this little happenstance." He glanced at his companions, as if just remembering he was not alone. "Have we wakened you?" The tone suggested he neither thought it was so, nor would have cared if it was.

"Yes, I was out like a baby," quipped Adrienne.

"Don't tell me you got caught again?" asked Frank.

Orion actually half-smiled as if the notion were humorous. "No," said he, "I have been verifying Attica being alive and here, and finding it to be true, I have returned to see what she wants; hence Cyprus can walk me alone and unbound to my prison cell."

"But…how is that possible that she is still alive?"

"Not 'still alive', but 'alive once again'. The Shades apparently have a way of catching spirits on their way to Eternity. She has been intercepted, changed, and returned to the living world – all for some grim purpose."

"Before I forget, what is the Kyrian Shore?" asked Adrienne.

Orion cleared a place for himself on the floor and slid down the wall slowly, folding his arms. "I will pursue our purpose here with Attica tomorrow, if given the chance."

"And the Kyrian Shore?" asked Frank.

"The Kyrian Shore refers to the Atlantean afterlife; you would say 'Heaven', although it is of course not a direct comparison. Suffice it to say it is a pleasant place where the 'good' dead go to suffer no more. But it is probably a useless gesture to invite Cyprus to read those Texts…"

"Oh?" asked Adrienne.

"I think his Kedassaic is rusty."

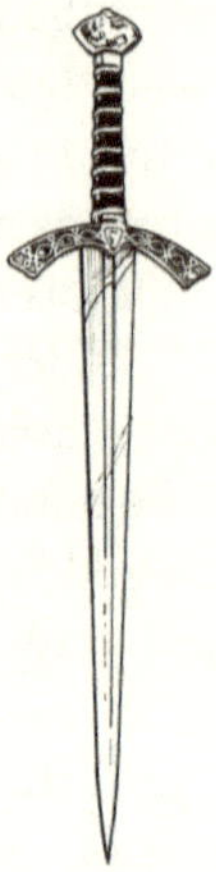

CHAPTER 15

"The Great Intrigue is all we have pursued since the Cataclysm sent that mighty civilization beneath the waves. Its fulfillment is all we have sought since that glorious day. It is all that matters."

~Memphis Shadowcloak

ᘐᘓ

At the end of her third forced march through the castle, Adrienne ended in the same room where she had first had met Attica. On the long table, Adrienne saw breakfast foods: some fruit, biscuits, plates set with sausage and bacon, and a bowl of hardboiled eggs. Orange juice was on hand. In a chair at the end of the table sat Attica, peeling an egg.

Among the most powerful women in the world, thought Adrienne, *and she peels her own egg.*

Adrienne sat, eyes on the food but afraid to eat. She had not consumed anything since the previous morning. But while the food distracted her, Adrienne looked only at Attica, marveling. Having worked in the fashion business, she had seen her share of beautiful faces and figures. Yet all those models of passed years paled next to Attica. Adrienne wondered if she had a mind to match, though everything she had seen and heard about this woman would confirm that.

At length Attica glanced her way. Hers was the voice of a gracious hostess, and Adrienne was almost offended at the tone, as if it suggested they had no history, however brief.

"Are you not hungry?" she asked.

"It crossed my mind."

Attica made a freeing gesture toward the food.

Adrienne was too hungry and too smart to pass up an offered meal. She had no idea when the next one would come along, and she thought it best to consume before Attica could change her mind. She took a banana and ate it in seconds, moving on to a warm biscuit which she lathered with butter and jam.

The two women ate in relative silence for a moment. Attica had not eaten multiple meals with another person in such a fashion for a very long span. Adrienne did not trust her counterpart enough to venture conversation, though she wondered at her own presence there. This uncomfortable silence, at least for Adrienne, went on for several minutes before the captive guest decided to chance a question or two. Frank could only tell her so much detail, and Orion was a very poor conversationalist: neither of them would or could tell her all of what she wanted to know about some things.

"Lady Triassa," she began, sounding as respectful as she could, "would you mind telling me about Shades?"

Attica merely glanced at her and continued using a knife to remove the rind of a fruit that Adrienne had not seen before. Adrienne continued at once.

"I know I haven't the right to ask, but perhaps you could indulge me…as an undeserved kindness…"

You laid it on too thick, girl, she thought. But Attica still did not respond, though she looked as if she were deep in contemplation, not just ignoring.

"I am afraid of them," admitted Adrienne, as if this were a secret. "Are you afraid of them too?"

At length, Attica spoke, asking a question. It surprised Adrienne.

"How well-versed are you in ancient history, Lady Blackman?"

Adrienne was reluctant, for Attica had a look in her eye. *Everything this woman asks feels like a trick question.* "I guess I know a little, I suppose." She had a small passion for certain aspects of the ancient world – she had visited Greece in her college years – but nothing she would admit to Attica. *A trick question that would end with some needless cruelty.*

"Do you know anything about Atlantis?"

A trick indeed. Adrienne hesitated, but then realized there was no point in playing such mental games with herself. Attica could do whatever she wanted, regardless of whether or not any mental fencing occurred.

"Not much," she acknowledged. "A city that was lost to the sea in some catastrophe. I think I read it was a legend originated by Plato, for the purpose of teaching allegory. Or Socrates, I don't recall which."

Attica gave her captive a knowing glance, and moved to put honey on a biscuit. "So nothing, then."

Not all of us waste our time learning useless history. Some of us still have to work for a living. She wisely wound up just holding her tongue. Being an insurance underwriter wasn't that glamorous anyway, and with law changes it was a dying career. Sarcasm was not so satisfying when the person one sassed could have one killed. Instead of responding, she ate.

"It is the first great civilization of Men," said Attica. "The Beginning. Orion could assuredly tell you more than I." For a moment she stopped, and Adrienne thought she looked perturbed, but the moment soon passed and she went on. "It was ages ago when Atlantis was lost beneath what is now the eastern Atlantic, not at all far from Spain, Portugal, and North Africa. Theorists who actually believe it once existed will blame what they assume to be either an earthquake or a volcano, but in the end it was more complicated than that."

Adrienne had to ask. "What was it?"

Attica leaned closer despite their being alone. "It was the Shades..." and she looked down at her plate, slashing the biscuit in two with a vicious stroke. She spoke again as if to herself, "...curse them all to the Abyss..."

If Adrienne had heard any of this not a week before, she would have laughed. But sitting there with Attica, having seen the shadows in her own yard and having met the people she had, she only sat and listened. *The most infuriating thing about this all is that I can never tell when any of these people are telling the truth or speaking figuratively.* Yet Attica went on, and she had left the metaphorical behind.

"The Atlanteans were an amazing people in their own right: the first to do anything that was worth doing. They had no competition in anything: war, finance, trade, religion, magic..." She glanced up at Adrienne again, as if to make sure she was paying attention. "That was their downfall, the magic. You have heard it said that with great power comes great responsibility. But this useless responsibility of the powerful is only desired by those who do not have the power in the first place. Absolute power is still the sweetest fruit of all. Great power leads to unlimited possibilities, and new frontiers, new gains, new species and new meetings. So it was with the Shades.

"The Atlantean priests and priestesses found the Shades in their own dimension ages ago, just by random accident, really. Just another realm of spirits the fools thought they could learn from. Yet the black shadows, unlike the previous others, were not just the random conjuring of sleep-deprived visions or hallucinogenic drugs. These phantoms were of their own dimension, their own empire, a mirror of the Atlanteans, really, only in their own realm. That realm they had filled to capacity; there was nothing left there to master. These shadows, these Shades as they came to be called, were far wiser and more learned than the greatest of the priests. Their civilization was far older.

"Over time, a relationship grew across the void between dimensions. The Atlanteans learned a great many things from the Shades, things that are now lost. They took it to be clean knowledge, so they used it and grew with it. Eventually, by the newly-learned techniques and skills they built a Portal, a gateway between the dimensions."

Adrienne was starting to shake her head, not in disbelief, but more in confirmation that like Attica she considered this a remarkably foolish thing to do. Having seen Shades for herself, it defied Adrienne's logic that someone would welcome their arrival and build a gateway for them to come. *Unintelligible.* Attica only looked at her with a glint in her eye, seeing the agreement.

"What better way to learn, Lady Blackman, than invite your teachers over to your home? There were no Shades on this planet or even in this Existence before the Atlanteans opened the way. The Shades themselves had tried to open the way here many times, but they needed a niche on this side. The priests gave them this niche, and while still limited in number, they came.

"There was just one at first. His name – its name – was Memphis Shadowcloak, a young diplomat of sorts. That was an age ago, when he came. Yet even today in the twenty-first century, he still walks our Existence disguised as a tall, wizened old man. Even disguised, there is something about him that people do not seem to like."

Adrienne involuntarily shivered. She did indeed remember Memphis, the tall man that she had been convinced was more of a shell than a real person. Recalling the genuine creepiness she had felt, this new revelation that he was a Shade explained a lot. Attica was not looking at her, and missed the expression of repressed terror at the memory.

"It was years before the Shades were integrated into the Atlantean society: at first they were the strange shadowy spirits only the priests and priestesses spoke to. Yet as the years went by, it appeared to the hierarchy that further wisdom could be attained from these creatures. They were seldom wrong in their counsel, and eventually they were allowed to be advisors to those of high rank. In time, even the Emperor of Atlantis had a Shade or two for counsel.

"Then came the war. The Shades had been hostile all along, to every race of mankind. Atlantis and her civilization were the greatest on the face of the earth! What if Atlantis fell?" She leaned forward, almost intrigued by her own storytelling. "The warped council of the Shades confused the Emperor, divided his court, his army, his personal guard. All of mankind would fall if their greatest civilization was destroyed first. Beyond Atlantis, other people lived in caves and dirt huts. How would they resist?

"Nearly every great country has had a civil war – even if they refuse to call it such. When the Shades killed the Emperor's son, factions broke out: the Loyalists against the rebel Separatists. Upon the outbreak it was immediately seen that the Shades had been bellicose since the beginning. And so, by their advanced arts the Atlantean craftsmen made up this…"

Here, Attica reached down and took hold of the necklace she was wearing, formerly Adrienne's. Adrienne could see the green gem dangling between the other woman's fingers. She remembered with new wonder what Attica had told her about the former ownership and magical qualities of the stone. Adrienne realized with renewed interest that Attica had only told her about the most recent ownership; not the archaic.

Attica noticed the recognition in her captive's eyes. "It was originally forged to keep Shades away, not unlike that idiotic myth about garlic keeping vampires away. At the time of the forging, it was powerful enough to hold most Shades at a distance. It was given to the remaining child of the Emperor, a daughter. Now, it is still powerful, but more so when one understands its use and purpose.

"This shiny green rock that once belonged to an Emperor's daughter, and then even to you, has kept you…not 'safe'…but 'safer' from Shades than you may have been." She stood up and began to slowly pace, as she was accustomed to do when she spoke for a long time all at once. "But that is not important now. What is important is that I have it."

"Why do *you* need it?" asked Adrienne, slightly intrigued.

"To keep away Shades, of course," said Attica matter-of-factly, as if it were a foolish question. A surge of anger flashed across her beautiful features, as if Adrienne had not been paying attention to her. She never could abide people that did not listen to her when she spoke.

"No, I understand that," said Adrienne apologetically with a swallow. "I mean, why should you care if Shades are around? I thought they were after me? After Frank?"

Attica laughed aloud, and a most spiteful, deep laugh it was. "After you? To what gain? They care only for the powerful, not common, insignificant people like you."

"Then why did they come to my house?" asked Adrienne, but then received an immediate chill: Attica's face assured her she'd said something frightfully wrong. Yet this had been the question behind her initial start of the conversation: no one in Dominos de Lumine had been able to tell her why Shades had come to their address. *I'd just like to find out what started this whole thing.*

Attica had stopped mid-word with her mouth still open and turned to Adrienne, her beautiful eyes ablaze with a shocked interest. She spoke slowly, clearly. "What did you just say?"

Adrienne was afraid to repeat it, but dared not alter what she said. Attica did not look as if she were in a forgiving mood. "The Shades…came to my house."

"Cyprus took you from the headquarters of Dominos de Lumine," said Attica.

"Yes, he did. After we came there from my house, which we left after the Shades came there."

Adrienne stopped short. *My word, she's afraid.* She had never expected to see how Attica appeared if afraid, but she realized this current state was quite possibly one of the only times she would witness it. Attica's beauty was already of a most light complexion, but she had quite suddenly turned rather pale. Yet her eyes kept their glaring intensity, though they left Adrienne and stared at nothing as she turned and walked a few paces. Her lips were pursed together and her hands had come together in front of her to tap her fingertips against each other as she walked slowly back to her chair. Yet there was never an instant that Adrienne saw any cowardice or a loss of control. Even obviously terribly shaken, Attica was still in command of herself and her facilities.

She sat only a moment but then called the guards, who came over at once from outside the doors. She gave them swift instruction, no longer behaving as if Adrienne were even in the room. "Take my Lady Blackman back to her quarters, and call a meeting, lieutenants only. Immediately!"

If Adrienne had the courage to ask what she had said wrong, she was not given the opportunity. To keep herself from being dragged, she stood and walked out with the men, offering no resistance on the way back to the cell. She never could get used to being led somewhere forcibly.

Behind them, Attica had returned to her seat, trying to finish peeling the hardboiled egg. She stopped in retrospect and stared at her left hand: it was trembling ever so slightly. She balled it into a fist and smashed it with resilience on the table. Then she got up and left the room, headed for her quarters.

⁂ ⁃

Cyprus locked the door with a snap and whirled toward the bathroom mirror. His black mood stared back at him with derision as he ran the hot water. His previous conversation with Orion outside the dungeon cell had been turning over in his mind ever since. Orion had always had gall. And his uncle had always stood in the way. He and his accursed Lords of Light.

If he will not join me, I will take the future into my own hands. His pride brings this on himself.

The mirror fogged and Cyprus focused. In a moment, once again his communicative thought wrote itself in the mist across the reflective glass.

I HAVE DECIDED UPON MY FAVOR.

As it always did, the response of Memphis was almost immediate in answer.

At last. Well?

Cyprus took a long breath and hardened himself. It was, after all, for the best. His best interest. A strong will assisted the longest thought-correspondence he had ever managed. It flowed from him, fueled by hate.

WHEN THE LAST GATEKEEPER IS SLAIN, WHAT HE LOVES MOST IN THIS WORLD MUST DIE WITH HIM. THAT IS MY FAVOR. THAT IS MY PRICE.

The following pause was longer than usual. Somewhere far away, Memphis was surely musing through his own dark thoughts, pondering what this request would mean.

You are certain this is your desire?

YES. IT IS.

What you ask is difficult but not impossible. It shall be done, though it may take time. Prepare yourself.

Cyprus turned off the water and smiled up at the mirror, swiping a cloth across it. A feeling of immense satisfaction swept over him. That he had wished such a thing upon his only remaining family troubled him not at all. Orion would be dead. What would it matter to Orion if what he loved most would perish also once he was gone? In Cyprus's calculation, Orion would be dead very soon. And that death would be a catalyst for Cyprus's own rise to power. He would be the true Lord of the Order of the Raven. Attica would kneel at his feet, would please him in any way he saw fit.

And now, his favor secured, Cyprus knew that the only other barrier to his assumed power would now be removed. Dominos de Lumine had been the only thing in the way of the Raven for years. Orion had created it, had put his life into it. He had bled for it on many occasions. His supreme love for his organization could not be denied. The fate of that organization was now sealed. Cyprus's black mood lifted, the anger that had spurred his request dissipating. Elation curved the corners of his mouth upward.

"Good-bye, my dear Lords of Light," he said aloud in his bathroom. "You've put up a noble struggle, but in the end, the best man has won."

୫୦ ୨୫

"You must stop asking," said Orion as he sat against the wall in the cell, "because I do not know."

Frank was lying on the bench after half-heartedly offering it to Orion, who refused. Orion had never been one for creature-comforts, even a bench in a barren cell.

"But the Shades must surely have some purpose for her, if what you saw is correct," persisted Frank.

"It is correct. Some things cannot be faked. Of course they have a purpose. We will not know till later. I must spend some time with Attica, and see what the Shades have been doing."

Frank looked up. "No offense, my friend, but I don't think she'll be spending much time with you anytime soon."

Orion spoke with a quiet confidence. "She will speak to me if she wishes me to fulfill whatever purpose she intends. We were married for over a thousand years. She'll talk to me."

"Speaking of over a thousand years, I wonder what's taking Adrienne. I hope they're feeding her. I don't mind not getting food. I know you don't mind it. But it's my fault she's into this. If she's abused or mistreated, I'll never forgive myself…"

"I do not perceive it is as much your fault as you believe," said Orion. "In a way, I find that most of it is my fault."

"Oh?"

"You heard Attica. She wants me, not either of you. She used you to get to me." He leaned his head back against the wall. "And now she has all three of us."

"Still…"

Orion's head bent to the side. "I hear footsteps."

In a moment his hearing was confirmed, for the door opened and Adrienne stepped primly into the cell before the hand on her shoulder could shove her in. She staggered but caught herself as the door slammed shut. Neither man in the cell made any effort to get out the door while it was open, though her husband stood and put his arms around her, welcoming her back.

She abruptly turned to Orion. "You're from Atlantis?"

He looked mildly amused. "Born and raised, my lady."

"But that's incredible! Why didn't you say anything?"

"It's not the successful anecdote you'd think it would be."

Frank, in need of a break in hour after hour of tension, laughed aloud. "Now *there's* a pick-up line."

Orion gave him a look that suggested he too would have chuckled if he was the sort.

But there the mirth ended. "Were you fed? What happened anyway?"

"Attica is a…very interesting woman," she said in answer to Frank's probing as to her absence. "You should have heard what we were talking about."

Orion stood up, his gaze intentional. "I'm listening."

To the best of her memory, Adrienne tried to recall everything Attica had said about Atlantis, the gems and the Shades. "I've not done it justice," she finished, but Orion plainly followed her history of Atlantis very well.

"The civil war," he said, reflectively. "I have not thought of it for some time. Long ago, and futile, like many wars. But while it destroyed Atlantis in the end, it was actually very beneficial."

"How so?" asked Frank.

"The Shades were intending to use the Portal for what it was designed to be: a doorway. But not just a door: a gate for an invasion force. They plotted to take over this entire dimension: it is their nature, and how they have operated for millennia. But the destruction of Atlantis resulted from the trials of the war. The Portal was sealed shut by the Gatekeepers, locking the Shades' dimension out, and trapping here the Shades that were already on this side. Any Shade you encounter here in this world was here from the beginning: they cannot go back and forth. The way is shut."

"She failed to mention that," said Adrienne.

"She undoubtedly would have if given the time. But it is a long tale. What else did she say?"

There was not much else to recall, but then Adrienne related how she had questioningly noted that the Shades had been to the Blackman home. She put into detail as closely as she could manage, exactly how Attica had responded to this piece of information.

"She was afraid, I thought," Adrienne ended. She looked at Frank. "Did I make a mistake telling her the Shades were at our house?"

Frank shook his head. "I don't know how. I wouldn't have known that would be a big deal." He looked at Orion. "Do you know what her problem was?"

Orion had stood there listening to Adrienne's account with great patience and kindness, but at the reference to Attica's concern over the 'house-call' he grew most serious. He paced for a moment after the question.

"Yes, I do know," he acknowledged when Frank repeated himself. He spoke no further and Adrienne rolled her eyes at having to ask for the revelation.

"Could you pass a little this way?" she asked.

"Attica has acquired the gemstone. She has done this to keep the Shades at a distance. But she has learned that the Shades came to your home. They were not looking for you, as I thought at the time. Plainly, they were looking for your gem."

There was a pause, as if Orion considered this his complete thought.

"You follow?" Adrienne asked Frank.

"I have to admit, I don't," said her husband with a shrug.

"Attica has been tied in with the Shades since she was returned to the Earth Realm, since her death," Orion continued. "Her acquiring of the gemstone can only mean one thing: she means to betray them."

"And their looking for the gem at our house throws her because..."

"The Shades were not seeking the stone for themselves: they were trying to beat Attica to it – and they nearly did. She is afraid because of what this means."

"But it repels them, how could they take it into possession?" interjected Frank.

"Recall they did not send one; they sent many. Teamed up, I believe a large number of Shades converged together would enable them to at least move it, which is all they would have to do. But to the matter at hand, Attica recognized this as the problem it is."

"What, because she almost didn't get it?" asked Adrienne.

"No. If they're trying to keep her from getting it, they know she is trying to get it in the first place: they somehow know she intends to betray them." He smiled grimly. "They're not supposed to know."

"So she is afraid they'll act on this knowledge," conceded Adrienne.

Orion nodded. "They have already acted upon it."

"This isn't good," said Frank. "Attica trying to throw the Shades for a loop? She's trying to outsmart the oldest creatures on Earth. And she's suddenly found she doesn't have the upper hand she thought she had."

Orion sat down on the bench, as neither Frank nor Adrienne was using it.

"This is wonderful," he said quietly, arms folded and legs crossed. A mere glance at his face told the Blackmans he was not being sarcastic.

"How can you say that?" asked Adrienne. "Your wife-"

The quiet gaze in which Orion enveloped her caused her to pause.

"-that woman," she continued, "is going to be in one heck of a spot. And by the way, we're probably going to be somewhere close by when it all goes wrong-"

"Oh, I sincerely hope so..." interrupted Orion.

"She's right," said Frank. "How is this wonderful?"

"She is aware that the Shades know of her treachery, and as a result will doubtless move her plans forward at once; immediately. The hard work I thought it would be to get to the bottom of all this will very quickly become unnecessary. If she is now in the hurry that I imagine she will be...she'll tell me everything I wish to know without even asking her to."

઼ ⍵

Frank was asleep and Adrienne was bored out of her mind. She had been taken from the cell for breakfast; by now it had to be about lunchtime. Adrienne had found in the years she had been married to Frank that sleeping was one of the ways he tried to ignore that he was hungry. She silently cursed herself for not trying to grab both of her cellmates some food from Attica's lavish table, but her hostess's sudden change in mood at the end of their discussion had so shaken her that it completely slipped her mind.

And so Frank slept on the bench while Adrienne finally tired of pacing and, not wanting to disturb her husband for a place to sit, found a remotely clean spot on the floor and sat against the wall. She found herself watching Orion, only because she had nothing else to look at. He sat across from her, elbows on raised knees, head tilted back against the stone blocks behind him, eyes closed. But he wasn't asleep. Each time she thought he was, he moved. *Perhaps he is meditating.*

She decided to ask him what she had wanted to ask Attica, but had not the courage. She did not necessarily believe Orion would give a good deal of detail, but she was not afraid to ask him. "How did you meet Attica?"

The eyes opened and stared ahead for a moment before redirecting their focus on the dark-haired woman across from him. He waited so long before answering her that she had given up on getting a response. Just as she was about to close her eyes to the one available activity of sleep, he spoke.

"We met in what is now Turkey," he said simply.

Adrienne was momentarily pleased that he had answered, but when he made no further sign that he intended to go on, she suddenly didn't care if she had to drag it out of him. "And?" she asked.

"The details would be merely tiresome for you."

Adrienne looked around the room, wondering if an immortal could suffer tedium or boredom like the rest of mankind. "Try me."

CHAPTER 16

"Spare no one, before the gods change their fickle minds."

~Agamemnon of Mycenae, 1184 BC

༄ ༅

OUTSKIRTS OF TROY, NEAR THE AEGEAN COAST OF ASIA MINOR. 1184 BC.

The traveler who many had taken to calling the Deathless Blade looked down from the hilltop and gazed at the city. Troy was a magnanimous and lordly city, home of great men since its inception of old. The traveler had met both Priam and Hector in years past, before the idiocy and immorality of Paris brought the Greeks to their shores. But the war was now in its greatest rage, the city in its death throes. It was now early morning; the night before, a hollow wooden horse had been opened in the main square. Now the gates had been opened, the Greek army pouring in. Slaughter, fire, and battle filled the streets of Troy. The traveler could hear the sound of it even from his hilltop.

Orion could not have stated clearly as to why he had taken the fork in the road the night before. He had most recently accomplished his own purposes in Egypt, and had been traveling for months through the Negev and up into Asia Minor. Whether fate or mere fortune led him to take the left fork or no, he would have been unable to decide. The war had been going on for years of course, and virtually all ancient ears had heard of at least the rumor of it. Finding himself close by, he had wished to look on the greatest war in ten generations.

The titanic conflict was nearing its end as the city had readily fallen once the Greeks were inside, and Orion was undeterred by the danger. He left the hilltop and made his way down toward the city, knowing he could easily pass for a Greek if worse came for worse – or for a Trojan for that matter – though he wagered the latter was unneeded. He picked his way among the stony hillside and drew gradually closer to the walls.

෨ ೞ

"Atty, what are we going to do?"

The slave girls looked at each other, both knowing it was a valid question with no pleasant answer. They stood in the main bedroom of their master's house, built partly into the walls of the mighty city. The lord and lady of the house had gone out the previous evening and not returned. The other denizens of the house, slaves and family alike, had scattered in hysteria when it was revealed by runners that the city was breached and the Greeks were taking it piece by piece. The shouts and yells and cries could be heard from virtually anywhere in the city.

Attica held the short sword that she had taken from her master's chamber. Having been there many times she had seen exactly where he kept it. It didn't matter now if he returned and could not find it, and she had no qualms or fears of what awaited a slave who stole. She perceived the stint of slavery that she and her sister had endured in Troy was over – but the likelihood of a new stretch abroad somewhere, or worse, was now pending upon her dealing with the situation.

"Just stay close to me," was all that came from Attica. She wanted to say more, to comfort her sister Triassa, but her mind was too distracted. Are those Greek shouts closer than they were a second ago? she mused distractedly.

She led the way to the bedroom of the eldest son in the family and immediately began stripping the large bed. Giving the weapon to her sister with a grim, "Watch the door," she pulled the Persian silks to the floor and began binding the ends together.

"Have you lost your mind?" Triassa half-exploded, "I'm not going out the window!"

"Do you have a better idea?" asked her older, beautiful blonde-haired sister. A fine time for your fear of heights, sister dear. There was really no better option available. If she was lucky she might be able to dispatch an armored invader in the streets as they snuck out – but she had not the skill to fight their way out. She wondered if any warrior in the world had the skill. Perhaps Achilles, she randomly thought, but then set her mind to the sheets.

The drop out the window was forty feet down. Attica had seen for herself, simply from cleaning the bedroom a hundred times. The illustrious bed had much upon it, but the sheets would not reach all the way to the ground. Still, they will reach close enough. "Help me move the bed," she ordered, and together the two young women began edging the sturdy bedpost closer to the window.

A loud bang made them both look up. It was repeated twice more before the sisters looked at each other in recognition. It was not the master returning home, assuredly. There was the rattle of bronze on metal and a Greek voice shouted out its intentions to any female in the home while still other voices laughed uproariously.

"Hurry!" Triassa hissed frantically as they pulled slowly at the bed. "They'll find us!"

"Good enough," said Attica, knowing it had to be. The bed was moved as close to the window as it was going to get. She made a frenzied knot about the bedpost and threw the makeshift rope of precious silk out the window. She had planned to look out and see if anyone was down below waiting for something like this, but the approaching Greeks changed her plan of sheets out the window from strategy to necessity.

"You first," said Attica, physically grabbing her sister and moving her into position. "Just hold tight and hand your way past the knots or you'll pull the sheets apart. Now go!"

Triassa handed the short sword to her sister and took hold of the makeshift rope, one foot out the window, one dangling into the room.

"Where do you think you're going?" asked a remarkably near voice.

Both young women looked up in absolute horror as first one, and then two and finally three Greek soldiers crowded at the door. They were bearded and bloody from forays through the chaotic city streets. Two had swords while a third carried a bow, which he drew on them.

"Go, Tri, go!" Attica demanded.

Triassa leaned hard and grabbed fiercely just as Attica heard the twang of a bowstring. Her sister's cry of pain echoed unreal in her own ears. To Attica's horror, Triassa faltered in the midst of the window ledge and slumped back against the side. The cry had not lasted hardly a second.

Attica pulled Triassa's limp form close to her chest, suddenly not caring if she were caught or not. Tears blurred her vision, but to her surprise Triassa managed to say one thing before closing her eyes.

"Atty, go…"

"Grab her!" roared one of the Greeks.

Attica never gave them the chance. Still clutching the short sword, she swept out the window in a much more nimble manner than her sister had tried. It had all taken so little time the archer had almost no chance to get another arrow off. They had wanted live prisoners anyway. The one rushed for the window just as she slipped off, her fall being much faster than she intended. She tightened her grip around the sheet in slight panic and was surprised to find that when she opened her eyes, she had stopped.

The rope of sheets jerked mightily in her grip and she realized the Greeks fifteen feet above her were hauling her back up. Knowing what it would mean, she descended rather recklessly to the end of the sheets and without hesitation let go, dropping the remaining fifteen feet to the ground. She landed hard and fell down the slope, narrowly managing to keep the sword away from her body. She slid to a stop about twenty feet from the wall and immediately got up and limped a bit but then ran, wiping her eyes callously as she went. She told herself she should be trying to do something purposeful to avoid the archer who was surely aiming at her anew, but all she could do in the moment was run.

If the archer shot, Attica never noticed. She was fleet of foot and put a good bit of distance between herself and the wall before falling to the ground amidst some bushes. Before she could even ponder what to do next, she was weeping uncontrollably. Spasms of sobs racked and shook her body. A minute or two passed and she began to master herself. I will take time to mourn later, *she promised herself. She could still hear sounds of battle, cries in and out of the city. Looking around she saw no immediate danger, but she could still see all types of people running this way and that. Some were Greek, some Trojan. Many were former citizens or just slaves like herself trying to get away.*

⅚ ⅛

Rounding the corner was death for one and a sentence of death for the other. Attica's senses were on maximum, tension and a controlled fear strengthening both resolve and her will to live. She rounded the corner as she followed the perimeter wall and literally walked into the Greek auxiliaries coming the other way. She had been creeping along the wall seeking a channel to depart the city, but much of it was open and being patrolled, and she had been holding back for her final chance.

She swung blindly at the sudden realization that she and her enemies were in close proximity. Her sword was a wilder swing that caught him completely randomly at the best place it could: his neck. Blood spurted and a choking gurgle escaped that was hardly heard or noticed as the seven that were with him sprang upon her with the eagerness of lions.

Attica had gotten one lucky swing off. She would not get a second; they were too close and adept at their business to let this slave girl deplete another of their number. One got her sword away from her body with some sparring that allowed the others to take hold of her and thrust her to the ground. A knee was put in her back and a hand took her long, blonde hair like a handle and kept her face pressed to the grit of the earth.

"What have we here?" *asked one in Greek.*

"Another one! She'll do fine," *said another.*

But a third counseled, "Not here. Let's take her to the grove there. I don't want someone on the walls dropping a stone on my head in the middle of it."

Attica did not beg; it would do absolutely no good. In her experience as a slave, lust-enflamed men were deaf to a woman's cries. But she didn't allow them to simply walk her to the grove of her eventual death either. She kicked and bit, punched and scratched. She drew blood more than once, until at last they wearied of having to manhandle her and tied her hands behind her back in cruel fashion. She gave a cry as her shoulders protested against their sockets. Her legs followed suit and in no time at all she was being easily carried over one's shoulder toward a grove of trees some way distant. The entire time all she could hear besides the distant cries were the voices of her captors talking of the sack, battle, and their plans for their third and prettiest catch of the day.

୫୦ ୋଷ

Orion had been doing what he did best for a very long time; multiple lifetimes. It became clear to him that, after leaving the dominions of lost Atlantis, he would neither grow old nor die for intangibly long years. He was still as fit and young as when he left. But he was wiser now, surely, with more knowledge than any one man could have gained in but one lifetime. In a way, he had been given a gift, one of which men would occasionally dream and eternalize: to walk through history and even influence it. With the proper training, education and skill, it was not hard to find the growing of power and become a part of it. To look upon the great empires of history in their infancy and help or hurt their sway was an intoxicating concept.

But the choice was whether or not to interfere with the supposedly trivial; to interrupt an important journey to save a beggar from a street gang – when the beggar will die from starvation tomorrow? To advise the good and decent king in his imperial advance when a rising power will take his lands in less than a decade, nullifying all his accomplishments? Or save a maiden from heinous assault today when, after Orion left the city, she would run into the same brigands tomorrow only to be subjected to every disgrace?

But these are not choices at all. The right decision was plain in each situation – but the choices were simple to one who was not nearly immortal. Surely, saving the girl in the dark alley was noble. But to save her tomorrow? Next week? Next month? Because she would need rescuing at those times as well, as would a dozen just like her in the city most recently departed. It was not a hard decision to make the first time, or even the second and third. But then he had been doing it for years, decades – centuries and eventually millennia. After awhile, he had begun to question the worth of what he did, even though the justice and rightness of it was never in question.

The traveler had been about for a long time, and was still not used to having the ability to make such choices. Regardless of going one way or the other, taking one action over another, he never became used to it. In the end, he never could live with himself for turning away from one in dire need. And so Orion determined he would help the young woman before he even ascertained where the small party was going. He could see the small band of seven Greeks making their way toward his little grove, from which he had been viewing all from high up in a tree. He could see they were bringing with them a bound figure carried over the shoulder. It was not hard to anticipate where they were going and what was intended. That there were seven of them daunted him not at all. Orion had dealt with worse.

୫୦ ୋଷ

It was Attica who had the best view of the foray that was to come. She was cast to the ground hard enough for her head to spin, and one knelt beside her almost at once. From her place on the ground, she could see the man up in the tree above them, unnoticed by the Greeks. The soldier beside her tore the front of her tunic but had no time to go further before the stranger had leaped from his branch; twenty feet straight down. In his hand was a shorter sword, pointed down as he came, and with his very landing he filleted the nearest Greek down the entire length of the man's spine.

The stranger's surprise assault lasted the death of but one man before the others noticed and rounded upon him. Attica was kicked and rolled back and forth in the stamping of feet and exchange of blades. The Greeks were yelling, shouting to each other, moving like ants on a hill. The stranger never said a word. He was too fast, and whenever someone would strike at him, he avoided the weapon with the most minimal of movements. More than once a spear passed between his body and his nearby arm, and yet missed him entirely. He moves like a god, *Attica thought,* like Ares. His sword always moved with surgical precision, blocking, thrusting, slashing; never a wasted motion, never strength extended where it did not serve a grim and bloody purpose. For a good minute and a half she was fully convinced that somehow Achilles had left the city and come to her rescue personally.

One soldier went down slashed across the throat; one's arm flew in one direction while his head went another. One was seized from behind by a strong arm while the stranger's other arm dispatched two comrades and took off a spearhead with one stroke. The Greeks were decreasing in number and getting nowhere. As far as Attica could tell, not one of them had managed to pierce the armor-less newcomer.

Three left. Two. Now only one. Attica watched from the ground wide-eyed with her hands trapped beneath her, knees bent to sturdy her. The battle had gone from an absolute frenzy to now a menaced waiting. The stranger looked grim. Now that he was not moving about like a hunting bat, she could get a look at him. His skin was not unlike hers; lighter than either Greeks or Trojans. His dark hair was long and kept neatly behind him and down his back. He was also very handsome, and quite tall for that part of the world. He did not even look tired. The Greek soldier, on the other hand, wanted nothing more to do with him.

He turned and ran, but the stranger was too fast. With one agile movement he dropped the shorter sword with which he had fought so ingeniously, and then snatched up a dropped spear. The motion with which he cocked the weapon back, gauged his target, and then threw the bronze-tipped spear was practiced and refined. There was a swift movement as the powerful arm launched the weapon through the air in a nearly straight arc before there was an abrupt sound of armor failing, and a Greek cry that was cut short before it even had time to enunciate. Attica from her angle missed the exact demise, but it was plain the stranger had brought down the running man from thirty feet away with a thrown weapon. It was impressive to say the least.

He did not come to her immediately, but took a few paces toward the last fallen

Greek, as if checking to make sure his throw had been aimed well enough. A second later he was beside her.

"I would have let him go," were his first words to her – and his voice was rich and deep, with an astonishing kindness that she was most unused to – "but he may have only gone to get help, and it would be best to make your journey alone." The strange blade he used made short work of her ropes and he pulled her to her feet with one arm.

Words failed her. "Thank you, sir, I – thank you," was all she could think to say.

A short contemplation made her realize that if this fellow desired it, she was essentially his slave. She was a former slave, then a war trophy, and now likely to be a slave again. She wondered at whether or not he considered this, but she promptly decided that as he had saved her life, she should submit to him. It was a debt to be repaid if nothing else. Perhaps servitude would not be so bad this time around – she could already see he would be twice the master the former fool was. And where, as a young woman alone, did she think she was going to go? Back to Germania, from whence she and Triassa were taken as girls all those years ago, as captives of a war that had destroyed their village?

"Neither of us should stay here," said he, looking at the devastation he had caused. "Do you have somewhere to go? Perhaps that is a foolish question."

"No...no, it's not foolish," she managed, brushing herself off. Her legs refused to hold her securely upright. "I cannot say I have anywhere to go. There are allied cities to the south of here but it is a long journey. There may be bands of Trojans that have escaped who I might find and join – but that would only be going back to slavery."

"You are alone?"

Under normal circumstances she would have debated answering that, but if he had wanted to take advantage of her, she would not be now free of her bonds. Besides, after what he had just done, she suspected this man could do as he liked with no fear of anyone. Fortunately, there was a kindness in his eyes; she could tell he was a decent sort at the same time. She had no fear in telling him she was alone. And after what he did to all those men, what would it matter if I had my own retinue?

"Yes, I'm alone." She hesitated but continued. "You have saved my life, my lord; I am indebted to you." In the experience of her life in servitude, it was the time to kneel, and she did. "I am your servant. Do with me as you will."

She did not see his expression because her eyes were now on the ground. Attica actually gave a little start as the man not only approached her but also knelt down in front of her. He took her delicately by the hands and stood up, pulling her to her feet a second time. Orion looked into the beautiful young woman's blue eyes and was, to his own surprise, suddenly very pleased he had taken the right fork in the road some miles back. She didn't shy away or flinch when he reached up and carefully smoothed her long silken hair out of her face. She was so lovely – but also had the demeanor of a gentle, quiet spirit as well; if he was interested in owning a slave, there was no doubt she would be perfect.

"There are many things I could use on my journeys," he said softly, "but a slave is not one of them."

Attica's heart sank when he said this. Slavery was slavery; but being a slave was all about who one's master was: the good ones took care of you, treated you well, and might even care about you; serving them was work but not unpleasant. Some slaves were practically family. When he had looked into her eyes and stroked her hair, she had dared to dream her life would suddenly not taste quite so bitter. She hid her disappointment, or at least she tried. I was a fool to hope.

There was a pause, as if he were debating. His decision came as if fated.

"I am Orion Keldir. You may accompany me if you wish. I cannot say I know specifically where I am going from here, but you will be safe while you travel with me. I can promise you that."

"You honor me..." she said slowly, but suddenly he chuckled and she stopped. For a moment she was afraid he had been maliciously teasing her with hope of unencumbered freedom. But he was laughing at himself.

At length he said: "Forgive me. In my pride, I phrased that poorly. You can indeed accompany if you wish – but when I said it I did not speak my own thought: it is my desire that you come with me, not as my slave but as a companion of your own free consent. I cannot offer you much in immediate accommodation, but we can remedy these things as we go. It is a long time since I have shared the road with anyone. Perhaps you would honor me instead..."

Attica was too proud to admit how her heart surged with unspeakable joy at this. She wished her sister was with them. But what she managed to say in a controlled tone was, "I am Attica...Attica Triassa, and I will share your road for now."

CHAPTER 17

"The Kedassaic Texts go back almost as far as Atlantean bloodlines. As generations and the civilization grew, so did the contents of the anthology. It is a collection of our history, names, events, genealogies, poetry, proverbial wisdom and more. There were many verbatim copies, as well-to-do families would seek to have their own book.

"I have recently learned that in the civil war, the Separatists and Shades introduced their own jilted history and added it to the Kedassaic Texts as fact. Loyalists also continued recording their own accurate writings. At that time, to embellish anything and offer it to the Kedassaic canon was beyond unthinkable to the true writers. It was a sacred obligation to be accurate and legitimate.

"And so there was a growing number of contradictory copies. Problems erupted. People became confused. The rebel Separatists weren't so bad? There was a valid reason for war after all? The Loyalists had done what? Separating legitimate text from blatant lies was lost on many, and in time became very difficult indeed without first person testimony.

"I just wish I knew which version of the Kedassaic Texts survived. The truthful one? Or the one that has been manipulated for gain? Even now I go to a summit regarding this very question."

~an excerpt from the diary of Talia of Lynsaelyn, Record Keeper of the Order of the Raven, 984 BC

⊰ ⊱

Attica possessed a remarkable self-control, but recently she was finding emotions creeping into her demeanor and attitudes. This change had been growing stronger ever since Orion had shown up at the castle. Still, as leader of a globe-spanning organization, one thing Attica had learned was to wear none of her thoughts on her face. She sat on the chair in the room that served as her office and looked at the large screen. Attica breathed in deeply through her nose and exhaled slowly, and then pushed the button.

The screen resolved into an image of Memphis, that twisted chief Shade who had manipulated its everyday appearance into that of a tall, thin old man. He – *it*, she corrected herself – looked even older and more careworn than the last time they had spoken, barely a half year prior. Well, for all practical purposes it was a he, she silently admitted. Those deep-set, dark and blank eyes looked at her with that same condescending stare, the long spindly fingers interlocked in an effort to appear more casually human as it sat.

"Memphis," she said simply, purposefully adding no title to enhance his status in her esteem. She could tell the lack of respect bothered Memphis. *Good.*

"Attica Triassa, you are late."

It was not long ago that she would have apologized, or would have at least pretended to do so. But now, no more.

"Life has many surprises, has it not?"

"Your flippancy is not amusing. And neither is what I hear about Larius Kiriath."

"Are my responsibilities now given to the maintaining of *all* your treacherous vassals?"

"Mind your tongue, slave," said Memphis shortly, and there was an intensity in the voice that made Attica swallow uncomfortably, her off-screen hand tightening into a fist as she vowed not to show any weakness. "Your impudence has caused us enough trouble already. Kiriath has been killed from beyond this existence."

By this Attica understood he meant the Different Place to which both she and now recently Orion had been – though only this latest tidbit about Kiriath solidified in her mind that Orion had indeed been there. That struck her for some reason, that he had left the world to find out about her fate. *At the least it seems I have Orion Keldir's full attention. But more telling is that he did not smash my orb along with Kiriath's.*

"And Kiriath is but one of many that have suffered the same fate," Memphis concluded.

"My heart breaks for them all," answered Attica, her tone and expression indicating nothing of the kind.

"It comes to my mind, *slave*, that so many of your fellow vassals have all fallen on the same day and yet you remain. Does this not…trouble you?"

She feigned concern at this rather well. "What can I do to assure you of my complete allegiance? Attend the respective funerals? Weep? I have everything I need here with the Order of the Raven; it would serve no productive purpose to eliminate others with the same immortal second-chance as I. Additionally, I have every means at my disposal to eliminate anyone I wish of my own accord. I have no need to use the dimensional Beyond to fulfill my designs." This was true enough. She tried baiting. "Do you not have everything well-in-hand?"

There was a long silence as the Shade stared at her. She found herself wondering exactly what was going on behind the dark, empty eyes. At length it spoke, and the tone was more of the sort to which she was accustomed.

"It has been too long, Attica Triassa, since we have spoken face-to-face. I will be coming to you soon. Much to your joy, I am sure."

Gauging my reaction. What does it expect, a smile?

"There are few things that bring me such joy. You know that."

"Indeed. While I am too distant at this time to make such an appearance terribly soon, I have already dispatched Arcanus to you. He should be there in a matter of hours."

Only Attica could have kept a cool appearance at this sort of announcement, and she did. But inside her heart skipped a beat and she shivered. She had intended to surprise the Shades with her own betrayal, not have them ambush her with some face-to-face for which she was not prepared. Much of Attica's clandestine plans depended on her own terms as far as timing. Still, flexibility and acting on the fly were also skills worth having. Yet a Shade like Arcanus was hardly the type to practice on. He was an old one, she recalled; Arcanus had been in the Earth Realm since the ancient initial contact, an original visitor.

"I look forward to his arrival," she lied, though her mind had already begun forming a plan to make the visit work out to her advantage. "There is much here I am sure he desires to see and discuss."

Memphis's face was blank of expression aside from the cold stare it always had. "You will concede and yield to his every request and desire."

It was all Attica could do to not break the connection then and there, but she wanted to keep up the appearance of at least a reluctantly obedient servant. It was best that Arcanus have no alternate understanding of their relationship status; under normal circumstances Shades regarded their human counterparts as at best hesitant in their servitude. But nothing more. Were he aware of Attica's true concerns, he would undoubtedly be on guard upon his arrival.

"Until next time," she said, and let him break the connection first.

A surprise visit...I'll give them a surprise.

৯০ ০৪

Cyprus stood and looked down at the old decrepit book. *Amusing*, he thought, *that something so dirty-looking and ill-kept could be so valuable.* That was how he had found them, the Kedassaic Texts, in the monastery library on Sicily. It was not the original; it could not be. The monks had found their own 'original' and copied it carefully, verbatim. It was written in Kedassaic and as a result they had not been able to read a word of it, but had considered it precious due to a misunderstanding. Not the first misunderstanding people of the Middle Ages had regarding a holy book. They considered it lost prophecy. *They never gathered how right they were.* He was unaware where they had gotten it, only that it had been in the monastery for over a century.

He turned a number of pages with exceeding care. The scripts were so beaten down with age and faint, he could have feared that breathing too hard might have scattered the words across the page. Cyprus spoke Kedassaic, or at least he had ages ago. It was a second language to all Atlanteans, coming from a contemporary that had been within the empire for many long years. One could write anything in Atlantean, but to write something *special* it would have been scripted in Kedassaic. A sacred language if ever there was one. And not ridiculously hard to learn, at least not until one got to a certain level.

That the Atlantean sacred books had survived at all was something of a miracle. Collected into one massive volume called the 'Kedassaic Texts' since their inception, contained within were histories, lineages, poetry, rules and regulations for the sacred orders, ancient proverbial wisdom on nearly all subjects, and of course prophecy. Many people scoffed at the very idea of prophecy, and Cyprus would have been one of them if not for the nature of the Kedassaic Texts. Magic as most people thought of it – real, actual magic – had no place in the present-day civilizations of the world. Even in what modern historians considered 'ancient culture' there was no actual magic involved. Egypt, Babylon, China. Well, perhaps a tiny bit of magic, but not much. Mostly chemistry, some early physics; potions; natural processes. Nothing that could not be created within the bounds of nature – nothing supernatural.

But the Atlantean civilization had been different. They had true magic, or *had* had it, as it were. That was why the Kedassaic Texts were not just some old, broken down, worthless pile of pages written by people long dead. He turned another page, scanning. These lines of ancient writing were the last solid link to the days when the rule of mankind was close to its zenith, close to acquiring its true potential. *All that potential has been lost once the wars ended,* Cyprus lamented there alone in the empty room. Now mankind had technology and progress; they would never seek out magic again – what was the need?

That was why the Kedassaic Texts were worthwhile. They held knowledge that was forgotten, and would never be gained again. While Attica was too foolish to see the worth in that, Cyprus was not. He could use these pages. He could become powerful. That it prophesied many things for the future was relevant, but not immediately so. The Kedassaic Texts had many things to say about the Gatekeepers, for example. Gatekeepers were after all included among the many authors.

Cyprus found solace in gazing through the book. It eased his mind when things took sudden veers from the path he had set: *like Arcanus showing up to force Attica's hand and get her to depart for the city before she intended.* Reading the ancient pages reminded Cyprus that one day he would incorporate the wisdom into his own empire. And that was most comforting. Attica would bow at his feet. She would beg for ways to please him before too much more time passed. That she was breathtakingly gorgeous only encouraged the daydream of a realistic future. All would be different when he was in control. He smiled. *That will be a good day, to be there when the Almighty Attica discovers a newfound humility.* That is, if he let her live at all. A use for her could be found, surely. *She is too beautiful to let completely go to waste.* Cyprus closed the book carefully. Another quiet reclusive meditation complete, he turned to other matters at hand. The Shade envoy had to be close.

ഔ ങ

He had to make it appear as if he had not known already.

"Arcanus is coming here?" asked Cyprus. "That is ill-news."

"Shadowcloak meant it to be," said Attica, "but I will turn it to our advantage. In the meanwhile, this pending arrival makes me wonder at what is brewing in that black heart."

"Mistress?"

"He has never trusted me," she said quietly, looking out the window of her bedroom at the glistening raindrops decorating the forest below. A cool pine-scented breeze gusted past her, billowing her long hair. "But lately he is even less-inclined than usual. It is as if he can read my mind, even though I know such a thought is absurd. It vexes me. He knows so much of what I consider secret."

"I cannot speak to this one way or the other," said Cyprus, glancing at her bed.

The words made her look at him, and Cyprus was suddenly jumping to his own mental conclusions about who fathomed what about the other. He was, after all, intending to replace Attica as head of the Raven, initiating a new era. The Shades had no place in his newfound power, though he would have to endure them for awhile yet. *Killing the time agents has not relinquished the formula Lumine uses for elapsation serum. I will need the Shade venom as long as the formula eludes me.* But now the way Attica had stopped and looked at him made him most uncomfortable. *What does she know? How much does she guess?* Simply because she was a woman did not mean she was less dangerous or devious than an accomplished male of the same deeds and title. In many ways, she was more perilous than such a man.

"I'm sure you cannot," she said, a little too readily for his comfort. She turned back from the window and began a sort of pace, hands behind her as she was accustomed. "We've been through much together, Cyprus, you and I. Yet we have not faced anything like all these nearing events just yet."

There were limited things to say on his part. "We will endure. We always have."

"Aye," she nodded once, and kept pacing. At length she took up again. "He spoke only of Arcanus. I do not know if he will be alone or no. If he is alone, he and

I will meet without any interruption. He is not what I would have chosen, but if I cannot do it now in these circumstances, there is no point going on."

With this comment even Cyprus had no idea as to what she was alluding. She had suddenly lapsed into talking to herself and not to him. She stopped abruptly and looked back at him, as if surprised he was still standing there. "He will be here soon. Prepare."

He blinked conspicuously, tongue wetting his lips with a flick. "As you wish, my Lady."

Cyprus departed and Attica remained standing in the room, where she returned to gaze out yet another window. She overlooked the courtyard and eventually saw Cyprus walk out beneath her, off to prepare for the Shade's arrival. He was some distance away when she spoke quietly to herself.

"We have done so much together, Cyprus," she repeated. "Are you not tired of me yet? We none of us have immortal patience, have we?"

She watched him go and then went over to a table, upon which lay Orion's sole weapon, his sword. It was still sheathed in the apparatus the Deathless Blade wore behind him, allowing him to draw it upside down. She freed it and held it for a moment before sheathing it anew in a standard scabbard, and then fixed it to her side. As she did this, she looked over at her bedpost where another sword was slung. It looked practically identical to Orion's, though it was of course not the same. This second sword – her own personal sword– was of standard steel but also had a special metal used just down the edges of tapering point. This unique, special metal had only come into Attica's possession very recently, and she had immediately committed its addition to the point of her own weapon.

But Orion's sword is fit for the task at hand: a Shade.

She smiled just a hint, but then grew grim. She could not have said whether she spoke to the blade or herself: "Patience, you'll have your taste of blood soon enough. When the time is right."

৪০ ୧୫

Within an hour after Attica had last talked with Cyprus, three limousine SUVs pulled onto the property of the Raven and passed through the open gate. The guard standing there watched them go by, seeing nothing through the tinted windows, and barely a glimpse at the drivers. They passed by and wound their way up the forest road to the fortress, passed beneath the great gates and into the courtyard, just as Adrienne had arrived hardly three days before.

As expected, a small entourage of Raven operatives stood there expectantly, awaiting their arrival. A presence of mind in the middle of the three vehicles noted their state of anticipatory reverence and acknowledged: *Good.* There was a moment's pause before the driver got out, walked around, and opened the side door.

A single individual emerged from the center vehicle. He was tall, very tall, and so thin he appeared spindly. In a way, he manifested very much as Memphis did – disguised in a human-looking shell but one that expressed itself contrary to nature. While Memphis looked as an old man, this fellow was not so aged. The blank face was middle-aged, but just as empty and cold. His sallow eyes were hollow, and his colorless hair like that of an albino was long and past his shoulders, and wispy. Like a caricatured undertaker of sorts. He was dressed in the same collar-less one-piece garment that Adrienne had first seen Memphis wearing a few days before, and underneath it could be seen a long straight sword.

This was Arcanus the Cruel, an ancient Shade of many centuries and the chief Shade in Europe. Arcanus had not always been an Elder among the Shades. In the days of Atlantis, the dark specter had filled the role of a soldier, a general. But there had always been a limited number of Elder Shades, a number that was to be maintained at all costs. The Gatekeepers were deadly enemies, and when on rare occasion an Elder was actually killed, a replacement had to be raised up. And so, many years ago, much to the chagrin of Memphis Shadowcloak, the bull-headed and sinister general left his legionnaires behind and joined the elite and powerful.

'He' had been the instrument and leader of the trans-dimensional beings in Europe since the crusades, and had been responsible for many an awful thing. Europe was only the latest of trivialities for Arcanus in his long stay in the Earth Realm. He had been many other places, done many other things. He was familiar with Cyprus originally not from his association with the Order of the Raven, but as an Atlantean from the days of the civil war and even before. Orion as well, though neither of these Atlanteans was on his mind at the moment. His sole purpose was to correct the course of the wayward slave Attica Triassa, to reassert in her mind who allowed her the privileges she daily enjoyed, and to purge away any rebellious thoughts or intentions. She had a role to play, as did every servant – and the Great Intrigue must soon succeed or fail. The Shades, or humankind. One race of beings would be victorious, and the other would fall into irrevocable ruin. Attica Triassa and the forces she commanded would have a hand in deciding which race fit which outcome.

80 C8

"It chills my blood to think what they are using her for," Frank said darkly.

Ten minutes earlier, Adrienne had been torn from her husband's arms and dragged up the stairs to the daylight.

"I should have fought them…"

"And if you had, instead of your wife doing whatever she is doing now," answered Orion, "it would be your widow doing it. There is a time to fight, friend. Now is not it."

"Some things are worth dying for. They could be hurting her!"

Orion remained unconcerned. "I think not. Remember she has a purpose here. Suffering is not it. And forgive me for just saying it, but if they were going to hurt her, you would be there to watch. You are not, therefore I think she is for the moment fine."

High overhead outside the castle, the Shade entourage arrived. Beneath, Orion stopped looking at Frank and stared at the wall, head cocked.

"What is it?" asked Frank.

As the Shade left the vehicle unseen above them, the newly-quiet Orion found himself pacing. Occasionally going all the way to the door and looking out as best he could, it was as if he expected to see someone coming. But he saw no one.

৪৩ ଔ

"My Lord Arcanus," said Cyprus with a low bow, "we are honored by your arrival. Please follow me."

Arcanus nodded once and walked after the shorter man, his hands behind him, his eyes looking neither left nor right but straight ahead. They never actually directly looked at Cyprus.

The way was not far. Cyprus took the tall brooding Shade through the winding passages at last into the Lounge that Attica had prepared. The middle of the room was wide and open, and there were expensive pieces of furniture spread around tastefully. The room would have been the perfect place to sit back and relax. That was not the purpose of Arcanus, however, nor was it Attica's. The Shade passed Cyprus up at the door and glided smoothly into the room. Taking no joy in luxury nor having the desire or need to rest, the tall lieutenant remained standing in the middle of the room.

"My mistress will be with you presently," said Cyprus, suddenly wondering if Arcanus could read his thoughts. *That would be disastrous.* But the Shade merely stood there, staring straight ahead from the blackness of those horrible eyes. Arcanus had not changed at all since Cyprus had last seen him; never blinked, never looked directly at anything, expression never changing. *He is like a cadaver with his eyes open.*

"I do not like to be kept waiting," said Arcanus in a voice so low it was inhuman. "She knows that. You will inform her I shall see her at once. We have a most interesting conversation in which to engage."

Even as Arcanus spoke, the Shade straightened as a twinge of discomfort twisted in his core. Showing no sign to the observant Cyprus, he only glared at him coldly. Yet under the collected exterior, the lurking sensation troubled the Shade.

"At once, my Lord," said Cyprus. If he noticed, he did not show it.

৪৩ ଔ

Orion could sense the Shade, the presence coming into range when this close. He had never quite understood this connection, this uncanny ability, but he had had it since the Atlantean war. He mused at times that it was probably due to

Atlantean magic cast during the war, given it was an advantage to sense enemies that often seemed to materialize out of nowhere.

He stood apprehensively there in the cell, his overtly intense countenance troubling his old partner. Frank now sat erect, watching Orion with a practiced eye. Orion was standing close by the cell door, gazing out and occasionally upward and pondering with unmistakable focus.

In his own mind, Orion debated for the first time how they might escape. He had at first been so intrigued by Attica's truly being alive that he did not wish to leave, wanting to know her purpose. Orion had an idea of what she might be intending, but he was not certain. Yet now with a Shade so close, Orion had seen his stay in the cell with Frank go from merely waiting confined to being utterly trapped. Should the Shade come down to the dungeon, there would be nowhere to go – and he did not even have his sword. *Perhaps Attica seized it for the very purpose of the Shades coming to her.*

Frank gave an approving nod as he saw Orion suddenly turn toward the door and put a massively solid kick to it, the wood trembling as the rumble echoed off the other cells outside. Despite these impacts, it remained whole and undamaged. He repeated the action twice more before turning away, dismayed. For a moment he stopped pacing and stood there, looking at the door, hands on his hips, a stance determining a cross between frustration and annoyance.

"Should I be trying to help you?" asked Frank from the bench.

He did not mention that he had already tried that: some men were stronger than others, some were trained in superior quality; Orion was both. In a way, he was really hardly human. Frank had seen him do more impressive things than kick down a door. But the door of their cell was designed specifically to withstand such pressures. It was four inches thick and could be both barred in two places and locked in three. Attica plainly knew the reputation of her most able prisoner.

"There are Shades nearby," Orion said, "at least one. It would be unfortunate if we happened to be in this cell and they decided to come down here. There would be nowhere to go."

Frank stood, their danger made plain. "What do you propose we do?"

Orion looked back at the door and realized he could not, by his own means, knock it down. He glanced back at Frank.

"At the moment," he admitted, "we hope they don't come down here."

೮೦ ೮ଽ

Attica leaned heavily on the dresser in her own quarters, breathing deeply. She opened her eyes to stare at her own reflection for a moment, her icy blues bearing a passion like she was hoping to see her own soul behind them. An hour could have passed and she might not pull herself away from the mirror, searching herself, telling herself she was looking for courage, knowing she was looking for an excuse not to go through with it. It was in essence the best opportunity for this particular sort of thing that she had ever had, and yet she was still debating whether or not to do it at all.

Cyprus appeared in her peripheral, standing at her open doorway. She turned the fierce gaze on him, but his pale face was not from encountering her.

"Arcanus is in the Lounge," he said, sounding slightly breathless. "He already considers you late, and he has in mind something specific to discuss."

She nodded once. Hearing that was what she needed to stiffen her nerve and resolve. "I would not want to disappoint him," she said grimly. "And the Lady Blackman?"

"As you commanded, she is in Communications with orders to listen well." He paused. "Are you going to go through with it?"

She did not answer, but left the dresser and walked toward him. He thought she looked as if she were sizing him up, her eyes boring into his face, and then away. Still she said nothing, but walked right past him on her way out. Reluctantly, he followed.

ഈ ൙

It came naturally to refer to Arcanus in the masculine, though Shades in actuality were sexless. Arcanus was a creature of immense patience. By his very nature, he had to be. In this physical dimension, he was immortal, as was his entire species. In his own dimension, he was an individual of extensive existence, and yet far from outliving his lifespan, if it could be called that. But even with the patience he had acquired from this physical existence, the female the humans called 'Attica Triassa' was beginning to wear on him.

Over the centuries, it could not be said that Arcanus spent much time on or with Attica, but he had become familiar with her. Being the chief of Shade affairs in Europe, even if her extra long lifespan was not due to the Shades, they would have had meetings before. The business of the Order of the Raven often coincided with that of the Shades, though rarely for the same ends. She was very guarded when they were in each others' presence, of course, for she was no fool; but they had had enough contact over the years that Arcanus had learned about her. And among the things he had come to know her for was at the very least punctuality.

Then again, he mused, *a timely arrival is what is expected of her.* Among other things. She had always, however reluctantly, fulfilled the purpose the Shades asked of her. Whatever they asked. It was part of the bargain; the agreement that had gone on and on down through the years. Standing there in the Lounge, Arcanus shifted his position, disliking the human-like form he assumed. The female was, some day, going to grow tired of such an arrangement.

Was there a queasy illness that he ached with just now, deep within him again? He frowned as it rose a bit, and then fell back down. It was troubling, for physical discomfort was not something regularly dealt with by any Shade.

In his time in the Earth Realm – the physical world as the humans infested it,

Arcanus had seen a handful of humans who were granted, well, not true immortal-ity, but as close as could be offered. The female Attica was one such individual, the males Cyprus and Orion were others. Some humans adapted surprisingly well to the extension of their own existence, beyond their own means. Others did not; some even went mad.

Arcanus had personally been amazed when the female Attica had not lost her mind. Surely, it demonstrated a monstrously strong self-will to maintain the com-posure she had, subjected to the things that had come upon her. *But that changes nothing*, he thought. If it were possible that a Shade could respect a human, he would and could respect her – but his disdain for all that form of life refused to let him; it was utterly impossible. Even so, he could not allow the underestimation of a foe to permit an unlooked-for defeat.

He heard the door at his back open, and a smile passed over his lips. At last she was here. And now, to see the look on her face when he confronted her regard-ing her treachery would be priceless.

"Here you are at last," Arcanus said, still facing away from the doorway in which she now stood, only twenty feet away. He turned slowly, menacingly as was his way, and stood there staring at her. She had not changed in centuries. "Memphis has told me we have much to discuss. Have you anything to say on your own behalf before judgment is passed?"

Would this accursed burning in his inner being not cease? If anything, it had grown worse in the passing minutes and now since the female entered the room it was quite intense. He suddenly found himself hoping that she would not have much to say, and that the business might be completed. Still, physically in appear-ance he appeared as eternal and unwavering as Time itself. No one could have guessed the Shade was in discomfort.

Attica said nothing as she passed into the room. Behind her the double doors closed with the help of unseen hands. She never took her eyes off the Shade, even as there were sounds of the doors being fastened – locked and barred. Arcanus was not troubled by this in the least, though he did wonder at it. There were two entries to the room, both sets of double doors opposite each other. She was having these locked, or at least someone was. Perhaps it was her own servants' fear of the Shade being there in the castle with them.

She was dressed in a loose but close-fitting outfit that allowed her a full range of movement without having any overly-long sleeves or pants that might snag or catch on anything. She was also barefoot for some strange reason. Behind her, her long blonde hair was entwined in a tight braid and put down the back of her top, where it would not flail or bounce around. Her eyes were a cold blue fire.

"In actuality we have very little to discuss," she said, coming only a little for-ward from the doors before stopping. "I would offer you the chance to answer for yourself before I hand down a little judgment of my own, but...I can tell you that even if you made a sincere effort to do so, I would have no ears to hear."

As she had come closer the powerful Shade was once again aware that the inner core of its being was troublingly burning with an intensity that was most disconcerting. For a being like a Shade wearing a physical-world guise, it was a sensation wholly alien; to be unable to focus, to actually physically suffer pain, to not understand what was wrong inside.

"You are the catalyst, my *Lord* Arcanus," she continued, and she spat the title as if it were distasteful. "The formality of a grand unveiled undertaking all begins here in this room with you. I am sure you are…honored."

"What madness is this, slave?" the Shade boomed in titanic baritone. Outside the Lounge anyone who heard the echo may have feared Attica was about to come to a bad end. "You forget your place."

She only looked prim and reached her hands slowly up about her neck, where she took hold of her necklace and drew it out from where it had rested hidden beneath her clothes. It was her magic necklace, formerly Adrienne's green jewel. She slowly came a bit nearer, and was inwardly pleased when the Shade took one look at the stone and actually withdrew a short distance. She took the treasure firmly in her enclosed fist and with an abrupt tug, tore it free of her neck. Attica wrapped the remaining broken chain around and around the hand, tucking the end away in the fist. She would not be dropping this trinket; to do so now could be fatal.

"You remember this pretty little rock, do you not?" she teased, enjoying how the magical trait of the gem still repelled even a powerful Shade, despite thousands of years gone by.

To be trapped in one place with the stone, with no exit in close quarters, had to be like a draining poison for the Shade. In her heart she praised the craft and skill of the Atlantean smiths, who had devised the magic.

"No doubt you are here to find out why I was searching for this adornment, and to get me to stop." She could not help but smile serenely and take a few steps more toward him. These cloaked creatures had enslaved her. Used her. *There is no mercy and no going back.* "You do wish me to stop, do you not?"

Arcanus straightened up to his full height, and there was such a murderous menace in the air of the room that Attica stopped smiling – though she did not stop in her steady advance. Even poisoned and slowed, the Shade was still a powerful creature, and now it was aware of its particular danger. It faced her instead of cowering. She recalled that before becoming an Elder, this one had been a soldier. However, it was in his black mind that previously Memphis had *not* informed him she had the Atlantean gemstone in her possession. He had been sent to remind her for whom she worked, not to be surprised by a deadly peril in close quarters.

"You can repel me with that accursed green filth," he rumbled at her, acknowledging. But at this he reached to his side and there was a long slow sound of metal on metal as the Shade drew out the long straight sword. "But you are going to have to come a little closer if you wish to do me actual harm."

This was actually a lie – but they would have to be there days and days with the gem alone, for the old magic alone to ultimately do him in. He would be in agony, but he would not cease to exist for a long time. Now it was the Shade's turn to be confident and self-assured. It hefted the heavy weapon of razor-sharp, chilling steel.

"Come a little closer and I'll tickle you with this in ways you'll wish your crusader friends had."

If Attica's eyes had portrayed a cold blue fire before he taunted her with this tidbit from her past life, now that it was spoken, her gaze was of scarlet lightning and pure ire. Her fist around the necklace adornment tightened and shook, and she drew out Orion's sword that had till then been barely noticed at her side.

So it was crusaders who did all those things to me. She had known it was European knights, but that they were specifically crusaders was new. *He must know exactly what happened to me the day I died. For all I know, he was there watching.*

She was done taunting. "You die now," she said darkly through clenched teeth.

Arcanus was still defiant. "Fool! That blade would have to be Atlantean steel to bring me harm. Only the Gatekeepers had such weapons."

"A weapon such as *Nemesis*?" she asked quietly. She stalked forward, downward sword tip audibly grating against the carpet and stone of the floor.

There was a stunned silence from the Shade before its eyes took on a frightening flare of rage, and then it raised its own sword to attack and began lumbering forward with a deliberate stride, closing the distance between them. But this wrath was met with an equal intensity as Attica cried aloud and rushed at the creature, her own fury escalated as she half-imagined a Templar cross emblazoned on the Shade's chest.

80 03

There were no more words in that duel; no more needed to be said. Attica had indeed planned to betray the Shades as a whole for a very long time, to sever her relationship with them. She despised answering to anyone, reviled the very idea of working toward something that was not for her own benefit. It had not taken long in her immortal state to grow tired of serving anyone but herself. And so plans for betrayal had been hatched early, but they had gone unheeded for many years. She had toyed with the idea at first. In the depths of her mind the challenge became a brooding goal – how would she accomplish it?

Then Cyprus had introduced her to the Kedassaic Texts, and a plot had been born. An intricate web of deceit and ambition had eventually formed, centuries in the making. But the specific plan to get a high-ranking Shade alone in a locked room while additionally cornering it with the Atlantean gem; that had only been in the making for a decade or so.

Ironic, she mused, *that so much work was required to set up something that will take no time at all in its execution.*

Capturing the jewel had been no easy task. As she had related to Adrienne

Blackman, the stone's historical narrative was scattered and incomplete. Only an organization like the Order of the Raven, or perhaps Dominos de Lumine, would have the knowledge and powerful assets to find the said gem again. Attica had not mentioned to her female captive exactly what her agents had had to go through to even find out about the magical artifact.

There was also the need to get the Gatekeeper's Atlantean steel, most readily available in the form of the famous sword *Nemesis*. She would use the Gatekeeper himself for the greater betrayal overall, later. That did not change the fact that the most efficient way to destroy a Shade in a form like Memphis or Arcanus was Atlantean steel. Such metal had originally been forged for such a purpose, tempered with the fire and experience of a fearsome war. The Gatekeeper weapon was *bred* to annihilate Shades. She could have shot them full of holes with a high-powered machinegun. She could have decapitated them. But these would not serve. Not for an ultimate and total destruction. Even a strong blazing fire – which would work against normal Shades – would not completely destroy the hierarchy, the strongest and most ancient individuals. For the very powerful Shades in their specific humanoid forms they manipulated for themselves, Atlantean steel was the best method of destruction. It had been since the great Atlantean Civil War in which both Cyprus and Orion had taken part.

Attica was a fine swordswoman, she truly was. Even when she was mortal, she had had ability. Training and drive, natural athleticism and the will to excel had turned her sword skills into a finely-honed mastery. Yet while she would have had a remote chance of taking Arcanus in a duel with blades alone – a remote chance – she would not have been pleased to undertake such a thing. Not by herself, and at the very least not without a weapon of the particular craft she needed: Orion's *Nemesis*. But above all this she would have been loath to attempt this kind of thing. The only thing different about this day was that she had the gem.

The magic alone was enough to heavily effect the Shade; it confused, slowed, annoyed, and confounded the monster. The ancient enchantment in the forging had been specifically designed to keep a creature like Arcanus at bay, to repel its approach. The elite old Shades could put up with it for only so long before their stamina waned, like being able to flex a muscle for a limited time. Eventually one had to stop and rest. In close quarters it would be only so long before Arcanus began to have the presence of the gem tell on him.

Attica was aggressive and quick. She thrust at Arcanus with a reckless abandon, her face the essence of hatred, her expression firm and unwavering. Arcanus hewed mighty strokes at her in return, but with the bauble gnawing at him he was not as fast as he would normally be. He could parry and block, but it was a very forced motion, barely ahead of the assault. Attica had chosen the field well. The battle ranged all over, with Arcanus constantly moving behind furniture and dodging her offense, while Attica leaped nimbly over things he cast in her way, swinging and stabbing.

It was really only ten minutes – a longer duel than she anticipated – before the gemstone, for a prolonged amount of time in an enclosed space, finally began to overcome the tall Shade. Leaps and bounds became staggers and almost pratfalls. Dodging and weaving became hardly swaying. Arcanus was slowing down more and more as if infected by some virus. Attica had her first real opening when she made a back-handed low sweep in following up a last ferocious exchange, and this time Arcanus was not fast enough to step out of the way. The closest thing was his right leg as he used it to push away from her for the hundredth time, and this time he was too close. With a sharp hiss of heat, the Gatekeeper sword shore completely through the manipulated physical limb four inches above the knee.

To evade a vicious assault while ailing terribly was one thing, but to do it while having only literally one leg to stand on was quite another. In fact, it could not be done, and Arcanus of course toppled over a chair and landed on the floor with a snarl of hate and pain. Attica was so close behind his fall that he could not even get his bearings before another swipe of similar nature parted his sword hand from the rest of the arm. The end of the severed limb smoked. The hand still clasping the sword fell bloodlessly to the floor of the Lounge and there moved of its own accord with the weapon, though without the Shade's strength of arm and shoulder the large sword itself moved hardly at all.

She stepped and stood callously on the remaining arm's wrist, and without hesitation put the point of her sword downward and rested it at the Shade's sternum.

"Any last words, vile apparition?" she asked, breathing hard but unable to not look remarkably pleased.

The face of Arcanus the Cruel was an unspoken and unheard agony. While in that shell of a physical appearance he did not breathe and had no blood or heartbeat, the body was still his identity and being while he wore it. The chest still heaved as if taking in air, but this churning was of the fire within. His voice was raspier than usual, but still deep as the canyons of the ocean. He spat the words at her:

"It will not be your lifeblood upon the Portal Gate, but it may as well be…"

Incensed at what she considered merely denial of satisfaction for a victorious foe, Attica drove the point of *Nemesis* down hard right through the chest of Arcanus, and pushed murderously until thwarted by the hard floor beneath. Hissing smoke and black ooze bubbled from the wound. A sputtering growl escaped for a few seconds, but soon ceased.

She breathed hard for an instant longer before wrenching up the weapon from the Shade, turning the point skyward once more, and slashing down with savage ferocity. The head rolled from its place and Attica sheathed the bloodless weapon. Any black ooze that clung to it immediately burned off freely without assistance, like dew in the sunlight.

"Meaningless threat," she answered the departed Shade, and then called loudly for Cyprus.

∞ ⋈

Outside the fortress in the courtyard where the three SUVs waited, their human drivers standing patiently nearby, all were unaware of what was going on within the building. But up on the parapets above the main entry, several members of the Raven waited expectantly. A radio crackled. An order was given. Without hesitation, they acted.

Only one of the three drivers looked up in time to see the business-end of a rocket-launcher peek over the banister up above the entryway. There was a sizzling sound and a smoking white trail hissed its way like a lightning bolt toward the first car, exploding it with brilliant incandescence. The second and third vehicle, in a matter of less than a quarter minute, also burst into oblivion, but any member of the Shade entourage was too busy being shot at to worry about the vehicles.

CHAPTER 18

"The Kedassaic Texts are the only thing we have left of our civilization. When the Lost Isle plunged beneath the waves, it was one of the few things we could truly save. I know the Shades of old had their own corrupted version to poison and mislead, but how can you suggest that our one remaining original copy actually is the tainted, Shade-induced heresy? You break my heart. Very few now living have a memory that reaches back to those days when these pages were initially written. How can we now tell if these accusations are true?"

~Talia of Lynsaelyn, Record Keeper of the Order of the Raven, 984 BC

ಌ ಐ

CHAMBER OF DIRMON, GATEKEEPER HEADQUARTERS IN IRATHA, ATLANTIS. 3653 BC.

The imperial palace had always been full of forbidden places. Now that the war had been ongoing eight years, such clandestine and prohibited areas had only grown in number. Could no one be trusted? Was nothing sacred? Orion realized he was being distracted as he stood there with the elite members of the Order of the Gatekeepers. Not a year past the Forum Lord of the Gatekeepers, one of three foremost Inner Circle members, had been found to be a traitor to the Emperor and his own Order. The roots of the Shades had grown strong, and men remained ever corruptible.

The Chamber of Dirmon was in the lower levels of the Gatekeepers Wing of the palace. It was square in shape with a deep, round pool of calm water in the midst of the floor, like a spa. Its one door was a narrow passage guarded by portcullis, locks, and guards at all hours of the day. Its ceiling was high, upheld by four strong pillars.

A pair of steps allowed one to move from the doorway down into the chamber itself, and then other steps would lead one down into the pool until he was fully immersed. Orion thought the water looked awfully cold, though that was presumably because he knew he would soon be in it.

It was impossible to explain the intricacies within the chamber – how old it was, its original construction, the power within, the nature of the water. Especially the nature of the water. Many years ago, the great explorer Harvor the Mariner had gone abroad, and had returned from the far West. He brought with him barrel after barrel of the water that was now in the Chamber of Dirmon's pool. He had also returned with two infants, claiming they had been grown men when they first set sail with him. The two men had led a scouting party into the peninsula's swampy wilderness. Upon immersing themselves in the strange pool they discovered, the water had reduced their years almost too far. Or so the story went – it had first been told hundreds of years ago.

Orion had always been skeptical of it, but he had been meditating on it a good deal lately. Ever since the remaining two members of the Inner Circle of the Order, the Orator and the Consul, had selected he and the other eleven Gatekeepers for the special task, he had not been able to dwell on anything else. Exactly what the special task was remained to be seen, but meeting in the Chamber of Dirmon revealed much in and of itself. No member of the Order of the Gatekeepers, be he standard Gatekeeper as Orion was or a leader in the Inner Circle, had set foot in this chamber for a century.

The conversation that had begun weeks ago in other places was picked up in the middle of itself there in the chamber.

"Your duty is plain," said the Orator to the twelve Gatekeepers standing there, among whom Orion was first. The Consul stood by, nodding approvingly. The Orator went on. "You will uphold the rulings of the Order of the Gatekeepers. You will hunt down all those who have been found guilty by the Order of the Gatekeepers. You will administer justice to them according to the Order of the Gatekeepers. Swear it, you men."

They all swore to it.

The Consul then spoke gravely. "That our civilization is endangered surprises no one here. The trials of the war and the sorceries of the Separatist armies – along with those damnable shadowed cloaks – have all conspired to convey our descent into the Great Salt Water. This cannot be stopped by any craft we here possess. Yet we have contrived a way in which the Order of the Gatekeepers will continue, and through which justice may have satisfaction."

The Orator and Consul went on to explain their plan: the waters of the pool were enchanted, as well Orion might have guessed. Anyone familiar with the history of Harvor could have jumped to that conclusion. The nature of the water was to decrease the age of the immersed, but the wise among the Atlanteans had applied their own magic to it. Without the magic of Atlantis, the waters would result in death by reverted age. Yet with the Atlantean magic, upon entry into the pool the properly prepared would not lose their age – they would simply not attain more. They would continue. It only made sense, really, that those sent upon the quest of upholding the order's justice would be granted a lifetime long enough in which to accomplish all these things. The enemies of the order and of the imperial throne were legion indeed. This was all explained to the twelve Gatekeepers who stood before the two remaining men of the Inner Circle.

"And when our task is accomplished," said one man to Orion's left, "what is to be our fate? To wander the earth forever, unable to die? To go on and on?"

"We have considered that plight, Halel," said the Orator. "You are not to be left to such an end. Ere you descend into the pool, within the confines of the ceremony you will select a methodology by which you perceive to bring about your end – when your task is accomplished and the time comes. This methodology must be different for each of you. Should an enemy discover your particular bane, had you all the same one, all of you might be killed easily in time. Yet if all of you have a different bane, then there is the hope that the order maintain itself down through the coming ages. Make your choice carefully and return here tomorrow night."

   

Six year old Kyla Sejarrian stopped short, staring at her current bodyguard.

"Are you listening to me, Master Keldir?"

His eyes went from the hands in his lap to his small ward. She was a pretty little thing, dressed as immaculately as a princess could be, hands on her hips as she copied her mother.

"Forgive me, princess. I have much on my mind."

Her magical green gemstone dangling from her neck as she leaned forward toward him over the small table at which she stood. The dolls in front of her lay suddenly ignored.

"Like what?"

Life and death. An ageless eternity. And an unending war. Standard fare, nowadays.

"Nothing important, your majesty. Forgive my being distracted."

She looked so much like her mother, the queen Mia. "Daddy says Gatekeepers are bad liars."

His mouth twitched but refused to smile fully. "The lord emperor is a wise man."

"Are you a bad liar?"

"Apparently."

"So what were you thinking about?"

"I need something…unusual and sharp, and I am not sure I know where to get it. And I have about two hours to find it."

"Did you lose it?"

Now he did smile. "No, child. I don't know what it is yet. It could be any number of things. I must choose."

To his amusement, she at once went to her wooden toy chest and began rifling through it as though something exceedingly precious were lost. At length she held up a play-sword of holly. He slowly shook his head. Disappointed, she dropped it.

Suddenly she brightened. "We can go the armory! It's full of sharp things."

"There are weapons there, dear. We need something that someone would not think about using for a weapon. The material it is made of must be unusual. Or unlikely."

"I don't understand."

She put her crown down on the table, wincing as some of her long hair caught on it. It was a slim, narrow length of silver with a blue sapphire set in the middle, curved so as to sit upon her head. Sapphire would have been the color of the magically protective gemstone if the emperor had anything to say about it, but the nature of the blue stone did not allow enchantment to be laid upon it so well. The green gem, carved jade from Zelada in the south, however, had many prized qualities.

The light caught the crown when she moved it, and Orion stared at it as she looked at him.

"What is your crown made of, princess?"

Kyla Sejarrian loved talking about her beautiful crown. "This blue jewel is called a royal sapphire, because only royalty like us is allowed to wear them. Gatekeeper Sashek told me it comes from the dragon caves on Lake Aspar – where the ground smokes! But we had it in the treasury."

"And the metal?"

"It's not metal, it's silver. That came from the treasury too."

"Most silver in the empire comes from Zelada, like the green stone of your necklace."

"Not this silver. This silver Daddy brought back with him before I was born, when he left our shores and went to fight the dark men. When he beat them, they gave him the silver so he would leave them alone. When he wanted something besides the silver, they told him there was nothing else like it in the world."

Orion leaned forward. "Is that right?"

"Uh-huh. It's like the sapphire. Only royalty gets to wear it."

"Sounds like your necklace."

She proudly held the bauble out on its chain. "The necklace stone is set with the same silver as the crown."

"You know a lot of things, your majesty."

"I'm the princess," she smiled. "I ought to know something."

That was what her mother always told her.

He got up and went to the table, looking at the small crown. The ends of it had a blunted sharpness, like his sister's knitting needles.

"Your majesty, may I…borrow your crown when I leave you tonight? I'll only be gone a short while, and I'll bring it right back."

❧ ☙

That night came too quickly for Orion. He returned to the Chamber of Dirmon, but not happily. The others did as well, moods unreadable. The Orator and Consul were there, both wearing their ceremonial swords. No one spoke for a long time, as it was a solemn occasion. In the back of his mind, Orion hoped that neither the Orator nor the Consul would attempt some long-prepared speech. Best to just get on with it, *he thought.* We all know why we are here.

The Orator and Consul stood beside the stairs that led down into the pool itself. With a nod at the man Halel, the indicated Gatekeeper stripped and came forward, descending down into the pool. It came a bit past his waist. In his hand was a knife-blade of obsidian. Standing in the water, he took instructions from the men of the Inner Circle.

"Draw blood with the obsidian. Your hand will do."

"Now clutch the weapon with the bleeding hand."

"Now submerse yourself fully and do not break the surface for a full minute."

The Gatekeeper disappeared beneath the surface and the men of the Inner Circle uttered some words in Kedassaic and tossed a handful of ground herbs over the surface. There was a hissing as the water grew hot, and the other Gatekeepers looked on entranced, fancying that it would soon be their own turn. Halel remained beneath the surface for a full minute as instructed, and at length surfaced. He was huffing and puffing, as if remaining submerged that long had been challenging. Perhaps with the sudden heat of the water, it was. He departed the pool.

"Show me your hand, Gatekeeper," instructed the Consul.

Halel turned to show his hand to the Consul, but in doing so he turned his back on the Orator. The Orator drew his sword – despite being ceremonial it was still lethally sharp and effective – and without hesitation put the point in the middle of Halel's back just to the left of the spine, and drove it inward as hard as he could go. Halel roared aloud as the blade slid into his flesh a good seven inches. His cry of pain lasted till he hit the ground down on one knee, but then he stopped.

"What are you doing?" demanded a Gatekeeper behind Orion.

"Treachery!" called another.

Orion himself just stood and stared, though his mind had shouted both statements. He fingered the young princess's crown in his own hands, which he had brought for himself. If he stabbed himself hard enough with the end, he would draw blood, but it was not an adequate weapon to take on men with swords. He wondered at how he might kill the Orator when the man turned the sword on the rest of them. Strange, very strange that the Inner Circle should have two traitors-

But the Orator was not a traitor. He pulled the sword from Halel and cast it aside, but then knelt down beside him and began speaking in a low voice. Remarkably,

Halel had fallen to his knees with pain and surprise, but he had fallen no lower. Indeed, he remained there for a second, his cry of agony not lasting. He was panting there on the floor, but he neither fainted nor collapsed. At length, the Orator was able to raise him to his feet, and he stood.

"Show them," said the Consul.

The Orator turned Halel away from the other Gatekeepers, showing his back. Where the sword had entered his body there was a scarlet mark, but it was neither open nor deep. It was a mere mark, as if someone had thrown a piece of red chalk and hit him in the back.

"See?" asked the Orator.

"Halel is now impervious to most weaponry. It may hurt, but no permanent damage can be done. Only with obsidian can this man be now mortally wounded."

There were a few murmurs among the Gatekeepers standing there. They had all known that something not unlike this ought to be expected, but actually seeing it occur and having proof was still powerful to behold. Halel in his own turn only began replacing his clothing. Behind him, the Orator and the Consul surveyed the remaining eleven men.

"Orion, you are next."

80 C8

Attica exhaled as if she had not breathed throughout the entire duel. Her chest was heaving like she had never used her lungs before, now that the immediate danger was past. Once she could finally accept that the broken up 'corpse' of Arcanus would never move again, she slowly breathed out, eyes closed. At length she opened them and turned from her place half-kneeling beside the Shade, and looked at Cyprus. He looked horrified.

"What have you done?" he asked, sounding shocked. His hands were spread as he asked, incredulous and blinking that twitchy tic of his. "Do you realize what you've done?"

With the tense moment passed, Attica stared back at him, and a smile slowly created itself on her mouth. But the smile faded as Cyprus refused to acknowledge she had made the correct decision. He continued looking as if a joke with serious consequences had been played in very bad taste.

"I have bought us the time we need to accomplish the task at hand. Now, prepare to leave within the hour. And signal the ship. The equipment should already be aboard. Have the Lady Blackman brought to me here, and then go do what I have said." *Before I use this sword to fix that twitch of yours.*

Cyprus turned his back on her, but she spoke again before he had left the room.

"And Cyprus."

He didn't answer, but stopped walking expectantly.

"Don't ever question my actions again."

Cyprus returned nothing, nodded infinitesimally, and left.

Left alone in the room, Attica looked back at the head of Arcanus. For an instant, she pictured it still casting that hellfire stare of his on her. She shivered involuntarily and turned her back on the battlefield. *A pity this was not Memphis as originally planned*. She would give orders as soon as she found someone to give them to; orders to have the Shade removed, the carcass burned to dust. The Shade was truly destroyed and the Earth Realm at the moment was by definition a better place – not that it had any bearing on Attica's purposes or cares.

The Shades had rushed her plans, arriving for the meeting earlier than she had anticipated. They had forced her hand. Of course, left to her own devices and timing she would have done the same thing, only later. If they had not come, she would have waited another few weeks before departing to the coast, for the brief ocean voyage.

But plans rarely go consistently as devised, she brooded silently. *I would be more concerned if everything went as intended.*

A short time later, two guards brought Adrienne to the Lounge and departed, leaving her alone with Attica. The young woman looked with distaste on the corpse and head of Arcanus the Cruel, and Attica could tell her mental processes were reckoning what she had heard earlier with what she could now see.

"You sat in Communications and listened to all that happened here in the past quarter hour?" Attica asked, though she knew well the answer.

"Yes," said Adrienne.

"And you heard this vile creature's words? All of them?"

Adrienne could not look away from the severed head. "I think so."

Attica's eyes locked on Adrienne's. "And? Did it speak the truth at any time?"

Adrienne had a good memory when she knew to not have one would bring great discomfort. She thought for a moment. Arcanus had spoken a little, making declarative statements only occasionally amid his already few words. She broke it down.

Yes, Memphis had truly told Arcanus there was much to discuss; that statement had been true.

Yes, the green bijou could repel the Shade, but the claim that it would have to be close in proximity to harm was a lie.

Yes, only Gatekeepers were known to carry such weapons.

"And there was something," finished Adrienne, "about crusader friends which I couldn't really tell was truth or lie-"

"Never mind that," Attica sniped hastily. "What of the lifeblood on the Portal Gate having anything to do with my own?"

"Yes, what was it talking about?"

Attica leaped over the dark corpse and took Adrienne by the shoulders with strong quavering hands. "Was it lying or speaking truth?" she half-shouted, angry at both the veiled threat that had been uttered as well as the gemstone not yet having granted her own immortal truth-telling abilities.

It will not be your lifeblood upon the Portal Gate, but it may as well be.

"I'm not sure!" Adrienne managed, cringing in the face of Attica's adamancy. "It wasn't entirely a flat statement of fact. I couldn't tell!"

A hand slapped Adrienne across the face, so suddenly she gave a short cry.

"Truth or lie?" demanded Attica, giving her a shake.

Adrienne had to pick one, and she went with her gut as her stinging cheek reddened. "Truth, Lady Triassa, truth."

 හ ග

Orion sat in the lead SUV of the convoy pending departure, feeling the steel that cuffed his hands behind him. *As if they expect me to try killing her if given half a chance,* he thought as he watched Attica come out the doors and approach the vehicle. She said something to a few of the guards, ordered Adrienne and Frank into another vehicle behind his own, and then came toward him. *If they only knew I tried to do as much less then twenty-four hours ago, only to fail.* Not breaking Attica's orb when he had the chance still haunted him.

It was not often that Orion found himself brooding upon failure. Over the years there was on occasion something that could have gone better; unforeseen happenstance, unpredictable twists in events, interference of the obscurely random. These were not excuses, but a man in his line of work was apt to run into something unexpected that changed one's course of action in an instant. But just plain and simple failure? That was a bit of an anomaly. Her magic globe, after all, had not escaped him or fought back, or even disappeared from his grasp; he had merely put it down.

He looked up as Attica entered the vehicle. Held for her entry, the car door closed as she reached her seat. She leaned forward to rap on the glass between them and the driver. "Go," she ordered, and sat back as the vehicle pulled away, beginning the entire convoy's departure.

Of all the available ways to travel at her fingertips, she picks this vehicle?

"Do you know where we are going?" she asked, not looking at him, but facing forward. She pulled a laptop from a black case at her feet and flipped the screen open to resume previous work.

He held her in a calm gaze that bordered on staring. "I could hamper a guess." He had a suspicion, but it was yet to be confirmed.

"Answer my question."

"West."

She smiled without showing her white teeth. It struck him as she did so. *There was a time,* he thought, *when the same smiling movement of her lips was both sweet and mischievous.* She was still a very beautiful woman, and a smile could do much to lighten face and mood. But it was not so now. The same motion on her part today came across as cold and superior, driven.

"You will find out in time. You will play your role and then we shall part company." She finally looked over at him. "It seems a regrettable waste, I know, terminating our relationship anew so soon after our reunion. It is for the best, I assure you."

"Who's best?"

"Mine is served, I acknowledge, but as a result a good many others too. The world would extol my name if they could comprehend the weight of what I have undertaken. I deserve freedom – and I shall have it very soon."

"You've changed." He looked out the window instead of facing her. It was troubling to look at her – and he could not stop noticing how gorgeous she was.

"Changed? Me?" She gave a musical laugh. "How so? In that I no longer find my contentment in your arms, Gatekeeper? In that I may want something more for myself than just a mediocre life, and have the will to pursue it?"

Now it was Orion's turn to chuckle, and he did. "Untold riches, command of thousands, beholden to none – yes, 'mediocre' is the word I would also use. Well said. A very mediocre life indeed."

Her humor evaporated. "The power behind the Order of the Raven is *nothing* if all it sums up to is an extension of some damnable Shade's right hand."

"So making it all your *own* damnable hand will set it aright…"

"You mock me."

"No, my lady, surely I do not."

Attica cocked her head. "How is it that a Gatekeeper does not see the virtue in seeking freedom?"

"What you seek is not freedom."

Her brow furrowed. "Were you this cantankerous in our years as husband and wife?" she asked.

He ignored the question. "You are seeking what is *called* freedom by many. True freedom, my lady, in its purest form must capitulate to rules; otherwise one's 'freedom' interferes with another's 'freedom' and removes it. What you are seeking is the unrestricted ability to do whatever you want; it is not the same."

"Call it what you will. What I have put into motion must be seen to conclusion."

"And so we ride to our destination. A port and ship, perhaps?"

"So you *do* know where we are bound," she said with an amused tone. Her hands worked the computer, and she gave no further sign that more conversation was necessary.

Silence was typically a comfortable state of being for Orion, but there in the car he had a remarkable urge to speak. *When*, he contemplated, *shall I have the chance to speak to her like this again?*

"I went to the Different Place," he finally said, recalling back to where he had gone at the same time as lying in a bathtub of ice. Her orb and his failure to destroy it flashed to life in his mind once more.

She didn't look up, but remained focused on the screen. "You said as much before departing yesterday. So you came there. And? What do you expect me to say?"

"I am not certain," he said truthfully, "but I can assure you I was not anticipating apathy. We are reunited after eight hundred years. Have you…have you really no desire to know how things once were between us?"

Attica looked at him with a cynicism that reasserted how different she now was from the woman she had once been. "I must have been a real piece of work eight centuries ago, that you should expect these pathetic little shortcomings from me. I am not the good little wife you picture, Gatekeeper. That weak, sheltered little angel of virtue."

He was not amused. "You are foolish to associate kindness and virtue with weakness. You were stronger then, in a way that you cannot now possibly understand."

The laptop slammed shut with a crack. "Yes, well, being gang-raped and having your throat cut can alter one's personality." She spoke brusquely, her blue eyes stabbing icicles at him. "But we all must rise above our circumstances, when presented with opportunity."

There was a long pause. Her gaze held him for a moment and then went forward again.

"Betraying the Shades is not an opportunity, my lady. It is a mistake."

"Any debt I owed to those hooded vultures I have repaid a thousand times by now. It was an unfair, manipulative bargain in the first place, and I have chosen to rewrite the rules. They won't stop me."

"How exactly do you determine to outsmart the oldest and most cunning creatures that walk the face of the earth?"

This logical question was met by scorn and an averted gaze. "I do not need to justify myself to you-"

"You determine to use me to bring about your own ends – but you will not speak as to your intentions."

"You will do what I bid when the time is right, I shall accomplish what is needful, and then we shall part ways. Permanently."

He had to ask. "And if I refuse?"

She just looked at him with that cold, humorless stare. "You are as weak now as I was then. You will comply."

In the many valid criticisms Orion had heard regarding himself, even his enemies had never seriously suggested that they considered him weak. His face portrayed that it did not register as credible, as it was not. She went on.

"You've a high sense of duty, don't deny it. It cripples you against doing what must be done. You may not be above suffering yourself but if I press those you care about, your precious instincts will take over."

I should have smashed your orb.

"And how will this twisted kindness of mine assist you?"

She looked sidelong at him for only an instant. "I can't torture you into doing what I want, but I can torture your friends and make you watch. Even you won't be able to put up with that for too long. Not with them screaming your name, begging you to make it stop-"

"I will not betray the whole of mankind to cease the pain of those you will kill anyway when your purpose is completed," said Orion, and the hardness of his voice was from his inner turmoil.

"The whole of mankind?" she asked coyly. "What is it you think I intend to ask you to do? But it is no matter. I'll take that bet. The Lady Blackman will be first. It won't take long for you to comply. All I have to do is submit her to the same fate you left me to…" and she turned and glared at Orion coldly, "…and this time you'll actually be there to have the chance to stop it. And if her cries don't convince you to yield to my demands, her husband's will."

With that, she turned back to face forward and tried opening the laptop again, but found the screen cracked.

"Of course," she muttered infinitesimally and closed it again.

"I came as quickly as I could," he said quietly in a low voice, not looking at her. "The way was long and my means were meager. I rode both horses in my possession to death in my haste to reach you."

Beside him, her cynical look glanced his way, expressionless.

"You were gone when I found you. I…I came as quickly as I could," he repeated. "I was not fast enough, and for that, Attica, I am sorry. Truly, I am. I would do much to make it otherwise, but I cannot."

"Do not apologize to me," said she.

"I never thought I would have the chance to tell you."

There was a pause, and her face bore no expression for her words, which were still stern. "I should not have taunted you just now with this episode from our past. Consider the matter closed and move on, Gatekeeper, as I have. The woman you loved is dead, you cannot bring her back."

Orion said nothing to that, but only met her eyes with an absent stare.

"Don't misunderstand," she continued, seeing the way he looked at her. "I still mean to complete my undertakings, and your role in assisting me remains the same. We have now been enemies for long years, and we remain so. Do not force me to make things more harsh than need be; do not try me."

He nodded soberly, meeting her eyes. "Rest assured, I can see now that my wife is truly dead."

"Clear your mind, Gatekeeper; you will need it today."

"My mind is clear for the first time in days. I know what I must do." *And you must forgive me when I do it, for I will not fail twice. Not with so much at stake.*

The look in his eye as he said this disconcerted her, and there was turmoil behind the blue ice that was her lucid eyes. "We all have our tasks…" she admitted at length, and turned to her own window.

80 03

Adrienne had always had a fascination with the ocean, had always loved it, had always in her heart of hearts desired a home near it. Perhaps it was the fact that she had come from a land-locked farming community, and the seaside was as different as one could get. Sometimes she thought it was because she was envious of her brother in Chicago, as he had his giant lake.

Regardless of whatever reason it was, any appreciative inclination she got near the sea was entirely vanquished when she was allowed to leave the car. She stood there beside the vehicle, hands cuffed in front of her and looking all around. About them large but dismal-looking buildings rose from the ground, leaving narrow aisles, loading docks, and truck entrances tearing through a concrete jungle. Not a living soul could be seen. Before her, the concrete abruptly ended and below the water was gray and only a dull green if the sun came out from behind the clouds, and was calm.

Docked in front of them was a ship: a one hundred fifty meter cargo freighter. The Raven had modified it and used the space and size for multiple purposes, but to the untrained eye it looked just an old crate. Cranes were still to be found on deck, and even as the limos pulled up, last minute preparations and supplies were being loaded into the hold. Frank found himself wondering what was in the large car-sized canisters that disappeared below decks.

Regardless of what it had once been used for, clearly the Raven had outfitted new specifications. Frank could see the wires, towers, and satellite equipment covering the tops of the roofs all over the deck. *Enough hardware*, he thought, *to run a communication headquarters if necessary*; and he could see Attica was perfectly capable of running any of her vast organization from anywhere in the world the ship might be.

"Not exactly what I had in mind for our first cruise," Adrienne whispered to Frank as they walked up the gangplank, following Orion, who was after Cyprus and a few guards. Attica had remained at the car for a moment, discussing something with a crewman.

"I'll make it right, someday, babe," he whispered back. *So much for my girl needing comfort.* The car ride had been spent agonizing over how to offer just that. Of course, the slight flippancy on her part was her own effort to make a heavy situation lighter. She smiled and kept walking.

It was nearly a half hour before the large ship started moving, and Attica's 'guests' were shown to quarters that were surprisingly pleasant, not unlike a roadside hotel; clean and adequate. Their handcuffs were removed, for they were not able to simply leave, but each individual was fitted with a GPS device around the ankle and a collar that fitted snugly about the neck.

Attica held up a small remote, like a garage door opener. "Not only do I know where you are at all times; I can control you at all times, with a small shock."

She thumbed something on the remote and instantly all three captives dropped to their knees as a jolt of electric pain pried rigid fingers into their brain stems. It was the most debilitating thing Adrienne had ever experienced, and it was close for Frank. Neither of them had ever been stabbed by a Shade. Both Blackmans gave involuntary but audible cries of pain, but Orion only managed a grunt between gritted teeth. For all the reaction, in the end the actual pain lasted an instant. It was the shock of what the pain had been which lasted.

"That is a quick press of the button," said Attica, looking down at them. "I can hold it down. Don't test me."

With that she walked away, leaving the prisoners on their knees.

Adrienne stopped clasping the collar and took a few staggering breaths. "I can't speak for you two…" she managed, "…but I'm doing my best to not give her a reason to do that again."

"That's debilitation to a high degree, I concur," said Frank. "Like being tazed inside your head." He looked at Orion, who was watching Attica. "Charming woman."

Orion got to his feet, still watching Attica's back. "She's been poisoned. Nothing more."

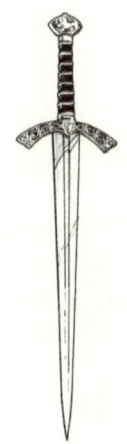

CHAPTER 19

"The Shades call it a 'Favor', but the Order calls it 'Deplorable Patronage'. One must wonder what kind of depraved service merits such hateful creatures to give one something one wants or needs? Elder Shades may be bound to deliver when they have granted a Favor, but do not doubt they will manipulate and corrupt its manifestation to their own ends, however they can – and always at the expense of to whom the Favor is owed."

~Frederick of Blois

ᙄ ᙈ

The ship made its way out into the Atlantic for a couple days, and the journey was uneventful. The prisoners were given relative freedom over a majority of the ship, and Adrienne and Frank spent much of the fairer weather walking around on the deck. They generally spoke of nothing important, but also at times of the crucial. Adrienne did not like the more serious of the talks, as it made her apprehensive for what was to come; Frank was agitated, most anxious of what would soon transpire. The premonition that any of them might die never left his mind.

"I don't want to talk about it, Frank," she said, looking up at him as she leaned on his chest with his arms around her. Her forearms were against his chest and she had her head against these. She pushed, gently. "I don't want to talk about it."

"We need to, Adrienne," was his answer every time. "I need to know you'll be okay if something happens to me."

She put her head back down and he had the inclination to tighten his arms around her. "Nothing's going to happen to you."

"But if it does-"

"Stop it, Frank! Just…please stop…"

He sighed a resigned sigh. "All right, okay, we won't talk about it."

After a few minutes, Frank's gaze moved to a distant figure looking out over the sea, ignoring the spray, stolid: Orion. Frank gave her a squeeze, pulled himself away from Adrienne, and moved to talk to his oldest friend.

"She's emotional," was all Frank said as he came up and stood beside the other man, leaning and looking in similar fashion.

"In these circumstances," said Orion dryly, "we would both be concerned if she was not."

"I mean she's too emotional to discuss the possibility that in a few days I'll be dead and she'll be a widow."

"Some things you can plan for. Some you cannot. This is called life, Frank."

Frank huffed. "Glad I'm not coming to you for sympathy."

Orion's answer surprised him. "Then why are you here talking to me, Frank, instead of spending all possible moments with your wife?"

Frank stood there staring back at the unblinking ancient gaze that had been turned upon him. The oldest man in the world was giving him advice. Something in the back of his mind told him to take it.

"Perhaps I'm fool enough to presume you had a plan, and that we might get a way out of this by working together," Frank finally offered.

Orion returned his eyes to the sea before them, stretching unhindered to every horizon. He said nothing for awhile, but at length spoke again. "I hope you're serious about that teamwork. Opportunities will be limited. It's Attica's game now. She'll do what she wants, and until I'm actually presented with a situational opportunity, I do not even purpose to stop her. To step in at the wrong time would negate future chances. Anyway, I'm still not sure what she wants, though I suspect. And if I am right, stopping her will be imperative, but it won't be easy."

"Stop her from what? They could write entire history books on events that never came to be because of Dominos de Lumine – and I daresay the two of us as well. Is this one of those times?"

"Stopping her might mean killing her," said Orion quietly, so softly Frank almost didn't hear. "I have already been responsible for her death once. And when given the opportunity of late, I could not bring myself to do it purposefully again. But the next time is on its way even now, and when it arrives my hand may be forced." He looked over at Frank. "I am not sure I could do it, even with the stakes what they are."

Frank cocked his head just a bit, face contorting just a hair. "Hey…let's keep it a little lighter than all that. You're the Deathless Blade for goodness sake, the man who always comes through. You'll find a way to get us out of this, you always do."

Those steel gray eyes bore into Frank Blackman.

"Perhaps not this time, Frank. This one is not about blowing something up and getting away," he said with a slow shake of his head. Then he leaned in a bit. "You need to understand that if I cannot do it when it needs to be done…you have to do it. Do you understand what I'm telling you? If that time comes, you will have to break the Rules."

In the business of Dominos de Lumine, Frank had had two cardinal rules: he would kill no civilian women and he would kill no children. Those were the Rules. There were other rules as well, but those two were paramount. To the best of his knowledge down through the years, he had never done a child physical harm – at least not on purpose. In the stress of war and instant decisions, he had ended many lives and among them were some women. But there were legitimate circumstances for virtually every such death.

A number of past occurrences flashed across Frank's memory. He looked back at his oldest friend.

"Let's be clear about this. Are you…are you asking me to kill your wife?"

Orion looked him in the eye. "Only if I cannot." Then, as if the stare were too hard, he turned back toward the water.

This is crazy, even for us, thought Frank. *Attica doesn't qualify as a civilian woman, but not killing your best friend's wife seems to naturally fit with the Rules.*

"Do you really think that's going to be necessary?" He looked around to see if anyone was nearby. "Killing her, I mean. She's the leader of the Crows, I get it, but-"

Orion's head snapped back at him. "Do not think for an instant that I would kill her simply for being the supreme leader in the Order of the Raven. That is not what this is about, Frank." He looked away again but turned immediately back. "My word man, what do you take me for?"

"Oh, well as long as we have an actual *good* reason, I can get onboard killing your wife. What do you take *me* for?" He paused. "Then what is this about?" He leaned closer so they were nearly touching foreheads. "Why do we have to kill her?"

"She is going to open the Portal Gate. We are headed for Iratha."

"Iratha?"

"The capital of the Atlantean Empire. It is the only course of action that explains everything she has done. The only thing of any modern relevance in Iratha is the Portal Gate. It is already sealed, and useless to the Shades in its present state."

"The Portal Gate…? That's the Shades' doorway into this dimension, isn't it?"

Orion nodded once.

"That is the real problem," continued the Gatekeeper. "What else is there to do to it than…reopen it?"

"Who in their right mind would *want* to reopen it?" Frank asked, incredulous.

"No one who understands what that would mean. She has a plotted course of action, but I believe she intends a different result. As you say, no one would want to reopen it. That is not what she is purposing; it is merely what will occur as a result of her action."

"Perhaps she is seeking something else in Iratha."

"I've debated that. It is nothing but a submerged ruin, for ages now." He shook his head. "I greatly lamented over its loss in those first long years after the Cataclysm. That was an evil day, filled with death and destruction. The innocent and guilty together, plunged beneath the waves..."

"Is there nothing else in the city but rubble and the Portal?"

"Oh, there was much that sank. For archaeologists or treasure hunters there might be something rewarding, I suppose."

"Attica doesn't strike me as being into antiques," said Frank. "And she's not exactly poor."

"She told me she was seeking freedom from the Shades. In the car on the way over here. That has to be the Portal."

"Could Cyprus have given her a faulty understanding of something?"

"Possibly, but the Portal is still the only plausible pursuit. Do you see now why she must be stopped, my friend? If we do not stop her, the very existence of mankind will face a serious problem."

A Shade-infested nightmare, thought Frank.

Orion went on. "I hate the very idea of stopping her with deadly force, but given the consequences if we do not...there is truly no choice left."

Frank's understanding of the overall situation took on a new light and he grasped the banister rail, staggered by the whole thing. He had obviously known it was a bit more personal for Orion, what with Attica and all, but the idea of having to kill her had not really come to mind. He looked back at Adrienne, about to disappear below decks, hugging herself against the blowing wind.

"I have some unfinished business," he said, turning away.

Orion stood there, unmoved and still looking out over the water. "Haven't we all."

⅚ ⅛

"All stop," she said.

Their journey stretched well into its fourth day when their destination was reached. Even without precise coordinates, that fact was plain. The sea around them had a few other ships in it, though none were as large as the cargo freighter. One had a crane and had lowered one and then another large canister into the water. These were the same canisters that Frank had wondered about the contents, seeing similar ones loaded on their own ship.

On the bridge, there was a general sense of apprehension with Attica being physically present. Having her onboard the ship at all was nerve-racking enough, let alone in the command center. The crew were all aware of their own roles, what they were attempting to accomplish, what they had to do; but her very presence raised the anxiety of all.

"What are our exact coordinates?" she asked.

Someone rattled off a series of numbers.

"And our heading?"

The same voice answered.

The beautiful woman in the captain's chair turned toward the chief officer and said, "If we are in the proper position, coordinate with the *Vulture* and initiate the sequence, captain."

The *Vulture* she spoke of was the ship three hundred meters away, lowering canisters. The captain contacted the ship and there were long minutes of back and forth. Attica was hardly listening as someone said something about submarines aligning canisters on the ocean floor. *This will take awhile.* After a tedious minute she tapped a nearby crewman with her foot and signaled with her hand at her own ship's cranes. He understood and a few minutes later, they were bringing up more canisters onto the bulk freighter's deck, preparing to place them on the ocean floor.

After operations had been going for a solid hour, a voice on the bridge said, "Activate the hydro-cells in quadrant four."

The activity of the crew on the bridge indicated that this was exactly what was being done. Attica sat and waited in a manner that for her was remarkably patient, eyes burning holes in the back of each crewman's head. At length, she noted that the people around her were no longer working as frenzied as they had a moment before.

"So?" she asked, drumming her fingers on the arm of the chair.

"Hydro-cells activated, my Lady," said the captain. "We have sixteen hours before the next phase can begin."

The allotted time irritated her. The drumming fingers stopped and rolled into a fist.

"Sixteen hours?"

"It is a detailed and delicate procedure, my Lady."

There was a pause, during which there was a hesitating silence over a majority of the bridge. A collective holding of breath permeated the atmosphere.

"Very well," she said at last, and rose. "As time progresses and allows, continue with the operation." Her piercing blue eyes locked onto the captain's. "Do it quickly. Do it right. If we have to reset *anything* or for some reason require more hydro-cell charges, we'll have a major setback." She turned to go and looked back over her shoulder abruptly. "I don't like setbacks."

"Yes, my Lady."

૪૦ ભ

Cyprus was in his cabin, satisfaction and impatience washing over him all at once. His mind continued to repeat the one thought that had not left since he had first conjured it: *When the last Gatekeeper is slain, what he loves most in this world must die with him.* Soon, the world would be a different place. Soon, Orion would be dead, and with him Dominos de Lumine – the foremost enemy of the Order of the Raven – would shatter and fall apart. And Cyprus would lead the Raven to glory over the smoldering ruins. *One era ends, the next begins.*

He had been in a foremost position for long years; complete control would be new, but it would be manageable as well. No more answering to Attica. *No more errand-boy, running off at some woman's whim.* No more gallivanting about on the business of another. *It is time for mine.*

He blinked hard and saw the face of Memphis staring at him from under his eyelids. Admittedly, the Shades were still about. That Arcanus was gone would be a setback for them, certainly. But another would ascend to take his place, just as he had ascended to replace his own predecessor back when the Gatekeepers were still periodically making examples of even Elder Shades.

He needed Shades around anyway, to continue. A strong dose of venom every century would see Cyprus's mortal longevity into the next – and he had not yet learned how to cope without it. And then there was the search for time agent serum – a waste of time after all that work.

As soon as I am in command, I will strike a new bargain with Memphis Shadowcloak. Then we will see to my supply of venom, see if there is a less dependent means to continue. And the ruins of Dominos de Lumine will have to be searched for elapsation serum too... Once that was established, the Shades in the Earth Realm could be hunted down and exterminated. He blinked heavily twice, tongue flicking out like a snake. *But first they will set me free of this lingering malady. It cannot be stutter-flutter. My new life is only about to begin, I am not going mad.*

›› ‹‹

On the bridge, the captain pointed at a green light on the console, his satisfaction evident as he proudly showed Attica the results of their earlier detonation of hydro-cells.

"See, my Lady?" he asked. "The ocean floor has risen almost three hundred fathoms. The calculation was correct. The vents beneath the surface were perfectly aligned to engage vertical seismic movement upon detonation."

Attica nodded quietly, saying nothing but obviously pleased. She had been in this reflective mood since giving the order to detonate the first hydro-cells six hours ago. Of course, as usual, even Cyprus was unaware of exactly what went on in her head. At the moment, she only watched the screen and then nodded once again.

"Initiate the second stage as soon as it is pertinent to do so," she said.

"At once, my Lady."

"How long?"

"Eighteen hours after initiation."

"Continue your work."

"Yes, my Lady."

஗ ௚

The time spent floating in the water, holding their position, was tedious for all parties. Orion, by looking up at the stars, determined they were holding their position, not moving. He spent the time on deck, looking out and staring at the other ships. For much of the tedium he preferred to go to the other side of their ship, to gaze out at nothing. Frank and Adrienne walked the deck together, as they had the previous days. Attica was nowhere to be seen.

If any of the three prisoners had been allowed to observe on the bridge, they would have noted that the operating crew was tracking the gradual movement of the ocean floor just off starboard and prow. Over the trailing hours, the bottom of the ocean had been slowly rising. Months before, when Attica's agents had reached the proper location and begun their work on the bottom, the ocean was nearly three kilometers deep. Through careful work in the use of hydro-cell technology and both a strategic releasing *and* increasing of volcanic pressures, the seafloor had begun its rise. Final stages had been within reach for a fortnight. By the time Attica's eighteen hour stretch was complete, in the remote distance off the ship, the smallest hills of land had just begun to peek up through the waves, vanishing and reappearing as the swells of the Atlantic churned over them.

It was Adrienne who noticed that these tiny islands had ever so slowly begun to grow larger with every swell of the waves. In time, they stopped moving altogether, or so she gathered after staring while leaning on the rails. Not at all long after she realized they had stopped rising, Adrienne noticed Attica ascending the stairs to the bridge and disappearing inside the doorframe.

No more than a minute later, as Adrienne gazed into the green and blue water in the direction of the small islands, she saw, deep beneath the surface but not too far away, orange flashes, small but defined. They began off to the right and distant, and one after the other slowly flashed through the water in the vaguest of semi-circles, making an arc from right to left. There were ten of the minute orange flashes, charges beneath the surface, barely discernible from the ship, but seen by Adrienne's sharp eyes.

On the bridge, Attica was assured of a mere ten hours to wait before completion. The process was enacted by the third hydro-cell demolition, whose flashes Adrienne had detected. Back on deck, Adrienne shivered in the November wind and leaned against Frank, whose attention she had just called to the islands.

"What are those islands?" she asked him.

"They are not islands," said Frank quietly.

"Then what are they?"

Orion's voice interrupted anything Frank might have intended to say.

"They are hilltops," he said, coming up beside them, looking out, resting folded hands on the rail. "Or what were once hilltops. By now even the highest mountains must be eroded and broken."

"So that is...?" she trailed off expectantly.

"The city of Iratha, capital of Atlantis," said Orion. "For the first time in millennia, Atlantis is going to be above sea level."

Adrienne stared in awe. "*All* of Atlantis?" she asked incredulously.

"Atlantis was not a city; it was a continent. Down through the ages a city was assumed, not an entire land. The Raven are using some specially developed depth charges to manipulate the old volcanic vents that helped sink the civilization long ago. What sent it below now allows it to rise: it is in the dead center of multiple tectonic plates." He paused and looked out over the water before continuing. "We must be dedicated in our business, Frank."

Frank nodded, arm around Adrienne. "I know. We are."

"We can hope that some other solution will present itself, but we must go forward as if none will."

CHAPTER 20

"The beautiful Lady Attica Triassa, on the rare occasions when she was able to hold her blazing lust for me in check, would grill me often about the Gatekeepers and their infamous Seal upon the Portal Gate. In the days when the Portal Gate was an open passageway to the world of the Shades, it was through this that the Shades gained entry to the Earth Realm. The Gatekeepers were able to place a Seal over the Portal Gate, like a door over a doorway, and the entry to our world was essentially blocked off. Anyone who knows anything would call this their greatest accomplishment.

"But even the Gatekeepers' greatest triumph is flawed, which given their arrogance is not surprising. The Seal is not impervious nor eternal as it stands today. It is like a dam that leaks; it serves its original purpose of keeping more Shades out, but the Shades already in the Earth Realm feed from what energy does get through. They would like nothing better than to see the Seal removed.

"The Kedassaic Texts are a time-honored and ancient work of Atlantean history, wisdom and philosophy. They speak of how things were then, and indeed even of how some things are now. Regarding the Seal, they state that only when joined with the lifeblood of an immortal will the gate between the dimensions be permanently sealed. Or so I told my pretty little angel one night upon a bearskin rug in front of the roaring fire – after making passionate love, of course."

~an excerpt from the memoirs of Cyprus Blackshaft

Attica appreciated that what she had in front of her were copies, and not the original. The Kedassaic Texts, the books of Atlantean craft and lore that Cyprus had gained for her on Sicily so long ago, were ancient indeed. She sat in the bowels of the ship, poring once more over the laminated copies of choice passages from the hoary old book. Skimming, highlighting, half-memorizing. She had spent hours doing this, and here in the ship she went on, reading and re-reading. *There must be no mistakes in the translation, no misreads, no misunderstanding.*

She had read the Kedassaic Texts in their entirety, of course. Multiple times. Not bad, considering it was in a dead language that only a handful of people in the world could even recognize, let alone read like a newspaper. Cyprus had only needed to assist her with some of the more grandeur of the vocabulary – and he never had to address the same word twice.

While the book had many things to say on a variety of topics, Attica's specific interests regarded both the Shades and the Gatekeepers. Both were of paramount importance to the legion of authors that had created the many pages, and over years of study Attica had learned much. In a world of obscure facts that most forgot, where truth really was often stranger than fiction, even she had to marvel. The Shades, however other-worldly, were still real enough. She still wore the green gem necklace at all times. The effect it had had on Arcanus was reason enough to keep the jewel close. The Eternal Order of the Brotherhood of the Gatekeepers, of simply the Gatekeepers, was the first of its kind. *And ironically*, she thought more than once, *they are still around*. But they were dying out, being down to their very last member: her own former love Orion.

Almost every culture had its own elite group, whether scholastic or military or even both. The Shaolin Monks, the Magi, the Hashishiyun, the Hospitalers, the Cult of Isis, the Praetorian Guards. In the modern world military associations like the Green Berets and Spetznatz, or MI6 were widely recognized. Yet the Gatekeepers predated them all, and in practically all cases had the best of what many such associations were known for: loyalty, philosophy, martial prowess, knowledge, daring, sacrifice. The list went on and on.

While she could admire the organization for its sheer ancientness, Gatekeeper demises were much more to her interest. Her fascination had nothing to do with bloodlust or hatred. It was just that Gatekeeper deaths were few and far between, and nearly every one after the fall of Atlantis was unique. The history of Gatekeeper deaths after Atlantis was vague, but she knew enough to form an understanding. Cyprus had aided her much, and even Dominos de Lumine had some records. They did not seem to mind dispelling what had happened once someone was dead; there was no disadvantage since no further damage could be done.

Thirteen men, a Consul and twelve Gatekeepers had been granted immortality.

The first among them had not died until a little over two thousand years later. In the seventeenth century BC, the first immortal Gatekeeper had taken mad with stutter-flutter and committed suicide. Over the next twelve centuries this happened twice more.

And then it gets interesting.

The Consul named Faeryn of Iratha, a foremost leader in the Gatekeeper order, had finally wearied of life right around the time Islam had begun its rise. But he was not taken with the immortal malady of stutter-flutter; no, his was an acceptance and capitulation that his years had run their course. And so he had come to the Different Place, and his secrets had been taken from him. Every remaining Gatekeeper's secret method of death was learned by the Shades.

Though it took some years for the Shade in the Different Place to pass on the information back to the waking Earth Realm, it was eventually done – and every Gatekeeper was in immediate mortal danger. Within a quarter century, three more Gatekeepers had been killed. Lists were sent out to enemies. Gangs of assassins, for once properly armed, hunted down the men who had hunted so many others before. Predator was at last prey.

Attica smiled. *Well…perhaps 'prey' is a poor word.*

More than once gangs of hunters had located a Gatekeeper and attempted to use a malady upon him – only to find they had the wrong man. Obsidian might work for the one Gatekeeper, but if another was cornered instead, the result was often that no assassin survived to explain to others what went wrong. Even mortal, Gatekeepers were still accomplished killers and knew their business well. Even if one knew what to stab him with – one still had to manage to stab him in the first place.

Attacking a Gatekeeper with the wrong weapon is a bad time to discover your mistake. Be sure you get it right, Attica silently counseled herself, *because you won't get a second chance.*

Still, Gatekeeper numbers had gradually dwindled. From around 1000 AD to the present-day, a Gatekeeper was killed on average once every two centuries. By that reckoning, Orion's death – last of the Gatekeepers as he was – was overdue. But he had been more clever than the others by half.

She thought back on the various methods the Gatekeepers had chosen to dispatch themselves. She could not recall every one. *Gold, pure bronze, obsidian, birch wood, unrefined iron, even a clay pottery shard.*

Some had gone with unusual items that were hard to get, and some had gone with standard every day items that one would not typically think of turning into a weapon. Orion had done both – and his genius was proven by his life remaining to that day.

Attica fingered the gem necklace with one hand as she pushed another laminated page aside and began skimming the next.

৪০ ৫৪

Over the hours the ship waited off the rising islands, land continued to push itself from the sea. The progress was slow, and soon most eyes had ceased to watch from the monotony of it all. What had appeared as small mounds were soon hills. Any land vegetation was gone, of course, as the hills rose anew from the sea. Instead of grass and trees, they were covered in mostly coral and tubeworms, some magnificently colored, so that one watching from the ship would see a virtual kaleidoscope of hues all mixed together. Other marine life that one might find at the bottom of the ocean could also be seen aplenty, for the rising island of Atlantis, or at least the section of it that Attica had isolated, was not at all small: the other side of it could not be seen from the ship. It was rapidly becoming a plausible island.

Perhaps it was some magic of old, or simply the incredible design of the Atlantean architects ages before, but there were remnants of buildings still to be seen: walls, arches, towers, gates, pillars; nearly all cast down and strewn everywhere. In places, intelligent construction and design over the desolation was obvious, and by squinting and some imagination it was easy to bring the city back to life in one's mind.

At length the process was complete and the island had reached its greatest extent above the waves. Adrienne was reminded of a trip to Greece she had taken as a student. The ruins of Ephesus, Athens, and other great ancient cities had filled her with both a delight and wonder. But what she had seen in Greece was dwarfed by what she could see now from the ship. They could see no end to what had surely once been a great metropolis, bustling with people, life and culture. Her eyes picked their way amid what had once been the heart of a mighty city.

৪০ ৫৪

Attica did not allow anyone the luxury of time to sit and stare. Her methods of bringing up the landmass had worked, and she was exceedingly pleased. But she was also aware no one had really done anything of the like before, and she was ever looking for something to go wrong, sending the fruits of her labor back beneath the waves. Because of this, she began organizing a departure to the island as soon as the process appeared complete.

Cyprus, who had not been seen for much of the journey or the elapsed time of waiting, helped Attica in this endeavor. Once she had decided to make her move, he could be seen on the deck giving orders to crewman, or with Attica on the bridge going over what proved to be a number of maps. Like Orion, he too was returned to his homeland, and while it had been a long time, he could still determine much of what had once been.

Between tasks, and while letting workmen accomplish various orders, he stood near Adrienne at the head of the ship leaning on the banister, pointing and speaking like the tour guide had in Athens.

"The great tower of Sothari stood there near those fallen pillars and rubble. She was the most beautiful and powerful queen to rule the empire. The pillars are what is left of her library," he would say, or "That wider area to the west, with the fallen columns, was used for athletic purposes, and had seats for ten thousand people: one could watch chariot races, athletic competitions, circuses, dragon duels-"

Adrienne stopped short. "Dragon duels?"

"Aye, dragon duels," he continued. "Great entertainment, that."

There were numerous cultures in the world that had some form of dragon in their legends; from China to Scotland, Russia to India. It surprised Cyprus that people today did not make this link to the past in which such animals may actually have lived. Cyprus had seen the creatures for himself. Not even so distantly in history there were numerous references to dragons. Modern man was constantly undermining eyewitness accounts as fanciful, as if he understood to a higher degree than one who was actually there. *Everyone who lives today thinks he knows better than he who lived yesterday. But there is nothing new under the sun.* Atlanteans had trained and used dragons for both military and recreational purposes. In city assaults it was remarkably convenient to have a living siege engine that would walk up to the gate by itself without having to be wheeled up hills or over rocks. And of course with properly trained animals the duels were truly fantastic. Cyprus had lost and won many a wager at the dragon arena…but many things had changed since the Age of Man was young.

Cyprus said little more, kept busy by Attica's orders to make ready to depart. Behind him, Adrienne stared with renewed interest. Despite her own kidnapping and all the disagreeable things that had happened to her, looking down upon the ruins of the oldest civilization of mankind on earth and having a local fellow point things out was utterly fascinating. Her own troubles were dwarfed by the wonder of Atlantis, at least until they left the ship.

෮ ෬

Two engine-powered RIBs – rigid-hulled-inflatable boats, each fifteen meters long – departed from the cargo ship. These highly-durable, hard-to-sink craft were piloted toward a rocky shoreline. Each craft held fifteen people, among whom were Attica, Cyprus, Frank and Adrienne, and Orion. The rest of the group was made up of crewmen; thirty people in all.

While Frank and Adrienne sat next to each other looking out over the waves toward their destination only a few hundred meters away, Orion did not share their apprehensive anticipation of setting foot in Atlantis. His expression was impassive, and he exhibited no more enthusiasm for their journey than one might have shown for a trip to the dentist. Each prisoner still wore the shocking collar, but Orion was the only one whose hands had been cuffed in front of him – with two pairs of handcuffs. *To ease my walk through the rubble and carnage*; behind his back would make his journey most awkward. He sat quietly in the back of the first craft, observing.

Attica had not given him a second look as she sat on the small box toward the front of the open craft. Orion forced himself not to watch her, but looked about. He had seen her carrying a number of maps rolled up carefully in sealed tubes, and among the other supplies he had seen no small number of flashlights, flares, and lamps mounted on headgear, as if they were going spelunking. Ropes and grappling hooks could also be seen in abundance, and he could tell that the Raven had come prepared to spend most of their time in the dark in passages that lay mostly in ruin.

Among the things that caught Orion's wandering eye as he tried to pretend he could not see her, was that Attica wore two swords. One was his, not in his crafted upside down sheath as he had always worn it, but in a simple scabbard over her shoulder with the handle in easy reach of her right hand. At her left side was a weapon of her own favor, obviously, and it was very much like his. It was a short, double-edged twenty-inch stabbing weapon with a rounded pommel and simple handle designed for one hand. In an almost humorous manner, aside from the ancient weapons on her person, she also sported a handgun on her right hip. From that distance at that angle, he could not tell what it was, but he guessed a .357. Attica's green gem necklace shimmered in the sun as she sat. Adrienne was looking resignedly at the bauble that had once been her own. She wondered why Attica had kept the jewel but gotten rid of the intricate silver casing that had formerly held it.

Orion did not marvel over why she was wearing swords in an age when warfare was reduced to pushing buttons or pulling triggers. Swords were archaic but could still accomplish much. A handgun would do little more than enrage a Shade, for example. But his Atlantean blade? That would dispatch such creatures. *The right weapon for the right job*, he had always believed. Hence it was no wonder she carried his blade. There was no telling what they might meet that was like the Shades, or even an actual Shade. It was best to be prepared, and she was. Perhaps her own sword was specifically designed to serve some purpose as well.

At length deciding that he could see too little from their current position as their modified crafts sped toward the pebbly beach that had appeared not four hours before, Orion sat back and closed his eyes. He did this just in time to miss Attica turning to look at him, her expression unreadable.

☘ ☙

The boats could be driven right up on the shore and partly out of the water to allow the occupants to disembark. When they had all set foot upon the shore per Attica's instruction, five crewmen remained with the boats. This left the three prisoners, Attica and Cyprus, and twenty crewmen.

Adrienne looked around and shivered in the cold wind. Each crewman lugged both a pack of supplies on his back, and over a shoulder carried a various array of firearms. Frank could tell there were a variety of automatic machineguns and small arms, but he didn't bother to tell his wife. She had never liked guns – despite her family upbringing.

Booted feet crunched on the pebbly beach as the company moved forward, the way winding between many large, worn stones. The air carried a distinct odor of dead sea life drying in the sun. Each person climbed over the first of many fallen pillars, like a giant log stretched across their path. Periodically, a burst of hot steam would vent off the surface or sizzle as the heat struck trapped saltwater. Adrienne recalled that according to some legends Atlantis had been taken down by a volcano.

The ground in most places was terribly muddy and wet. Cyprus led the way, followed by Attica, a couple crewmen, the prisoners, and the rest of the guards. It was all natural, wild. Frozen, dry, crumbling sea life like coral was everywhere, crackling underfoot or catching a loose garment as one walked by. There was also the occasional stranded fish lying beached on the stone, or feebly moving in a shallow pool among the rocks. Marooned jellyfish lay like blobby, white softballs.

Orion kept his emotional connection completely unexpressed as he once again set foot upon Atlantean stone for the first time in millennia. Their short walk had taken them to what had once been a main thoroughfare through an outdoor market and business section of town. The remains of buildings were now clearly around them. *This road leads back beneath the carnage and would take us to Mount Aliah if we went far enough.* He recalled the next sharp corner was where the blacksmith and the other metalworkers had congregated.

Before them, the path of cobblestones was smooth and worn over with time. Dark doorways gapped at them. All was a cool whitish stone, like marble. Columns lay cast upon the ground, or half-erect but broken off like jagged marble teeth. One stump of a pillar stretched twelve feet across. The lines of buildings were broken up by side streets that crisscrossed the main thoroughfare.

Cyprus too showed little if no sentiment as he looked upon the ruins of his homeland. But to Frank it seemed his jaw was set a bit tighter, and he looked more pleased than aggrieved at the status of the broken city. Orion walked to a large pillar, slightly away from the group, two or three of the crewman following him with the barrels of their weapons.

Orion at length touched the smoothness of the stone. He stood there showing for the first time that he might, after all, have some connection to the destruction. He stood there for nearly a minute, some of his companions watching him quietly, others unable to take their eyes from the magnificent civilization around them. At length Cyprus spoke loud enough for Orion to hear from where he stood, doubtless intending to get him to return.

"This way," he said simply, and started walking.

If Adrienne had been awed from the ship, she was utterly floored by personally standing amidst the ruins. Beside her and holding her hand Frank walked along, equally impressed. He had never been to tour ancient sites as his wife had, but he had always wanted to. Now, walking through the ruins of a newly-arisen city of the Atlantean continent, he could not turn away.

The only one plainly unimpressed with much of anything was Attica. The only time she looked at the city was when she glanced up from a map, which she took out and inspected whenever they took a periodical break to get bearings. Only Orion had concern in the back of his mind when he looked at her, consumed as she was with all in her mind. In their married days, she had never been a driven woman, never more goal-oriented than what she intended to do from day to day. Yet now she was more focused than he had ever seen her, and in a most discomforting manner. He also noted that she had not looked his way since departing the cargo freighter.

At length, Cyprus halted at a major crossroads. The grand street they had followed now crossed perpendicularly with another tremendous road of equal girth. In the middle of the crossroads was the circular basin of a large fountain. Despite its diameter, there was still a wide space around the perimeter for passing traffic and people. In the middle of it there rose a pedestal, and upon the stone stood a towering statue of a figure thirty feet tall; a man of athletic build with a large barrel tucked under his arm and another over his shoulder, the mouths of which both leaned down. Cracked and crumbling sea life covered him, and there was immense wear and tear; the face was entirely worn away. At one time the statue and its barrels had fed the fountain, which even now maintained a little saltwater that did not drain away.

"The Crossroads of Harvor the Mariner," said Cyprus with satisfaction. "It has been long since I looked upon this fountain. I did not think I would ever see it again."

"Nor me," said Orion quietly, looking up at the terribly worn face. Only a few looked at him at first, but when he went on, all eyes turned toward him. "You'll want to go north, I imagine."

Attica's eyes especially bore into him. "And how did you know that?"

"We are going to the Portal Chamber, no?"

"Very good, uncle," said Cyprus. "But how did you come to that conclusion?"

"Where else would we be going, nephew? There is nothing here of value any longer. The throne you meant to usurp will do you little good now."

This last remark was obviously a shot at Cyprus and the old insurrection that had been mentioned, when the two men had taken different sides in what became the Atlantean civil war. The war the Shades had introduced their true colors to create, which had ended with the utter destruction of the continent.

"You can hold a grudge a long time," said Cyprus, "but I have other loyalties now." He blinked hard twice.

"Yes, and why shouldn't you?" asked Orion dryly, eyes on the horizon. "The winds have changed."

Cyprus turned practically scarlet at that, but Attica interrupted both of them.

"Peace!" she snapped, eyes on the map she had unrolled carefully upon a boulder. She ignored how both Atlantean men did not stop staring at one another, but continued studying the map. At length she spoke again, to Cyprus. "How long till the imperial palace?"

"Due north an eighth mile: not more than five minutes," said he, still staring at Orion.

"Then let's get moving. I want to gain the imperial gates soon. Then we'll see what condition the lower levels are in."

"And if you cannot enter them due to the destruction?" asked Orion.

She glared at him as if a child in the class had asked a stupid question. "Then your friends had better hope you know another way in."

Adrienne looked from Attica to Orion, from storm to calm, and she clasped Frank's hand tighter. She had hardly let it go since they had reached there. Atlantis was beautiful and amazing, but there was an inescapable dread in the atmosphere about them. They were walking through a dead city, nothing living but themselves. It was an eerie sensation. *As if feeling cold isn't enough. I'd turn around and look back, if I wasn't afraid I'd catch something watching us from one of these black doorways.* While she admitted this to be a silly fancy, her spine tingling was quite tangible. The talk about 'lower levels' did nothing to assuage her nagging worries.

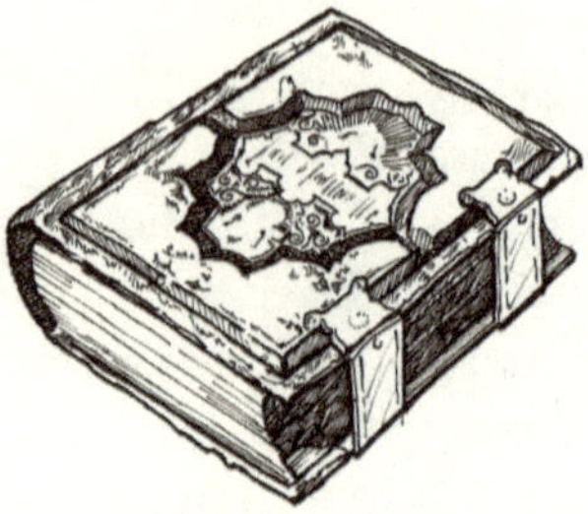

CHAPTER 21

"Nothing upon the face of the Earth lasts forever. Even the Eternal Brotherhood of the Gatekeepers shall one day have a final member. Their Seal over the Portal Gate must be joined with the lifeblood of an immortal if the Way is to be forever closed. Only then can the Earth Realm be free of the brooding darkness that seeks its destruction and the enslavement of every soul within her. Woe to them that remain should the Seal ever be broken – for then the black tide shall cover the Earth Realm, and darkness reign."

~an excerpt from Book 23 of the Kedassaic Texts – said by some to be the Compromised Passages.

ꟿ ꟿ

Adrienne was not the only one who did not care for the mention of the lower levels. Though he showed no concern outwardly, Orion's mind was conjuring every last memory he could recall from the old days. It had, after all, been a long time since he walked anywhere in Atlantis, let alone the dark passages and halls beneath the imperial palace. Even before the Shades had introduced themselves to the most legendary civilization of mankind, there were generations going further back, and these remnants of old kings and rulers still left their mark. There were other cultures here too, in the foundations of the city itself, deep and remote – untouched since years before the civil war or even the empire itself, before the imperial line of the Sejarrian Dynasty had conquered the continent and put its peoples under one political system. The Sejarrians had been a noble house, but not all their ancient predecessors had been as cultured or civil

It was to the legends of these uncultured predecessors that Orion's mind found itself wandering as he walked in the procession northward. They now walked consistently uphill, but Orion's thoughts were dragging him down. He caught himself once again checking the armament of Attica's thugs, counting the firearms, curious if they had extra clips. He wished the list of their defenses went on, but it did not.

ꙮ

In time they could see their destination. As they rounded a soft corner, an especially wide berth of destruction altered the horizon. At the top of the gentle hill they had been climbing for a solid five minutes, there was, or at least had once been, a mighty wall. In its glory days, the wall had stood fifty feet high, the perimeter wall of the imperial palace. Their avenue led them straight to a gaping hole in the barricade where gates must have surely been at one time.

Of course only Cyprus, Orion and maybe Attica fathomed that the entire city was built around a gently rising hill upon which sat the square of the imperial palace. They reached the end of their path and paused for a moment before the southern gate. About the palace and right at the feet of the wall was a tremendous trench. Thirty feet below them water filled this trench, hiding its true depth.

The street they had followed ended at the trench and transformed into a decrepit-looking stone bridge. It had once had banisters on both sides and snarling stone lions as large as elephants facing out toward the city in silent warning. One lion's upper half had fallen off and lay in ruin, and the second lion had vanished completely. Across the short stretch of bridge, there awaited the shadowy mouth of the south gate halfway filled with rubble and sediment, and beyond at the end of its dark but brief tunnel, they could see daylight shining on the courtyard beyond.

Attica was unconcerned at the age of the bridge, though she sent Frank and Adrienne across together, as if to see if it would vanish from beneath their feet. When nothing happened, the rest of the party followed. Only Orion looked down into the trench, reminded of the lower levels that awaited them all. Attica noticed that he was not moving quickly, and her glance at one of the guards got him a gun barrel in the back to get him plodding along faster.

The courtyard of the palace was but one of many. Once inside the gate they could see that the wall was some forty feet thick, and had stables and barracks built into it. Orion looked about. *There is no perfectly-kept grass here now. Just stone and muck, and water-logged earth.* Behind them was the gate, and after a wide gap of open space for the courtyard itself, some wide steps went up into the palace itself.

That section of the palace itself rose several stories above them. The places in the palace that looked out over the wall would have allowed the viewer to see for miles in every direction. The complex was huge, and beyond the steps the high roof was upheld by a row of tall columns. Beyond the cavernous hall was darkness with occasional stabs of sunshine like slender, slanted golden pillars; their way forward was for the first time covered with a roof.

Frank stopped to stare at an eighteen-foot shark that lay unmoving on its stomach nearby, beached in the courtyard when the city rose from the sea. Nearby, Cyprus spoke to Attica. In the silence of the courtyard, all heard what he said.

"I can take us no further. I have been in parts of the palace long ago, but never from this direction; it is too large a place to try and find our way without getting lost."

"Very well," said Attica quietly. She glanced at Orion, who was looking up the steps to the columns and the way forward, wondering what had happened to the stone lions that had once been there. She ordered him with confidence. "Take us to the Portal Chamber, and do not delay."

Without looking at her, eyes still taking in the ruins before him, he held out his cuffed wrists. He said nothing.

"Those remain where they are," said Attica, knowing he meant for her to remove them.

"Then so do I," he said, lowering his gaze until it finally met hers. He was firm.

Her eyes strayed to Adrienne, standing beside her husband. They took her in from head to toe. "Do you remember our conversation regarding the Lady Blackman?" she asked coldly. Adrienne straightened. "What I would have done to her if you refused me?"

Now Frank looked up and held his wife tightly.

"I am not refusing you," said Orion evenly, "I am saying I would like the use of my hands. I assure you it is for the good of passage to the chamber."

There was a moment where the two merely stared at each other, but at length Attica nodded to one of the guards, who removed the handcuffs.

"Keep in mind I can have it done, should you feel obligated to abuse your freedom," she hissed at him as he walked past her, headed for the steps. "Or I can shock you."

He spoke over his shoulder. "If I am suddenly met with a need to use my hands," he said, "rest assured that at that moment in time, I will be the least of your problems."

Attica glared, but did nothing as they all fell in line behind Orion, Frank trotting to catch up a moment before returning to Adrienne. His instinctive role as husband would be protective, despite the likelihood that their captors would stymie his efforts. *I've got to know if something unpleasant is going to happen.*

"Expecting troubles in a city with nothing alive in it?" asked Frank.

Orion paused at the top of the steps, standing between two giant columns. Before them was a smooth floor that stretched into darkness; they were about to enter a cavernous hall filled with pillars. On one side large statues could be seen lining the wall, but these were abruptly lost in darkness. Droplets echoed in the empty night ahead of them.

"The lower levels beneath the imperial palace have many things within them, my old friend," he said, looking back at the sunlight as if he would miss it. "And most of those things were put there with the purpose of keeping the unwanted visitor out."

He stopped speaking at the sound of Attica's footfalls as she climbed the steps behind them, leading the rest of the expedition.

"Look out for your lady," ended Orion to Frank, and began walking into the darkness of the hall. The others reluctantly followed him, one by one.

∛ ∛

Orion led them on a trek of winding and climbing around fallen debris through grand rooms. They passed through the first hall and into the shadows where they found a massive entryway that at one time would have had tall narrow doors filling the space beneath the arches. The doors were now gone, and a few crabs scuttled out of the light of the headlamps and electric lanterns which seven of Attica's crewmen had activated. Attica herself carried a flashlight, and a few others did too. Orion walked without the aid of the light, and they had to keep up with him or lose him in the darkness.

Cyprus crept along behind, as he could see in the dark as well. He found himself looking behind them periodically, listening to the sound of dripping from the ceiling, or the clicking of crab legs on the stone as the crustaceans scattered out of their way periodically. He also watched Attica, wondering how well she could see in the dark, as the other present immortals could. She had never divulged completely to Cyprus exactly what abilities her Shade-given lifespan had allowed her. *That was wise of her.* He wondered if his uncle may have been considering the same thing.

Orion took them through a span of four large halls, all deserted and ruinous. The darkness was absolute, and the flashes of headlamps made one almost sick after a while. They had ventured away from any windows or lattices. Occasionally they had to go around massive blocks of masonry that had fallen from the ceiling. Here, no beams of sunshine managed to stab down into the eternal night.

Attica held her flashlight and moved it about with one hand, the other hand resting on her sword-hilt. She allowed herself a few fleeting glimpses of the magnificent ruins around her as she and her companions traversed through them. Yet always her eyes returned to Orion's tall and silent form as he moved down the corridors and through the halls. *After all*, she pondered, *he does not need the light. All he has to do is vanish around a corner and leave us all here.* This fear kept her alert, eyes consistently on her former husband. Cyprus would have been some good to have around, perhaps, but he had never been in the very depths of the palace, or in the lower levels where Orion was supposedly leading them.

Adrienne and Frank had locked hands since passing into the darkness, and neither was even close to letting go. They walked in silence, trailing some crewmen and followed by others. Yet even the crewmen were on edge enough to hardly be concerned that they might actually be called upon to guard any of the prisoners.

The looming size and lonely darkness of the palace had a sobering and distracting effect on the men.

Frank had realized potential opportunities to escape and slip away into the labyrinth about them, but he did not seize any of them. When it came right down to it, he had to recognize they were on a small island hundreds of miles from anywhere. He had no means of communication and the only passage off was on a Raven freighter. With Attica's entourage or alone, they were trapped; they might as well stay with the people who owned the boat.

"How much longer?" asked Attica at length.

Orion's quiet question infuriated her. "Until what?" he asked without turning, still walking along.

"Until we are at the Portal Chamber, of course," she snapped. "We haven't descended a single level since entering-"

"At ease, my Lady," he said, again not turning, which only added to her angst. "You shall have your lower levels soon enough." He pointed into the darkness. "See? We approach the Bottomless Stair."

Cyprus's voice came from behind them all. "At last!"

The others turned their lights in that direction. At the end of the hall there was a vast black opening, like an old railway tunnel. Beneath a high arch, wide and shallow stairs led down into the dark.

Adrienne leaned close to her husband. "I don't like the sound of 'Bottomless Stair," she said quietly.

Frank nodded and squeezed her hand. He didn't care for it either. Judging from the mutterings of the men around them, not many others did. Cyprus and Attica, on the other hand, were quite pleased. Attica even allowed them a ten minute break before continuing.

"How deep is it really?" Adrienne asked Orion as the group sat, some on fallen rubble and others at the bases of tremendous columns. *It can't be truly bottomless.* As he answered, he was aware that most of those present were anxiously anticipating his reply.

"I do not truly know," he admitted at length. "I have never been to the end of them, nor has anyone else that I know of. I have only been down twenty-three levels at the deepest."

"Right," said a nearby crewman, rolling his eyes. "Maybe it really *is* bottomless." His suggestion got a couple chuckles from his crewmates, if only to release some of the tension. But Orion only continued:

"No one I know of would have the curiosity to go all the way into the depths, at the same time having the fortitude to climb all the way back up. The Stair was not made entirely by Atlanteans, but by previous monarchs and dynasties. Undoubtedly its lowest reaches are rubble by now. Even the path we mean to follow will take us far below what was once ground level." He paused in telling this to Adrienne, but then added to the crewman as an afterthought, "You should save your clever wit for the coming time when the path grows truly dark."

℘ ℂ

The stairs were broad and shallow, spanning the whole descending passage. They curved to the right, gently, as if they were slowly walking down inside a giant hollow pillar of stone. No longer were they surrounded by the lighter stone of the palace; no marble or alabaster here. Now all was gray rock, cut in drab squares. The walls were unadorned with an occasional removed block for what Orion said were places for candles, or originally brackets for torches, long since rotted and gone.

When they had been walking downward for sometime, they at last came to a place where the stairs stopped temporarily in a landing. The stairs went on and passed down into the dark, but to the right was a black passageway.

"The armory was once down that passage – the royal armory," said Orion, nonchalantly.

"Is that where it was?" asked Cyprus conversationally. "We never could find it. It must have been well-protected."

"Aye," agreed Orion, "by the girtas."

Cyprus hesitated, looked into the blackness once again, and then back at his uncle, who had begun to head down the Stair once again. The others in the company looked up at his unveiled apprehension. "Girtas…" he repeated to himself, and blinked heavily twice.

"Surprised that the Emperor should have the foresight to protect his family and possessions, nephew?" He paused and went on down the stair, talking over his shoulder. "You know, I have always wondered exactly what wound up corrupting the girtas. For a time they were so efficient."

"Their corruption…" finished Cyprus, thoughtfully licking his lips.

"The Keepers should have anticipated, but complacency is comfortable. Well, think nothing of it. Those barbaric little monstrosities are probably gone by now…"

Attica was glaring at Cyprus, mostly because his fretfulness was beginning to make her uneasy. She slowly turned her back on the dark entryway and continued walking with the group. No one was anxious to remain standing before that entry.

One of the crewmen had to ask. "Probably gone?" He turned to a compatriot. "I thought this place was deserted for thousands of years. How could anything live here?"

Orion's voice echoed back up the passage, sounding amused. "Your definition of what qualifies as 'alive' seems narrow."

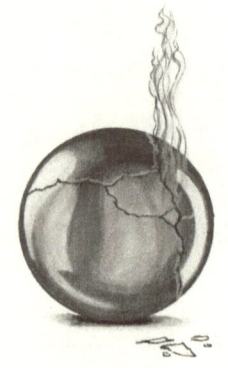

CHAPTER 22

"Do not speak to me of the girtas. I wish to sleep tonight..."

~Atlantean Crown princess Kyla Sejarrian

ᘓ ᘔ

A midst the murmuring of both friend and foe, Orion continued to lead the procession on down the stairs. They descended for nearly a half hour, just a steady pace, a gentle walk. Time after time they came upon another landing, usually complete with a black opening, some large enough for an elephant to pass into, some merely man-sized. Occasionally the natural decay of the place had cast rubble and fallen masonry over what had once been a door. With a difficult climb, they squeezed past one by one it to continue their way. Orion plodded along in no hurry at all, and all they saw was his back in the electronic light. His pace and manner were perfectly at ease.

But as usual, Orion's outward appearance completely masked his inward processes. His hearing was strained to its peak, listening for any rustlings in the dark aside from the footfalls of those with him. He wanted to have a warning, if anything was lurking there in the dark. The realization that the city had been sunk below the waves of the ocean for eons of time did nothing to dissuade Orion from fully expecting that they were not alone in the city.

He searched back in his old memories as far as he could reckon, trying to pull up recollections of the times he had ascended and descended the Stair. The Stair was so long that periodically there were levels set aside purely for the purpose of allowing stair-climbers to stop and rest for the night. He tried to recall the places in the palace that could not be reached by anything except the Bottomless Stair, which was really like a central axis around which the palace itself was built, and from which it extended out. As the steps descended, safer places were left behind and only the more perilous lay below.

"How much longer?" called Attica again, after quite some time.

Orion only slightly turned his head to speak over his shoulder as he kept going. "I really don't remember. But we must be close, at least to our exit level."

"I do not relish the climb back up," muttered a crewman.

"Aye," said a few others.

"Keep your comments to yourselves," growled Attica.

Adrienne walked close to Frank, silently agreeing with the crewmen, lamenting the momentous climb back up. *I hope we don't have to climb these stairs in a hurry.* Beside her, Frank was dreading the same thing.

Another hundred stairs and they reached what was around the tenth landing, and here Orion stopped. The entryway was large enough for five to walk through shoulder to shoulder, and the arch of the passage was well over their heads. He paused and looked around the crowd of people until he saw Attica.

"This is the level," he said, gazing at her evenly. Again Adrienne was amazed he could look at her without betraying the slightest hint of what had passed between them over the years. He neither looked as if he loved or hated her. He was expressionless.

"Good," she conceded, as if reluctant to praise him. "How much further?"

"Not more than one hundred fifty meters, barring any destruction that may block the way."

∞ ∞

The corridor of stone that Orion now led them down was wide enough for eight to walk abreast, with high stone walls and an unseen ceiling. Occasionally other passages intersected their own, and they would have the choice to go left or right or both. But Orion led them straight on for quite some time until their corridor emptied into a tremendous room, a hundred feet to a wall.

The large room was perfectly square with a doorway set in the middle of each of the walls. The first doorway through which they entered was the west door. The others, to their left, right and straight ahead, were completely walled off by large single pieces of smooth stone. Each rounded stone door, about ten feet in diameter, had an intricately carved symbol on its face. The ceiling in the room was unseen hundreds of feet overhead. In the southeast corner of the room was a circular gapping hole with nothing surrounding the edge. Staring into the hole revealed nothing but blackness. Down from the ceiling stabbed a pillar of sunshine, allowed in by either design or decayed flaw. While it illuminated much of the room with a terrifying brightness after so long in the darkness, it revealed nothing in the well in the corner.

"What is this place?" asked Attica.

Cyprus answered her, looking at the symbols on the doors. "The Guard Room to the Portal Chamber. In times of old, a company of Gatekeepers would hold a permanent barracks here. But now all that was here except the bare stone is gone... how barren it looks without their company." He pointed to the blocked passageway straight ahead, the east door. Even from across the whole room, he could see the eloquent ancient character carved on it. "That is the way to the Portal Chamber."

"You know much of a place you were never allowed to be in," said Orion over his shoulder as he slowly approached the eastern door, the way forward.

"What lies behind these other doors?" asked Frank as the entire company crossed the room.

No one said anything.

At length, Orion said, "Well? Tell him, nephew, since you know so much of the Guard Room."

"Just other passages," said Cyprus at length, and with some hesitancy.

"Yes yes, that is not our purpose here," snapped Attica with typical impatience and bite to her voice. "Orion, why is the passage blocked?"

"Do you not suspect why?" he asked.

Only Frank could detect the slightest hint of dry humor. He hid a grin.

"Answer her," ordered a crewman. A machinegun cocked in the relative silence of the room.

Orion gave him a glance, looking not quite unlike a disappointed father. At length he turned back to the east door and said as he faced away from them all, "There are no Gatekeepers here, so the Portal Chamber must be protected in their absence. It is blocked and indeed locked to keep out people like *you*."

She called over to her shoulder to one of the crewmen with a large pack: "Blow it."

Orion turned quickly. "I wouldn't do that..." he said.

She rolled her eyes and fixed him in her cold blue-eyed stare. "I'm listening."

"Forcing the east door without opening the lock may force the north and south doors open."

"So?"

Orion looked not at Attica, but now at Cyprus. The elder local's gaze was steely, but the younger was apprehensive. But both looks agreed they did not want the north and south doors opened.

"I like the room the way it is now...deserted." was all Orion said.

"Can you open it?" she asked.

"Given some time and peace..."

"Then get a move on." She turned to the rest of them. "All right, we'll take a rest here, then."

಼ ಣ

Twenty minutes later Orion was still standing beside the door, looking with concentration at a square flat area in the wall beside it. Frank leaned on the wall nearby, wishing he could be more helpful.

According to Orion, the circular hole in the floor was a well. On the other side of it, Attica and Cyprus spoke in low voices. The crewmen were scattered standing around the room, or sitting on blocks of fallen rubble and masonry. Adrienne sat on one such block of stone, not far from one of her guards, who had passed her a bottle of water. She sipped and stared at the floor, pretending that Cyprus wasn't staring at her, his eyes occasionally squeezing shut as if trying to clear themselves of debris.

"A bit complicated?" Frank asked Orion, even as he wondered if he should say anything at all.

He surveyed what Orion was looking at for the third time in twenty minutes. The flat patch in the stone was divided many times into small boxes, each about two inches square. Each had a symbol etched upon it. Very occasionally, Orion would reach out and push one of these squares inward toward the wall, and it would insert itself a few inches into the stone into which it was set. Franked watched with interest. *He's punching a sequence into the most ancient keyboard in the world.*

"You might say that," Orion consented as he pushed yet another key and then lowered his hand to study what he had done. Before him, given the keys, he had around one hundred choices. He had pushed in seven blocks. "I just have to remember the sequence, that is all."

"So far so good?"

"Given all of the keys have remained where I push them, yes, so far so good."

"What, don't you get a second chance if you push the wrong one?"

Orion stopped and gave Frank a condescending look. For the first time in twenty minutes he looked at something besides the keypad of stone. "No, Frank Blackman, I do not get a second chance if I push the wrong stone key. Now, do you mind?"

"Hey, sorry."

"Thank you."

Orion turned his attention back to the wall before Frank spoke again.

"What happens if you hit the wrong one?"

A lesser man would have snapped at him by then, but Orion only spoke with the slightest of annoyances. Frank had heard him speak to children with less tact. "If I push the wrong one, either that south door," and he pointed to the blocked passage to the right of the room, "or that north door" and he pointed to the other, "will open. The door I want to open will not open. The east passage we just came down – the way out, if you recall, may close. Now, that none of that has happened yet means that I have not yet made a mistake. Now, if you please…"

"But what if-"

"Frank."

"Yeah?"

"Shut up."

જી ભ્

A full forty minutes after Orion had set his mind to the sequence of opening the passage on to the Portal Chamber, he had pressed a total of twenty keys. He had once again paused in his study of the keys, reviewing the order in which he had progressed, and was also completely ignoring Attica's questions.

"How much longer?" she called from across the chamber, after another long pause.

"You ask that far too much," he said, not looking at her.

"We've been standing around for-"

"If I make a mistake this deep into the sequence, woman, we will all regret it."

"Then what is the hold-up?"

"I've one more key to press."

"Then *why* don't you press it?" she half-yelled, exasperated.

He turned to glare at her, his voice rising in surprising anger. "Because I cannot decide which one it is!" He stepped away from the wall a few steps, ticking on his fingers as he spoke. "It is one of three characters: tari, ephelos, or landir. Do you know which one it is?"

Silence met this question, as it had been asked with the intensity of a verbal onslaught.

"Well, nor do I," he said, and turned back to the keys.

"Just guess and let's get on with it," suggested a crewman.

"Yes, guess," said another.

"I cannot guess," said Orion quietly but rather menacingly, "because a mistake this far into the sequence will-"

"Make your pick," snapped Attica. "We've wasted enough time."

"You don't understand."

"The city will not stay above the waves for good," said Attica. "Eventually this will be under water again, we cannot sit and wait."

"I cannot just-"

"Do it!" three voices shouted at him.

"I am innocent of your blood," said Orion with a simmering menace, and turned to the keys. At length he reached out, having made a decision. "Landir…"

There was a soft click as it sank into place. It was his best guess, but he was far from sure. Of course, not being certain about it, he would have had to pick it anyway in the end. Some memories came back to him if he concentrated and waited long enough.

There was a moment of silence when nothing happened. Then there was a clicking behind the central door Orion was trying to open, then a very distant boom, as of great machinery moving in the walls, though what could have survived for so long, no one could imagine. And then the doors on their right and left, *not* the central passage door, slowly began to grind open, as if moved by tremendous gears in the walls. Slowly they ground back, beginning to reveal black passageways beyond.

Attica watched them open and then turned to glare with savage ferocity at Orion, as he stood there in front of the sealed door. Orion was expressionless, and if he was sorry he had not accomplished his task, he certainly did not show it. If it was possible to shrug not with his shoulders but merely with his eyebrows as he stared Attica and then Cyprus down, he did.

"Perhaps *tari* would have been wiser," said he.

Cyprus did not take it nearly as well as the others. "You fool!" he exclaimed and leaped to his feet in so arduous a fashion that several of the crewmen took their guns off their shoulders. Adrienne was not the only one briefly reminded of his former hesitancy to declare what was behind the other doors, now open.

Both Frank and Adrienne had stood with expectancy, looking at either opened door in turn, and though they did not purpose it, their hands met and clasped. Around them, there was a moment of quick chaos as everyone – or at least the crewmen – got to their feet or took some form of readiness.

A half minute of staring at the opened passageways passed, and nothing happened. Only Attica and Orion showed virtually no concern at what might decide to come down the passage and join them in the Guard Room. Or at least not on their faces. Attica, after an angry glare at Orion, loosened her sword in its sheath and freed the safety on her sidearm. Orion looked around the room, as if surveying the best place to be, and then slowly walked toward Frank and Adrienne.

The atmosphere in the Guard Room was one of such tense waiting that no armed crewman cared to stop Orion from walking over to Frank and saying a few quiet words in his ear with a hand on his shoulder.

"Fire-drill, old friend."

Frank nodded once, acknowledging their old saying for the needed evacuation of an area. *We need to get out of here now.*

"Where to?" he asked quietly.

"Back the way we came in. And don't look back. They'll want me first."

"Who will want you? The guards? Attica?"

"No, you'll see. Now that I consider it, after the other immortals, they'll want you next; have your wits about you when they come. Under no circumstances let them bite or sting you."

Frank nodded once and held Adrienne's hand tightly, wondering what exactly Orion was talking about. But the old Atlantean only turned away and walked toward Attica.

"What was that all about?" whispered Adrienne, as she hadn't heard much of it. Something in the atmosphere of the room told her not to just ask aloud in the quiet expectancy. She tugged at her shock collar uncomfortably.

"Just be ready to follow my lead," said Frank, and kissed her forehead.

Attica's glare had changed back to her cold stare that was typically reserved not for just Orion, but all parties. By the time he had come close enough to speak to her quietly, she had placed her eyes on the newly opened passageways.

"Attica," he said, "there is something you should know about what is going to happen in the next few moments."

She sounded annoyed. "I suppose you're going to tell me."

"Attica, listen to me."

Something in his voice actually made her turn and look at him.

"When it begins, know that they'll be coming for everyone – but in particular, Cyprus, myself and you."

"Who?"

He lowered his voice and leaned a bit closer. "The girtas."

Her eyes narrowed, as if anticipating that this was a trick of some kind. "Why?"

"We three are the oldest. The girtas do not eat flesh, they consume life."

"So…"

"So being for all practical purposes immortal as we are and having existed the longest, we are the…choice fat of the flock, so to speak."

She rolled her eyes. "Oh, fantastic. And I suppose they're immortal too."

He was now close enough that he could have leaned in and whispered in her ear if he wanted. But he only went on. "Practically. At the fall of the city they were able to feed continually. But assuming they haven't eaten since then…" and here he paused thoughtfully, "…we might look at them as coming off a fast." He walked around behind her, and spoke to her other side. "A very long fast."

"So they are starving," said she.

"Absolutely ravenous."

Attica's right hand had reached across her body and rested on the sword-hilt at her side, fingers caressing the pommel with familiarity. If she was frightened, she did not show it.

"And Cyprus?"

"Anything I have told you that he does not know, he has forgotten."

And with that Orion reached out and took the sword – his own sword – strapped to her back. Attica twisted around and in the same motion drew the blade at her side. The guards stirred and aimed weapons at him. Only Cyprus saw the newly-opened doors as more engaging.

"Fool!" she snapped, arm extended and pointing the blade tip at his chest. "Did you think my guards would not wrest that back from you?"

Her hand fumbled for the shock collar remote, intending to bring the trio of prisoners to their knees – but her hand closed on nothing. She looked down to her side where it had been, and looked up in time to see Orion casually toss the device into the well.

"That will cost you," she seethed between gritted teeth.

He remained undaunted by the threat of her wrath. "I am the least of your problems."

She glanced away and then back at him, scowling.

"And you need me to stay alive, do you not?"

"Don't bet on it," she said, teeth gritted.

And in the next few seconds everyone's attention was abruptly drawn from the immortals' quarrel to the passageways.

CHAPTER 23

"To reach the Portal Chamber, no cost is too high. If lives are sacrificed, so be it."

~Attica Triassa

୫୦ ୧୫

Of the origin of the species called the girtas, only a few Atlantean sages and a handful of lore-masters kept the knowledge. Some of the wise men held that the girtas had been found in the depths of the earth when the deepest foundations of Atlantean civilization were first being crafted. Others maintained that the girtas were actually a species specifically made and engineered to serve the royal lines of Atlantis.

Orion, though he spoke of it to no one at any time, was of the latter opinion. The girtas did not feed as men, or like any other known creature. They took no physical sustenance their entire lives, which could be eons and eons long. What they did consume, as had been proven many times, was life. Life itself. The creatures would latch onto their meal with vampire-like efficiency and – no one discerned exactly how they did it. Few had ever had the courage or resolve to watch.

In appearance a girtas was small, like the size of a throw-pillow. Not unlike oceanic stingrays in general appearance, they had flat almost square bodies that included leathery wings on which they could only glide over short distances. From beneath their bodies sprouted eight spidery legs whose joints were many. Two red eyes could be seen atop the body toward the front, and from underneath the front of the body an apparatus that might pass as a mouth on some species could be found. In the makeshift mouth were no teeth, but only the pointed end of the life-sucking apparatus that few living had now seen in operation. Behind them was a long whip-like tail, all black like the rest of their bodies, though maybe a sickly-gray-black-green when seen in sunlight. Down in the depths below the palace they were black. At the tail's end was a poisonous sting, not unlike a scorpion.

The emperors of Atlantean civilization had used the girtas like guard dogs, to watch places of special value; the treasury, the armory, the council chambers. In such places of vigilance, dozens of them would hang from the ceiling like bats overhead, ready to drop upon whatever invader might enter in. There was a time when they easily recognized friend from foe, when there was almost a psychic link between the emperor and his creatures, making it possible for the welcome to pass and the unwelcome to be set upon at once. In their days of greatest-efficiency, it was said that they could even sense the intent of a trespasser, and if there was no malice in the mind of the invader, the paralyzing sting could be used, and not the life-taking apparatus of the mouth. Orion, for one, was never certain this was true.

But those days had faded into the past, even before Atlantis itself had. There was no explaining it, why gradually over time this link and efficiency for accuracy was lost, little by little. Eventually, the girtas completely wore out their usefulness, trading it for a ravenous and destructive appetite for life itself. Men like Orion and other Gatekeepers of the Portal Chamber – learned men, and well-studied, all of them – had suspected that the species' abilities and intelligence corresponded directly with the first contact with the Shades.

Orion had never liked the girtas and had always distrusted them, as a parent might not like to see a child play with certain breeds of dog. The creatures were other-worldly in appearance, like the Shades, and had always struck him as belonging Somewhere else. In another dimension even, like the Shades themselves. Yet neither he nor the other Gatekeepers were the Emperor, and so the girtas had remained in the palace and other important places.

80 C03

Orion had always known that there were girtas near the Guard Room for the Portal Chamber. The Gatekeepers had been trusted servants, but even they had had the potential of meeting their match, especially when civil war broke out and the possibility of armed rebels entering the palace was a reality. He was not exactly certain where they were in the proximity to the room, for over the years their rabid little packs may have roamed much or chosen to hibernate elsewhere. But they could not be far, and the smell of life had to be driving any within sensory range absolutely mad.

Now, as the men of the expedition stood there in the Guard Room looking towards the passageways, there came a clicking and buzzing. Only Orion and Cyprus gathered exactly from whence it came. The girtas could not fly, and so they ran along the stone floor with their eight chitin legs. Occasionally, in their hurry to traverse the passage toward the smell of life more quickly, they leaped from the ground and their wings buzzed like those of locusts, and they whizzed along close to the ground for a brief span. Their greatest leap might have taken them to chest-level, but they could also climb walls faster than spiders and could leap from the highest points in any room.

Then one crewman began firing his machinegun into one of the passageways, then another and another. A moment before all men began firing their weapons, the girtas spilled into the room like an infestation of insects. There were hundreds of them. The air was full of their clicking and buzzing. The creatures themselves made no noise, except the slightest stirring of the air when their mouths opened and their life-sucking apparatuses shot out like frogs' tongues trying to catch flies.

Adrienne shrieked involuntarily over the sound of gunfire as she first laid eyes on them, for they were hideous indeed. Frank stood beside her and was doing his best to put himself between them; their captors had given them no weapons. He was grateful when he suddenly found that Orion had come to them.

Quite a few of the creatures were cut apart by the machinegun fire and lay either dead or twitching on the stone, which was soon stained with a blue-green goop, their lifeblood. Yet despite their losses, on they came, undaunted by the ferocity of the defense fed by modern weapons. One might have thought the noise in that enclosed space alone may have dissuaded some of the creatures: so many guns fired in close proximity for minutes at a time – it was like they were standing beneath aluminum bleachers in a pounding thunderstorm of biblical proportions. But heedless of the hail of lead, the girtas ran and leaped and twisted through the air on their way to the life scattered in the room before them.

One man blew away two as they approached him, but a third cutting through the air hit him in the gut and he went down screaming. Several others immediately leaped to the kill, blood spurting, limbs flaying. This scene was everywhere, though more men hung on, standing their ground. One such individual was Cyprus, the only near-immortal to not be sporting a blade. He calmly stood there near the middle of the room, turning round and round to keep the things from leaping upon his back or shoulders, aiming and squeezing off burst after burst, clipping and wounding some girtas, bursting others into little piles of gooey slag that reeked like rotten eggs. Yet more came through the passageways all the time.

Orion and Attica had their hands full with their swords. Orion had been right; the girtas were attacking everything in sight, but in particular they were unswervingly drawn to the two sword-handlers, and Cyprus as well. To Attica it was almost like practice, in a twisted and dangerously morbid fashion. If someone had stood about twenty feet away and whipped black Frisbees at her in a frenzied fashion, the sword-work would have been much the same. The girtas leaped and dived at her incessantly, and she twisted and arced her blade like a master, winging some, slashing others completely in half, pausing only an instant to stab straight down at the wounded on the floor as they scurried at her feet. At one point she turned around just in time to have to stomp hard through the skull of one with a sickening crunch.

Orion's sword never stopped moving. His motion was like a consistent all-in-one maneuver, twisting and turning in a lethal figure-eight, his footwork making it so that anything that flew at him from above the waist would cast itself into a windmill of slashing steel. In this fashion he cut many down as they came for him, the oldest of all as he was. At times he too had to pick up one of his feet as the whizzing of air sounded and a mouth apparatus tried in vain to latch onto him. He even once managed to swipe through the long green tongue, leaving the twitching biological machinery to flail on the floor while the former owner bled profusely from its face and eventually stopped moving.

It was not long into the foray that Frank managed to find a bloodied machinegun. He picked it up, ignoring the stickiness of someone else's blood on his hands, and stood there much as Cyprus did, calmly blasting anything that came close. Adrienne stood behind him, per his instruction keeping one shaking hand on his shoulder so he was to know where she was at all times. The two were at this point nearly backed into a corner – it felt strategic but Frank wondered if it would be beneficial when he ran out of ammunition.

The battle was fierce and did not pass speedily. The girtas were numerous and starved, and had no regard for their own safety or that of their own species, if they even looked at it as a war in which to take sides. Many stopped in the midst of the violence to feed, and in only a few minutes eleven crewmen lay on the ground, covered with the vampire-like little creatures. But on more of them came, until even when they stopped emptying into the Guard Room there were still too many with which to deal.

Always they came especially for Cyprus, Attica, and Orion. It was well for Cyprus that so many of his comrades had been slain, for spare machineguns were to be found in abundance, and he was able to keep up his masking fire sometimes with two firearms at once, his face deathly grim but always calm. His clothes were speckled with the blood of both friend and foe alike, and a blue-green blotch colored his right cheek; all that was left of the one girtas that had gotten to within touching distance. A sucking apparatus dangled harmlessly and severed from where it had reached out and latched at his waist; that one had made it so close before he'd blown off the back of its head from an inch away. It had inserted into his outer clothing, but its death had come too readily for it to puncture him.

"So run!" Orion shouted to Frank through the flying gore and over the sound of cries of death and beating wings. "Get out of here!"

Frank nodded, and reaching over his shoulder to clasp Adrienne's hand, began to make his way across the battleground and headed for the doorway through which they had entered. Up until that moment in the attack, he had not really had much of a chance to do more than stand his ground and hope he was able to shoot whatever came upon them. Before he had not really entertained trying to escape, but that was before an immediate danger was actively present. The situation had changed.

Behind them, Orion continued to weather the assault, though the creatures were beginning to thin out a bit. *It makes them hesitant...and crafty...*he thought, and in a way it was better and in a way not. In a particularly awkward moment, he found his sword only slightly out of place, and barely managed to twist it in time to impale the nearest girtas as it skimmed across the floor and leaped for him. The thing impaled itself the long way on the sharp Atlantean blade, but was not to be dislodged in time for Orion to stop the next creature.

The next creature, thankfully for Orion but unfortunately for Adrienne, leaped at her as she and Frank ran by. Neither she nor Frank saw it coming. The air was too full of noise for an out-of-breath warning to be heard. On its way to Adrienne, the girtas passed by Orion's left shoulder as he moved aside before realizing it was purposing to attack her and not himself.

Orion did the only thing he could; as it whizzed by, mouth opening to extend the apparatus into Adrienne's spine as she ran, he took a hold of the tail as it went, fingers sealing their grasp just above the sting at the end. It was well that the girtas was not a large creature, for its momentum could have taken him with it. Instead, being a taller and stronger man than most, Orion held fast and the girtas came to a complete stop in mid-air. The girtas then found itself hoisted by its tail up and over his head, like a weight on the end of a rope. It impacted the stone with a smack as he whirled it about like a sling and whipped it down, crushing one of its brethren and injuring a second.

Orion then quickly planted a boot on the head of the creature he held by the tail and stabbed its own stinger into its back as well as the injured one nearby. He then looked up in time to see a mouth apparatus lunge at his face, and dodged barely enough to let it miss. The effort cast him backward and onto the floor where he twisted and rolled to keep the ravenous little creatures away.

Adrienne was trying to keep up with her husband as he pulled her by the hand through the melee. All around them was death and the dying. She could hear the emanating but now periodic roar of gunfire, the screams of crewmen, the flitting of the girtas as they whipped through the air all, sometimes coming for her. She could hear their alien, miniature shrieks as time and again they were torn apart by sprays of lead, sometimes by her husband, sometimes by the men around her. One of the creatures came hurtling at her so fast, she ducked hard enough to fall to the ground as it whistled immediately overhead.

"C'mon, sweetheart, get up," she heard Frank say as he stood nearby, unable to help her out because he was too busy shooting at the girtas that had suddenly noticed her prone position.

She clambered to her feet amidst the gunfire, teeth gritted, her frightened eyes trying to ignore how not seven feet away a mob of girtas had felled another crewman. The dead man's bloodied gun clattered to the stone near her splayed hands. Without hesitation she picked it up, but then Frank had grabbed her by the wrist and yanked her to her feet again as they began to run once more.

They were almost to the passageway through which they had entered. The girtas were thinning, but so was the number of people they could pick out to attack. Suddenly Frank gave a cry and Adrienne realized with horror that a girtas had sailed on its wings right between them and alighted on his right shoulder. He reached up a hand to dislodge it and grasped a corner of the bat-like wing, the stretched skin crunching in his fingers. He had no choice but his own hand; his firearm raised blindly over his shoulder may have put a hole in his wife as well as the creature.

The tail whipped itself erect in the air above the girtas and flashed down at the grasping hand. The needle of a stinger disappeared into Frank's wrist, and she heard him shout aloud with the pain. Without an inkling as to what she was doing, Adrienne brought the butt of her gun down hard on the girtas. She heard a crunch, but the force of her blow put Frank to his knees as well.

"Sorry, baby," she said in his ear as he groaned, the girtas falling lifelessly to the ground, a punctured exoskeleton decimating its back.

"Nnnnn," was all Frank could manage, but staggered to his feet as this time his wife did the pulling.

Across the room, Attica could see the Blackmans departing, and she shouted at the nearest crewmen, even as she stabbed yet another of the scampering vermin while it made for her leg.

"Stop them!" she ordered, but the demand was unheard. The Guard Room was slowly thinning, but there were still cries and gunfire. Thirteen crewmen had fallen, seven remained. She looked off to the left at the man nearest to the Blackmans, just as three girtas got there. Six.

Snarling exasperatedly in her throat, she slipped her foot under a fallen machinegun and expertly flipped it into the air high enough to snag with her free hand. Swinging it around with a remarkable amount of skill and calm in the midst of the turmoil around her, Attica extended her left arm its entire length, aiming at her fleeing prisoners. Her right still clasped the sword, which she dared not put down. She sighted down the barrel and squeezed off a shot.

The weapon jumped in her hand abruptly, as she had expected, but at the same time several things happened. Firstly, by a remarkable coincidence just as she centered on Frank's back and pulled the trigger, a girtas leaped up into the air on its way to a crewman. Her bullets took it out from across the room, and she could see the spurts of blue-green blood burst from it as she brought it down inadvertently. Secondly, although she held the trigger down, the gun ceased bucking in her hand, out of rounds.

"Gah!" she burst out in spite of herself, and clubbed one of the creatures with the empty weapon. Her rage was hardly cooled as she saw an instant later that Frank and Adrienne had both cleared the room and disappeared up the entry passageway. She paused to disembowel one creature as it sailed ravenously toward her, and then in her frustration hacked the still flying dead body in two before it passed out of her reach.

She momentarily locked eyes with Cyprus from across the room where he stood, at this stage of the battle being able to have a second to himself. The foray was definitely cooling, and now instead of hordes of the hideous girtas, there were only a handful of them still leaping about. Some found dead bodies or were fastening on the writhing stricken. Those that did so were easily shot at close range by the now four remaining crewmen. Sixteen men had fallen, though not all of them were quite dead just yet. The writhing of the fallen living only served to attract the vermin all about them.

Cyprus glanced at Attica and followed her searing gaze to where the Blackmans had just disappeared up the passageway. She flicked her head in their direction. He gave the briefest of nods, picked up a new gun and ran after them, checking the clip as he went. As he turned in pursuit, his eyes blinked like shutters and his tongue darted out and back in like a snake's.

Attica was positively seething with rage as she lowered her oozing, bloody blade and locked her murderous stare at Orion, who was on one knee, sword point on the stone, plainly tired from the assault. As the oldest of the immortals, the girtas had taken him for the prime-rib of their dinner course; he had been busy holding them off, and had slaughtered many. He only looked at her as the empty firearm clattered at her feet, thrust with the anger of the moment.

The two stared at each as in the background the last of the girtas were shot. The Guard Room was littered with the corpses of sixteen men and countless girtas. Their blue-green guts were everywhere, like a failed painter had tried to brighten the gristly scene but run out of paint, smearing what little he did have in all directions. Gradually, the room quieted. Attica remained glaring at Orion, but at a sound off to his right, he lowered his gaze and walked over.

A single girtas was feeding upon a prostrate crewman who lay crumpled, dying. He was wheezing and shaking uncontrollably. The girtas paused as Orion approached, hissed at the old Atlantean, and took a flying leap at him as he drew near. He expertly hacked it in two the long way as it sailed at him, and then he was beside the man. The fellow may or may not have been aware as to much of anything at that point. He was young, too young to be doing these sorts of things. Orion laid his sword aside and knelt beside the fellow. At that stage of an attack where girtas were concerned, the man was going to die – there was nothing to do for it. Orion did what he could; he found the quivering hand and held it for the remaining minute or so of life, until it stopped shaking. He then removed his shock collar – the first chance he had where more important matters did not demand his attention.

Attica watched her former husband do all this, her anger gradually cooling. Pity was not something that moved her; the events in her own life that needed pity from others had not received it from them at the time. Still, Orion could not have cared about this young man at all, she thought. There were fifteen others dead on the floor as well – though these others were already dead when most of the violence ceased.

While Orion was preoccupied with his pathetic heartfelt triviality, at a motion from Attica one of the remaining crewmen picked up his lowered sword and brought it to her. Orion did not look up until his immediate concern was over, but remained crouched beside the last fallen man. If he was the type to say 'I told you so,' it would have been the time to say it, but he did not. Instead, he was given to the moment at hand.

"That last wave had a good many of them," he said, "but there are surely more girtas about. We should not stay here. If you have any sense, you will return to the ship."

"I have not come this far to turn back now," she said. Attica turned to some of her men. "Grab some supplies from the fallen, particularly the water bottles and weaponry. We'll not pause long."

"What about the other two prisoners?" asked someone behind her.

She looked at Orion and smiled just a hint. "Cyprus will take care of them, I have no doubt. And you, Orion, where did you pretend they could go? This ruin is an island, and barely that."

"I did not want them eaten alive," said Orion, "and there are few I would wish that fate upon." He reached out and closed the eyes of the last fallen crewman, and only then did he rise. "The knights that hurt you when I was not there," he said looking at her, "they deserve the judgment of starving girtas, not these poor men here."

The remaining men of course had no idea as to what hurt Orion was referring, but it was obvious they heard him. Attica stiffened at this but said nothing.

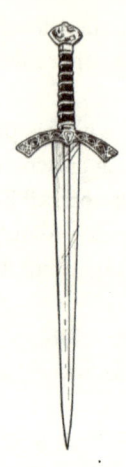

CHAPTER 24

*"Those who pursue freedom merely as a license to do what they wish
will only discover that true freedom adheres to rules that must be
obeyed."*

~an excerpt from the foreword to the bylaws of Dominos de Lumine.

ଚ୍ଚ ଔ

Frank's left arm was completely numb from his fingertips to the elbow, and the tingling sensation was slowly, ever so slowly, crawling up what was left of his arm toward his shoulder. It left behind nothing he could feel; and that alone was beginning to scare him. The foul creature had stung him in the wrist when he went to remove it; the icy fire had injected into him as he reached for it, but ever since then the icy numbness had spread.

Adrienne was under his right arm, having put it across her shoulders in an effort to help him to his feet. She had not let go since, and he could hear her labored breathing right beside him as the darkness closed in around them in their flight. They ran along as fast as they dared, for the passage was very rapidly becoming dark, and finally utterly black. The Guard Room they had left behind had been lit, after all, by a shaft of sunshine and a few Raven battery-powered lanterns designed for just that purpose.

At length they stopped, and he realized that her breathing was not from being so much out of breath as it was from the terror of the battle. He also determined that while not making much noise, she was still crying ecstatically. Her hand that clutched his was shaking uncontrollably, and by the sound in the darkness beside him, her emotional state was beginning to make it a challenge to even breathe, like she was panicking.

"All right, sweetheart, all right. Just breathe for me, c'mon, just breathe."

He heard the gun she was carrying drop to the stone floor and he put his arms around her, pulling her shaking body in. He had to make-do with his wounded arm, and wound up swinging it and catching it behind her with his good one. It was cold and lifeless in his own hand.

Her intake of breath was like a severe case of the hiccups, or like the shuddering crying that shook the shoulders, like he had not experienced since early childhood. It was, in a vague way, almost – *almost*, he thought, *like she's relapsed into being a young child.*

Frank held her gently but firmly in the same way, occasionally whispering kind things and telling her just to breathe. Some young soldiers, freshly after intense combat, broke down in their own fashion; post-traumatic stress was more common than most people thought. And if a soldier who'd been hardened in the trials of boot camp could break down and cry like a child after being shot at in the thick of fighting – so could a thirty-two year old underwriter with no warfare experience. He knew it was tragically unfair for her to be trapped below the surface in an ancient city, smeared with the blood of slaughtered men all over her from the closeness of the fighting. Beyond that, also being attacked by nightmarish, life-sucking monstrosities that looked as if they belonged more in a horror movie than in real life.

It was no small wonder she was crying and having a hard time taking full breaths; it was to her credit that this had started now instead of sooner. Adrienne's shoulders were shuddering with every breath, but she was gradually mastering herself. They stood there in utter darkness, hearing the fighting in the distance behind them fade. Abruptly and with a grunt of disgust, she removed her shock collar, nearly tearing it off.

Then Frank heard something he did not wish to hear; one of the last things he wanted to hear in that place. It was the voice of Cyprus.

"Do you tire of my company already?" came the sly and smooth-sounding words up the tunnel. "Where are you going?" It took on a taunting air. "Oh, please come back."

In his arms, Adrienne stiffened and caught her breath. Frank let her go and reached with his right hand down to the floor where the barrel of her dropped machinegun rested against his foot. He was grateful that at least one hand had its dexterity.

"Take my left hand," he whispered to her, and pointed the barrel back down the passageway. He could see the small rectangle of light; the end of the tunnel where it reached the chamber. And walking steadily up the passage, barely discernible, was the vaguest of shapes as their pursuer followed them.

Gunfire erupted in the tunnel as Frank shot off a few rounds down at Cyprus, if only to keep him from coming for a minute or two. The shape of him disappeared as the Atlantean stepped to the side and pressed himself against the wall. Breathing hard, Frank started walking, his left arm tugging in the socket as his hand was drawn back in the act of leading his wife into the utter darkness. He tapped the side of the tunnel lightly with the barrel, inching his way forward. He could remember that the passage down to the Guard Room had several tunnels branching off to the left or right.

They were now trotting their way back up the tunnel in utter darkness, following along what had been the passage's left side when the whole company had walked down the corridor originally. In Frank's memory, he thought that the left side held the first opportunity they would have to get off the beaten path. He had his confirmation when the sensations of the tapping in his right hand stopped and he realized he and Adrienne were walking past one of the side entries. He turned sharply, ignoring Adrienne's quietly startled cry as he pulled her along.

Frank's blindness to the dark was now amplified by no longer having the vaguest idea where he was going. He had only the most random hope that before Cyprus reached their new tunnel, he and Adrienne would be behind yet another corner, and so out of sight. *Hell's bells, I wish I could see in the dark.* Cyprus could, a distinct advantage in their situation. He pulled Adrienne along at a most unsafe pace, so anxious was he to get away.

He was in no position to challenge Cyprus. Even on equal footing in the daylight with even weapons, Frank would have hesitated from such a conflict. But down in the depths of Atlantis he was most assuredly at a disadvantage. For one thing, his left arm was now completely dead at the shoulder. He could not move it of his own accord; the only way he could tell Adrienne was holding on was the gentle pull when she tightened any slack as she followed him. That and he had no light, no way to see where he was going; even if he had been able to see, he would not have known where he was going. It bothered him most that Cyprus could see in the blackness without assistance. Not for the last time, he wished the ability on himself. *Why, he could be right behind us, toying with us.* The thought irked Frank very much.

Just as Frank was sure Cyprus would come around the corner of the main tunnel and see them scampering down this secondary one, his groping hand passed into nothing as it met a gap in the wall, and he immediately pulled Adrienne into it. He put his back to the wall, trying not to breathe as loud as he was. Beside him Adrienne's own muted breathing was aided by having pulled her shirt up over her mouth and nose in an effort to quiet it.

The only thing to do at the moment, Frank concluded, rather than continue to flee blindly and risk noise, was to wait and hope Cyprus didn't pick this tunnel.

80 ⟡

The gathering of supplies did not last long, for the expedition's numbers had been much depreciated. Orion had walked back to the stone keys he was pushing before the attack began, either unaware or ignoring how Attica now watched him. There was still a fierce glare to her countenance, but her goal was closer than it had ever been, and that helped her mood.

"Blow the door," she ordered after a moment of solace.

"What about the creatures?" asked her nearest fellow, even as he knelt to pick some concussion grenades from the salvaged pack. He clearly remembered what had happened the last time a door opened, but at least he was still acting to do her bidding *while* he questioned, instead of just questioning and not acting.

"He said there would be more around..." added another.

"All the better reason," said Attica, walking over to the kneeling fellow, "to keep moving and not wait for them here!" And she grabbed him by the collar, wrenched him up and shoved him toward the circular stone door. She was strong for a woman of her size and build, and assisted by her extended near-immortal state; he staggered a little.

As terrified of the girtas as they are, Orion brooded, *they are more terrified of her.*

It was not unheard of for a Raven commander to execute an insubordinate underling on the spot, and each man was convinced Attica was not above this sort of thing. Of course, in the everyday running of a professional organization of the caliber of the Order of the Raven, insubordination rarely occurred. But the power of life and death was often with those in command. They obeyed her.

Still, as the fellow set the grenades at the base and clamped toward the top middle of the door, he looked nervous. He took one lingering glance back at Attica, as if hoping she would renege upon the order. But her face was like iron and at a nod from her, he armed the explosives and trotted away to a safe distance. Orion had also left the stone keys behind and moved to an angle behind a protrusion in the wall, away from ricochet. Attica was a safe distance but still stood nearest, as if unconcerned at this stage that something might happen to her. The inner drive was spurring her on, heedless of harm to any party including herself. Her goal was so close, and now that she was about to fulfill it, *nothing* would stop her.

A tense wait of about ten seconds left them holding their breath, and the resulting twin explosions shook the chamber. If the girtas had not already come, they would have then, doors up or not. The Guard Room itself trembled as its eastern stone door was slammed with fiery power. The stone crumbled and fell apart like poorly fit puzzle pieces. In a moment the orange bursts of energy subsided to smoking and charred stones and burning-hot shrapnel. In the wake of the demolition Attica had ordered, the circular stone door that had blocked the way to the Portal Chamber was not completely destroyed, but it was sufficiently cracked and broken to squeeze passed. It would still be quite a tight fit for the larger of the crewmen. Ironically, the south door – one of two that had originally accidentally opened to allow girtas to enter – rumbled closed.

"At last…" said Attica to herself, and was the first to push her way through the east entry.

On the other side, the door opened out onto a stone terrace, covering a small area that would not have held more than ten people crowded onto it. Where the terrace ended, a fall began. Carrying her light, she walked fearlessly to the edge and looked over the waist-high stone banister. Before her and below her stretched black oblivion: to the left and right stretched a vast canyon as if the city and all it held stopped abruptly there and this was the penultimate edge: no ceiling could be seen above, no floor could be seen below. Off in the distance to the left, sunshine stabbed down into the dark, but nothing else could be seen.

Curious, she shined the light down to see if she might make out the bottom; nothing but a foggy blackness enveloped her light totally at its furthest stretch. Reaching into her pack, she took an eight inch plastic glow-stick and cracked it as if starting to break it in two. Of its own accord the rod glowed neon green in the dark, and she tossed it over the side.

Attica counted multiple heartbeats in waiting for the green glow-stick to stop twisting through the air. But at length it merely disappeared into the darkness, the fall being too great for its light to endure the journey back to her. Impressed by the mere size of the place, she stepped back and waited for the four crewmen and Orion to pass through the shattered remains of the door.

It was not a dead end. In the middle of the terrace was a bridge of stone about six feet wide without banister or rail; smooth and polished. It continued the passage floor on into the dark, stretching out over the dreadful fall below them. She once again shined her light, tracing the bridge out as far as the powerful beam would go. At its furthest reaches, she could see that the bridge connected to an identical-looking terrace across from them.

"Come," she ordered without looking at any of them. "I've waited a long time for this; I'm not stopping now."

CHAPTER 25

"The Shades may be wise in many things, but they will never understand love."

~Amelia of Persia, wife of Godfrey Hammerhand, AD 1268

℘ ℭ

Adrienne stood with her back to the stone, one hand clutching her husband's cold and dead fingers; she wondered why they did not entwine readily with her own. Her other hand held her own neckline up above her nose in an effort to quiet her intense breathing. She was beginning – just beginning – to recover from the ghastly horror of the Guard Room, and her heart was beginning to slow down again. But their role as hunted quarry in the pitch dark did little to alleviate her anxiety.

Beside her, Frank could not feel her next to him at all, though they stood shoulder to shoulder and she clasped his hand; his left hand, arm, and shoulder were completely dead to touch and sensation. All he could sense was a dull weight occasionally tugging. Near the left side of his neck, there was a chilling tingling that burned at the same time; this same sensation also crept over his left side down his ribs.

He held the machinegun ready, not daring to shine a light – but also wishing he had a light to shine, actually – ready to pump full of lead whatever came around the corner. He caught himself holding his breath as the two waited in complete darkness. The only thing he could hear was their breathing, and maybe in the echoing distance of his own ears, his own throbbing pulse.

The three minutes spent standing there erect in the dark were the longest

Frank and Adrienne had ever spent together, let alone apart. Neither dared to speak, to relax, to even breathe until forced by necessity. At length Frank began to believe they had at least temporarily put themselves from the dangers of immediate pursuit. But he knew Cyprus was somewhere close by looking for them. There could be more Raven henchmen joined in the hunt, though he doubted it; Attica will need all the help she could get keeping Orion under her sway. Most of the help would remain with her.

They both stiffened as they heard the distant boom of the concussion grenades when Attica had the way forward demolished. The distant reverberation must have been deafening at its source. *The floor is trembling beneath our feet,* Adrienne silently noted. *Does anyone else think this could be a problem?*

She did not speak, but she held his hand tighter, curious as to why he did not respond; she was holding onto dead cold fingers that did not squeeze her own back. Looking at him in the dark with a confused look but of course not being able to see his face, she lifted the weight of the dead limb and rubbed the back of his hand against her collar bone. When he failed to respond to this, she touched her cheek with it. It was very cold, too cold – for some reason it had felt much warmer to her hands.

If there had not been utterly dead silence in the tunnel, she would not have been heard: "Frank."

He was still facing away, looking back up the way they had come, ready for pursuit. His answer was equally quiet. "Yeah."

"Baby, what's wrong with your hand?" Her other hand reached across herself and took his elbow. "Geez! And your whole arm?"

"One of those things stung me. It started then and only now has the numbness stopped spreading. I can't feel anything from the shoulder down." He decided not to worry her about the deadening of his upper left ribcage as well.

"But the rest of you is okay…"

Well, he could function. "Far as I know. We'll see."

"So what are we going to do?"

"I don't suppose you have a light on you."

"No, but you do."

"What?"

"On the end of the gun. I saw it fixed under the barrel, like a bayonet."

He realized if he had had two hands to hold the weapon properly, his sense of touch would have allowed him to discover this for himself; having seen it in the light and not looked for a lamp, it had escaped his memory that each machinegun was indeed fixed with a light on the end; the Raven men had been prepared.

He passed her the gun. "Help me find it; I've got one hand only. But point it at the floor. I don't want a big beam of light all of a sudden letting anyone close by know exactly where we are."

It was a frustrating minute or two before Adrienne found the switch, which had passed beneath her probing fingers several times without being identified as the proper button. It was not by any means a spotlight that came from the light fixed just beneath the barrel. Yet in the long darkness they squinted for a moment, grateful for the small but adequate glimmer.

80 ○8

Attica followed Orion across the open expanse, sparing not a care for the oppressive darkness or hideous fall to her right and left. Behind her, the men stepped carefully; it was cold and misty here, and not long before all had presumably been underwater. The stone was very smooth and more wet than dry, and the bridge's width of six feet made a perilous plunge never more than a few feet away.

She was troubled at how Orion had conducted himself in the Guard Room; his compassion for the dying and especially his words thereafter irked her. An unwelcome but strong urge swirled in her mind; to ask about their past life together, to know what she herself had been like. *I may not have been as strong as I now am, but perhaps I was happy.* But she was not going to ask. Not in front of her own minions, not so close to the Portal Chamber where their time together would come to an end. Again. *It is my respect for him that keeps me from asking him now, so close to severing this latest relationship of ours.* A worthy enemy did not deserve games. *It would be cruel, like baiting him, to think I have feelings at this point. He is obviously past me as well.*

This internal debate in and of itself made Attica irate, and she simmered in silence. A twinge of doubt at her decisions refused to be ignored, resisted the push back down out of her thoughts. She began to justify her actions mentally, even as she screamed at herself that she need not justify anything to anyone. *That is why the Portal must be sealed – so I do not have to answer to them any longer. I will answer to no one but myself.* A few seconds passed. *Perhaps by that time I will have learned to stop questioning my own methods.*

The bridge passed beneath them as they walked, and still Attica brooded. She grew more enraged as the mere thoughts passed through her head. For the first time she found herself purposefully focusing on the day she had died not quite a thousand years ago, if only to keep her imagination from picturing how Orion may not have been an awful husband. She had not given it any thought either way, but her plans were made difficult if Orion was a good man. It was one thing to plot a man's death without ever having met him. It was quite another to have met him, spent time with him, and then be following him toward the place where one purposed to spill his blood.

It was the Shades, she thought as she walked, having gone from mildly annoyed to utterly seething in a few short minutes. *They have forced this deed upon me.* She had been under their thralldom far too long. Even as the bridge shortened before her, the Portal Chamber approaching, her emotions turned from turmoil to victory. They had kept her in their power by way of their 'choice' which was no choice after her own death, but she had at last found the way to settle all. The Atlantean scriptures, the Kedassaic Texts, had provided the answer after all those ascending years. She had at last discovered it for herself not that long ago.

An immortal's lifeblood applied to the Portal will permanently seal it – and then I will be at leisure to hunt the remaining Shades all down like dogs. Every one. Do you hear me, Memphis? You will be last. Only after you have lost everything will I end you.

୫୦ ଓଃ

Orion spent the careful walk across the bridge wondering only briefly of Frank and Adrienne's safety. Frank was completely capable of getting himself and his wife out, and while that concern was set aside he had a decidedly larger one to contemplate. He was actually a little grateful for the distraction of the possible fall being all around him – an immortal was just as prone to gravity as anyone else. He walked his slow confident stride to give himself more time – time to think. *If Attica persists in her purposes, if she does not relent, I will have to stop her. For the good of the entire world, I will. But I just found her, how can I lose her again?* A sober minute passed. *If I return to the surface alone this day, I will sever this mortal coil of mine myself. My time will have come. Or perhaps I will not return to the surface at all, but stay with her body until the sea reclaims this place. I will not live without her. Not again.*

He reached the other side of the bridge first and stood upon the little landing. Before them was a simple open passage that was mostly covered by a massive stone crashed down beside it. There was barely room to slip by for a man of his size, but he moved past it and the others hurried to assure they didn't lose him. They walked easier, more confidently. One laughed, tension disappearing once the bridge was cleared. Surely the most perilous part of the journey was behind them.

୫୦ ଓଃ

Where are they? In the darkness, Cyprus stood quietly, alone and frustrated. Blackman had fired at him and he had stepped to the side of the tunnel, pressed into one of the recesses behind a pillar. When the firing had stopped and he had looked around to see from where the weapon had been discharged, the two fugitives had vanished.

But where had they gone? They could go further up the hallway, which he doubted because he did not see them, and it was a long way to go before being able to get out of sight. Or they could have gone right or left, down the side passages. He had stood at the junction for some time, listening intently. In reality, Frank and Adrienne had gone right, but Cyprus could not see them huddled behind the corner twenty meters away. He took the left passage and went on a moderate distance, listening.

He was only slightly concerned that Frank could pop from around a corner and empty the machinegun's clip into him point-blank. He was for all practical purposes immortal, but not invincible. *Someday, something excessive will do the trick.* Neither was he impervious to pain. What would it take…a decapitation, or being ripped apart, or melted? Cyprus suspected there was no small number of brutal combinations or circumstances that would bring the end.

His watchful eyes did their heavy double blink, and his tongue pushed in and out between gritted teeth. What was it Orion had said when Cyprus brought him to the cell? He was talking about eternity – and Cyprus entering it in the *blink of an eye.* That had unnerved Cyprus more than he cared to admit. Obviously his uncle had noticed his quirk. He had blinked strangely for years. Decades. *Everyone blinks. That doesn't mean it's stutter-flutter. My uncle blinks…doesn't he? Stop dwelling on it. Focus, man…*

The Blackmans. He must find the Blackmans. Frank had an automatic weapon. *Think on that.* Getting shot was excruciating. He could withstand it physically, though he avoided it when he could: just as a normal person would shun a nail-gun emptying its contents into one's kneecap, so no immortal just stood there to be shot at; some things were worth evading, no less so just because they were non-lethal. In most cases, it was worth avoiding the pain. A non-lethal affliction could still be very much worth dodging, and so he had chosen to stand behind the pillar while being shot at. *Just as Orion would have.*

His mind would not shut up. *Orion blinks. So do I. That doesn't mean I have stutter-flutter. It doesn't mean I'm losing my mind, just because I blink.*

Yet now, as he walked down the passage quietly, listening intently and hearing nothing save a distant water droplet fall to the floor, Cyprus grew impatient and angry. *This was my own home city,* he thought, *however long I've been away.* The very idea that Frank Blackman and some female could escape him in the darkness grated on his pride. The darkness through which he could see adequately, no less. He grew more grim even standing there in the darkness as he stopped and listened. And blinked again.

Two fists clenched. *They will not get away.*

CHAPTER 26

"He had stutter-flutter, that's how we knew. That twitching, compulsive double-blink like he had something in his eye…ever the scourge of immortals who have outlived their own sanity. Happens to the best of us. And the worst. Never cares who it picks to go mad, stutter-flutter."

~Halel of Caeladon, 464 BC

೮೦ ೮೪

F rank's mind raced. *We can't go too far wandering through these passages, but I've got to put some distance between us and that psychopath. I'm no match for him like this.* Surely their pursuer had taken the wrong way, but Frank respected his enemy's intelligence. It was reasonable to assume the man would soon figure out he was headed in the wrong direction, and would rectify the situation.

Beside him and holding the machinegun, Adrienne was holding herself together reasonably well, given the circumstances. They had debated who should hold the weapon, but where the girtas had stung him, Frank's arm was completely dead to sensation. The spreading chill had stopped, but the arm was now a useless weight. Randomly in spite of all the dangers about them, he wondered if this was a permanent change. Frank held the light which they'd detached from the weapon, and Adrienne held the firearm.

Still afraid that pursuit was too close to risk excess talking, they walked along in silence. Frank was alert and looking about, paranoid they might lose their way and thus never would make it out. Not that there was too much worry for that; the passage they followed went straight on after the one turn, and they did not leave it. There were rooms that opened to either side, but after the girtas, Frank was also quite concerned about meeting any more of the creatures – or anything else.

Adrienne was actually grateful when the corridor they were following ended in a chamber. She was both tired and frightened, the former of which caused by what had been a rather constant state of the latter. She completely understood Frank's concerns of keeping clear of Cyprus, and had also been mentally prepping herself to maybe even shooting him if they met. Frank had confided to her in their dungeon cell that killing someone was not easy, and she had believed him. Still, she wanted nothing more than to sit in reasonable safety and just wait.

"Could be worse," said Frank quietly, voice shaking the silence they had walked in for perceived hours, though in reality was hardly twenty minutes.

He was referring to the chamber they just now entered. It was square with only the one entry, the stone doorframe that they stood beneath now as they looked in. The walls were unadorned and of cold gray stone – like all the lower levels they had looked upon so far. The space was bare, the walls very high, a domed ceiling at the furthest reaches of their light.

In the very middle of the smallish chamber whose floor space and width of walls was not large at all, there rose three steps. At the top of these there was a small platform, like a dais or place for a throne: yet this space was circular and only about three feet in diameter, rising above the rest of the floor. There was nothing else in the chamber.

"I wonder what it was used for," commented Adrienne, her curiosity getting the better of her. Their peril was dire, but they were also gazing at the first great civilization of people in history, largely unspoiled; it was worth a look.

Frank took a step into the room. Until that moment, they had been standing in the doorway going in. Now, as he stepped into the actual room, he received such a shock that he dropped the flashlight he held, and Adrienne nearly squeezed off a shot reflexively: upon Frank's entry, the entire room lit up bright as day. Appearing instantaneously as he came on were hundreds of bright gold orbs, and from them came the light that so surprised the Blackmans. Each gave off light as if it were an electrified bulb.

The orbs were in some cases the size of beach balls, at other times the size of golf balls. Most were somewhere in the vicinity of basketball size. They appeared out of nothing and did not move except for the slightest of almost drifting, as if caught in the same very slow invisible current. The globes were everywhere, from inches above the floor to high up beyond what had been the reach of the tiny flashlight – which had thankfully not broken when Frank dropped it in surprise. As if it was needed any further in this particular room.

"Frank!" Adrienne hissed, "Get back here!"

But Frank was taken up in the wonder of the room. His eyes were only just beginning to adjust to the light, and he almost didn't want to look back at her to give her a reassuring sign it was okay. He stared, up and down, all around, gaping in absolute awe. He'd not seen anything so beautiful before, and he was convinced it could not be a weapon of any design. The Atlanteans had been able to design things that would have killed them both by now if entry to the chamber was forbidden, he was sure.

"It's okay, Adrienne," he said, his voice almost as if he were in a dream. The globes moved out of his way in order for him to pass, and then moved back into place when he had gone by. He found himself drawn to stand on the slight rise, the pedestal, in the center of the room.

Behind him, Adrienne watched apprehensively. She was beginning to get the same drift of thought Frank was, that the globes were not dangerous, but she was still concerned. She'd seen too much in the past week or so, too much to turn her back on anything strange and new. She said nothing more, and after another minute or two, moved cautiously into the room after Frank. The globes parted for her as well. She would not have done it if they did not slowly move out of her way. At length she sat down on the steps near the entrance.

"Amazing," Frank heard himself say, his voice sounding distant to his own ears. He had reached the pedestal and stood among the floating golden orbs, chuckling as a remarkably childish burst of imagination struck him. It was almost as if he were some sort of master wizard in a fantastical setting, about to conjure something astounding.

Curiosity utterly annihilating any further hint of caution, he put his hesitant normal hand out toward a softball-sized globe. To his amazement and delight, the globe aptly sensed his longing and glided smoothly to his palm. Still reluctant to touch it, as it came within a foot or so of his hand, he pulled back, and instantly the sphere stopped its approach and gradually began to drift back to its original place. Impressed, he again put his one good hand out. The globe once more came near, and this time he touched it.

He could hear Adrienne's intake of breath as his fingertips and eventually his entire palm settled on the top and side of the globe. It was so smooth it was almost frictionless, and for a moment he could not tell that he was actually touching it. He not only touched it but rested his entire hand on it, and it bore the weight.

Adrienne opened her mouth and said something, but Frank never heard.

Seeing nothing but his back as he stood there, she repeated her statement, louder.

"Frank, *be careful!*"

She took his silence as a wordless ascent to the advice, and told herself not to nag him. She sat back, looking slightly annoyed, content to rest. If he wanted to stand there agog at the floating globes – and she did admit they were eerily beautiful – that was fine.

But Frank was no longer in the room there with his wife, or so he thought. *Have I teleported somewhere?* Upon resting his palm fully upon the floating sphere, the room melted away into bright sunshine, a stark contrast from the dimness of the sunken city. He blinked in surprise and took in a gasping breath that was short more from shock than anything else.

Instead of a room of gray stone full of floating globes, Frank saw that he was suddenly standing in the middle of a marble floor, or of some polished whitish stone. He was in a lavishly rich, high-ceilinged room, arches over every doorway, with some pillars too. To his left was a large doorway whose dark wood doors were closed, and to his right, at the other end of the large room, there was no wall but arches and pillars. Beyond these lay a magnificent terrace upon which many could stand at once. And beyond the terrace banister was a bright blue sky shining down on a green landscape, and on the horizon sat snow-capped mountains.

The landscape outside was astonishingly beautiful, but Frank had no time to stare in awe, because even as he was taking in the room, he saw that it was full of people, numbering around twenty. A very tall, bald man of tanned skin tone sat on a throne: it was a great chair of stone, padded and high-backed, sitting on a dais. His clothing was of red robes, wrapped about his thin but firm frame in a most remarkable fashion. Frank had never seen a getup like it. *Adrienne would love to see these clothes.* The man's look was one of concern and concentration, one hand holding his chin as he leaned forward, deep in contemplation. Beside him on a small pedestal was a small orb that looked remarkably like the one Frank was touching in waking life. Its light gleamed with a throbbing glow anytime someone spoke.

On the floor and indeed all around Frank were other men. He gave a violent start as one passed through him as if he were a ghost. They were all men, a few being bald and exquisitely dressed like the man on the throne. Others wore a simple-looking, blue tunic with a rose embroidered on the breast. Their hair was long, arranged in tails behind them. These latter men were more robust in appearance; hardened, muscular, athletic, a breed apart.

Frank had been standing there for all of five seconds when he realized that the man he took to be a king, as well as everyone else in the room, was looking at one man in particular. This fellow attracting all the attention was speaking. Frank looked where everyone else gazed, and he could not help himself; he gawked, incredulous.

"Orion?"

It was true. Orion himself stood there in the room, and yet it was a different Orion. He still appeared to be himself, but while his look was the same he was indisputably younger; perhaps thirty. His hair was much longer, the tail behind him ornamentally wrapped around his torso in a fashion that Frank wanted to laugh. And yet at the same time it was plainly a distinguished look to the culture of which he stood a part. His brow was less care-worn, his countenance not so tired as Frank recognized the man to be now. This younger Orion before him was not nearly as grim. *The years have changed him since these forgotten days here.*

He stopped staring and started listening. No one, after all, had paid his spoken question any mind at all, as if he was not there.

Orion was addressing the group, looking in particular to the lord on the throne. "And furthermore, the rebels have taken Kel-Monsir," he said, and his voice was not quite as deep as Frank was accustomed to, nor was it as emotionless. "That outpost, however small, will surely allow them to disrupt the shipping to the supply-lines holding the eastern mountain passes." He paused and murmuring traveled slowly through the room. The king said nothing. Orion went on. "It is the counsel of the Gatekeepers, my lord, that a division or fleet be dispatched there, to either take it back completely or blockade it from the sea."

The murmuring went on, but the lord on the throne nodded in acknowledgement of Orion's report and looked through the crowd of men. His deep voice asked a question.

"What say you, Councilor?"

"It is an interesting notion, your majesty..." came a sly-sounding voice from Frank's left, and at the recognition of the speaker, he spun and stared. Very, very close beside him and stepping forward between the shoulders of other men on the floor, Cyprus came into view. He was dressed in a manner similar to that of the bald men, and he also was a younger man; perhaps no more than twenty. He had a snide smile on his face, of the sort Frank recognized and always wanted to wipe off with a dose of lead. He walked right beside Frank and spoke on. "...yet we must look at all options when the war presses in so many places. There are many regions in the empire that could use a division or naval fleet."

Orion wore an unmoved expression, though something in his eyes condemned the statement of his nephew, and there was disdain behind his words. "If my lord's enemies take the eastern passes – as they are in a perfect position to do, Councilor – they will in turn be able to cut off *Iratha* herself from the supply routes." He paused an instant and almost smiled, almost, and then went on. "You would not see his majesty *starve*, would you?"

Frank, still enamored but beginning to understand what he thought was happening, lifted his hand from the globe on which it rested. The scene before him, in which he himself was standing, faded. Once more he was in the middle of the chamber lit by the glow of spheres around him, and the globe he had been touching was withdrawing from his reach, slowly returning to its original place.

He turned around and looked at Adrienne. She had not seen his face the entire time and so had no inkling of what was going on, though she had heard a quiet question. She looked inquisitive at his expression.

"You have *got* to try this, babe."

౭౦ ౪

Cyprus had grown tired of the corridor he walked slowly down, listening for his quarry. He headed back the way he'd come, reaching the crossroads where originally Attica's entire party had passed down, on their way to the Guard Room. Upon reaching it, he looked only for a moment to the right, down toward where the battle with the girtas had taken place, and to the left, from where the party had come originally. And straight on, eying the new corridor down which Cyprus assumed the Blackmans had fled. He began walking once more.

Despite the role of a hunter that he was undertaking down the hallway of gray stone, Cyprus could not help but get the slightest hint of amusement and hopefulness. This hopefulness was not only the anticipation of finding the Blackmans, but also partly from the nostalgia of walking the old passages. He had forgotten when the party had first traversed the corridors of that particular region of the city, but as he started down the new hallway, he came to recall what a special area it was. He found himself looking through the darkness with more and more anticipation. The Chamber of Records should be ahead. He had never been there, but it was rumored to be located strategically close to the Gatekeepers' barracks. *It must be around here somewhere.*

The art of the ancient Atlanteans was not only well-advanced beyond other ancient civilizations, but amongst the more crowning achievements they had an aspect unparalleled: magic. While the societies of history waited till their alphabets and written languages developed to leave records, the Atlanteans *recorded* their own important councils and worthwhile discussions, all for posterity. The records were stored in magical golden orbs, which could grow in size given the length of their contained discourse.

One could view the crowning of a ruler seven generations past, critique the war councils of a hundred campaigns, or review what different parties like the Councilors or the Gatekeepers or the Courtiers had determined to be fitting advice in times of imperial distress. It was a most enlightening experience for those who wished to learn. Such education was equipped in every way – even to the point of translating the language for the observer. The magic used was strong, and it had to be. The Atlantean Empire after all, was home to several languages. *A pity*, he randomly thought, *that those cursed Tyrians had never been forced to learn the local vernacular.*

Cyprus was not a scholar, but the Chamber of Records could be enjoyed by many types of men. After the Blackmans had been recaptured, perhaps he would search through the records and find some councils over which he himself had presided. There had even been a time that his role as Councilor had remained for a short time into the civil war – before his treachery, trial, and his own joining of the rebellious Separatists.

CHAPTER 27

"If you want to meet a Gatekeeper, son, meet that one over there. That is Caladan the Cunning – he is the chief spell-caster of the Gatekeeper order. If you can answer one of his riddles, perhaps he'll speak further with you."

~Rehan the Barkeep, owner of the Castle Tavern, reputable establishment and host to many an off-duty Gatekeeper.

⁘

"What now?" asked a man's voice.

Attica stood at the head of her escort of four crewmen. She paced beneath the arch entering a wide hall, one hundred paces long and half that wide. It was empty, completely barren. The smooth stone floor was clean of even dust, having been beneath seawater for age upon age. The immediate entry they stood in was like an enclosed narthex that was not a true part of the hall. They would have to take further steps forward to actually enter the larger room.

She had surveyed the empty room for mere moments and then, from experience, began scanning the walls and doorway under which she stood. Her blue eyes fell upon a nearby stone panel set in the wall with written script upon it in row after row. Lines of Atlantean runes ran foremost across the top right to left, and beneath these there was other lettering from other languages. Even to the unschooled crewmen, it was plain that the various lines of letters were of different origin; three cultures were clearly portrayed.

"What do these say?" a crewman asked Orion.

Attica ignored them all, looking carefully at the panel. *Atlantean at the top...
Kedassaic in the middle...and some other dead and useless tongue on the bottom.*
She could read but not understand the Atlantean, as it used the same characters
as Kedassaic. But the Kedassaic itself she could understand well enough. The third
line she had no inkling of; this was the Tyrian language, and like the Kedassaic it
was representative of an Atlantean contemporary.

Orion stood a little out into the hall facing away from them; the enclosed
area was a bit crowded with five people standing in it. No one noticed that his
trench-coat wafted a little bit as if with a draft, though there was no movement of
air in that place. He turned back and looked just a bit coy – but in his own way.

"Can you not read it, my Lady?" he asked.

She sniffed derisively. "A riddled warning about disturbing the Portal
Chamber," she said after a moment's contemplation: "Love thine own time or be
ever lost to mine."

"Is that what it says?" asked one.

"What does it say?" said yet another.

Attica read it again, to herself. *Love thine own time or be ever lost to mine.*

Orion did not look remotely amused at this point. "It is a good translation," he
said, "and you should heed what it says. Come no further, at your own peril. You
should not even be here, this close."

At this point she had a long stare at Orion, looking into his eyes. It went on for
a good minute, taking so long because she could not see what she wanted to see;
a bluff. *How does one read a bluff in the eyes of a man who never has to make one?*
she asked herself. She wanted to see there was no actual danger, that the warning
was merely to scare off the superstitious. This answer she could not read in his
gaze, and it made her less sure of herself. Deep-seated need made up her mind. *I
would rather be dead than continue living under the sway of the shadows. This is why
I am here.* Looking ahead, she could see flickering, glowing light from behind the
opposite doorway; they were almost there.

"Think on it, all of you," said Orion. "I'll not say it again, come no further."

Concluding that he must somehow be trying to protect himself, she left the
alcove and walked with confidence across the barren floor. The others, one by
one, followed her. Attica was twenty feet out across the floor when she heard the
raspiest of cries, as if the throat that attempted to call out had gone dry. She turned.

The man nearest her, a few feet away, was on his knees and clutching at his
chest. She cocked an eye at him. *This is no time for a heart attack*, she thought.
Ironic; he's so young. He could not be over thirty-five. The hurry she was in and the
enormity of her task left her sympathy at a distance. But, then again, the presence
of genuine pain could not be denied– *is his hair turning colors?*

The roots of the man's hair were turning gray, then white and then rapidly progressing up the strands to the ends, until his entire head was a shock of white. The
transformation of the hair startled Attica, but she did not know horror until she

looked down at his face, from which the hair had distracted. She now gazed upon a ridiculously aged old man. The former fellow was gone. Time had desecrated his youth. He rasped something at her and fell forward, ancient hand clasping at her pants leg in desperation.

Mortified but controlled, Attica pulled back with mouth half open, and as she took a step back the grasping arm was pulled free from the body, completely separated. Without hesitation she kicked herself free of the limb and the body. Even as she watched, before her very eyes it debilitated down into nothing but a vaguely-shaped pile of a dusty ash. She stared at the pile, unable to speak, amazed; he had aged hundreds of years in a matter of seconds. Nearby, Orion stood looking at the pile, and then her, and then the other men. There was no sign of satisfaction on his features, just the sad resignation that was always there when terrible things happened.

She looked and saw her second and third men were rapidly approaching the same state; at any rate, both were quite dead. It had happened so fast! She had not even had time to look up and witness the grim sight. The fourth man had merely been slow to leave the space beneath the arch of the entry. He was in the midst of a wordless scream, Attica watching with some understanding as he put a fist in his own mouth to help stifle it.

She looked down at her own hands and exhaled in relief: not a day over thirty. And of course, there was Orion standing there unaffected. She thought on it. *Love thine own time or be ever lost to mine.* The last crewman was in such shock he had yet to notice, or did not care to speculate, that she and Orion were apparently immune to the magical trap in the room. She understood what the vague warning had meant. Quite plain when one could see the end result, as with many riddles. One's own time, one's own life, should be treasured by coming no further, or an accelerated passage of time in that enclosed space would cause the life to be lost.

She opened her mouth to call to him to merely wait for her as she went on – the others were a regrettable loss, but what was she going to do now, turn around? – when she noticed that like Orion's trench-coat, the loosest parts of her clothing were also gently tugged by invisible unfelt drafts. The still air of the place was alive with enchantment. It was so strong it was almost tangible, now that she was standing there in the open space.

"Pleased now, are you?" she asked Orion, and he could have sworn it was somewhat softer than to what he had grown accustomed. It sounded closer to an honest question than a biting retort.

He looked at her. "No," he said simply. "Are you? Did I not warn them?"

She turned her back and proceeded toward the glow of the Portal Chamber; one could see the faint light even from where they stood. His voice followed her.

"Your compassion is inspiring. I see service to the Order of the Raven is its own reward..."

That made her stop but she did not turn around. He watched her back as if expecting a response, but she gave none. Her shoulders moved like a sigh, but he could not be sure. Orion turned and walked toward the last crewman, back in the alcove. The poor man was rocking himself back and forth, sobbing like a baby. He hardly even acknowledged that a tall man was standing over him, looking down at him with a stern but not unkind expression. Orion looked back at Attica, but she had vanished, having gone ahead into the Portal Chamber. The light from the doorway flickered like a giant television in a dark room. The crewman was too shaken to look up.

"I would depart from here, if I were you," said Orion quietly, and then walked out into the hall, headed for the Portal Chamber.

The man watched in shocked awe although he had already seen it, almost waiting for Orion to debilitate into a pile of gray dust. But the tall Atlantean showed no such signs, and made his way uninhibited across the floor. Trembling, the crewman waited until Orion had disappeared inside the opposite arch, and then at first crawled, then staggered, and finally ran from the accursed chamber.

What made no sense to Attica's henchmen made perfect sense to Orion, who had seen it all before. Attica had made it safely across the deadly cobblestones, and for the exact same reason that he did. It was too simple to conclude that the crewmen had been affected by the magic in the room while Orion and Attica had not. On the contrary, the two survivors had been affected by it; and to a greater extremity than the now dead men.

Attica, at the time of her entry into the newly arisen Atlantis, was roughly-speaking three thousand years old. From her time in the enchanted time-accelerated hall before the Portal Chamber, she was now possibly around four thousand years old. Being for all practical purposes immortal, time had no effect on her body. She could be one hundred thousand years old and from the outside she would not appear to have aged a day.

It was the same for Orion. He walked across the chamber, knowing he was not immune to the magic per se, though as for negative effects he was completely free of harm; his existence was dragged out another thousand years, taking no toll on his physical makeup. He paused and took a breath before entering the Portal Chamber, a place sacred to the Atlantean civilization and undisturbed for over fifty-six hundred years.

Who is the naïve one now, he mentally confessed, *that I would hope for a phantom solution to simply manifest?*

Orion, in his extraordinarily long lifetime, had killed many people. Some he had known personally, some he had not. He had known the names of some, and others he had not. In the years after the Atlantean continent had been destroyed, Orion had for a time hunted down the traitors to the imperial crown. Cyprus alone had escaped his wrath, but at the time it had been complicated. Family was like that.

I may be a killer, but I am not a murderer. There was a very clear difference in his mind, and guilt had never plagued him over what had gone on in the years of his existence. *My cause has always been just. All my long years I have been a man at war.* Any casualties of warfare conflict were not murder victims, they were merely sad statistics in a brutal but necessary game which was played for the welfare of the many.

That said, Orion paused before the entry. *Attica is no longer the woman she once was. She must be stopped.* She was no longer his wife, more the pity. She had plainly lost her mind, commanded a ridiculous amount of power, and had virtually no moral scruples. She was, in short, exactly the kind of person he had dispatched a hundred times before; though in this particular case it was not only a woman, but a woman who had at one time been dear to him. She still was dear to him.

It is the just thing to do. It is the right decision. If I do not stop her, how many millions of others will be lost? But could he do it?

꜡ ꜡

As Orion entered the Portal Chamber, his natural intuition tingled. *We are not alone in here.*

The floor plan of the Portal Chamber was a perfect circle, about twenty meters across. The stones on which they walked were wet and slick. Water pooled in some places next to the walls. The ceiling was too high overhead to be seen, and somehow – Orion recognized ancient Gatekeeper craft – the entire place was lit as if it had its own lights. There were none to be seen, of course, but the room was indeed lit. The Portal Gate was there in the middle of the room, and it was the sole reason the Gatekeepers had originally decided that eternal, omnipresent light was necessary. It would not do for some things to be left in darkness, where one might stagger blindly.

The Portal Gate was two columns of stone six feet apart and twelve feet high, connected at the stop with a sweeping arch. If it were all merely stone and nothing else, one should have been able to gaze between the pillars and see the other side of the chamber. Instead, what appeared as a rippling, shiny blue sheet of heavy plastic stretched succinctly to cover every inch of the space beneath the arch. Occasionally it would tremble, like the canvas of a tent when someone on the inside pressed the wall outward. In one moment of stark horror, the outline of a many-fingered hand pressed out against the surface.

Attica stood before the Portal Gate, hands on her hips, taking it in. Orion neared her and stood almost beside her. Many heartbeats passed as each pondered the weight of the moment. Pending death for one, savored freedom for another. Perhaps neither. Or perhaps both.

"That is a Shade's hand," said Attica, watching the blue Seal of the Portal Gate grow taut against the inner pressure. "Does it sense our presence?"

"I do not know what their perception of our dimension is like from the other side," he answered. "I could not hamper a guess."

"It is a tribute to the craft of your order that it has endured intact for so long."

He said nothing to that, but could not help the thought: *Now would be the time to take her, when she is facing away. At the least I should take back my blade. Frank is not here to do anything for you, you need to act.*

As to her precarious situation, she either did not care for her own safety or it had not crossed her mind that he would harm her in such a fashion. She spoke on in a musing sort of tone, blue eyes reflecting the rippling magical surface a few meters in front of them.

"In a way, we are here to eternally solidify the work of your order. The manner in which we will do so is perhaps unfortunate, but I assure you it is the only way." She turned and looked at him. "Are you aware as to what I refer?"

Orion stepped closer to her so that they were standing nearly toe to toe. He was looking down at her and she was looking up at him. *Now is your last chance to act in stealth.* Even as he contemplated it, he knew he could not. Not so swiftly and suddenly, unprovoked. Regardless of what she had become, she deserved better. She hadn't actually tried to kill him yet – how could he just reach out and kill her outright?

"What you are intending will not bring about the results you seek," said he.

Her mouth opened to respond, but before she could a third voice grated into the air. It was a wispy croak, like a parched, thousand-year-old raven:

"I smell the blood of two immortals. Have you come for the Seal?"

Orion's head snapped up and Attica whirled around to face the Portal Gate. Yet the voice had come not from the gateway, but from the other side of the room, where they could not see because the Portal was in the way. Sword in hand, she gave the Portal Gate a wide berth and walked around to view the speaker. Orion came around the other side of the structure in the middle of the room. There against the wall opposite the chamber's one door, was a strange creature.

It was the size and general shape of a tall, lanky man. It had not two but four arms, one pair from the shoulders and one from what would have been mid-rib. The head was like a deformed skull with large, entirely black eyes. Its whole form was covered with a black-green-grayish, clinging flesh like that of an old corpse. Its arms, legs and neck were manacled to the stone, and it had a minimal array of motion.

"What…is it?" asked Attica.

"It is a Shade unmasked," said Orion darkly, looking at the monstrosity with loathing. He had truly forgotten about this being, but could remember every last detail now.

The Shades had at one time managed to infiltrate the Portal Chamber. This sole individual now chained to the wall, nameless then but referred to thereafter as *Accursed*, had been caught by Gatekeepers as it sought to open the Portal Gate. The success of Accursed would have meant certain doom for the Earth Realm – but instead the thing was captured. Narrowly escaping a death by incineration, it was instead decided that incarceration would serve as a more direct message – incarceration there in the Portal Chamber, forever unmasked and exposed.

It was meant to see if they could go mad, as we can, Orion thought as he looked at Accursed, still chained against the wall like the animal it was. *And now we can see if it is so. No one knew the imprisonment would go on for this long.*

"Unmasked?" she asked.

"Those we see in robes are disguised; this is their true, naked form. It is discomforting for them to appear as such in the Earth Realm – they desire to be cloaked and hidden."

"But how did-" she began, but stopped.

There in Orion's hand was the Gatekeeper sword that seconds before she had had over her shoulder. She had drawn her own weapon from over her side, and forgotten about his own at her back. He had obviously snagged it when she whirled.

"Clever," she acknowledged at seeing it, "but in the end, futile. You could not bring yourself to disable me earlier, did you really intend to *stab* me now?"

The sudden and previously-forgotten voice had thrown him off his game; grabbing the weapon was second nature and had been a subconscious reaction. But she was right. What did he intend?

"Listen…" said Accursed, black eyes staring through them, head bobbing as to unheard music. "The Seal is calling for lifeblood. Can you not hear her? For millennia now I have listened to her plea. Satiate her. Now."

Still a good ten meters from it, the two immortals looked back at the Shade. But even as they did so it would not look at them. For all they could tell, its black eyes could not see a thing. They could also not hear any voice coming from the Seal. *It has gone mad after all,* thought Orion.

"It has taken leave of its reason," Attica unknowingly agreed. "You have your blade; kill it. Its voice is a plague on my ears."

"Fool, I have no lifeblood here in the Earth Realm," growled the Shade. "You cannot use mine. It must have yours."

Randomly, the floor trembled beneath their feet. Dust and tiny debris loosed from the walls in wafting clouds. From a small gap in the paving stones of the floor, water spurted upward in a vapory gust. The air tasted of salt. A large puddle oozed from the gap, spread like a nebulous amoeba for a moment, and then sucked back down. A more distant rumble met their ears.

"We do not have time to debate," said Orion.

"So finish it!" she snapped, and walked toward the restrained Shade.

"Have you not ears to hear?" asked Accursed. "My blood will not do!"

Its mind and everything it says is permanently occupied with the opening of the Seal, mused Orion. *It cares nothing for itself. It does not understand.*

He approached it, sword point leading the way. As he drew near, the Shade's attention went from centering on nothing to focusing on Orion. Seeing or unseeing, the head turned toward him and the black eyes stared through him.

"I smell a Gatekeeper." There was an inhalation of hideous breath, like drowning snakes. "The...*last* Gatekeeper."

"How do you know this?" asked Attica, also coming forward.

The creature only sniffed again. "When you are slain, what you love most will die with you," it said to Orion. "That has been decreed it has, he decided on his Favor. It won't be taken back, no, no, no..."

"What does it mean, Gatekeeper?"

"I do not know," Orion confessed.

Accursed carried on, as if randomly quoting. "It is difficult but not impossible. It shall be done. Prepare yourself. Last Gatekeeper. Slain. Love dies too. Love dies too. What you love most dies too."

"Do not take me for a fool," said Attica, "what game is it playing with you? Of what does it speak?"

He turned fiercely to her. "I do not know!"

"Rubbish!"

"We owe him a Favor, we owe him a Favor-"

"Silence, apparition!" snarled Attica, and lunged forward with her blade.

Her sword sheared from right shoulder to left hip with a downward slash. The upper right arm of Accursed came clean off to dangle there still tethered with chains, and a gash was carved down the front of the shriveled body. Amazingly, the slit flesh grew back together and the Shade cackled.

"Kill the Last Gatekeeper," it garbled at her, "and what he loves most will perish as well! You must not fail us, slave. Feed the Seal lifeblood, grant the Favor of Blackshaft."

Orion stared with revulsion at the instructive captive. *So they are all telepathically linked together, even this isolated one. The old theory is true. But to what events does this one speak unknowingly?*

Attica stood there staring at it, a scowl on her beautiful features. "Cyprus Blackshaft interferes in my affairs...I might have known."

Accursed shifted focus back to Orion. "When the Last Gatekeeper is slai-"

The Gatekeeper sword came straight down on the crown of the ugly skull, passed between the eyes, through the mouth, through the throat and its manacle, carving into the chest cavity and finally tearing itself free at the top of the legs. One stroke from the Gatekeeper-enchanted steel, and the Shade was cut in two – the long way. The chains still held the limbs which, free of restraint, now dangled like meat in a butcher's window. Now truly dead and in a dimension to which it was unnatural, the remains began smoking and burned away into disappearing ash. A few seconds later and there was no sign of Accursed. The empty chains clanged against the stone walls.

Orion looked at Attica, straightening after his sword strike. "You should carefully sift words that such a vile creature would utter."

There was blue fire in Attica's eyes as they bore into him. "I must close the gaps in the Seal, Keldir, you know that."

"Attica, did you hear nothing it said? Its *only* desire was for you to put immortal lifeblood upon the Seal. That will open it, not close it."

"The broken words of a mad Shade, nothing more. The creature did not know what it was saying. Your own Kedassaic Texts declare an immortal's lifeblood will permanently blockade the Portal. Do you deny its words? The power of the Shades in the Earth Realm will be entirely cut off – and then I will destroy them all. Then I shall have peace."

"The twenty-third book of the Kedassaic Texts," he acknowledged. "Have you not heard it called the *Compromised Passages*? The book is beyond old and not some incorruptible canon, it has been manipulated."

Her face was serious. "I know what I read, we are not going to argue about this."

The floor shook again and the water spurted out once more, lingering longer this time before sucking back down. The hole in the rock itself made noises like the gasps of trapped souls.

"If you put immortal lifeblood on the Seal, you will open it, not cut it off."

"Keldir, we cannot-" she sternly began, but then surprisingly softened and started over. "Orion, do not make this harder than it needs to be. What we once were or had is irrelevant to what must happen in the here and now. Put aside your weapon; do not resist me. In the end, you know this will be better for the world as a whole."

She will never believe the truth, not now coming from me. "Attica…" he began, but words failed him and he fell silent.

"Put down your weapon and stand beside the Portal, Orion. That is how this will end. I will strike cleanly, you have my word."

"I love you, Attica."

She cocked her head just a bit to the side, long blonde hair swinging. "You *love* me?"

He said nothing to that, her tone indicating she was not honestly asking. She continued.

"Ah. 'She's a woman, my talk of love will no doubt stop her in her tracks.' Is that it?" She came forward, brandishing the sword. She twisted the steel in expert fashion and finished with the point directed at his chest. There was ice in her voice now. "If you are going to make this difficult, we might as well get on with it."

Orion sighed. "Forgive me for this. I see now there is truly no other way."

She still advanced. "You force my hand, Orion Keldir."

The Gatekeeper weapon came off his shoulder and into a usable position. "No, Attica Triassa, you force mine. As you say…let's get on with it."

80 03

Frank was so enthralled with the watching of the Atlantean historical records that the pressing issue of his and Adrienne's predicament was in the back of his mind. He had paused and glanced around at Adrienne periodically, and to his delight had discovered that the recordings were not real-time: he could watch one for what seemed a good hour, but in reality only a minute or two had passed. This illusion of the passage of time made Frank relegate the danger behind them as further and further away.

This was a purposeful design of the ancient Atlanteans. It was recognized that they could not expect one to learn the history of a particular aspect of their civilization and still assume that scholarly individual would have time to put his knowledge to use. The aspect of the magic automatically translating the languages for the observer also had a good deal to do with the idea of not wasting his time in unnecessary disciplines such as learning new languages. Also, it made for the most excellent excuse that Frank, millennia later, was not really keeping Adrienne waiting – as if she had somewhere else to go. She, at any rate, was not nearly as anxious to 'view an orb' as he had thought.

Adrienne was content to sit on the steps at the entry to the room they now occupied, the machinegun laid across her knees, looking both reflective and bored. The shock of the experience had left her; she'd been through quite a bit of late and was more than happy to just sit quietly. Seeing that she was neither angry nor annoyed, her husband had no qualms about poring through the orbs.

Frank stood fifteen feet away from her on the small circular rise in the middle of the floor, almost like a conductor above the orchestra pit, the golden spherical occupants all at his beck and call. In no time at all he was searching among them like a trained veteran scholar, dismissing some and taking in others, probing for something that might catch his particular fancy.

After hardly a few minutes he found one, and one could not truly fault him in the ecstasy of enthrallment and discovery of an ancient and undiscovered civilization. His entire awed attention was upon the scene before him, in which he was standing and had a part. It was an overpowering experience.

The aspect of the Shades initially drew Frank's attention when 'scanning' the various orbs by touching each briefly one by one. His chosen scene had the physical location of a throne room, possibly *the* throne room for the Atlantean monarchy. It was grand indeed, and from one end of the hall to the other, a football field could have fit inside. Yet Frank had grown so accustomed to the high ceilings and mighty pillars and smooth light-colored stone, that these things held almost no awe for him any longer.

Central in this latest scene was the tall thin man that Frank had decided for himself to be the Atlantean emperor. He was seated on a stone throne of such majesty that those he listened to were six feet away and yet still standing *beside* the chair itself. It was lofty and raised, and of such shape that the man who sat upon it was truly set apart. There were various councilors and such before the throne, but mixed among them were the Shades themselves.

Three were standing there to the left in a place of belonging. One of the three stood ahead of the others, foremost. Frank in amazement realized this primary fellow was the Memphis he had met in his own waking life, though it had been years since he had actually seen the Elder Shade. Someone among the Atlanteans was speaking his thought to the general council, and all were giving him heed, the Shades included. Indeed, Memphis himself looked almost as an old grandfatherly type, standing there with a not unkind but still stern expression. Hands behind his back and hood thrown back behind his tall and narrow shoulders, it was as if perhaps his grandson had hit a baseball through his window and was desperately apologizing.

It rattled Frank to be standing in a room so close to Memphis, even though it was really a memory and not an actual scene. Even when he grasped that the Shade was not actually before him, he flinched with apprehension, and his mind even played tricks on him. He could swear Memphis had for a split second glanced his way and looked directly at him. The only thing that took his attention from the Shade was Cyprus.

Cyprus came into Frank's perceptive view from the left behind the Shades, who did not turn or acknowledge him in the least. He walked into the emperor's presence respectfully, drew close enough to the throne to be seen, to bow, and then made his way toward the councilors on the other side of the dais. This path brought him right in front of Frank, who did not move, being accustomed to having people pass right through him.

Frank could not help but look at his old nemesis, though he had seen him countless times scattered throughout the records. And in the split second that he did look at Cyprus as the Atlantean passed by, so very close, he noticed two things at the exact same time. For one, Cyprus was not dressed in clothing according to the ancient period. Secondly, Cyprus looked him in the eye.

Frank's realization came too late to not afford Cyprus a free-shot, which he took and made count. As he walked by, he paused mid-step and abruptly slammed his elbow and forearm hard across the side of Frank's head. The blow caught him entirely off guard and snapped his head around, a small thread of blood trickling down the side of his face. The impact sent him reeling and he strayed backward, feet looking for somewhere to go. He was on little platform above the floor of the chamber, and his feet found only emptiness when they stepped from it. He staggered off of it backward and fell hard.

"You show your age, Blackman," Cyprus chuckled, standing where Frank had been, gazing down with his hands on his hips, looking pleased with himself. He took an instant to enjoy Frank lying on the cold stone in obvious pain before leaping down to land beside him, and then putting a hard foot in the other man's ribs. "You get out of this game for too long, and you start embarrassing yourself."

He stepped over Frank. "You lose reflexes…" another kick, "…you lose competitive drive, you forget the simplest things…" yet another kick, "…and my personal favorite: everything starts to hurt more."

Frank groaned as the sharp kick of Cyprus's foot dug into his side again, searing pain poking as if it displaced a rib or two. He stomped on Frank's chest once, decisively, as if to make sure he wouldn't move for a moment. He then took a step back and retreated openly toward the steps of the entry. Frank strained to see Adrienne, and finding a new strength to ignore the pain, he propped himself up on the elbow of his good arm.

"I can see why you retired," his enemy continued, and Frank's blood pressure rose as Cyprus sat down on the steps beside Adrienne, putting an arm around her.

Adrienne could do nothing more than look at her husband, regret in her eyes. A pillaged backpack had been opened and freed of its duct tape. She sat on the steps with their captor beside her, legs in front of her wrapped at the knee and ankle, hands behind her and undoubtedly taped securely, a couple additional strips easily covering her mouth. Her eyes were apologetic, but Frank angrily blamed no one but himself.

"I admit," said Cyprus, reaching down and picking up the machinegun, "the Chamber of Records is a pretty amazing place. Why it could distract a man long enough to…let someone sneak up behind his wife, grab her when she's looking the other way, and tie her up." He smiled as Frank got to his feet, making no move toward their adversary despite the murder in his eyes. "Funny thing about viewing the records, Frank, is you can't hear anything else. Why, someone could be not twenty feet away and screaming your name," and here he found himself curling some of Adrienne's medium-length dark hair around the fingers that clasped around her shoulder, keeping her close, "and you'd never know it." She grimaced, eyes tightly closed as he leaned in and inhaled deeply. His tongue flicked beneath blinking eyes, and he smiled without showing his teeth.

Frank was in no mood to be mockingly lectured or to watch another man caress his wife. Especially an old foe taking such pleasure in it. He was in no position to better the situation – though he randomly realized that his tumble actually stung his limp and newly achy wounded arm, no longer numb above the elbow.

"So what now?" he asked at length.

"What do you think, sweetheart?" Cyprus hissed at Adrienne. "Any ideas?" Unable to speak, she said nothing. Cyprus gave Frank a specific look and then licked Adrienne's ear. Then he stood up abruptly, hauling her violently up by one taped arm, ignoring how she winced, the hint of an involuntary moan escaping the tape. "Good idea, love. Let's go back to the Guard Room."

CHAPTER 28

"How do you combat love? What defense could you possibly employ?"
    ~Amelia of Persia

☋ ☊

When Attica had ceased speaking and unleashed her first blow, the strength of it made Orion think. He stopped the downward cut with his own weapon, but if he had missed and been a normal person, her sword would have come down through his shoulder and only been halted by his ribcage. There was a pause as the two looked at each other underneath the crossed steel.

"Do you really mean to resist me?" she asked. The sound of her voice indicated she was putting strength into pushing her blade down toward him.

"Do you really mean to see this plan through?" he answered. The strain did not tell on him yet. He had the strength of many men. She was strong, but not compared to himself.

She broke off and came in hard with two more strikes, fast as lightning.

"What choice do I have?" she snarled as her third strike hit nothing but air.

His voice was stern, his mind made up. "Then I will not resist you."

That caught her by surprise and she stood off for a second. "No?"

"No. Forgive me, Attica Triassa, but you leave me no choice."

She made a straightforward lunge and was parried. "We do not have time for this game, Orion."

Her weapon raised again, but she instantly had to change her plan because he came swiftly in with an assault that blurred the air. The aggression was so fast and precise, she hardly kept her blade ahead of his. The last block was away from their bodies, and with the opening provided he put his shoulder and the weight behind it into her sternum like a load of bricks. It was like being rundown by a linebacker, and Attica was knocked flat. He remained a few feet away, looking down at her.

"That's more like it," she said with a smile, rubbing her chest with a free hand. But the playful response was a mask to show she was not afraid – his one exchange had bested her with what appeared little effort. For the first time, she saw the possibility of her own failure. *I had not counted on his being armed with his weapon of choice.* Her defeat was not guaranteed by any means, but she had now witnessed the capability of the man she intended to best – it would not be easy.

"You are not going to kill me, Attica." He came forward and she scrambled to her feet and kept ahead of him. "But because of what you are going to do, I *will* have to kill you. Forgive me, I see no other way."

Her face hardened. "Just as long we understand each other," said she, and flew at him.

From their genesis in the ancient days of yore, the Eternal Order of the Brotherhood of the Gatekeepers had not been a place for the weak of mind or body. Entry was limited, training and testing were constant, and shortcomings were unforgivable and often painful. The men of the order were known to be hard, strong, sagacious, but especially – deceptively composed in manner and mood.

While many armaments were used to train, the sword was the penultimate choice. The order's fondness for the weapon developed into officially designed and sanctioned techniques and forms for devices that were in themselves works of pure art. Every soldier had his preferred methodology. The fast and precise could use the Diving Falcon form. The feinting and calculating often opted for the Sea Merchant form. Those who favored a paced, relentless but tireless approach employed the Red Stag form. And then there were the devastatingly strong and ruthless. The Cornered Dragon form. A true master adopted and mixed all interchangeably, and there were many forms from which to choose.

Orion was a true master, but he was a Cornered Dragon man at heart. It had nothing to do with personality or temperament; in close quarters, his preference was to end the conflict quickly and irrevocably, often with extreme prejudice. The efficiency of such an approach was undeniable, and his natural size and enhanced strength complimented the method superbly. As a teenager in training, one of his teachers had head-butted him in the nose and then pressed a foot to his throat as the blood ran down onto the boot. *This is not a dance, boy*, the old warhorse had spat at him before kicking him hard enough to break a rib. Not something an impressionable lad was likely to forget.

The encompassing flurry of the Diving Falcon had brought him into Attica's personal vicinity just now, but the Cornered Dragon's impact at the end had virtually put her on her back. After years of practice and multiple lifetimes of using his sword, most maneuvers were second-nature. He did not have to think or plan most of the time; a certain position allowed for a plethora of applications and one would jump forward and perform itself. And so Attica had been cast to the ground.

But now she was up and back at it with fire in her eyes. She had neither his training or teachers, but she acquitted herself well. She was lightning fast, and fierce as any lion. The chamber echoed with the ring of steel on steel, their interlocked shadows moving back and forth on the stone of the floor and walls. The masonry about them trembled periodically with a distant rumbling, water spurting and vanishing over the one gap in the floor.

She had not taken me as a serious threat until just now, Orion decided. *It was unwise to disclose my intentions – she is guarded against them now.*

It was true; her knowing his intentions mattered. He could feel the difference in her attack. His initial flurry had taken her by surprise and wound up with her on the floor. But now that she knew he could move like this, she made a conscious effort to not allow him such an opening. Parries and blocks left little space in which to work something else. The way she stood and allowed her body to be exposed made another body blow difficult to land.

There was one thing she had in greater capacity than himself; her speed. Orion really was very fast for his size and constitution, but she was more fleet. She was making use of it too, thrusts and slashes and the angles she could take or correct. More than once his dodge was only a hair ahead of her weapon – though these lunges risked putting her in precarious positions of full extension that invited counters.

This is all just a waste of precious time, he admitted to himself. *Her steel won't kill me, even if she runs me clean through. So why can't I let her do that and finish her while her weapon is extended and useless?*

It was true. As a Gatekeeper he was impervious and resistant to many things; a standard sword would hurt, but the wound would seal itself up as soon as the blade was pulled free. Attica would have no defense if her one weapon was embedded in her opponent. It would be easy to surprise and finish her in a quarter second if she was up close and her sword was gone.

Have I really been reduced to such a charade?

How she sensed his inner turmoil was impossible to know, but after another fierce exchange she kept the space between them and gave him a strange look.

"Do you toy with me?"

Yes, but not willingly. The truth would infuriate, but what he could say instead would be a lie. He said nothing, but that only seemed to irk her more.

"Is this just a game to you?" she shouted at him. "Finish it or let me!" The mist of spurting seawater was damp in her hair. "We do not have time for some accursed game!"

Frank had led Cyprus and his captive back to the Guard Room at the point of a gun. Adrienne remained restrained and gagged, but her legs had been cut free. Cyprus walked with one hand pointing the gun at the base of Frank's spine while the other steered her by the back of the neck.

"Hell's bells," said Frank, quietly.

The rampant destruction in the Guard Room, the scene of the battle with the girtas, was enough to send shivers up Adrienne's back. She was thankful that there were no living girtas in sight. They had apparently retreated back from whence they came when there was no further life to feed on – and there was none left. The mouth of the well, looming black and ominous only added to the mood

More than a dozen grown men or the remains thereof lay strewn across the floor of the chamber like pieces of trash scattered across a parking lot downtown. A small fortune in military equipment lay in bloody aftermath with them: grenades, side-arms and automatic weapons, some quite usable and some surely never to fire again. The gooey blue-green guts of the girtas spattered everywhere, amid their own shattered bodies as well. The meal provided by the human beings had been quite costly; a tribute to firearms technology.

"Imagine how swift the slaughter would have been without our modern weapons," said Cyprus, left hand on his own firearm, his right on the back of Adrienne's neck, under her hair. "This is worse than Tavern Street."

He said this last part with a smile and looked over at Frank, who looked back without humor.

"I wouldn't know," said Blackman, locking eyes with Cyprus before flitting briefly to his wife's, and then back to the room. "And I doubt you would know either," he added as an afterthought. He was absentmindedly massaging his injured arm at the elbow: from the shoulder to the elbow was painful and tingling; below the elbow was still dead to sensation. This was, in actuality, an improvement.

"I'm well-traveled," said his adversary, and, steering Adrienne in front of him, began to navigate across the floor toward the blasted hole Attica and Orion must have passed through earlier.

Adrienne, of course, did not recognized the reference to 'Tavern Street', nor would she have wished to know. What would have surprised her the most, however, was that of her recent company, only Orion had actually been physically present for the Massacre on Tavern Street. For Orion's contemporaries who heard what had happened that bloody day, it came as no surprise that as the only living witness to the carnage, Orion spoke of it to no one. It had been the only time he had ever lost control.

Through the silence, running footsteps traveled toward them from the gap in the stone door ahead. In the grim desolation of the room, the coming of footfalls struck the listening occupants as sinister. Frank straightened and looked around for a weapon, at the same time wondering what Cyprus would do if he went for one. He hesitated to do so, but looked anxiously toward the shattered door.

Cyprus in turn snaked his entire arm around Adrienne's neck and pulled her up sharply in front of himself like a shield, and thrust his machinegun barrel toward the door. He ignored the woman's breathing, accentuated and labored as it was due to the tension of the moment and the duct tape not allowing her to breathe with her mouth. He glanced behind him from habit, expectantly.

The last of the crewmen, whom Orion had directed to depart, staggered through the rubble of the door and collapsed wheezing on the floor. He was badly shaken; indeed, Adrienne even heard him crying. Cyprus gestured at Frank with the weapon as he came slowly forward.

"Pick him up."

Frank obeyed, not nearly as sympathetic as his wife at seeing this former captor reduced to a childlike state. With his one good hand, he took hold of the clothing and then an arm and pulled the fellow to his wobbling knees, and then to his feet. With a glance from Cyprus, he hesitatingly remained standing beside the fellow, putting his own valid right arm around him; the man was tipsy and teetering, ready to fall back down.

"You look like hell, man," said Cyprus, looking him up and down. "What happened? Well? Out with it!"

"Ramón and Pierre are dust!" the crewman blurted out, leaving his newest companions staring at each other. Not receiving the reaction he had apparently been looking for, his voice grew higher and more adamant. "They're dust, curse you! Elias too! They turned to dust right before my eyes!"

"Do you know what he's talking about?" Frank asked Cyprus.

"Must we discuss everything?" snapped the Atlantean.

"Ah. So 'no.'"

"Are you even *listening* to me?" yelled the crewman. He pushed Frank aside and lurched for Cyprus, ignoring the machinegun and practically pulling Adrienne out of the way as he took hold of the front of Cyprus's clothes. "They're *dead*! Just like *everybody* else!"

"Unhand me, fool!" Cyprus snarled callously, but the crewman was half-mad with fear and shock, and the two men grappled for a moment.

The violence of their action and her closeness to the conflict resulted in Adrienne being suddenly shoved aside. Cyprus had freed her legs to enable her to walk, but her hands remained taped behind her. The floor beneath her feet was smooth stone, and slippery with the blood of two species. It was also scattered with debris; she reeled and fell flat on her back.

Adrienne's collision with the stone floor was stopped only by the body upon which she fell. It was an unpleasant business, even as she realized what she had to be lying on. Her clothing was already smeared with blood all along her back and a bit on her cheek, her feet slipping in the goo of a dead girtas as she kicked to right herself. Her hands squelched in something soft and terribly sticky. Still, in reality it was the corpses that kept her unprotected fall from seriously injuring herself on the hard floor.

"Let go!" demanded Cyprus, at last finding an advantageous hold by which he thrust the man away from himself.

The crewman faired no better than Adrienne, and slipping and staggering about he landed amidst some old comrades on the floor. He got up at once, squirming like the smeared blood physically burned, and he glared fiercely at Cyprus. "Their blood be on your head, Blackshaft!" he said abruptly, and then ran across the chamber toward the room's west door; back the way from which the whole party had originally come.

Cyprus watched with scorn as he went. "Well, he won't get far without a light." He turned just in time to see Frank stand up from where he had crouched down on the floor – to retrieve a handgun from one of the bodies. Both men brought up their prospective firearms together as they simultaneously and without a word aimed at each other.

Frank was first, having seized the moment when Adrienne was momentarily away from their captor, and the weapon was right at Frank's feet. He knew a shot wouldn't kill him – unless he put one in his head, but even that was an assumption. *Wish I had two hands for this.* Frank pulled the trigger as his bad arm continued to weakly tingle.

The click of an empty chamber was all that met his ears, and his heart sank.

∞ ∞

They slashed and cut at each other, lunged and dodged. Attica was a wild animal, her energy never wavering; she was agile and fast, recovering smoothly from any overreach as she attacked him again and again. Orion was ever the rock of impassivity, countering her aggression with solid and firm maneuvers that frustrated her every assault. He could be deceptively agile as well, just not all the time as was she. They had been mostly even with few recognizable moments for either to get the upper hand.

At one point they had crossed blades overhead and as she stood to the side, she had tried to kick his legs out; her shin had placed itself hard against the back of his knee. She might as well have tried kicking an oak tree. His knee had bent a bit, the leg itself moving only a few inches; but then with that extra strength of his, he had straightened it so forcibly that her shin was pushed away. Before she could put her foot down, he'd parried her sword out of the way and slammed the base of his free palm against her upper chest. She had gotten a guard up at the last millisecond and what was meant to hit her square in the sternum had collided forcefully with her softer pectoral.

My entire torso is going to be black and blue by the time we're through, she randomly thought. Her chest ached from his strikes; despite her best efforts to avoid them, he had still landed four. Three had knocked her flat.

This was again the powerful Cornered Dragon technique, which became more and more favored as he tired. He had fractured sternums before with that strike – the *battering ram*; it was good for ending confrontations. She had reeled backward from the blow and pointed her sword at him to stop him coming too close as she massaged the area of impact, wrinkling her nose an iota. He'd not followed her, and after a second's pause she had charged once more.

Now in the Portal Chamber, the ground again shook beneath their feet and there was a distant rumbling emanating from the walls about them. Orion paused mid-strike and stepped away from her, pondering this turn of events. The strength of this latest tremor dwarfed the others.

Attica made a conscious effort to not rub her sore chest.

"Surely you did not think your beloved city would rise above the waves for good?" she asked. "The ocean is looking to reclaim Atlantis for the depths once more. You may have to hurry in your work here, if you wish to have the satisfaction of my death before the saltwater takes the privilege from you."

"Would that please you?" he asked.

I would have fewer worries if I were dead once more, she admitted silently to herself. But what she said was: "There are worse fates to be had than perishing here, like remaining a pawn of monstrosities like Memphis or Arcanus." She paused. "And you...are you not afraid to die?"

She did not give him time to answer, but instead drove at him hard with her blade, swinging and striking. The fury of her assault made him give ground, which she followed up at once. But try as she might with all of her intensity and skill, she could not get the steel to reach anything but his own sword in return. Orion was simply too fine a swordsman. They pushed apart and Orion answered her question, ever the stoic.

"I will die today, that is so."

"If you are so resigned," she panted, "why do you resist my assistance?"

"Whether I finish you or you finish me, I will not return to the surface. I am the last Gatekeeper. What better place to end my mortal coil? It has gone on long enough."

"Speak plainly, Orion Keldir."

"I've lived thousands of years. I'm tired." He sighed. "Stopping you from igniting this destruction upon the Earth Realm will be my final act as a Gatekeeper. Once I have done that, I will remain here and return with this great city back into the depths of the sea."

There was a distant thundering, as if the city itself approved of this plan. Reverberation trembled in the soles of their feet, even through their boots.

She snorted. "Do you call that noble?"

"I lost you once. It nearly destroyed me. Now that I have found you again, do you really think I could lose you once more and then go on with my life as if nothing had happened? No, not this time."

"You forgot to say 'I love you,'" she said, and held her blade out to the side, completely exposing herself to a mortal strike. "Finish me now, then, my old love. Run me through if that is all that keeps you alive." She walked right up to him. "Just remember to wipe my lifeblood upon the Seal and cut off that accursed flow of energy upon which our cloaked enemies feed." Her eyes were locked onto his. "That is the only reason I am here. Even if I do not live to see them whither like a branch severed from a tree, I would still have the deed done. My quarrel is not with you; I hate *them*. Do it, or do not and I will. I will not live as a slave."

A voice inside her roared at her. *What are you doing? What about the plan?*

Her offering of herself was at first a sarcastic calling of bluff, but when faced with the possibility of her own death, Attica realized she was not truly opposed to it. A simpler, more resolute realization answered her own psyche's objection. *I am tired too. Slave or free, I am tired too.*

Attica's arms were up and her eyes were closed as she finished giving Orion her ultimatum. The space between her breasts tingled as she fully anticipated a point of hard steel to be rammed irrevocably into it. Precious seconds passed. But no death-thrust came. The chamber trembled and rocked.

Did he lie to me?

She opened her eyes and found he was standing there in front of her, sword point downward.

"I cannot…" he finally said. "I must…but I cannot."

"Then I must," she said.

"I'm *immortal*, Attica. You cannot destroy me, and you cannot seal off the Portal with my lifeblood. My sword is tempered Atlantean steel, and the wound would seal instantly. What good will yours do?" asked Orion quietly.

Attica's sword arced expertly in a brief instant before it found itself poised right at Orion's chest. She hesitated a half instant to look into the gray eyes before her, and Orion thought he saw for an instant a sign of regret in her beautiful blues. Hesitation, if it was that, lasted a matter of seconds. She took a step forward to help empower the pending thrust she intended, but she now held it there instead of driving forward.

"There is no other way…" she said softly, looking up at him. But her arm did not move.

A crack louder than anything they had yet heard erupted directly behind Attica, and the stones upon which she stood surged upward without warning, rising a suddenly abrupt two feet. Her weight was planted strangely as she had stood there in front of Orion, and when the floor moved unexpectedly, she was pitched forward into him. As sudden as it was, her movement was reactionary and involuntary – and she inadvertently drove the sharpened steel into Orion's lower chest.

She stared in shock at her hand as it clutched the handle, and then she looked up at Orion's face, and then back down. Attica let go of the handle and took a few steps back, face unbelieving what she had not intended. But she began to recover and drew near once again.

"Your sword may be tempered Atlantean steel, my old love," she whispered, "but mine is tipped with Atlantean silver from the gemstone necklace." Her hands found his face and held it softly as she spoke. "Don't you see? I had to. It is better for both of us."

Orion looked at her with an expression that was a cross between exasperation and patronization. As if what he had been saying all along had been utterly ignored, and now the result of this snubbing of his excellent advice was needless pain and discomfort. But actually the only real trailing premonition in his mind in that instant was that her weapon was now out of her hand; he could recover from his mistake in not striking her down earlier. Perhaps there was still a chance at saving the Earth Realm and countless lives.

He took a step toward her, honestly uncertain of intent, but two things suddenly happened. The first was that his hand suddenly failed to maintain its grasp on his sword handle. It fell, clanging on the stone beside him. The second was that as he took the step, his planted leg decided it had no strength and promptly buckled.

He sank to one knee, rather than toppling over. His eyes looked down at the blade protruding from his chest. There had been so little Atlantean silver available she must have had to barely trim the blade's point with the stuff. Blood poured from the wound, painting the front of his clothing. Orion grew lightheaded.

Attica approached and knelt down beside him, her expression firm but bearing no sign of satisfaction of any sort. He had no strength to resist her in the slightest, but all she did was slowly remove the weapon and ease him to the floor. Blood pooled beneath him but he maintained consciousness.

"There is enough old magic about you that you are not bleeding out as easily as a normal man," she observed. "But you, Orion Keldir, are now mortally wounded. Forgive me for this, but I must have some of that lifeblood."

One of her sleeves had been badly ripped near the shoulder in the midst of their duel with sharpened steel. She now easily pulled it free and began using its absorbable properties to staunch the bleeding. It grew wet and red as she watched.

Look at his eyes, he does not despise me even now. A reminder of the imprisoned Shade's words crept into her psyche: *Kill the last Gatekeeper and what he loves most will perish as well.* She pondered them, not for the first time. *And now Dominos de Lumine is doomed. A poetic way of saying his organization will never survive without him. How true.*

The Order of the Raven had known for long years that every Gatekeeper had specific weaknesses. In 617 AD the Gatekeeper Consul – the highest rank available – had allowed himself to die after intangibly long years of life. He was the only man alive who knew what would kill each individual Gatekeeper, and he had taken his secret to the grave with him. But he had come to the Different Place and the Shades had learned his secret. At their earliest convenience, they had publicized it in the Earth Realm. And Gatekeepers had begun to die at regular intervals. The years 623, 628, 647, 1006, 1276, 1534, 1537 and 1711 were etched in Attica's mind. Three had died before these years, but those had gone mad with stutter-flutter.

She had read of Orion's particular bane, Atlantean silver, and had known from years earlier that he was likely to be the last Gatekeeper; his element was rare and hard to come by. Atlantean artifacts in and of themselves were unusual, and they were the most likely place to find the special metal. Mines had been opened. Museums purloined. A synthesized element was even attempted. All for minimal gain. Some, but very little.

The gem necklace clasp was of Atlantean silver, and at Attica's first chance, she had melted it down and made it into the tip and furthest edges of her sword.

There in the chamber and unknown to Attica, Orion's mind recognized as his body began failing him after receiving the wound. He lay there looking up at her, feeling the red stickiness of his life leaving him ounce by ounce. Randomly he recalled their first meeting, the early blossoming friendship and later romance, the joy of their wedding night.

Attica gave a start as his hand came up and clasped hers around the wrist. All that remained of his strength was devoted to that grasp, and she could not at first free herself from it. Their eyes met.

"Orion, you must not stop me now," said she, not unkindly. "Forgive me, but I must do this."

"Perish…too…" he managed, hardly audible above the distant rumbles. "You too…perish."

Her brow furrowed, though she recognized he was also remembering the words of the Shade.

"Yes, the Lords of Light shall soon be finished without you. There is nothing either of us can do for it. Now, let go of me." His grip was like a vice and she grew angry. His precious blood was seeping. "Unhand me! There is no time!"

I must get to the Portal and place his lifeblood upon it.

She stood, her strength raising him from the floor as he held on like a bulldog. With a concentrated effort she finally managed to pull free, but with such exertion that she staggered once more to the floor. Placing one leg so as to better rise, she suddenly paused. A pain was growing deep in her torso.

What now?

She went to come to her feet once more but as she did so the pangs within blossomed excruciatingly, tenfold as to their first murmuring. She cried aloud and fell to her hands and knees. She reached within herself and leaned back on her knees to get off her hands and face. Looking down her front, red blood spilled across her torso.

"What is this? What have you done?" she snarled in her agony. Attica cast her gaze on Orion, who lay there six feet away staring back.

But one glance at his eyes confirmed that he was no longer seeing. He did not move, but lay there. His one hand was still curled as if to clasp her wrist, the blood-stained other hand futilely covering the wound. As she looked upon his latter hand, she realized that their wound locations were identical.

She sat for a second, breath short. Fallen from her hand was the blood-soaked cloth she had sought to take to the Portal. She looked at it for a second but then ignored it.

What is the point of sealing the Portal now, if I will never leave this place?

She knew it to be true; she was covered in her own blood and could barely move from the torturous anguish within. What was she going to do? Crawl back across the bridge, past the girtas and up the Bottomless Stair, through the city and to a boat? The thought almost made her laugh.

I've not the strength to make it out of this chamber, let alone anywhere else. But how did I come by this wound? She looked around the Portal Chamber, blinking away some tears that had pooled in her eyes at the realization: *What a forlorn place in which to die alone.*

Well, not quite alone. Orion was still there, though not entirely. He was gone. Though every jolt was a fiery agony within her, she edged toward him and at last collapsed beside his body.

The Last Gatekeeper had indeed died...*and what he loves most will perish as well.* She lay beside him on the cold floor, looking at his still face. The clear thought came to her: *And you, Attica Triassa, are perishing as well.*

"You were not supposed to love me," she whispered, almost unable to get it out.

Only seconds later, the Portal Chamber was once again without life. The immortals that had broken the age-long siege of emptiness and entered the great room in the depths of the city had now left it once again. Their bodies they left behind, one beside the other.

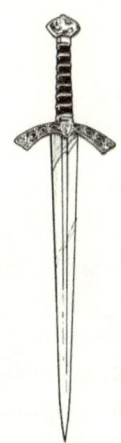

CHAPTER 29

"How is it you agreed to grant this desire of Cyprus Blackshaft? How is it within our power to destroy that which the man Keldir loves most?"

"Blackshaft's favor was an unsought boon. It is a fortunate coincidence that what he wanted was already under way. Blackshaft is under the impression that he has willed the destruction of Dominos de Lumine upon the loss of Orion Keldir. But the death of Orion Keldir will mean opening the Seal, and with our new invasion realized, the society would be doomed nonetheless – along with the rest of Earth Realm. Our Favor is granted and Blackshaft will never know it would have happened anyway."

"And what if Orion Keldir loves something more than his precious Dominos de Lumine?"

"Don't be naïve. What gives him his unnatural power is gone. What is left for him to love but the Lords of Light and all they offer?"

~From a conversation between Memphis Shadowcloak and Arcanus the Cruel

๛ infinity

Cyprus had the discipline and reflexes to not fire, and his stern face broke into a leering grin. Those purple eyes twitched, blinked, and focused again. He held his own weapon trained on Frank for a few seconds before looking down at Adrienne, her expression hard to read with the duct tape over her mouth. He gave Frank one fleeting look before reaching down with his free hand and hauling Adrienne up by her hair. She found her feet promptly to keep him from having to actually pull her to a stand.

His hand is shaking, she thought as it gripped her locks.

"Costly mistake, Blackman," said Cyprus to Frank, enjoying Frank's expression as it was plain his mortal enemy of long years was positioning his wife to stop a bullet. "Where do you think she'd like it? I'll let you choose, as a courtesy of old times."

"You pull that trigger and no amount of lead left in that gun is going to stop me from getting to you," said Frank darkly, and Adrienne had never seen him so angry.

Adrienne was half facing the man as he gripped a firm hold by her long dark hair. She looked at her husband who, understandably, did not have an immediate answer for the situation. He was too enraged to look apologetic. But there was of course nothing he could do to stop Cyprus, unless the Atlantean took his own sweet time. He had pulled her up from right before him, always looking at Frank, and had once more pinned her against himself while she and her husband locked eyes.

"Watch now, Blackman," said Cyprus, "we only get one take at this type of thing." And he laughed cruelly as he pressed the machinegun barrel to the side of Adrienne's head. For Frank, time stood still.

A gunshot exploded into the quiet intensity of the room.

"Adrienne, no!" was all Frank could yell at the top of his voice.

But it was Cyprus's face that changed terribly at the sound of the gunshot. His entire expression contorted and he erupted with a roar of pain as a volcano. He let go of both the machinegun and Adrienne involuntarily, and as she fell away and turned her body, Frank saw with utter relief that firstly she was still alive – but secondly in her taped hands behind her back she had a smoking handgun.

Adrienne had planned it of course, but not as neatly as it came out. Among the many things her tied hands had brushed and grasped when she rolled on the ground amidst the corpses was a variety of weaponry. Her right hand had reflexively closed neatly on the handle of a Beretta, before she had the state of mind to know what she was doing. It had been to steady her at first, but just as Cyprus came forward and picked her up by the hair, her grip had tightened as the pain surged at the top of her head. The strong hold on the gun helped to pull it free from the midst of the twisted pile in which it lay, and Cyprus had never looked at her as he hauled her up and turned her to face her husband – and had in so doing placed her firearm in a very convenient position.

The bullet Adrienne fired from her bound right hand entered the top inside of Cyprus's leg at an angle and went through his kneecap on its way to exit the left side of his calf through the bone. Half the impact of the assault was that it was completely unlooked for. The other half was the blinding pain and crippling of a limb important for mobility. His leg was suddenly useless – at least for a little while yet – and it buckled beneath him as he fell. Frank didn't know how Adrienne had managed this, nor did he particularly care at the moment.

"Adrienne! Get clear!" was all he shouted at her.

Frank had failed to pick up a loaded weapon once already. *I won't repeat that mistake.* The instant he had had the chance, he picked one up and checked it; even one-handed, it took him hardly any time at all. He got back to his feet and leveled the gun at Cyprus, who was looking with murderous intensity at Adrienne. Only when Frank drew the hammer back did Cyprus's slowly blinking eyes leave Adrienne and look at his old adversary.

Cyprus had nothing to say, but that was just as well because Frank was past listening. The Atlantean sat up and was so fast he had nearly reached his feet by the time Frank fired reflexively. Cyprus was blown off balance and cast to the floor. Frank was slowly coming toward him, pulling the trigger and putting a piece of lead into him every second step. The clip held eight shots, and over the next ten seconds, Frank put each in Cyprus. By the third he had stopped trying to rise, by the fifth he was moving feebly, and the seventh and eighth left him crumpled on the floor – but still very much alive.

Frank let the weapon click empty in his hand before tossing it aside, but immediately he looked around on the floor for another one. He grimaced at a sudden pain in his bad arm; it ached above the elbow, had a sharp pain at the point, and tingled down the wrist. The ends of his fingers were numb but a gradual restoration was undeniably occurring. He actively began trying to incorporate its use to encourage recovery. He did not realize it, but an unfelt flesh wound from a stray bullet graze was helping to bleed more of the girtas venom out of his body. Additionally, Adrienne had smashed the creature in the middle of its dosage application; he'd not received a full injection.

Even as he looked about for a gun he saw a stray boot-knife and used it to cut Adrienne free. He was then immediately back to seeking firearms. She tore the tape from her lips with an involuntary expression of smarting pain. Cyprus was on his back about twelve feet away, groaning. His chest smoked, and each shot had left its small circular hole in his torso. He was not going to get up any time soon, but he was certainly not dead.

The ground shook beneath their feet and Adrienne grabbed Frank's left arm and he winced again.

"Frank, let's go."

"In a minute, Adrienne," he said firmly. "I'm going to finish this." She pulled on his arm but to her surprise he held firm. "Should have finished it years ago. If I don't he'll just show up on our doorstep someday. Now, let go, Adrienne."

"You can't kill him that way, can't you tell by now?"

"The hell I can't," said Frank, looking around and occasionally squatting amongst the dead men. "He can take it – but not indefinitely." He glanced up at Cyprus, who still wasn't doing much more than groaning. "Ain't that right, Wonder

Boy? You can only stop 'em for so long. Today's the day, my old friend. You try and put one in my wife? I'm gonna put one in your-"

Adrienne's anxious whisper made him turn and look at her. Her voice had changed.

"Frank!"

He looked at her and then followed her eyes to one of the entryways. The softest of fluttering came to his ears, and after some careful looking he saw that a lone girtas had returned to the Guard Room. It was slowly flap-hopping amidst the carnage. He saw another flit into the room behind it.

Without a word, Frank was on his feet, grabbed Adrienne's hand, and together the two ran from the room. Headed back up the passage from whence they'd come, he paused only to grab an empty machinegun nearby, for the mounted flashlight. The cavern shook and trembled all around them even as they left.

Their path was not hard to follow; they went straight back up the corridor they had originally come down, until at last they reached the Bottomless Stair, climbing up to the left of their passage and downward to the right. They paused for a moment, breathing hard from the run.

Adrienne groaned. "This is going to be fun," she said with a roll of her eyes. "How long did we spend walking down? An hour? How long is it going to take to get up?"

The city shook again, violently this time. Behind them in the passage from whence they'd come, a thunderous crash sounded, and it was apparent some masonry had fallen in with the rumblings. Far off in the distance, down the stairs, both Blackmans heard the rushing of water.

"The city's flooding again," said Frank after a second. "We've gotta move."

"Lead the way," she managed, taking a deep breath, far from pleased about the prospect of climbing the stairs in a hurry.

The broad and shallow steps passed swiftly beneath them as both began running upward at a pace that was just short of frenzied. The understanding that the city was flooding made it a very easy decision to push oneself to his or her limits. They went on for about ten minutes' hard going before pausing at one of the many landings.

"So what…about…Orion?" asked Adrienne as they paused, breathing hard.

Frank panted alongside her, hands on his knees. "He knew…what he was doing. Always did. I don't know what he's up to now…but I'm not worried." He crouched and took a deep breath. "Always could handle himself…I'm more concerned about us."

"How are we going to get back on the ship if we don't have any thugs with us, or Attica? I mean, it *is* her ship…"

"I don't know," admitted Frank, "but right now all I want to see is daylight; then we'll worry about that."

"I hear water."

"Me too. Let's go."

୫୦ ୫

Cyprus watched several girtas that flitted and crawled about the Guard Room. He hesitated to try and move; for one thing, his injuries hampered his efforts immensely, and for another he did not want to risk the girtas targeting him. He was pleased there were not too many, but even a small handful would be his match in this condition. Cyprus gritted his teeth, his breathing labored. He could already recognize his immortal's body beginning to fuse the bullet wounds in his torso, though it would be a lengthy process. It had been a very long time since anyone had managed to put an entire clip into him, and the world of pain he was in felt slightly new to Cyprus, though certainly bearable. His leg would be tender for weeks.

But the girtas complicated things. That, and the trembling of the city. If he strained his utmost hearing, Cyprus fancied he could hear the movement of water in the outlying distance. He imagined that below him the ocean was trying to reclaim the city; he would not have been surprised to know that beneath the bridge spanning the magnificent gap between the Guard Room and the Portal Chamber, the seawater was indeed rising. Attica had done an efficient job raising the city to daylight once again, but her solution had not been permanent. Her technology had served its purpose and expunged its energy; nature was taking back what had belonged to her for so long; the city was sinking beneath the sea once more.

Which meant this was a bad place to be – *is that girtas looking at me*? He could not tell at first, but with a slowly rising concern, Cyprus began to realize that it was indeed looking at him in particular. The vile creature's red eyes glinted in the darkness, and it leaped into the air, wings buzzing as it came on its way toward him.

The hunk of stone he threw at it disrupted its flight and it crashed to the ground not far from him; but the other handful in the room could not have missed this action. Cyprus saw them all head his way now, not necessarily speedily, but certainly inevitably. Not caring about the pain that protested his movement – and it did scream at him – Cyprus got to his feet, groaning aloud.

He turned his back on them and staggered and hopped toward the shattered doorway that Orion and Attica had passed through on their way to the Portal Chamber, the eastern door. It was the nearest exit by far, the only option. *I've got to get out of this room without the girtas following me. If even one notices...* Cyprus found himself growing angry even as he did so; they would follow him, as surely as the sun rose every day. They were bred to follow him, but at the moment, this particular path was the only place to go – literally. He would never reach the western door where the Blackmans had fled.

The awkward gait in which he was forced to move was excruciating and humbling, but in no time at all Cyprus had reached the bridge. Behind him fluttered and scurried the girtas, and there were additionally several more now. Straight on before him spanned the bridge itself, and to the left and right as he stood upon it was endless darkness. Far, far below in the depths was the sound of water. He paused on the bridge, debating.

He could cross the expanse, destined for the Portal Chamber and whatever Attica and Orion were doing there. But both legend and rumor cited traps ahead which only Orion's presence would help avoid; Cyprus had never been this far into the realm of the Gatekeepers before; not being of their order, he was in great peril. Ironically the one trap left would not have hurt him in his near-immortal state, but Cyprus did not know that. He looked back at the girtas. Two had left the Guard Room and were crawling toward him. Others clustered around the doorway. There were now close to ten.

His eyes convulsed shut in a longer and heavier blink, but with a gritting of his teeth he forced them open. *Maybe it is stutter-flutter after all. Is this what it's like to go mad?* He had heard it theorized that stutter-flutter was an immortal body's subconscious way of telling him or her that it was weary of gazing upon the world, and was making an effort to no longer look. The condition itself didn't kill– it was a visible symptom of a deeper problem. He looked at the girtas.

If they feed on life, perhaps madness carries a unique taste to it. What would I taste like?

It was a terrible decision; be eaten alive by the girtas – and with few in number it would take considerably longer – or limp in great pain across the bridge to be no doubt eviscerated by some sadistic trap of severe cunning. Even then the girtas would follow over the bridge. It was a choice that was no choice. In his heart he was certain they would catch him before he crossed the vast span of bridge. No doubt about it. The nearest girtas leaped for him, mouth apparatus opening almost in slow motion as it sailed through the air toward him.

One for my memoirs.

And Cyprus leaped from the bridge into the black oblivion below.

ಹಿ ೧೩

"Faster, Adrienne, faster!"

Frank and Adrienne had been climbing hard for quite some time, pausing only when utterly necessary, knowing that saltwater followed up after them. The city would tremble and shake so violently at points that it was a wonder to either of them the whole place didn't just fall in. Yet the architecture remained sound enough, and rarely did something actually come crashing down.

But now both of them could hear and see the saltwater rising up after them. Their steady, non-panicked pace turned very speedily into a race against time. Frank had no intention of letting himself or his wife drown in the enclosed Bottomless Stair; he made her go first and stayed on her heels, encouraging her on with all speed.

Their legs burned and breath had been short for awhile now. *It doesn't matter what's behind us, I can't keep this up for much longer,* Adrienne admitted to herself. Beside her, Frank was beginning to realize it was a race in futility; the stair was too high and the waters surging too rapidly. As he raised his left leg to gain another stair, his right was suddenly soaked to the knee. His next step soaked his other leg to the thigh. He shouted at her to leave him and run but even as he did so the rush that enveloped Frank swallowed her as well. Just as her legs were yielding to collapse under her own weight, the water was at her waist and then over her head. They were picked up off the stairs and rushed upward as the surge of saltwater threw them against the ceiling of the narrow little passage. It was well that the roof itself was slanted, for both were pushed against it and they could almost crawl along it upside down as the water carried them upward. This went on for a terrifying minute, but ended just as Adrienne felt her lungs would implode.

The stairs came to an end, and the violent surge of rising water vomited them out of the archway and spat them across the floor. They tumbled disoriented, saltwater stinging their eyes, swallowing some as they were spilled over the flat stones. Suddenly the water receded just a bit, leaving them exhausted and panting on their hands and knees, looking at each other with relief. Another wave of water issued from the Bottomless Stair entry and knocked Adrienne down as she tried to reach her feet. He was pushed away as he tried to help her. Then the level of water found equilibrium and was content to lap about their ankles, only a few inches deep for the moment. They had once again gained the level of the palace from which they had initially started down. Though a few hours before, it felt like weeks ago.

The water spilled over the top of the stairs after them, but given the immense capacity of the hall in which they now stood, it spread but did not deepen noticeably. Despite the danger, upon reaching the top, both husband and wife practically collapsed, panting, teeth chattering, leg muscles aching. On top of this, Frank's wounded arm was sore and tingly, sensation gradually returning. He could move his hand and work the fingers, but as of yet had no sense of touch from the wrist down. Above the wrist there was a strong ache that made him miss the deadness.

"That was close," gasped Adrienne.

"Yeah, but we're not out of the woods yet."

"Frank, I'm not going to be able to go on like this much longer."

He put his arms around her. "Yes, you can. You must. We'll make it; we just can't give up." He smiled and glanced back at the stairs. "I worked too hard to get up those stairs to give up now."

She somehow managed to return the smile, weakly. "Well, we can't hang around here for long."

"I think it's this way."

੪ ୡ

It was well for the Blackmans that the city was not sinking as rapidly as they surmised. The close proximity of the Bottomless Stair and a particular concentration in the depths below had caused the water to rise rapidly up the stairs themselves, but once it had room to spread out, it only very slowly began to cover the stone floors, and then to accumulate depth. Now that they were not climbing, moving in itself was not so exhausting.

They went on for some time; Orion had led the group for quite a while, following his flawless memory. It was impossible to expect any first-timer to recall the way back through the palace, especially in such poor light. At uncertain junctions, one could not just stand there and take the time to decide. A turn left or right was decided upon within a few seconds and did not always turn out to be correct. In no time at all they had left the path Orion led them upon and struck out on their own, unintentionally at first. By the time they realized it, it was far too late to try and backtrack. There was daylight cracking through periodically from the ceiling and occasionally a wall, but they were searching for an actual exit – or something that could pass as one.

The water was mid-calf and cold. Numbing, even. They splashed along, occasionally consulting over which way they ought to go when presented with several choices. After a good half hour, it was distant daylight that spurred on a new direction. They came to a large hall, and could see blue sky through the archways on the opposite side. It was a moment of near unspeakable joy.

"So far so good," said Frank, grabbing her hand, trying to ignore how the water was a little over his knees.

"I was beginning to worry," she said, splashing along behind him. Her voice was weary beyond measure.

The light they saw was from an open terrace which made up the entire side of the vast room. Starting some way from the edge of the terrace, the water about them was taking on a current toward it. As a whole, the entire surface of the water around them was making a steadily faster course toward the open edge of the room. Frank realized this was because it must be spilling over the side – and even as he noticed this, both he and Adrienne were finding it was hard to stand upright; the current was pulling them toward the fall, and quite strongly.

"We're in trouble," said Adrienne, drawing the same conclusion as her husband.

"Hold onto me," he answered, and tightened his grip on her.

They were swept across the hall on the strong current of now nearly waist-deep water, now both soaking wet and shivering. By a remarkable coincidence, they both managed to steer toward one of the pillars at the end of the hall, and caught it about a few meters before they would have been either smashed into the banister of the terrace or simply swept over the side.

"Now what?" asked Adrienne.

Frank looked around the pillar, toward the edge. With the angle, he could not see how great the fall off the terrace would be; but they would not be able to go anywhere except over it until the water stopped flowing, by which time it would be too late to care any longer for their safety.

"I was hoping you'd tell me."

There was a moment's pause as both looked around, realizing they had nowhere to go but over.

"We can't just sit here," she finally consented.

"I don't know how big the fall is," he said, partly annoyed with the tension of the situation and the hopeless outlook he had.

"Well, that makes two of us. So what?"

"I don't want to lose you, that's what!" he snapped sharply.

There was a silence where she was looking at him and he was looking anywhere but her.

"I'm sorry," he finally said, still not looking at her. "I just don't want to lose you, Adrienne-"

She put her hands on the front of his shirt, gripping it tightly, and pulled him in for an interrupting kiss of the sort Frank had not experienced for what felt a lifetime.

"You won't," she said, looking into his eyes. Then she hauled herself backward, pulling him along, taking both of them out from behind the pillar and into the full stream of the current. An instant later they were both swept violently over the banister and off the edge of the terrace.

CHAPTER 30

*"I have heard that my old foeman Frank Blackman has retired from
Dominos de Lumine, apparently in order to marry. I've lost some
respect for him, given that. He has fallen far if he does not realize he is
sacrificing near-immortality and endless glory for the sake of being with
some woman. What woman is worth that?"*

~an excerpt from the memoirs of Cyprus Blackshaft.

༄ ༁

In retrospect, Frank acknowledged it really was the only thing to do. The
ocean would only have kept coming until the waters over the edge of the
terrace had risen to that level, by which point the entire city would be going
under. Still, he would have preferred another manner than simply being pulled
unprepared into the rapid current. It was good to find, however, that the fall was
not too great, and that it emptied into deep water.

Sometime in the forty foot fall, both Frank and Adrienne lost hold of each
others' hands. In the time the fall took, Frank at least could tell that below them
was a courtyard surrounded by high walls, some steps going down and up at opposite ends, leading to other parts of the massive palace. Then he was cast below the
frothing surface at the foot of the falls, and for a moment he could see nothing but
bubbles and horribly stinging white water before his eyes. Adrienne was nowhere
to be seen, and it worried him for only an instant, until he recalled she was actually
a better swimmer than he had ever been.

She was treading water on the surface, waiting for him when he came up. They
exchanged only a look before simultaneously heading for some stairs that climbed

out of the foaming pool that now made up the courtyard, the pavement of which was some way below their bobbing feet. Exhausted, the Blackmans climbed the stairs out of the pool and stood at the top of them, looking through the archway before them that led out to the top of a wall.

A minute later they were standing on top of the perimeter wall of the Atlantean imperial palace, gazing out over the ruins through which they had journeyed from the original drop-point by boat. This viewpoint was now to the south. They had come west from their original entry into the palace. They were above the rest of the city, viewing it all from the palace on a hill, and could see far and wide. If not for their immediate peril of the island itself sinking back into the sea, it would have been breathtakingly beautiful.

The day itself was cloudless and bright. The full sun of the late afternoon shone down on the familiar lightly-tanned stone columns and deserted buildings. Yet the cobblestone and paved streets were now different; most of them had water running down them and some could not be seen at all. In some lower places only the tops of half columns and pillars could be seen. The city was unmistakably sinking, and more readily than wading through the palace had let on. The sea crept in from the outer edges while the Bottomless Stair had become a spouting fountain.

Both Frank and Adrienne had had their fill of the magnificent architecture and ancient civilization. While the marvelous site was not lost completely on either of them, both were far more distracted by other matters. Much to their relief, they actually did spy the modified RIBs the initial party had taken from the cargo freighter Attica had used as a main vessel. Had they emerged from the palace where they had come in, it would have been quite far away, but their getting lost amidst their departure had actually served a purpose: now, when they emerged to the south of the ruin, the part of the palace they stood on was actually significantly closer to the boats.

The water was rising fast enough that it would have been an eventual swim if they left the high perimeter wall and tried to make their way through the city. They walked atop the wall to the southwest corner that was closest to the boats, and Frank waved his arms high over his head to try and get their attention.

"These are the same people that imprisoned us in a dungeon and tried to kill us," said Adrienne and pushed her long wet hair back for the ninth time, looking at him signal. "Do we really want to flag them down?"

"Do you see another boat?"

She let go of his arm and only watched with slight surprise as he took off his shirt and used it to help signal the craft about three hundred meters distant. The men on the craft noticed them at once; they had anticipated the return of *someone* for quite some time, and in a city showing no other signs of life it was not hard to see the *one* fellow trying to get their attention. A man on the foremost craft waved back, and Frank stopped signaling.

Pleased enough, he sat down on the edge of the wall, feet dangling, and looked almost smugly at his wife. Removing his shirt had reminded him of the shock collar he'd not removed since he had just the one useful hand until lately. Recovered enough to remove it, he did and tossed it off the side.

"I guess we wait for the water to be deep enough for them to come here and pick us up," he said, sounding elated, for indeed he was. He could handle being captured, opposed to drowning while trapped in an enclosed room.

"Oh, I can't wait to be handcuffed in the brig again," Adrienne answered, folding her arms across her chest. "Great fun, that."

Frank looked at her, smile gone. "You got another ship we should have flagged down? Or perhaps we should just tread water once the island's gone from beneath us, and wait and *hope* for someone to swing by? Did you see the size of that beached shark in the courtyard? I don't fancy treading water long knowing something like that might be around."

She sat beside him, watching the distant craft float offshore waiting for a lane to open in order to come get them. It would not be long before such a channel became deep enough for modified RIBs. The city would sink and the palace they sat near was upon a hill in the middle; they would soon be a remote island in the sea, and all that would need to happen would be a leap to the boats.

"We don't know where Attica is, Frank. Or Cyprus," she said. "She could already be aboard, she might be trapped in the city, she might be dead. What are we supposed to do? Show up without her? Even with her, we might as well be dead."

Frank had not been worried about this half as much as he had been considering the disappearance of Orion. Cyprus he assumed to be dead, as he had been left behind wounded and alone with girtas in a chamber of stone soon to be flooded. Frank had no problem condemning the man to such a fate; he had known Cyprus for decade upon decade – he deserved worse.

Yet Orion was his oldest friend, literally and figuratively. A better man he had never known, nor a more resourceful or capable one. Still, if Frank had known beforehand that he could escape a sinking city while Orion could not, he would not have believed it. But there he was with Adrienne, with Orion missing and quite possibly, though he regretted the very thought of it, dead.

"One dilemma at a time," he said to Adrienne after a few minutes' silence, watching the distant boats find their channel forward and slowly make their way toward them, angling through the ruins of the city.

"What are we going to tell them?" she asked.

"How about the truth?"

"That won't tell them whatever happened to Attica – she could be onboard even now, though I doubt it. Baby, they're not going to believe the truth."

"No...I guess not. But do you have a better idea?"

She shrugged and remained content enough to watch the boat get closer.

80 03

Close to an hour later, Frank and Adrienne were aboard the small craft as it approached and was attached to the large cargo ship. If either had had any assumption that they were to be treated differently in the absence of Attica and anyone else they had come with initially, they were disappointed. They were allowed to remain together, but were immediately handcuffed and treated in a far from kindly fashion.

They stood side by side on the bridge of the cargo ship, watching from a safe distance as the very last vestiges of Atlantis sank below the surface. The last thing either saw was a long rock covered in coral that had been on the northwest side of the imperial palace. Then, just as the sea had lain undisturbed before their arrival, so it returned to an unbroken wavy blue-gray-green plain to the horizon in every direction.

The captain watched the last of the city disappear and then turned to them.

"One more time: what happened?"

Frank told him. Again.

"What, no goblins or elves to add?" the bearded captain said condescendingly upon the conclusion, which took them all the way up to getting picked up once more by the boats. "The very idea that you two alone could escape that many armed men is ridiculous. What do you take me for?" It was grimly humorous they were trying to get him to believe it – but that did not negate the fact that he had lost two superiors and twenty men. An assumed twenty, anyway. Frank could not account for the one crewman who had scuffled with Cyprus and taken off in the direction of the Bottomless Stair. Still, it left the captain in charge.

"The question is," said the first mate over Adrienne's shoulder, "what do we do with these two?"

"Throw 'em overboard," said another.

"Aye. Overboard," came still another voice.

Adrienne's intake of breath was audible.

How civilized, thought Frank, but was smart enough to say nothing. He hoped he did not look scared of this, as he recognized it as a real, valid threat. Actually quite likely. *I'll save telling them about our hostage value till they actually decide.*

"You men underestimate prisoner value," said the captain, confirming Frank's own plan. The man was looking at Frank. "This one goes way back with the High Command. They were telling me about him. Even with the Lady Triassa and Blackshaft gone, I'll wager Triassa would not have us discard this one." His eyes moved to Adrienne and took her in, though she noticed he wasn't really interested in looking her in the eye. "And I'm sure we can find uses for her."

Adrienne had been in the presence of enemies too long to even grimace at that veiled threat to her honor. And she was aware how her soaked clothes clung to her in the cool air. Instead of cowering as he would have liked, she only glared at him. Disappointed at her reaction, he sat back, glowering.

"Put them in the brig."

ဆ ၄

Three days was a long time to sit in a brig, even together. Rations were provided, however scant. When it came right down to it, Frank had to admit to himself that he was simply glad they were just still alive, given what they had been through. He sat there with her leaning against him on the bench, arms around her, mind wandering. His foremost thought as the days went by was that thankfully the captain's vague hint about finding a use for Adrienne was apparently just that; an empty threat; they were left alone.

He also thought of Orion, beginning to fear the tall Atlantean was gone forever. He brooded on Cyprus, wondering exactly what had transpired after they had left him to his fate – and whether he met it there or not. He thought a little of Attica, wondering if anything had occurred between herself and Orion before the end. More than once he recognized that the world as he knew it had not ended, and so concluded that something substantial had occurred between the immortals before the end.

Adrienne spent much of the time quietly thinking, though her reflections did not turn to the immortals she had met. At least, not as much as her mind turned to her family. This year they would have Thanksgiving with her parents in Nebraska, no excuses. And she would watch a Bears game with her brother Andrew in Chicago. She could write that book she'd been wanting to – she had experienced what she considered a moderately good plot in the past week – but she stopped in the middle of her deliberations.

She realized she was beginning to picture her coming life as a second chance. And perhaps that's what she had been given. Ironically, suddenly and fleetingly, she contemplated being pregnant. The idea hovered and then vanished. She gave herself to Frank's arms around her and began daydreaming about what she had learned about him; having missed a couple hundred birthdays, no longer wondering why he had no family, and finding a strange new attraction to his capabilities in a dangerous situation.

"Frank."

"Yes, love."

"I want to go home."

His arms adjusted themselves. "Working on it."

"And I want to have a garden when we get back."

"Okay."

"A nice garden, with steppingstones and a good variety of flowers and vegetables."

"Okay."

She smiled. "And a baby."

"Well…"

"And a Ferrari."

"Now you're just being silly."

"And the world on a platter. A silver one. With maybe some gold trim and set diamonds. Are you writing this down?"

He kissed her on the cheek. "Oh yes, every word, madam. Your every wish."

She laughed, grateful for the release of tension. They were, after all, still in a brig.

"But we can start with a garden."

"No squash."

"I suppose…"

CHAPTER 31

"You are amongst the eldest of us. What is the key to your sanity remaining intact?"

"The madness is slow to come when it knows you have no desire to avoid it. Immortality is about time given to accomplish a task, not living on and on in pursuit of vanity and riches. When our task is done, no one will be more pleased to enter the great Beyond than I."

~excerpt from a conversation between Reldir of Susa and Orion Keldir

୬ ଓ

The vast Raven cargo vessel brought them right back to the exact same port and dock they had left roughly a week before. It was now much the same, even to the point of being marched down the gangplank at gunpoint and put in the back of what may very well have been one of the same cars in which they had formerly arrived.

The crew of the large boat saw them to the armed guards that put them in the car and then watched them drive off without a second thought. The limousine they were in was spacious and comfortable, thick glass separating them from the driver and the armed man that sat in the front. They said nothing to either prisoner upon their entering the car, as if they were under orders, and neither of the Blackmans objected.

୬ ଓ

On the roof of one of the warehouses about two hundred meters down the wharf from the docked Raven ship, a man dressed in black lay on his stomach, watching the whole scene through the scope of a sniper rifle. He observed all: the identification number on the cargo ship that docked, the license plate on the lone limousine that pulled up, nearly all the individuals who showed themselves; especially the handcuffed man and woman that were marched down the gangplank to the waiting car.

As Frank and Adrienne got into the car, he turned his head down just a bit to speak into the transceiver inside his left collar.

"They're back and headed for checkpoint two. No Keldir."

℘ ℘

Frank wondered if they would be brought back to the castle they had left initially. His understanding of it had been that it was a personal retreat of Attica's. *Attica would have shown up by now if she were still alive. Everyone else must be dead, just as I feared.* It served little purpose to return to the fortress with Attica gone, what with all the secure places the Raven had at their disposal. Also, he recalled the violence and confusion involving their initial departure, and wondered if it would not still be considered a hotspot.

℘ ℘

A most average-looking man walked a black Labrador retriever down the wet street, whistling an old tavern tune and smoking his pipe. He gave every impression of not noticing as the Raven limousine passed him and turned left into the city. He kept walking till they had been out of sight and then spoke into his own collar lapel:

"Checkpoint two. North on Ferdinand. North on Ferdinand."

A block later, a van for Cadfael's Flowers pulled into traffic after the limousine passed and followed at a discreet distance.

℘ ℘

They had driven for an hour when the car slowed and through the front windshield both the Blackmans could see they were gradually stopping in a long line of traffic. Up ahead, traffic was slowly going through tollbooths. The limousine pulled into the right lane, joining a few other more distinguished-looking vehicles. Frank guessed it was the express lane for those that were either paid ahead of time or willing to pay more. It struck him as odd at the moment that the Order of the Raven of all people would not have their own lane to just drive right through this sort of thing. Perhaps it was due to the construction about them that they did not have a special road.

Frank was watching the exchange between the driver and passenger ahead of them. The glass was soundproof as well, but it was obvious the latter fellow was unimpressed with the former's choice of route. The argument went on for a half minute, but by then they were surrounded by traffic; their path was fixed. The glass opened in front of the prisoners as the guard poked his head up to the small little window he'd shifted over.

"Don't get any ideas," he growled at the Blackmans. "First one to try and get noticed by *anybody* at this booth up here stops a dose of lead. Don't think I won't."

Then he slammed the window again and turned back toward the front. Adrienne looked at Frank. He patted her leg. "Don't worry, and do what he says, babe."

"But Frank, this could be our shot."

"Trust me."

৪০ ০৪

The time dragged on for both captives and captors, but eventually the limousine pulled up to the booth. As if to add to the congestion along that particular trek, a construction crew was pulling up asphalt not at all far away, a forklift was driving back and forth, and a truck was backing up. Men shouted at each other. Adrienne absentmindedly watched a particularly strong-looking fellow smash a sledgehammer down to help break up what was being cleared away.

The driver rolled the window down, pulling a card and some money from a compartment between the seats. He handed it without a thought to the tall man at the window, who took it with a courteous smile. There was a moment as the man behind the counter stamped the sheet in the appropriate place, took his time getting the correct change, and then handed it back.

The driver took it and dumped the coins loudly into the dispenser, hearing an extra loud *tink!* as he did, and then glanced at the card. His brow furrowed: the red ink date and time stamp for the same old toll booth pass did not read as it always did. No date or time. It had a single word instead. He stared at the word.

Adrienne straightened as she looked out the window toward the construction. "Frank, I think the forklift guy is lost."

Frank looked. "Or drunk."

This time the ink on the card simply read: *Sorry*. The driver shouted in surprise as the limousine itself jolted violently, and then to his horror the back of the car rose off the ground. He looked in his rearview and then physically turned his head and looked, even as he floored the accelerator.

The forklift from the construction site had crossed the short distance, approached the back of the car, put its extensions beneath the trunk and rear axle, and lifted the entire vehicle's rear end off the ground. The remaining grounded wheels spun uselessly as the driver tried to speed away. The car didn't move, securely hung up on the forks.

"Rodrigo!" the driver yelled, looking over at the gunman next to him.

The guard was facing away from him, apparently not in the least interested in what was going on. The driver grabbed him but as he turned to face him, he stopped short, gapping. The armed guard Rodrigo sat slumped in his seat, eyes open and staring right through the driver, a bullet hole in the middle of his forehead, perfectly aimed. The driver looked to the windshield and saw the tiny hole where the bullet had come through, and realized the extra loud *tink!* he had heard when he carelessly let the change fall was the bullet entering the car – and Rodrigo.

"Adrienne, look out!" cried Frank, and threw the coat lying across their legs over his wife's head as her window suddenly spider-webbed over its entire surface as a heavy blow struck it from the other side.

The construction worker with the sledgehammer had walked over, right behind the forklift, and smashed the window with his tool. Frank saw that the window was unbroken, but the heavy hammer raised again, and he covered his head alongside Adrienne as the man hit the window again, exploding it inward with flying tiny square pieces of broken glass.

No sooner was the window broken in than the man smashed the hammer down one last time atop the locking mechanism. His strike was surgical, and when this was done he reached inside and was able to open the door from within. He grabbed Adrienne by the arm and pulled her not too roughly from the car. "C'mon, love, move," was all he said. Frank followed.

In the front, the driver fumbled for the firearm kept in the glove compartment, but he stopped as something hard and small pressed against his back in an introductory manner. A Scottish accent spoke over his shoulder.

"Haven't you had enough fun for one day, lad?" The driver stopped and the voice went on. "Because if you take that piece out of the glove-box, I'm going to have to paint the inside of this pretty car with…you."

The driver sat gradually back in his seat, very slowly raising his hands and putting them on his head, interlocking the fingers.

"Good lad. Stay right there. And remember the sniper is watching you. I've been doing this for longer than you've been alive, and I've never seen Killian miss. Behave yourself."

While the man with the sledgehammer had taken Adrienne rather emphatically from the car, as soon as she was free of it, he guided her without force to the tollbooth and there let her sit with her back to it. He'd said something that may have been polite, but there was a lot of background noise all about them and she missed it. Frank never left her side, and the man only dug in a pocket and tossed something small to Frank as he turned away. Her husband caught it and looked in his palm; a small pair of skeleton keys, undoubtedly for the handcuffs.

Frank set to freeing himself and his wife, but Adrienne only sat dumb-founded, watching the forklift hold the limousine where it was while the driver was yanked from the front. She never saw what happened to him; he was very quickly taken out of her sight. One of the construction workers at once set about hooking up the Raven vehicle to a tow-truck, which had blended in perfectly sitting at the

construction site. More than once she saw one of their rescuers flash an identification badge at nearby civilian drivers and wave them through.

The door opened next to her and out of the tollbooth came a tall, burly man
with red hair and a beard. He had a sawed-off shotgun in his hands. Adrienne had
been taken so many places by so many different people that she almost didn't care
exactly who these people were, just so long as they were not friends of the Raven.
Obviously they were not. She looked up sharply when the big man spoke with a
Scottish accent.

"Now, Frank, you really didn't think the rest of us were going to sit this one
out, did you?"

Frank smiled. "Never crossed my mind."

"Is this the wife? She's way too pretty a lass to be with you."

Frank grinned. "Yes on both counts, Trego."

To Adrienne's surprise, her husband stood up and embraced the tall Scot, who
only chuckled when Frank added, "Nice work."

Adrienne stood and Frank turned to her.

"Babe, this is Trego. We go way back. He's with de Lumine. Trego, this is my
wife, Adrienne."

"Pleased to meet you, lass. But if you'll excuse me, we need to clean up the
mess. If you'll be so kind as to get into that flower van over there, you'll be on your
way home."

"Standard operation?" asked Frank.

"Aye," said Trego. "We weren't certain they only had one vehicle, so we were
ready for a little more overkill. But as it is, it turned out well enough. The Network's
confirmed Triassa's operations here for months. It all came to a head when you
and Orion went missing for a bit, after he left me a second time. That reminds me:
where is Orion, anyway?"

Frank patted the big man on the shoulder. "I'll explain on the way."

CHAPTER 32

"Our traitor at Dominos de Lumine was afflicted with an acute case of greed. Ironic that what caused us to depart from the Order of the Raven all those years ago should still haunt us today."

~Bohemond LIV

໖ ໖

hile Adrienne had enjoyed mostly luxurious travel conditions when in the hands of the Order of the Raven, she had to agree that Dominos de Lumine left her wanting nothing. Their rescuers – who turned out to be an organized team of thirteen – saw them to a five-star hotel in the downtown area, the penthouse and top three floors of which served as a local headquarters.

Between the time of their arrival in the afternoon on the day they were rescued to their departure in an armed convoy at ten the next morning, both Frank and Adrienne enjoyed having whatever they needed. For the first time in what seemed months but in reality was almost three weeks: hot showers, changes of clothes, restful sleep, a catered meal.

The hotel was only a place to stay for the night. Without even having to request it, Trego had organized their stay and their departure on one of Dominos de Lumine' own jets, having its own hangar at the airport. By the time the plane landed in their own home state, they had slept, had two full meals, watched three out of two hundred movie choices, and Adrienne had won a couple games of cards. Frank jokingly placed his two defeats on the loss of feeling in the thumb, fourth and fifth fingers of his left hand stung by the girtas. Sense of touch had not returned to these digits. Once in the country they switched to a chopper.

Adrienne leaned against her husband in the helicopter as it headed east. She was well-rested but still exhausted, as was he. She listened to the relentless hum above them as she looked out the window, enjoying how they were over a rural area, reminding her of her childhood. Again she was reminded of the commitments she had mentally made to her family in the coming year. It was dusk.

"I hope you don't mind us making a stop before getting home," he said quietly. "I know it's been a long trip, but I need to sew up some loose ends."

She nodded, almost too tired to make the effort of talking. "It's fine. Just glad to be back in the right country."

"I hear you."

"But where are we going?"

"Dominos de Lumine headquarters. Same place we were when you were taken twenty days ago."

"A lifetime ago, if you ask me."

"I know."

She sat up suddenly. "My gosh, my boss is going to kill me!" He paused half a second and put her hand up to her mouth, genuinely concerned. "And Giovanni's probably starved to death!"

Frank actually laughed at her. "I wouldn't worry about that."

"Why not?"

He leaned in and kissed her cheek. "You don't imagine a world-spanning secret organization can't drum up an alibi for you? Or feed the cat, like it's hard?"

She sat back. "I hadn't thought of that."

"Because you've not done stuff like this before. Relax. They've already been sent the information. You're probably not expected for a week yet."

"Nice...but what loose ends are you sewing up?"

"Bohemond needs to know what went on. It's called 'being debriefed,' and I promise it won't take long. You can sleep in the cottage if you want-"

"Frank, if you don't mind, I'll stay with you this time around..."

"Oh, yeah...sure. Of course – oh, being debriefed *and* I owe it to Bohemond on a personal level to tell him what happened to Orion."

"You don't know what happened to Orion."

"I've got to tell him what I do know, then. And about Cyprus too; he's still the likely candidate behind the time agent murders. I've got to ask him about the mole in the organization too; that's the last piece that will let me sleep soundly. But about the other things, Bohemond can draw his own conclusions."

৪০ ৫৪

The funeral of Orion Keldir was the talk of many throughout the world when it occurred rather nonchalantly on a Tuesday two and a half weeks after his death had supposedly taken place. It was generally accepted that the death had indeed happened, though the manner of his passing was debated long and with great speculation. Orion's reputation remained behind him and many wondered at what it had finally taken to end such a man without his direct cooperation. Of course, there were no witnesses to testify to exactly what had happened to the greatest champion Dominos de Lumine ever had. The man who had known him best, Frank Blackman, did say a few words at the podium. The Lord Bohemond also spoke.

Around one thousand people filled the largest de Lumine building in the city. Not everyone present was aware of all Orion's special qualities, especially his age. It was mostly recognized that a senior operative had passed, and respects were to be paid. Dignitaries from almost virtually every corner of the globe had come. All four Dominos de Lumine leaders were present: Bohemond, Frederick, Godfrey, and Robert. There was such power, such influence and leadership in the place that for a solid week beforehand security had gone over every inch of the building, and a virtual small army stood guard in and out of doors. The Order of the Raven was not to be trusted at any time, but on their own end they had also lost their greatest leader and were in disarray; a strategic strike to kill a number of high profile enemies never took place.

Adrienne stood and watched as Frank, the four lords of Dominos de Lumine, and the man Trego carried the empty but heavy casket from the doors of the building to a waiting car. She had thought Frank took the whole thing rather well. He hadn't choked up once giving his speech, which was pretty good considering he had known the man for so many years. He had only had to pause briefly at the worst of times, and had maintained his composure well throughout.

There were three hours of chat and discussion after the service itself ended, for there were many people that wished to speak to Frank. That and the four leaders of Dominos de Lumine had not been together in the same place for longer than most could remember. The funeral, as such an event often could become afterward when all respects were paid, turned out to be quite a social convention. No one lamented this aspect.

It was Bohemond that caught Frank at a rare unengaged moment. He had been absentmindedly moving fingers on his left hand, finally beginning to accept that his left thumb, fourth and fifth fingers would never regain their sensation; he could use them and they maintained their strength except for the pinky, but he could feel nothing with them. His second and third fingers had some sensitivity to them but were dull compared to his right hand. Standing off to the side, the old man spoke so quietly that Frank had to lean in to hear him.

"We have lost not one but two recently," said Bohemond sadly. "I must inform you that Doc Helms is no longer with Dominos de Lumine as well."

"Not Helms too!" exclaimed Frank. "What happened?"

"I'm afraid it's worse and yet not as bad as you might think."

"Oh?"

"There was a reason he could never trace the mole online. He *was* the mole."

"How did you catch him? I suppose he could doctor what evidence there was to hide it all anyway…"

Bohemond shook his head, taking no pleasure in any of the discussion. "While he was away recently, he had asked his wife Stephanie to access an account. The information she used to call up the account was taken from the wrong pile on his desk at home. Instead of opening the account he wanted her to, she linked up with a security account through the wrong IP address. Well, it was right for what she wanted to do, but essentially when she called it up, our security caught her straight away. She had no idea she was opening something contraband – or that accessing from her end bypassed all the safeguards Helms used to not get caught opening it."

"What kind of account was it?"

"Cayman Islands. It was opened on one of security's sites and they questioned an agent opening up a foreign bank account with a low seven figures in it."

Frank whistled. "How'd she take it?"

"She had no idea. I feel badly for her; her marriage is over. Once Helms was identified in this underhanded role, many things fell into place and it was easy to discover that he was the mole in the organization as well." He shook his head. "Poor man. I trusted him with much! How true that power can corrupt. I wonder at how his compensation was not enough for him; he was paid well for his duties."

"So he was the mole all this time…"

"Yes, my new tech man Maurer confirmed it. Without Stephanie's accessing all that and setting off a chain-reaction of double-checks and investigation, we may never have caught him. He defected to the Raven, I'm afraid – which also explains how your wife was so easily kidnapped on that night not so long ago. They had inside assistance. And it seems this would also be how Blackshaft located so many time agents in such rapid succession."

"So what has happened to Helms?"

Bohemond was silent for a moment. "I could not bring myself to order his death. I have had him for so many years…even though high treason before the Society is a crime punishable by death, I could not sign the order. His wife will have their first child in two months. She and the child are both innocent. I thought there were better ways.

"Wretched fellow…he broke down crying when I revealed to him all that we surmised. I'm sure the Raven promised him much. His memory that contained the highly secret and sensitive information was wiped, just as yours was upon retirement. He still remembers what Dominos de Lumine is and certain things that were done when he was here, but he can betray nothing important anymore. Essentially he was terminated and the ill-gains that we know of were confiscated, as they essentially came at our expense. In a way he was cheated by the Raven: he had some gains but these were not tantamount to what was pending. The events at the Atlantean capital must have cut short any negotiation and whoever was supposed to get his complete payment to him is either dead or has bigger problems right now.

"There is no doubt in my mind he will find able employment elsewhere, given his technological skills. He will be monitored for years to come; if he crosses a certain point, he will not get a second chance at life." He sighed, sad. "I would not have chosen this way, that his wife should know he had betrayed one of the last bastions for good in the world. She did no wrong; the Society will look out for her. Perhaps that would be punishment enough for him, knowing what he has thrown away. I wonder if he had seen the loss of his wife coming, if the money would still have been worth it in his mind. Somehow, I doubt it."

"And now he has neither," said Frank.

"But let us speak no more of this. Justice is served, at least for the most-part. Now, let me give you this. It is something Orion would have wanted you to have." He smiled, chuckling. "Even if he knew you would share that story about him liking Big Macs and Cherry Coke at his own funeral. Somehow, I had him pegged as a gruel-man."

With that, the old man handed Frank a large sealed manila envelope and walked away.

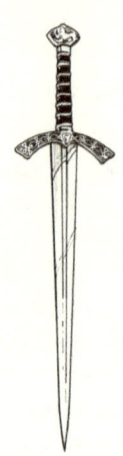

CHAPTER 33

"You would throw this life away to be with her?"

"I would throw everything away to be with her."

~an excerpt from a conversation between James Talon and Frank Blackman

෨ ෬

Around six months later, Adrienne walked in her own door and collapsed immediately into the armchair nearby. She kicked off the heels and dropped her purse on the floor. She took off her earrings and was too tired to retrieve it when the one slipped from her grasp and disappeared somewhere beneath her in the chair itself. She leaned her head back and sighed.

Frank poked his head around the corner, and she was almost too stuffy to enjoy the aroma of his making dinner. Stir fry, perhaps. He was drying his hands as he walked in to the living room, having heard her come in.

"Hi."

She sighed. "Hi."

"Rough day? You look-" he began, but she cocked an eye, "-tired," he finished.

"You could say that. I don't know why I keep this up, Frank. If I'm too generous on my pricing, I'm costing the company money by writing bad cases. If I'm too strict on my pricing, I'm costing the company money by not letting them write any cases. And even good risk goes bad if a group hires someone in awful health – typically a week after I approve something. Sometimes this job is just too much, you know?"

"I felt the same way about mine. Course, I don't have the hours you do, Milk or apple-juice?"

"No wine?" she joked.

"Rough day indeed," he laughed, "but I'm afraid not."

"Milk, please."

He smiled deviously. "Does that body good…"

She frowned playfully, hands going to her stomach. "Don't talk that way in front of our daughter."

"Son, sweetie. We're going to have a son."

Her eyes closed and she sat back. "Did you know for short term disability, they classify pregnancy like a *disease*? But I'll get leave from work, at least."

He nodded. "But look on the bright side: if I was getting a steady check for twelve-grand a month for the rest of my life, you could quit your job."

"Frank, don't tease me about quitting. You know we can't afford that…"

"Anyway, I've got a surprise for you Saturday."

"Good thing it's Friday."

He smiled. "Aye, good thing."

"So, you're not going to even give me a hint?"

"Why, you want one?"

Her voice took on a playful whine. "Fraaaaaaank…"

"Okay, okay. We're going to go to an open house."

She stopped short. "I said a hint, not to just give it away."

"I didn't tell you what house."

"You hate open houses."

"Yes, I do."

She smiled. "Oh, that's sweet."

"Yes, yes it is." He walked back into the kitchen. "Dinner's ready in five."

− −

Adrienne had expected more people at an open house; they were in a rather nice area, and the houses were expensive but not too oversized or extravagant – but they were still well beyond what she would ever tease herself as possibly being able to afford, even in a fantasy. The house they pulled up to was one of those; something she would have settled on for an imaginary holiday and not for real. It was large with a flat, green, well-kept lawn and stonework as well as some shrubbery. A birdfeeder could be seen in the backyard as they walked up, sheltered by a crabapple tree that was just ending its gorgeous bloom. It made her own home look rather dull, really. And honestly, poor. She wondered briefly if she had or had not seen any signs about the yard. She could not recall seeing any notice welcoming them to the open house.

"Why do you tease me about these nice places?" she whispered to him as they walked arm in arm up toward the front door.

"I know you like doing this stuff, so I thought I'd give it a shot."

The front door was six-paneled hardwood and painted red with a golden knocker set perfectly. It was also closed. Not having seen any signs, Adrienne hesitated, and bit her lip when he opened the door without knocking.

"Frank, do you think we should?" she asked quietly.

"C'mon. I'm sure it's fine."

The house on the inside was just as she might have imagined from its outside; hardwood floors, solid dark colors on the walls, well-painted and beautifully built – but it was stark empty.

"I don't feel right about this, Frank."

"Adrienne, relax," he said, at complete ease. "Look, there's some paper on the counter over there. I'll bet it's a note telling us to take our time and go wherever we want."

"Doubtful," she said, walking over. She looked at the paper and gawked. "You've got to be kidding me."

She looked over at her husband, who was smiling profusely.

"Why would I do that?" he asked mischievously.

"Frank, this is a…"

"A deed. For this house and property. In our name. Yes, it is."

She stared at the paper, then stared at him, then at the paper again. "Is this some joke you set up with those Society friends of yours? Is Bohemond going to come from upstairs and say 'Gotcha!'?"

"No, but he did leave the grand piano in the sunroom around back."

Her expression was a silent blank, stunned.

He came beside her. "We had driven through this neighborhood five years ago, and you had commented on how nice it was, and how you'd like a place around here. I hope that's still true."

"Frank, this is a seven-hundred thousand dollar house."

"I know," he said simply.

What he had done was sweet, but fiscally foolish: "We can't afford this, baby-"

"Couldn't."

"What?"

"Couldn't afford. Past tense."

He was still smiling, so genuinely that for a moment Adrienne found herself believing him. In her heart she was overjoyed, but her mind would simply not let her make the illogical assumption that they had bought the house.

"Dare I ask what the payments are?"

"No payments. It's all paid off."

"What?"

"It's paid for. No mortgage. No loan. It's ours." He laughed.

She poked a finger in his chest, warningly. "Franklyn Jonathan, if you are playing with me…"

"Remember how I was talking about the twelve grand a month for the rest of my life, and how that would let you retire? And how we could do other stuff, obviously, with that kind of money?"

She was suspicious. "Yes…"

"Recall Orion's funeral six months ago?"

"Yes…"

He put his arms around her and held her the way she had always liked. "Bohemond gave me some paperwork. Some of it was tied in with Orion, but most of it was just plain mine. Some financial arrangements the Society has made."

She was beginning to believe him. "What kind of financial arrangements?"

He chuckled again. "My pension for over twenty-decades of service to Dominos de Lumine. That and something Orion had setup. He had absolutely no one left, really, so I was his pick as a beneficiary. Combined, it comes out to around one-hundred-forty-four grand a year. For good. And it transfers automatically to you if something happens to me – but don't get any ideas."

"Frank…"

"I had always known I'd have some sort of pension eventually, but it was up to me to take, and I wanted to surprise you one day, but I had no idea how to explain it, and I didn't know exactly how much it would be…"

"Frank…"

"So in the long-run, there was a down payment missing, so it's been all squared up – and I got this house with it. Hope you don't mind."

She twisted around in his arms so she was facing him, and he saw she was crying.

"Something in your eye?"

It was sometime before she could speak, and even when she had regained the ability, she said nothing. The two just stood there by the counter, arms around each other.

"I love you, Adrienne. Do you love me?"

"Frank, what's the matter with you? Of course I do."

EPILOGUE

The sun showed down on a spectacularly beautiful white beach. Perfectly marine-blue waves broke gently upon the sand in an endless display. The smooth, clear water offshore dazzled the onlooker, shining like diamonds, clear to the bottom. A pleasant but not overwhelming breeze kept the temperature warm and yet cool all at once. The sand was undefiled; no broken shells, beer cans, or rotted seaweed could be seen; just sand. The beach ran to infinity in both directions, up and down. Inland, one could see the trees about fifty meters from the water's edge. Few could find a better place to be anywhere. Once there, no one would seek to be elsewhere. A sense of eternity without match permeated the very air.

Placed in the sand as if it had at first appeared in midair and then been thrust down, was an ancient sword. Its ivory handle and grip were well-kept and well-loved, but well-used. It was plunged firmly into the sand a good way, so as to stand by itself for a long time – it would kill no more; danger and aggression, violence and peril were unknown here.

Slung over the handle and resting on the hilt, dangling against the Atlantean steel in the breeze was a necklace of gold with a bright green gem carefully set. The jewel was of the magical sort that kept evil creatures at bay; that kept the wearer safe from their approach. It was hung with care and yet, abandon – it was not needed for protection anymore. Not here, where deception and danger had no place.

Two sets of barefoot tracks walked away from the makeshift memorial. In the distance, walking down the beach hand in hand were a man and woman, a couple, too far away to clearly make out. They no longer needed weapons or protection. The long lives they had lived before were now viewed as a mortal prelude; here they found life to be only beginning. They had come to the Kyrian Shore, and regained not only their immortal lives, but each other as well.

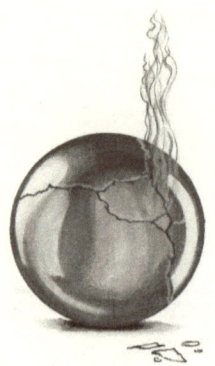

APPENDICES
THE HISTORIES AND ORGANIZATIONS
OF THE LAST SON OF ATLANTIS

Some dates are exact, others are generalized.

I. **Atlantis** – 5000 BC to 3648 BC
  A. 5000 BC – Human Civilization begins on Atlantean Continent.
  B. 4800 BC – Atlantean Continent becomes a united kingdom of one race.
  C. 4500 BC – Magic is discovered.
  D. 4240 BC – Separate dimensions are discovered but not visited or contacted.
  E. 4000 BC – Atlantean civilization is the most powerful nation in the world.
  F. 3747 BC – Shades contact Atlanteans from beyond the Earth Realm.
  G. 3741 BC – Portal Gate is conceived and construction begins.
  H. 3706 BC – Portal Gate is completed, Memphis alone enters the Earth Realm.
  I. 3692 BC – Eleven more Elder Shades enter Earth Realm via Memphis's wishes.
  J. 3675-3661 BC –Portal Gate allowed to become a true highway and some thousand non-elder, legionnaire Shades enter Earth Realm.
  K. 3661 BC – Shades turn hostile, imperial heir murdered. Atlantean Civil War begins and Atlantean history begins a downward spiral. Portal Gate sealed by Order of the Gatekeepers.
  L. 3648 BC – Atlantean civilization ends when the Cataclysm occurs and

the continent sinks into the depths of the sea. Select few escape; most do not.

II. **Atlantean Civil War** – 3661 BC to 3648 BC

A. 3661 BC – Sides are chosen when Elder Shades are driven from the capital, Iratha. Loyalists like the Gatekeepers side with the Imperial Monarchy. Others, many downtrodden or resentful of high-handed imperial tactics, listen to Shade lies and join the rebellion, the Separatists.

B. 3658 BC – Mount Aliah: Memphis and Elder Shades bestow a sort of prolonged mortality on men like Cyprus and the like, whom they deem to be their most powerful allies in the struggle against the Loyalists.

C. 3655 BC – Separatist armies take 3 principal cities of the East that turns the tide of conflict from one of typical defeat to the rebels really having a chance. The Shades' now immortal henchmen are pivotal to the campaign.

D. 3654 BC – Dandralian Campaign seeks to cripple the Separatist forces in their strongest regions.

D. 3653 BC – The Order of the Gatekeepers takes special care to make their own immortal soldiers, and men like Orion are empowered in this way.

E. 3650 BC – Shades beneath Mount Aliah seek to activate a dormant super volcano for the controlled purpose of using it against the Loyalists. But activation occurs and controlling the phenomena is beyond their ken. Tremors begin across the continent. Some flooding.

F. 3649 BC – Separatist armies begin a press in earnest to take Iratha. Fighting and battles are fierce and cost many lives. Earthquakes grow in intensity, initially occurring on the outskirts of the civilization and making their way toward populace areas. Sometimes battles are interrupted by the growing volcanic tremors. During this period, Accursed the Shade infiltrates the Portal Chamber and attempts to open the Gate. Interrupted and captured, it is imprisoned in an attempt to learn more about Shades themselves.

G. 3648 BC – With the Separatist army two days' march outside Iratha, the super volcano at Mount Aliah has subterranean eruptions and the entire continent is torn apart and plunged beneath the sea. Select few from both sides of the war see it coming and escape via ships. Atlantean civilization ends.

III. **The Order of the Raven**

The Order of the Raven, in memory of the Atlantean battle standard, was begun by a handful of Loyalist exiles from Atlantis in the year 3646 BC. It was formed for the express purpose of defeating the Shades in the Earth Realm. Some thoughts of revenge, surely, may have been present in the beginning. But in the years to come, vengeance was superceded by the understanding that stopping the Shades was more imperative for the security of mankind. A council under a single leader led the order.

As time went by, the Order of the Raven became both powerful and rich. Initially these aspects benefited the cause, but left to themselves they began to fester. The year AD 1204 is infamous as the year the organization originally split, but there were at least three occasions in the years prior that small factions had split off, or feuds were settled. What made AD 1204 so different is that on that occasion, it was the Order of the Raven that changed its philosophy, and the "renegade" group that split off – the Lords of Light – was really the one that kept the Order's original intentions.

And so after the split the Order of the Raven became a usually legitimate organization that was dedicated to its own gain, while the newly-born Lords of Light determined to continue their war with the Shades. The Raven maintained power and influence and riches, forming a thousand cover organizations to deal with their legitimate businesses, names any average person would know. Criminal enterprises as well were soon to be born.

Attica Triassa entered the Raven legitimately in AD 1206 and swiftly came to a leadership position. Her unfailing youth and Shade-enhanced skills led to her being recognized as special. In the AD 1230s she had earned her way into the inner circle and by the AD 1250s she was leading the inner circle. By the end of that decade, she succeeded the standing leader when he died, some say under mysterious circumstances.

For a time Lady Triassa was content to live a luxurious and successful lifestyle at the head of the most powerful singular organization in the world. But eventually she tired of pure success and began to take more and more angst at the services Shades periodically and continuously insisted upon. By AD 1400 or so she was actively searching as to how to end the Shades' influence on her life.

IV. The Sacred Order of the Brotherhood of the Gatekeepers

While the Gatekeepers were originally begun by Atlantean royalty to serve a multitude of purposes (including majordomos, bodyguard, councilors, administrators, etc), the following history will be devoted to their actions after the fall of Atlantis in 3648 BC. Note for reference: the term "Gatekeeper" did not originate around the order's creation of the Portal Gate. Rather, the title is older and is more speaking to the role of service and protection over a household, namely the royalty of Atlantis. That they later designed a magic gateway is purely ironic.

Gatekeepers were to be seen among the founders of the Order of the Raven, but they are two separate organizations and from the beginning it was plain to all parties that the Gatekeepers would always seek their own purposes before those of the Raven. In those early days, their purposes were often one in the same and there was no conflict of interest, but as time went on, there were occasions when Gatekeepers went about their own business.

In the beginning years after the Cataclysm that sank Atlantis, the primary business of the Gatekeepers was the arrest and prosecution of the remaining Separatists. These individuals had, after all, been legally condemned of high treason and were owed their due punishment as prescribed by the courts. The pursuit by Gatekeepers was not considered vigilantism; they were lawfully-sanctioned agents of an official state, working to mete out Justice upon those whom the courts had found guilty. In no time at all, the number of remaining Separatists dwindled to the point of just down to the Shade-venom-infused immortals like Cyprus. While the Order of the Raven bore these individuals no love and would certainly kill them if given half the chance, it chose to pursue the Shades more directly. The venom-infused Separatists were an affair for the Gatekeepers, and as long as they did the Raven no particular harm – usually they had the sense not to invoke the order's ire – the Raven did not seek them out.

The standing Consul of the Gatekeepers for long years was a man named Faeryn of Iratha. He knew every Gatekeeper secret method of death. If a Gatekeeper somehow became unable to speak or write for whatever reason, it was wise to have a fall-back.

With captured Shade venom modified to do away with certain ill-effects, Faeryn was allowed unnatural long life like many others of his time – an original time agent pioneer of sorts. In AD 617 he grew weary of the mortal strain and allowed himself, of sound mind, to no longer tarry: he stopped taking the venom – which had by now been turned into a more wholesome serum.

Taken to the Different Place, mortally weary and unprepared to meet Shades, Faeryn's knowledge was extracted from him before he gained the Door of Eternity – and so the enemies of the Gatekeepers came to know their weaknesses. It was not until AD 622, when the Different Place aligned with the Earth Realm as it did every 10 years, allowing Shades to go back and forth as they wished, that this knowledge was able to be shared with the Earth Realm Shades.

Three Gatekeepers were killed within the next quarter century, and after that on average one in every 210 years or so. By the close of the 18th century, Orion Keldir was the last Gatekeeper. His choice of demise was known to his enemies – but the metal he had used was for all practical purposes extinct and could not be found. And so he endured, the last of the oldest organization in the world.

Immortal Gatekeeper Death Count

3653 BC – immortality ceremony

1648 BC – first Gatekeeper killed by suicide after onset of stutter-flutter (11 left)

1085 BC – second Gatekeeper killed by suicide after onset of stutter-flutter (10 left)

465 BC – third Gatekeeper killed by suicide after onset of stutter-flutter (9 left)

AD 617 – Faeryn of Iratha allows his own death (9 left)

AD 622 – discovery of the Gatekeeper banes by the Earth Realm's Shades (9 left)

AD 623 – fourth Gatekeeper killed legitimately (8 left)

AD 628 – fifth Gatekeeper killed legitimately (7 left)

AD 647 – sixth Gatekeeper killed legitimately (6 left)

AD 1006 – seventh Gatekeeper killed legitimately (5 left)

AD 1276 – eighth Gatekeeper killed legitimately (4 left)

AD 1534 – ninth Gatekeeper killed legitimately (3 left)

AD 1537 – tenth Gatekeeper killed by suicide after onset of stutter-flutter (2 left)

AD 1711 – eleventh Gatekeeper killed legitimately (1 left)

Present day – twelfth Gatekeeper (Orion Keldir) killed legitimately (0 left)

Just as the numbers of Gatekeepers lessened in time, so also did the immortal Loyalist traitors. Even newly vulnerable, the justice of the Gatekeepers was not easily held at bay, and sentencing and executions still occurred efficiently. As the primary business of the Gatekeepers was concluded (or so they thought), most of them turned toward the affairs of the Raven and the Lords of Light, and once again goals became unified.

v. The Imperial Gemstone

The enchanted imperial gemstone of Atlantis was the brainchild of the Consul of the Gatekeepers, Faeryn of Iratha. Around 3665 BC, after being ignored or mocked for suspicion about the Shades, he secretly came to the best magic-users in the land, in particular those whose loyalty was not in doubt. And he made long counsel with them.

There was some mining within the confines of the empire, particularly in the mountains south of Aliah. Much of value was to be found beneath the peaks, but gems were rare. Among the local gems that were available were the green stones from remote and dangerous mines in the very south tip of the landmass, a region named Zelada. Emerald-like in appearance but not true emeralds in actuality, green stones from those lands were rare and beautiful, referred to as Zeladic jade. Additionally, it was found that Zeladic jade had a quality within its molecular makeup that was a natural repellent to Shades; the dark creatures shunned close contact with such elements, and prolonged contact could eventually kill after an agonizing process that could only be described as withering.

Faeryn chose a large Zeladic jade from the royal treasury and took it to the magic users. By their arts, they enhanced the repulsive characteristics, magnifying the stone's natural ability to repel Shades. Additionally, they empowered the gem so that its keeper would be protected from natural occurrences; falls, strikes, accidents. Not impregnable, but protected. Lastly, by Faeryn's insistence, the magic users also charmed the stone to enable its keeper to mentally divine if an immortal was lying. Faeryn distrusted Shades very much, and in those times it could be very useful to determine if an immortal was lying. Immune to disguises, the stone could determine.

If the stone was to be taken by force from its keeper, it could surge out in power, protecting itself. As a willing gift its enchanted abilities would be passed along to a new keeper. But if the gemstone were taken by force or manipulation, the protective characteristics and ability to determine truth would be sluggish at first and only after some time would recover.

This stone was then crafted into a necklace of strong but feminine chain, and was quickly given into the keeping of the emperor's last child, his daughter Kyla. In shape the jewel was a rectangle, two inches tall, an inch wide, half an inch thick at the middle.

In the days of the war, it fell to the Gatekeepers to pose as bodyguards to the imperial family. A young girl in her formative years, Kyla had a Gatekeeper with her or immediately outside her quarters at all hours of the day. The war played out the way it was fated to play out. Kyla escaped with other imperial exiles from the deluge and lived out her days in what was later to be Egypt. The gemstone was to be passed down from generation to generation.

From Egypt, the jewel went throughout the world, often with keepers but not always: Egypt to Babylon, to China, to the Americas, to Spain, to Germany and the Hapsburgs and to France around the First World War. From France it was taken back to Germany and there remained until the Second World War, at which time it had come to the hands of the last known Atlantean traitor that remained, Falcius Kiriath.

Orion Keldir, of course, caught up with Kiriath in Berlin during the war and took the gem into his own keeping. The heirs of Atlantis had died out amid the early Persian Empire, and there was no specific person to whom it might be entrusted. Additionally, it would be foolish to keep it on his person for long.

Eventually, Orion would give the gemstone to Frank Blackman, who gave it to his fiancée Adrienne Kelly. It would remain in her hands until our story begins.

VI. The Kedassaic Texts

This ancient document is really a collection of seemingly sporadic writings. The Kedassaic Texts were begun around 4800 BC and are a recorded history of Atlantean civilization. Historical record, names, events, genealogies, personal correspondences, proverbial wisdom – much like the Bible, actually. Throughout the history of Atlantis, the Kedassaic Texts kept up with the advance of the civilization, recording most everything.

The development of magic, the design of the Portal Gate, and the arrival of

Shades were all recorded and described in the Kedassaic Texts. These documents were kept by the well-to-do, especially in the monarchy, and were copied by professional scribes. That is not to say that everyone had a copy, but there were multiple copies floating about, supposedly all the same because of the way they copied, like the Jews copy the Torah.

Amid the travails of the civil war, one of the things the Separatist forces did, guided by Shades, was write their own jilted history; this twisted accounting they introduced as fact into the Kedassaic Texts. The Loyalists, of course, recorded things as they truly were (to embellish anything and offer it up into the Kedassaic canon was beyond thinkable to the true writers). And so there were contradictory copies. Problems erupted. The well-to-do would read and become confused. So the Separatists weren't so bad? Had they a valid reason for war after all? The Loyalists had done what? Separating true copies, and truth from fact, became easily confused. No one had ever manipulated the sacred texts before, and there was not a firmly established way to sort genuine from fallacy. Good copies were just as numerous as bad, and addressed virtually the same period of time.

Amid the greatest lies incorporated were those that addressed the Portal Chamber. The Gatekeepers that had sealed the trans-dimensional gate had made opening it possible only with immortal lifeblood. The Shades changed this in their malicious text to immortal lifeblood being the only way to *seal closed* the gate.

This event was recorded by both a truthful and a malicious writer, and copies of each account were mixed. One told the truth; that immortal lifeblood would break the Seal and open the Gate. One told a lie designed to bring about the former anyway: that immortal lifeblood would permanently close the Seal and essentially destroy the Gate's use. Over time very few, like the Gatekeepers, remembered which way it really was.

Most people understood that there were two types of Kedassaic Texts; one with verbatim records and one with Shade-enhanced lies. What was harder to determine was which was which. So Book 23, the section that really started the history of the Shades and the last few hundred years of Atlantean history, was called the Compromised Passages.

Multiple copies of each kind of Kedassaic Texts were taken with exiles when the island sank. Even the traitors had a couple among them. The Order of the Raven even continued to write some history, starting Book 24. Time went by and eventually most copies were lost. A good number of them were destroyed when the Library at Alexandria was burned. Some remain but they are mostly decrepit and getting worse. When Cyprus discovered a copy, it was the perverted dark version, but even he did not know which it was.

Attica was of course unaware that there are two versions of the book.

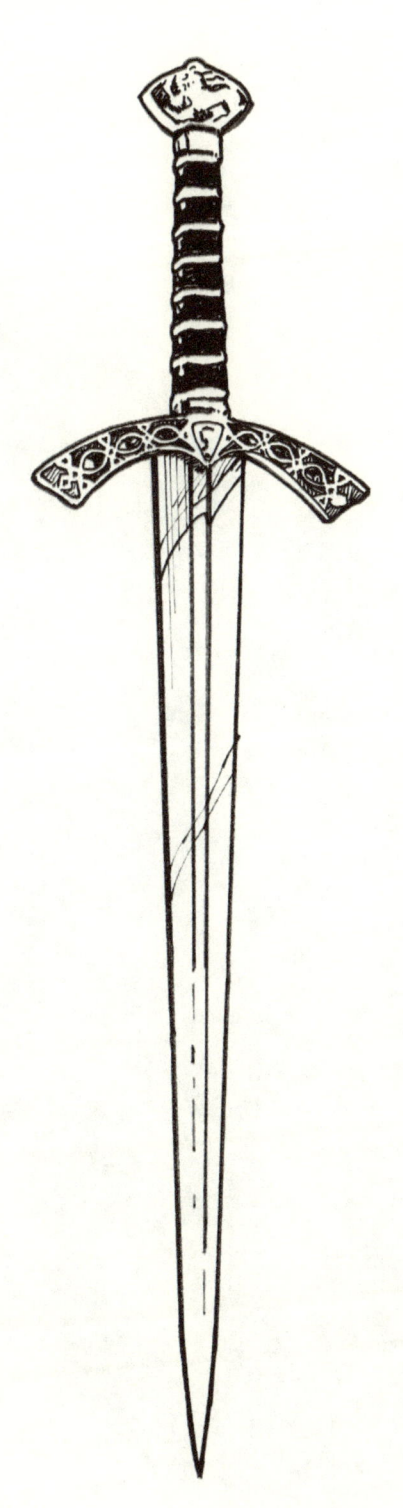

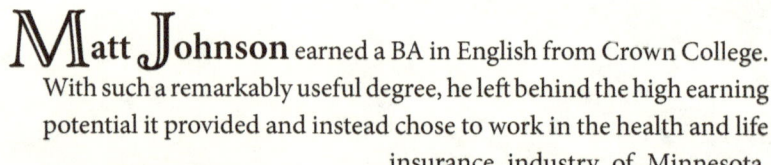

Matt Johnson earned a BA in English from Crown College. With such a remarkably useful degree, he left behind the high earning potential it provided and instead chose to work in the health and life insurance industry of Minnesota. It is exceedingly glamourous, but he manages. Matt lives in the Twin Cities with his gorgeous wife, and a dog and cat who qualify as children when no one serious is asking. He enjoys writing medieval fantasy, collecting swords and playing piano for fun and church.

Photo by Amanda Anderson